The One After the One

Cass Lester spent many years at CBBC having a fabulous time making award-winning programmes including *Jackanory*, *Big Kids*, *Kerching!* and *The Story of Tracy Beaker*. She has published a number of children's books and is now having a fabulous time writing adult fiction.

THE
ONE
after
THE
ONE

CASS LESTER

CANELO

First published in the United Kingdom in 2022 by

Canelo
Unit 9, 5th Floor
Cargo Works, 1–2 Hatfields
London, SE1 9PG
United Kingdom

A CIP catalogue record for this book is available from the British Library.

Print ISBN 978 1 80032 541 8
Ebook ISBN 978 1 80032 540 1

Look for more great books at www.canelo.co

Printed and bound in Great Britain by Clays Ltd, Elcograf S.p.A.

1

For Elle

Prologue

Sometimes, out of the blue, the fates like to choose you to mess with, and completely ruin your whole day. Sitting in a vast and beautifully ornate Tuscan church in the middle of a wedding, Charley Taylor was blissfully unaware that this was going to be one of those days.

Although strictly speaking, *blissful* wasn't an accurate description of her mood since, much as she loved weddings, she was finding this one bit of an ordeal. The service was in Italian, obviously, and she couldn't understand a single word, so she was impossibly anxious she'd do something glaringly wrong and make a complete spectacle of herself. She glanced around nervously at the surrounding sea of faces. There were literally hundreds of guests and, apart from Ricky, sitting next to her, she didn't know a single soul.

Perhaps sensing her unease, Ricky slipped his hand over hers, gave it a reassuring squeeze and then, leaning close to her ear whispered, 'I love you.'

She could feel the warmth of his breath. 'I love you too,' she mouthed back.

The two of them had only flown in from Bristol the previous evening and Charley hadn't had time to meet any of his relatives properly. Although she'd been introduced to his sister (the bride) and all the bridesmaids, his parents and a vast array of aunts and uncles and cousins, everyone had been swept up in the whirlwind rush of wedding preparations, and she could barely put a name to a face. She turned her attention back to the ceremony and reminded herself to focus on meticulously copying what everyone else was doing. *Oh my God*, she thought, *how utterly mortifying would it be to make a fool of myself and embarrass Ricky in front of his entire extended family?* Funnily enough, less than an hour later, she found out.

–

It was while everyone was traipsing into the grandiose medieval lodge for the reception that the fates decided to start having fun. Buried in the middle of the tide of guests surging into the entrance hall, Charley found her right heel had suddenly caught in a metal grating in the floor and promptly stuck there, yanking her to an abrupt halt. The crowd surrounding her carried on obliviously, sweeping her irresistibly onwards, but without her shoe.

Bloody hell! She grabbed Ricky's arm and hissed, 'I've lost my shoe!'

'What?! Oh!' Ricky immediately turned around and, loudly exclaiming, '*Scusi, scusi!*' he tried to force their way against the oncoming waves of relatives whilst, she assumed, rapidly explaining her predicament in Italian.

Instantly, and with an astonishing degree of melodrama and noise, at least twenty well-meaning people dropped to their knees to try to rescue the shoe which, despite the efforts of several men and the heated advice of even more women, proved to be irretrievably wedged. Cheeks burning, Charley begged them to leave the shoe and let her and Ricky deal with it. But they didn't understand her English and so the commotion continued until one particularly determined young man grasped hold of the offending article and started twisting it ferociously.

'Please don't force it!' Charley pleaded, 'You'll—' A loud cracking sound interrupted her. '—break it,' she finished.

Beaming triumphantly, the young man proudly presented Charley with her shoe, minus the heel, which was still jammed in the floor. Spontaneous applause broke out so, slapping a cheerful look on her face, Charley thanked the lad profusely, then slipped the remains of her shoe onto her foot and resigned herself to making even more of an exhibition of herself by spending the rest of the day limping heavily. *Bloody, bloody hell! Why? Out of all the hundreds of women here, why did this have to happen to me?*

The fates hadn't finished with Charley yet, intent on turning the reception into an absolute nightmare for her. To start with, Ricky's mother was determined to introduce Charley – or more precisely 'Ricky's girlfriend' – to each and every guest in the entire room. Charley hobbled along dutifully as she and Ricky were endlessly paraded around until she'd completely lost track of who was who, who was related to who, and how. She just hoped to God she wasn't expected to remember any names. Naturally, everyone bombarded her with questions, mostly in Italian for Ricky to interpret, and she began to feel like a broken record continually repeating herself. 'No, I haven't hurt myself, I've just broken my heel… Yes, I live in England… We've been together about six months… We met at his bike shop… I run a Prosecco-themed shop…'

At last, having completed the marathon tour, Ricky's mother patted Charley's cheek affectionately and drifted off, no doubt to resume her multiple duties as mother of the bride. Which would have been a blessed relief for Charley, except Ricky was immediately annexed by a gang of his friends and relatives. Watching his face light up with every embrace and re-union, she couldn't blame him; he hadn't seen most of them for years, since he'd moved to England. Nevertheless, it left her trapped in the corner of a crowded room, hemmed in by people she didn't know and couldn't even talk to.

She was just about to do what any smart woman would do in those circumstances – bolt to the Ladies' and hide – when she was pounced upon by a gaggle of older women who, with much fluster and arm-flapping, herded her into a group of young women and girls corralled in the centre of the room. Before Charley could grasp what was happening, Ricky's sister had leapt onto a chair, turned her back on the room, and blindly hurled her bouquet into the throng. There were squeals of delight as a host

3

of hands shot up into the air to catch it, but to Charley's horror the bloody thing flew straight at her face. Instinctively, she put her hand up to protect herself – and promptly caught it.

There was a deathly hush, during which several hundred people turned to look at Charley, and then the entire room erupted and everyone within arm's length grabbed her and kissed her on both cheeks, including Ricky's mother who had somehow pushed her way through the throng to sweep her into an ecstatic embrace.

Oh brilliant. Why? Why did you do that? she cursed herself furiously. All but drowning in a tidal wave of strangers, her eyes frantically scanned the room for Ricky. She found him, beaming sheepishly, amongst a bunch of cheering lads who were all slapping him on the back. Shooting him an imploring look, she saw his face immediately cloud and he tried to break free and push his way towards her, only to be enveloped into a hug by a huge bear of a man and disappear from her sight once more. *Bloody, bloody, bloody hell, could this afternoon get any worse?*

As it turned out, yes, it could. Acutely aware that she was still clinging onto the wedding bouquet and no doubt looking either optimistic or pathetic, or possibly both, she tossed it irritably onto the nearest table – and promptly knocked over a bottle of wine. What seemed like gallons of dark red wine flooded all over the pristine white tablecloth. A chorus of horrified cries rent the air as a dozen or so people all dived into the scene, busying themselves with righting the bottle, mopping up the wine, and generally making a crisis out of a drama.

'Oh my God! I'm so sorry!' wailed Charley, immediately trying to help, but she was shoed away by multiple reproachful hands.

To her dismay, her eyes started prickling and she realised she was close to tears, and then she felt a firm hand suddenly take hold of her elbow and gently pull her away from the melodrama. Assuming it was Ricky, she turned gratefully, only to discover an elderly lady in his place. Calmly and majestically, the old woman steered Charley across the room, the mass of people miraculously parting to let them through. Then, pausing only to casually pick up two glasses of sparkling white wine and hand one of them to Charley, the woman led her outside. She headed for a stone bench, under the shade of a wooden pergola running along the side of the building and, taking hold of Charley's arm with her free hand to steady herself while carefully holding her wine glass with the other, she lowered herself onto the seat and then patted the space next to her. Charley sat down beside her.

'I do not speak English,' the lady informed her slowly, shaking her head apologetically.

Frankly, Charley was infinitely relieved – at least she'd be spared another interrogation. 'I'm sorry. *Non parlo Italiano*,' she replied, shrugging helplessly and pretty much exhausting her Italian.

'Ha!' The older woman rolled her eyes good-humouredly, then she tapped her chest to introduce herself. '*Nonna di Ricky*. Grandmother.'

Charley made the same gesture and said, 'I'm Charley. Ricky's girlfriend.'

'*Sì, sì*,' nodded the woman, and Charley felt vaguely ridiculous since it was patently obvious everyone knew who she was.

The elderly woman raised her glass in salutation to Charley, then she leant back, sighed happily, and waved her arm at countryside in front of them, clearly inviting Charley to take in the fabulous views. Charley happily obliged. After all the minor disasters and unwanted attention inside it was bliss – sheer bliss – to be sitting in the fresh air with the warm May sun on her skin and enjoying a generous slice of peace and quiet. Charley's eyes roamed across the Tuscan countryside in front of her, taking in the small villages and churches peppering the hillsides and the vibrant patchwork of fields, some of which she guessed were vineyards, all bordered by the characteristic tall, thin trees of the region. Occasionally, Ricky's grandmother would leisurely lift an arm to shade her eyes, casually wave the glass in her other hand to indicate something in the distance and utter a word or two. Whether she was naming the villages, or the types of trees, or a passing bird,

Charley had absolutely no idea, a fact that didn't seem to matter to either of them.

Shortly afterwards Ricky came looking for her, full of apologies. His grandmother instantly berated him in a tirade of Italian, with a lot of head-shaking and finger-wagging, leaving him looking like a scolded child.

'She's telling me off for not looking after you properly,' he told Charley, crouching down in front of her and pulling a face. 'She's right, and I'm sorry.'

'No. It's fine,' Charley assured him hurriedly and leant forward to take hold of his hand. 'I know you have a lot of people you want to catch up with.'

He smiled at her gratefully then after a moment asked, 'Are you ready to come back in?'

Charley looked across to the old woman, serenely comfortable beside her, and then turned back to Ricky. 'Do you mind if I stay here with your gran a little longer?'

'Of course not,' he replied and then, raising her hand to his lips, he kissed it, which won him an approving nod from his grandmother and made Charley melt inside. He gave them both a deeply loving look before he stood up and headed back indoors.

The two women sat peacefully in the May sunshine, in an oasis of calm, sipping their drinks and sharing the occasional comment, in the full understanding that neither of them understood a word the other was saying, but not caring a fig.

Chapter One

It's going to be complete and utter bloody chaos when you get in.

Painfully early the following Saturday, Charley cycled through the streets of Bristol, heading to the shop. It was barely seven thirty so the city hadn't entirely woken up yet and, since their flight had been delayed and she'd had less than six hours' sleep, Charley hadn't entirely woken up either, but she'd forced herself to rise and shine. Or at least rise. Her bleary-eyed face in the mirror made shining a little optimistic.

Waiting impatiently at a red light, she glanced at her reflection in a store window – a woman in her early thirties, wearing jeans and a loose shirt, perched on an old-fashioned pale blue bike. Her dark curly hair was falling out of its topknot and she started to rescue it but a curt beeping from behind warned her the lights had changed. Pushing off, she immediately starting worrying about the takings while she'd been away. She hoped to God they hadn't plummeted. The turnover wasn't brilliant at best of times – she still hadn't figured out how to turn the inevitable troughs into the more elusive peaks, but then she hadn't even been open a year yet, so she wasn't going to beat herself up for that. She'd been torn about whether to go to Tuscany with Ricky at all because it had meant leaving her shop in the hands of her colleagues. Not that she didn't trust them, she just didn't know if they'd cope without her. But, having worked pretty much 24/7 for the last few months, she'd desperately needed a break. Which was a shame, since it hadn't exactly been the stress-free getaway she'd hoped for.

Peddling over Prince Street Bridge towards Wapping Wharf, with the city's colourful docks spread out on either side, she was imagining only too vividly the dire mess that would greet her when she arrived at the shop – jumbled displays with products piled higgledy-piggledy, the litter bin overflowing with packaging, and the till table plastered with Post-it notes listing a litany of disasters she'd have to deal with almost before she'd put her bag down.

Unlocking the shop door, she cast an eye around and was pleasantly surprised to see everything was pretty tidy. Most of the shelves were fairly well stocked. The baskets of bath bombs were almost empty, there were gaps in the display of Prosecco flutes and she couldn't see any tealights, but over all, it wasn't too bad. A glance at the floor told her that someone, probably Pam – no, definitely Pam – had even found time to hoover. Both of her co-workers were part-time, and in fact one of them was *extremely* part-time, infuriatingly so, frankly. Whilst Pam came in every afternoon and all day on Saturdays, Charley's mate Tara only worked mornings (after she'd dropped her little girl at school), term time (no holidays, not even half term) and absolutely no weekends (because of her daughter's countless hobbies). Charley could hardly complain since the business wasn't doing well enough to pay either of them yet.

She dumped her bag behind the counter and made a swift mental note of which displays needed replenishing the most. Charley's Prosecco Pop-Up was in the trendy Cargo area of Bristol's docklands where the shops were made from converted lorry containers. The glass-fronted units were small, leaving little room for storage, so her spare stock was either stashed under the display tables or stacked on top of the white-painted wooden dresser that filled one entire wall. Grabbing a chair, she lugged it over to the shelving unit and clambered up. Almost immediately she heard the shop door open behind her. *Dammit*. She'd meant to re-lock it again until opening at nine.

A cheery voice called out, 'Welcome home!'

Charley whipped round to see a woman in her early sixties clutching two take-away coffees and a pack of pastries from the deli, deftly closing the door behind her with her heel.

'Pam!' She jumped off the chair and went to embrace the woman warmly. Gratefully taking a coffee and helping herself to an almond croissant she added, 'You are an absolute star!' Then, eyeing the clock on back wall, which, despite permanently proclaiming it to be 'Prosecco O'Clock', more helpfully informed her it was barely ten past eight, she added, 'You're also very early.'

'Yes, well, I was worried we'd left you too much to do when you got in,' said Pam, looking around anxiously.

'No! It looks brilliant!' Charley said, peeling the lid off her coffee. 'And you can take the money out of the till for these,' she added, before taking a mouthful of warm croissant.

'Absolutely not! It's my welcome home treat!'

'Mmm, thank you,' Charley mumbled around her pastry.

'So how was Tuscany?' asked Pam, putting her coffee down and switching the till and the card-reader on in one move.

Before she could stop it, a brief grimace contorted Charley's face. She recovered quickly, but not before Pam had noticed and raised a querying eyebrow.

'Fine, it was fine,' Charley said, momentarily putting her pastry back in the bag.

'Only "*Fine?*"' queried Pam mildly.

'Well, more than fine,' Charley corrected hastily. 'It was lovely… wonderful. Really!' She smiled brightly at Pam in an attempt to reassure her, or possibly to reassure herself.

Then she kicked herself. Why had she said '*Fine*', for crying out loud? Who says a holiday was '*Fine*'? Anyhow, she reminded herself, some of it had been idyllic. Ricky showing her round his old haunts and taking her to her the parts of Tuscany the tourists never found, the time they'd spent together, just the two of them, had been fabulous.

'Tuscany is beautiful,' she enthused. 'The countryside, the colours, the cute little villages… I loved it. Absolutely loved it. And the wedding… Oh my God, lavish or what? Hundreds of people, gorgeous locations, and the food! Mountains of the stuff, and gallons and gallons of wine. It was a miracle anyone was still upright at the end of it! So it was all lovely…' She hesitated and Pam looked at her quizzically.

'But?' the older woman prompted.

Charley let out a sigh. 'But being presented to every single member of Ricky's *entire* family, and not just at the wedding, but day after day afterwards, was a bit… wearing.' *A bit wearing? It had been a gruelling, week-long Ordeal by Family.*

Pam pulled a sympathetic face. 'Poor you.'

Charley wouldn't have been that indiscreet with everyone, but her relationship with Pam was exceptional. She was actually Charley's mother-in-law, or rather her *former* mother-in-law. Not her *ex*-mother-in-law, because Charley's marriage to Josh, Pam's son, hadn't ended in divorce, but when Josh had died, unbearably young, leaving his mother and young widow harrowingly bereft and heartbroken. Their joint bereavement had thrown them together, paired survivors of an appalling disaster. Over the last few years, the two women had grown as close as any mother and daughter, and closer than many.

Even so, wary of confiding too much out of loyalty to Ricky, Charley tried to make a joke of it. 'Honestly Pam, I met his parents, his sister, his brother-in-law…' she intoned, listing them off on her fingers. 'Then his aunts and uncles, his cousins – and there are dozens of them, literally *dozens*. Then I had to meet his grandparents, and his grandparents' parents…'

'His grandparents' parents? Seriously?' Pam flicked Charley a look.

'Yes,' fibbed Charley seamlessly before continuing, 'and his grandparents' grandparents…'

'Charley! They'd have to be about a hundred and fifty years old!'

'I know, even older than you,' deadpanned Charley, nodding solemnly.

Pam threw a Prosecco-themed cushion at her. 'Now I know you're exaggerating!'

Charley automatically plumped up the cushion before putting it back in its place on the dresser and for a while, both women turned their attention to restocking. After a few moments Pam asked, 'So what are they like, his family?'

She shrugged lightly. 'They seem very nice. His parents don't speak a lot of English, but they were extremely...' She searched for a tactful word. 'Welcoming,' she finished, mentally awarding herself an Olympic gold in understatement. Out of the corner of her eye, she could see Pam busying herself stacking chocolate bars.

'And his mother?' prompted Pam.

'What about her?'

'Oh, you know... Does she work? Is she retired?'

'I have absolutely no idea!' Charley admitted with a laugh, vaguely wondering what was going through the older woman's mind.

'And is she... tall and glamorous, or short and dumpy? Does she seem serious-minded or full of fun... or what?' continued Pam casually, and suddenly Charley guessed what was going through her mind.

Stopping what she was doing, she looked squarely at Pam. Taking in her mother-in-law's short, slim figure, her practical clothes and sensible shoes, Charley said carefully, 'Ricky's mother is tall and plump. Stylish but not glamorous, and, judging by the fact she's definitely got wrinkles rather than laughter lines, I'd say she's probably more serious-minded than full of fun. But above all, she is absolutely *nothing* like you. But then nobody ever could be!'

'One does one's best!' replied Pam with mock modesty.

The shop door opened again and Charley was about to give her standard '*I'm sorry but we're not quite open yet*' spiel, but it was Ricky, followed as usual by Carlo, his large grey lurcher.

'I was going to offer to get coffee, but you've already got some,' he said, crossing to Charley, sliding his arm around her and kissing her.

Charley had expected Carlo to come over to her for his regular ear-scratch, but instead the dog went up to Pam and nudged her hand with his whiskery face.

'Er… excuse me?' said Charley to the dog, affronted by his blatant disregard.

'You abandoned him and left him with me for a week! What do you expect?' demanded Pam, straight-faced.

'Undying love and loyalty!' countered Charley.

'No chance. He'll adore anyone who feeds him.' Ricky grinned then, turning to Pam, handed her a hessian tote bag. 'A thank you for dog-sitting.'

'You shouldn't have!' Pam took the bag nonetheless and peeked inside. 'Real truffles!' she gasped. Delving further in, she pulled out cheeses, olives and a bottle of white wine. 'This is too much!'

Ricky's eyes flicked to Charley and they shared a smile. She'd told him Pam would think him too generous. 'No it's not,' he said. 'Kennels would have cost a fortune and he'd have hated it.'

'Well, I'm very grateful. And touched!'

Pam gave him an affectionate hug, which Ricky returned with his characteristic easy charm then he kissed Charley again before heading for the door, Carlo following him like a shadow, but at the doorway he turned back to her. 'Supper at mine?' he asked and without waiting for her reply went on, 'I thought I could do the spinach and ricotta gnocchi you like – unless you've had enough Italian food for a while!'

Personally, Charley doubted anyone could have enough Italian food, but she heard herself say, 'Actually, would you mind if I give it a miss tonight? Only I've got a lot of stuff to catch up on,' she waved her hand vaguely round the shop, 'and to be honest, I'm all in. I could really do with an early night.'

'Of course not. And in fact I'm not surprised. A week with my family's enough to wear anyone out.' And, calling Carlo to heel, he left.

Through the shop window Charley watched him striding off towards his bike shop, three units down, with the huge lurcher plodding along faithfully behind him. As he passed the florist's, Ricky waved cheerfully and called out to Del, the owner, and they both laughed, and Charley couldn't help smiling. She loved his easy manner and the generous warmth he extended to everyone because she loved *him*. So why, she wondered, had she wanted to duck out of seeing him tonight?

Chapter Two

Letting herself into her flat after work, Charley kicked off her shoes to ease her aching feet and padded into the kitchen. Opening the fridge, she pulled a face because, as usual, there was bugger all in it – partly because she'd not had a chance to go food shopping since she'd got back from Italy, but largely because she could rarely be bothered to cook. In her defence, she was usually either too knackered or too busy when she got back to grab anything other than a quick snack, and she spent most of her evenings either doing paperwork or making deliveries. Any nights she did manage to take off she spent at Ricky's. Fortunately, he was a far better cook than her and could conjure up a meal from a handful of pasta and, apparently, just about anything. Only very occasionally did he stay at her place, but it was nothing to do with her cooking. It was more because she still lived in the flat which she and Josh had bought just before they got married, and inevitably, the ghost of Josh still hung around the place. His face beamed out from their wedding photo in the living room, and from the picture she kept on her bedside table – a grinning Josh in Bermuda shorts, shades and a suntan on holiday in Ibiza. On the few instances when Ricky had spent the night in her bed, she'd hidden the holiday snap in a drawer beforehand, although the gesture always felt like an act of betrayal, as if she were packing Josh away to make way for someone else. She refused to remove her wedding photo, however. Her marriage to Josh was part of her life, part of who she was, and she wasn't going to hide that.

Shutting the pitifully empty fridge, she grabbed her bag and nipped to the mini supermarket round the corner and bought a small quiche and a pot of fruit. Back in the flat, slobbing out on the sofa with her feet on the coffee table, she ate with her fingers and made the most of the solitude. Which, now she came to reflect on it, was testament to how much she'd moved on. In the early years after Josh's death, five years ago, the loneliness and the endless solitary evenings she'd had to endure without him had almost crushed her, and she'd have sold her soul to have someone, anyone, to talk to, if only to share the inconsequential minutia of her day. All those empty nights spent in an empty bed, marooned in the aching void of loss. But now there was Ricky, she reminded herself, and the days and nights of loneliness were over. The thought immediately struck her as disloyal. Ricky could never replace Josh. He had been, and still was, The One. She turned to her wedding photo where Josh beamed back at her, forever cheerful, hopeful for a happy-ever-after with her.

She finished eating and, although she'd have loved to just crash on the sofa and make the most of an evening to herself, idling it away with a TV quiz show or a rom-com, she dutifully took her laptop into the kitchen to try to catch up on the multiple tasks she never quite managed to keep on top of. Granted, it was worse because she'd been away for a week, but she had piles of stock to order, online orders to plough through and dozens of requests for party bags to sort out, not to mention bunch of emails she knew neither Pam nor Tara would have dealt with – Pam because she lacked confidence and Tara because she couldn't be arsed.

Mentally rolling up her sleeves, she slogged away doggedly for an hour or so until, mercifully, her phone rang. It was Tara. Charley happily discarded her computer and slipped into to the living room to curl up on the sofa to take the call.

'And how was Tuscany with *The Lovely Ricky*?' her mate demanded instantly.

Tara's nickname for Ricky always amused Charley. 'Tuscany was lovely, and *The Lovely Ricky* was even lovelier. It was wonderful being with him and when he—'

'And I'm going to stop you there, caller,' cut in Tara, 'since a) I can't stand the gloating tone in your voice and b) I don't want to hear the ins and outs, if you'll pardon the pun, of your no doubt disgustingly passionate holiday!'

'You're a fine one to talk. You and Baz are forever taking fancy holidays!'

'Yes, but we always have a nosey ten-year-old daughter chaperoning us from the room next door!'

'Bad luck!' laughed Charley but, feeling the need to confide and offload the niggling anxiety that had been plaguing her for the last few days, she added lightly, 'I'll tell you what wasn't so lovely... Ricky's family.'

'Why?' Tara's voice was tinged with concern. 'What happened?'

'There just seemed to be this assumption that Ricky and I were... well, practically engaged, and that we'd be the next couple walking up the aisle. I mean, why else would I be dragged round half of Tuscany to meet his entire extended family? And then, when I accidentally caught the bouquet—'

There was an explosion of laughter from Tara. '*Accidentally!* Yeah, right!'

'Oh don't you bloody start!' wailed Charley.

'Is that all?' scoffed Tara. 'I thought you were going to say they hated you because they wanted him to marry some local girl instead. God, imagine what a nightmare that would have been.'

'No thanks!' joked Charley, but her unease remained, especially when Tara bluntly told her she was naïve to expect to pitch up at Ricky's sister's wedding without *certain assumptions* being made by his family. Reluctantly, Charley had to accept the point, especially since Ricky had specifically asked his parents to invite her, and he had apparently never taken anyone home to meet them before, ever. So she should have seen it coming, they both should, and perhaps he had. Either way, she couldn't really blame his family.

'I'm just not sure if I want to marry Ricky. We've not even been going out that long and...'

'You don't have a choice,' Tara informed her. 'Monnie is *desperate* to be a bridesmaid.'

'I'm not going to marry Ricky just so that Monnie can be a bloody bridesmaid!' laughed Charley.

'No, you're going to marry Ricky because you love him, and he adores you, and because you have great sex... and don't even start to deny that any of that is true, especially the last bit.'

Charley didn't even bother to try.

In contrast to Charley enjoying her meal-for-one and an evening of solitude, Pam was girding her loins to face another depressingly lonely evening, despite being in the process of cooking a meal for four. She poured a generous slug of olive oil in a large frying pan and set it on the stove and then, when it was hot, she slid in a finely chopped onion, which gave a gratifying sizzle. Turning the heat down, she left it to soften while she fetched the risotto rice.

A little over a year ago she'd been happily married, sharing her home and her life with her husband. As it turned out, she'd only been happy because ignorance is bliss, and the discovery that Geoff had been having an affair for several years with a former colleague of his had abruptly and traumatically ended their forty-year marriage. A chillingly sobering visit to a lawyer had informed her she would probably lose the house if they divorced, which had distressed her far more than the thought of losing her husband. The house was Josh's childhood home; years of memories of him were imprinted into its walls and she couldn't bear to give it up. Wisely, she'd put the divorce on hold, kicked Geoff out, and moved back to the house alone. Short of money, she'd started hosting foreign high school students via a language academy in Bristol. The courses, and therefore their visits, were very short term, lasting just a few weeks, but they ran regularly and the school was a prompt, no-quibble payer. Currently she had three sixteen-year-old lads who were apparently from Germany although, since they barely said a word to her, they could have come from outer space, for all that mattered.

The onions had softened, so she stirred in the rice, put the vegetables to simmer in chicken stock and carried the plates and cutlery into the dining room. She'd naively imagined that having youngsters around would be good company, and had pictured them noisily flocking round the table for meals, setting the table, and cheerfully practising their English with her. The joyful fantasy had quickly dissipated when the first batch had arrived. She blamed mobile phones. The teenagers barely spoke to one another, let alone to her, with their eyes glued to their screens and their thumbs furiously working the keys, and all her attempts to engage them in conversation had faltered and failed. The most she usually got out of any of them was a brief 'thank you' for the meal, and very basic details about where they were going the next day, whether they'd need a packed lunch, and what time they'd be 'home'. She couldn't blame them, she supposed; she was old enough to be their grandmother.

The risotto was ready, so she carried it through to the dining room, pausing at the bottom of the stairs to call up, 'Boys, supper!'

A nano beat later she was rewarded by the thump of three pairs of feet eagerly thudding down the stairs like a small herd of wildebeest and she smiled to herself, the stampede reminding her of Josh and her other son Luke at that age. The lads clattered into their places and she dished out their food and tried to start a conversation, not for her own entertainment, but because she was supposed to, as part of her hosting duties.

'So what did you all do today?'

Three mute faces turned to her, and then to each other in panic-induced silence, until one of them, clearly having lost the eyeball battle, was forced to reply.

'We went shopping,' he managed.

'Oh?' Pam tried to look interested. 'Did you buy anything?'

'No.'

She glanced across to the other two, who both shook their heads hurriedly but said nothing.

'Oh, okay,' said Pam then valiantly tried again. 'Did you have a good time?'

More uncomfortable looks ricocheted between the boys but eventually one of them plucked up the courage to say, 'No. It was very boring.'

'Oh, okay,' repeated Pam, defeated. *Right, well, we'll leave it at that then.*

The conversation having stalled into silence, the boys immediately retreated to the comfort zones of their phones and, not for the first time, Pam reflected on how lonely you could feel in a room full of people.

After they'd wolfed down the risotto, followed by large slabs of her home-made sticky toffee pudding with hot caramel sauce, the youngsters fled to the sanctuary of their rooms. Pam cleared the table and stacked the dishwasher, thinking that if they'd been her sons she'd have expected them to help. Pouring herself a mug of tea she wandered through to the living room where she switched on the TV and, not caring what was on, sank onto the sofa to while away the evening until she could reasonably go to bed. The images flickered in front of her eyes but she was barely aware of what she was watching, her thoughts having drifted to Charley and the conversation they'd had about Ricky's family. She turned to the photo on the windowsill of Josh and Charley at their wedding. Her son beamed back at her broadly, his eyes brimming with joy, and she remembered how confident the two newly-weds had been that they were going to be happy for the rest of their lives. But now Josh was dead, and Charley had found someone new, and the thought cut Pam like a jagged knife. She didn't for one second begrudge her widowed daughter-in-law the chance of a happy future after Josh – a future without Josh – because Charley, lovely, adorable Charley, had made her son's short life complete. Yet the knowledge that the young woman she had grown to love would soon become part of someone else's family, and no longer any part of hers, broke her heart.

'I'm going to lose her,' she told Josh sadly.

She knew it was probably inevitable one day, but Charley's trip to Tuscany had brought the loss one step closer. The old adage sprang to her mind, 'You're not losing a son, you're gaining a daughter'. *Well nobody warned me that if I lost my son, I'd lose my daughter-in-law too.*

Her thoughts were interrupted by her phone ringing. She wasn't entirely surprised. Zee, her oldest friend, had taken to calling her more frequently since her separation from Geoff. She muted the TV and reached for her phone.

'Is this your responsible citizen, "Care in the Community" call?' she asked dryly as she answered.

'No, it's my nightly check-up on the aged and decrepit.'

'How very dare you! You're older than me!' spluttered Pam, her spirits lifting, as they always did, chatting with Zee. The two of them had been close friends for decades.

'How's things?' Zee asked lightly.

'Oh, fine,' replied Pam, equally lightly.

'"Fine" as in really fine, or "Fine" as in "actually a bit crap but I don't want to go on about stuff like a broken record"?'

Guilty as charged, thought Pam but she managed a laugh before admitting, 'I'm just a bit low.'

'Any reason in particular?'

For a moment Pam considered confiding in her old friend her sadness about losing Charley, but thinking she would sound selfish, she lied.

'No, just the usual. Except – and can you believe this? – I'm missing that damn dog!'

'Seriously? You only had him a week.'

'I know. How insane is that?'

In all her sixty-plus years, Pam had never owned a dog and she was surprised at how quickly she'd got used to the lurcher's lumbering, lovable presence. She missed having him follow her around like a faithful shadow, and the warmth of his rough body as he heavily plonked himself down next to her on the sofa, heaving melodramatic, heartrendingly soulful sighs designed to let her know how much he was missing his beloved Ricky.

'Why don't you get one?'

'I'm tempted, honestly I am. A dog would be better company than the school students, bless them.'

'Better company than a husband too,' replied Zee, much to Pam's amusement.

'Definitely more faithful!'

'So why don't you?'

'Because I'd have to send it out to work to pay for the food and vet bills!'

Maybe she should get a dog, she mused, after Zee had rung off. Other working people did. At least the house wouldn't feel so empty. Plus, she'd have company, and good company at that – the kind that wanted to be with you, that actually wanted to share the sofa with you, if nothing else. Then she realised that she was literally missing a dog she'd only lived with for a week more than she was missing the man she'd lived with for forty years which, when she thought about it, spoke volumes. Idly, she wondered whether she should consider getting a permanent lodger instead of a series of temporary students. At least then there'd be a sporting chance of some interesting company in the evenings, but she baulked from making a long-term commitment to living with someone she barely knew and might not even really like.

Her previous dejection soon reasserted itself, a low level depression sliding back into her stomach like a dull weight. She seemed to be having a constant battle with it these days, and nothing she did could banish it. Ever self-perceptive, she knew what had triggered it today. It was the thought of losing Charley, as well as having lost everyone else. Luke, her eldest son, had moved away for his career, Josh had died, Geoff had left her, and now Charley was slipping away from her. It wasn't surprising she was left feeling unwanted, unnecessary and abandoned.

Chapter Three

Oh, for crying out loud, seethed Charley, as the ditzy young woman who'd just spent twenty minutes sniffing every single bath bomb, body wash and bottle of bubble bath in the entire shop left without actually buying anything at all. Charley wasn't usually so easily irritated but, in her defence, she was not having the most brilliant morning. As she was cycling into work the heavens had opened, drenching her completely, and she was still steaming softly, with rain dripping off her curls, and desperate for a coffee – but she couldn't leave the shop to get one because Tara was even later than usual. She was just about to text her mate to see if she was actually going to show up when an insistent rapping on the door distracted her. Looking up, she cursed silently. Possibly the most unhelpful delivery man in the world – dubbed 'Jobsworth' by Tara and Charley – stood outside, in the pouring rain, with a huge pile of boxes on a sack truck.

Charley groaned as she went to open the door. 'Can't you wheel them in?' she pleaded. 'Just this once? The boxes are getting soaked.'

'Nope. I'm only supposed to deliver them to the building,' he informed her, with undisguised pleasure. 'It's not in my contract to move the goods around inside the store.'

'But it's only another metre.'

He eyed her unflinchingly. 'I'm not insured to enter the premises.'

Charley was pretty sure he was lying but, not wanting to antagonise him further, she said brightly, 'Oh, but that's okay, then. I've got ten million pounds' worth of public liability insurance, so that'll cover you if you have an accident in the shop.'

'I'm not going to have an accident in the shop,' he replied, shoving the bottom box off the sack truck with his foot before adding smugly, 'because I'm not coming in.' Then he turned his back on her and walked off.

'Bye! Have a nice day!' Charley called, deliberately chirpily, to his retreating back. *Look on the bright side*, she told herself, *at least you're not married to him.*

Eyeing up the stack of heavy boxes, the cardboard already sodden, she briefly considered nipping round to the bike shop and asking Ricky if he'd just carry them in for her. But she was pulling in enough favours as it was and besides, he had his own shop to run, so she braced herself and starting hauling the boxes in one by one, hoping the cardboard wouldn't disintegrate and silently cursing the delivery man under her breath.

She'd just finished lugging the last of them into the dry when Tara finally arrived, nearly two hours late, but Charley couldn't say anything, since her mate was an unpaid volunteer.

'It's pissing down!' cried Tara, a tad unnecessarily, before taking off her wet coat and slinging it onto a chair. 'I'm late because I had to catch Monnie's teacher at school. Honestly, teachers! They're so precious about their time, I swear to God it'd be easier to get five minutes with the bloody queen.'

Swallowing her resentment, Charley said, 'No worries. But is everything all right with Monnie?'

'Yes, yes.' Tara waved a dismissive hand. 'Just a misunderstanding about homework.' She headed over to the pile of boxes. 'Come on, Charley, let's get this lot sorted. The place looks a right mess with this lot piled up in the middle of the floor.'

In all honesty Charley agreed, but that didn't stop her inwardly bridling at Tara's implied criticism. *Whatever.* She held her peace, and the two friends instantly slid into their well-practised routine with Tara unpacking and Charley logging the items on a spread-sheet.

'Twelve tea towels with the slogan, "Don't cry over spilt milk – it could have been your Prosecco!" Oh my God, I love that!

We should get it printed onto T-shirts!' said Tara gleefully before ripping open the next box. 'Twenty bottles of Prosecco and raspberry bubble bath. Ooh, mind if snaffle one?'

'Of course not.' Charley was only too happy to be able to give her mate at least some recompense for her time.

'Two dozen boxes of Prosecco and vanilla truffles,' continued Tara, and then she frowned. 'I thought we still had a stack of these stashed behind the till?'

'Have we? I thought we'd sold them all. I'll see if I can return them.'

'Or I can eat them, if that would help,' deadpanned Tara.

Charley grinned, then told her to take a couple of boxes home with her since she'd clearly ordered too many.

They went on companionably tearing open boxes and logging the contents, breaking off only to deal with the slow but steady stream of customers who came into the shop looking for that perfect Prosecco gift. Tara was just unpacking a cushion emblazoned with the legend *Relax! Prosecco's got your back!* when she glanced up at Charley and casually wrecked her day. 'Don't forget it's half term next week, so I won't be in.'

Dammit. Charley hadn't even been aware that it *was* half term next week. Not having any children, she wasn't au fait with the school timetable, but that never occurred to Tara, whose entire life was dictated by Monnie's calendar and assumed everyone else's was too.

'I hadn't forgotten,' lied Charley, but her heart sank since, after Tuscany, she was massively behind with her admin and had planned to catch up in the shop's quiet moments. More than anything, she needed to catch up with the dreaded accounts. To be totally accurate, she needed to start them. She'd intended to faithfully do them every month but somehow they kept slipping to the bottom of her fire-fighting list and then falling off it completely.

It would undoubtedly have been a lot easier for Charley to keep on top of the work if she wasn't effectively running two businesses. Well, one and half. A year or so, ago when Charley had been made redundant, she'd taken a bar job, which she'd absolutely loathed, and also launched a small business selling Prosecco-themed gift bags to local pubs and hotels, which she'd absolutely loved. Building on that budding venture, she'd taken the hugely adventurous step of ditching the bar job and starting a gift shop, but she still ran the party bag business as a side-line.

It would also undoubtedly have been a lot easier for Charley to keep on top of the work if Tara came in more. Still, she was good value when she was in, as Charley often reminded herself, and not just because she was free labour. The woman was a born salesperson – far better than Charley. Breezily buoyant and assertive, with a Teflon-coated self-confidence, Charley reckoned her mate could sell inflatable water wings to lifeguards on Bondi Beach. Whereas Charley preferred to hang around unobtrusively at the till, ready to deal with any queries, Tara always leapt straight in. Watching her enviously, Charley wondered how she did it.

'Morning!' Tara trilled as a sodden and thoroughly miserable-looking middle-aged woman plodded gloomily into the shop. Charley suspected the poor woman had only come in to get out of the rain, but Tara clearly wasn't prepared to let her leave without buying something. Chatting away nineteen to the dozen, Tara pounced and then swept her unsuspecting prey round the shop. 'Ghastly out there, isn't it! Have you seen our range of Prosecco-flavoured chocolate truffles? They're the perfect pick-me-up on a dismal day…' By the time she'd finished the customer had happily bought a box of the Prosecco and vanilla truffles, a pack of Prosecco bath bombs, and a couple of sparkly tealights.

–

At the end of the morning Tara waited until Charley had bought herself some lunch from the deli before sloping off. 'Are we still on for drinks at yours on Friday?' she asked, pulling on her raincoat.

'This Friday?' Charley queried, not recalling any plans.

'Yes, this Friday. Your place. You, me, Angie and Nisha,' intoned Tara pointedly. She locked eyes with her mate. 'You'd forgotten, hadn't you?'

'No!' Charley tried to look wide-eyed with innocence, but she knew Tara had rumbled her and she felt a twinge of guilt.

The friends usually met up at Charley's once a month to catch up, drink cheap fizz and put the world to rights, and she was well aware the get-togethers were just as important to the others as they were to her. For workaholic Nisha, it was the one night she prioritised her social life over her business, and for Angie, it was an oasis of calm away from her four young children, while Tara just loved the banter and camaraderie of getting the gang together.

'Liar!' retorted Tara good-naturedly. 'Honestly, woman, you are losing the plot!'

'Sorry!'

'Well you can't back out. Angie will be gutted, Nisha will shred you, and I will never let you live it down.'

'I wouldn't dream of it,' Charley promised, but the second her mate left the shop she called Ricky. 'About our date night on Friday...' she started awkwardly. 'I've sort of double-booked myself. I'd forgotten Tara and everyone are coming round to mine.'

'No worries,' he said. 'The lobster will wait.'

'Lobster?' Charley wailed, mortified that she'd messed up what was apparently going to be a special meal and a very expensive one at that.

'I'm joking! It's only prawns and they're in the freezer.'

'I'm really sorry—'

'Charley, it's fine,' he broke in lightly. 'Honestly. Have fun with your mates. Don't worry, there's always another night.'

'Yes, of course.'

Charley rang off and slipped her phone back into her pocket, feeling unexpectedly uneasy. For some reason, Ricky's phrase – *There's always another night* – remained in her thoughts. His casual assumption that there was always going to be 'another night' for the two of them tripped her up – how was it so simple for him to assume that? Perhaps more to the point, why wasn't it so easy for her?

—

Pulling up outside her flat on the Friday evening, Charley cursed. She was late for her own drinks do. She'd completely forgotten an order for fifty pamper bags she needed to deliver to the Avalon for a hen party that weekend and since the hotel was her biggest client, she didn't dare let them down. Fortunately, they'd phoned just before she'd left the shop so she'd managed to compile the bags, but she couldn't manage them on her bike – well, not without them getting trashed. She'd had to cycle home to get the car, and then the traffic had been chronic... so here she was, nearly fifteen minutes late.

She slipped off the seatbelt and leapt out of the car, locking it as she ran across the road. When she got to the top of the steps down to her flat she could see her mates already standing on the doorstep. 'Sorry, sorry, sorry!'

'For goodness' sake, Charley!' admonished Tara, as Charley arrived at the bottom of the steps.

'Is everything okay?' Nisha asked. Charley nodded and pushed her way through them to open the front door.

'No worries,' said Angie, patting Charley's shoulder as they all trooped inside.

Moments later, they were clustered round the coffee table in the living room, Nisha and Tara on the sofa and Charley and Angie squatting on floor cushions opposite them, each happily clutching a glass of fizz. Tara was eagerly outlining the list of outings she'd lined up for Monnie over half term.

'A trip to London with shopping at Westfield, a day on the beach at Weston if the weather holds, a movie... the zoo of course – we always go to the zoo, or the aquarium if it rains. A bike ride somewhere... Oh, and Legoland.'

'Is that all?' Nisha asked dryly.

'We were going to go to Center Parcs for the week, but Baz put his foot down.' Tara pulled a face. 'Tight wad! Anyhow, what are you doing with your lot, Ange? D'you fancy coming to Legoland with us?'

Angie had looked increasingly astonished by Tara's holiday plans; now she seemed caught on the hop by the invitation. 'Oh... er, it's lovely of you, but we're saving big trips like that until all four of them are big enough to remember going.'

Angie's eldest was only seven, whilst her youngest was still a babe in arms, so it was a plausible excuse, yet Charley wondered if it was actually because Angie couldn't afford it.

'Oh, I meant to say, Ange, I sold a couple more of your canvasses this week. I must settle up with you.' Charley doubted the money would cover the cost of a trip to Legoland but every little helped.

'You'd better get cracking on some more,' Tara told Angie. 'We haven't got many left. Do some really large ones. A bloke came in last week and he wants some this big.' She held out her arms to indicate the dimensions.

Nisha snorted. 'That's not large, that's outsize.'

'I don't have any canvasses that big!'

'Get some!' Tara narrowed her eyes Angie. 'You know what people are like. They don't know anything about art, but they like to buy it by the metre!'

Angie's Prosecco-themed paintings were good sellers, and Charley could have easily sold way more than her friend could ever supply. The vibrant, brightly coloured pieces featured foaming glasses of fizz, or bottles of bubbly, and they always attracted compliments from customers browsing in the shop.

'Can't you just knock off a few pieces over half term?' demanded Tara, causing Nisha to raise an eyebrow, Angie to flush pink with indignation, and Charley to protest that Angie didn't just 'knock off' her artwork.

'No, I can't!' Angie put her flute down sharply on the coffee table. 'I might not be taking the kids on countless day trips but I've still got to entertain them!'

'Get Will to look after them,' replied Tara.

'I wish! Ofsted's looming and Will's like a cat on a hot tin roof.' Angie's husband was a lovable, big bear of a man and a great dad, but he was also headteacher at a primary school so he couldn't always drop everything to look after his children.

'I'd offer to babysit but I'm up against deadlines,' Nisha said apologetically. Cool, elegant and 'happily divorced', Nisha ran her own marketing company, and her free time had long been a victim of her significant success.

'I can't either, Angie. Sorry,' said Charley, without even needing to explain why. 'But don't worry about it, Ange. You can only do what you can. The sky's not going to fall down if a customer has to wait a couple of weeks or so for a picture. It's not like he's waiting for a vital organ transplant!'

Angie shot her a grateful smile, but Tara instantly wiped it off her face. 'That's not the point. We don't want to disappoint our customers.'

Angie flushed, and Charley could have happily thumped Tara, but fortunately for both of them, a coffee table laden with glasses and snacks was in the way.

Nisha stepped in to defuse the tension. 'Meanwhile, in *other* news...' She paused for dramatic effect before announcing, 'I've been headhunted!'

'Bloody hell, Nishe,' beamed Charley. 'How exciting!'

'Fantastic! Who by?' Angie asked.

'Wait!' ordered Tara, immediately recovering her good humour and leaping up from the sofa. 'Hold that thought! I need to know too, but I'm getting more fizz!' She dashed into the kitchen to get the second bottle she'd brought. Tara never arrived anywhere empty-handed. Tonight she'd brought two bottles of fizz, a cheese selection pack, a box of fancy crackers, a large bag of tortilla chips and three different dips. Charley had long given up protesting at her mate's over-generosity because she knew treating people was Tara's way of expressing affection. This was due, Charley had long surmised, to Tara having had an impoverished childhood, brought up by a single mum who, her mate would fiercely insist, had more than made up for a lack of funds with a surfeit of love. But even so, treats had been thin on the ground and now Tara could afford them, she loved to spoil those she loved every chance she got. Anyhow, tonight Charley was only too grateful. She hadn't had time for supper and was eagerly hitting the dips and chips.

Rushing back in with the other bottle of Prosecco, Tara proclaimed, 'You may proceed, Nisha!'

Laughing, they all held out their glasses for a refill, while Nisha carried on.

'So, there's this upper echelon PR company, based in London, but they have offices all over the country, including Bristol. They do global brands, celebrities, televised events and so on, and they have invited me – yes, little old me – to meet to "discuss opportunities"!' She pulled a self-effacing grimace as if she couldn't believe her luck.

'What do they mean by "discuss opportunities"?' Tara asked shrewdly.

'Good question,' replied Nisha. 'I won't know until I meet them. But it's tempting. Ten years on and running the business still hasn't got any easier.'

Charley's hand froze, her glass poised halfway to her lips. *Bloody hell*, she thought. *Ten years and it's still a struggle? And that's with Nisha at the helm*. How much longer was it going to take before her business got any easier? Evicting that disturbing thought, she raised her glass to Nisha cheerily. 'Well, it sounds fantastic! Good luck.'

'Good luck!' chorused the other others, clinking glasses.

–

The evening broke up earlier than usual with Angie being the first to leave because Will had, unusually for him, texted her an SOS.

'Sorry, Charley, but Lily is the demon baby from hell at the moment. She's teething and Will says she's been crying solidly for thirty-five minutes, poor little mite.' She pulled an apologetic face. 'I'm going to have to rescue them from each other!'

Nisha took Angie's exit as her cue to leave too since, as ever, she had a mountain of work to get through when she got home.

After seeing them out, Charley wandered back into the living room where Tara was clearing up the remains of the snacks.

'Take the cheese back with you,' she told Tara, 'I'll never get through all of it.'

'I'll take the Stilton,' said her mate, wrapping it up. 'It's Baz's favourite and it'll be a useful sweetener for when he sees the credit card bill after half term!'

Charley inwardly rolled her eyes. Like Tara, Baz was the soul of generosity, but even he baulked at the amount of money Tara lavished on their daughter.

'The trouble is, he never used to see the holiday fund when I paid my credit card bill myself. But now there's no pulling the wool over his eyes anymore!'

Although her friend's tone was jokey, Charley flinched inside. 'I'm sorry the shop can't afford to pay you yet—' she started, but Tara cut her off.

'It's not a problem! I love working with you. It's a hoot. If I'd wanted to carry on earning a wage I would've stayed working at the Avalon.'

'If you stayed working at the Avalon you'd be doing life for murder by now!'

Tara had loathed her previous boss, once describing him as 'a pimply prick of a micro-manager with the intelligence and people skills of a plastic garden gnome'. Having met him, Charley could vouch for the accuracy of the description.

'Highly likely,' agreed Tara.

Although she was smiling, Charley still felt the usual onslaught of guilt when her inability to pay her colleagues came up, not least since both of them had invested in the shop to help Charley stock it in the first place. Pam always maintained that the five grand she'd put in was a gift and she didn't want anything back. Tara, on the other hand, had invested three grand, with a view to getting a share of the profits at a future date. The trouble was, Charley had absolutely no idea when that might be and, judging by Nisha's earlier comments, it might turn out to be a lot longer than either she, or Tara, hoped.

Chapter Four

The following day, Charley did a minimal clear-up and re-stock after closing the shop, then cycled round to Ricky's, still riddled with embarrassment at having stood him up the previous evening. She let herself in through the side gate to leave her bike in the back garden as she usually did, and found him crouched down, stripping an old bike frame. Carlo lolloped over to give her a warm, whiskery welcome, and she gave his rough grey head a scratch.

'New find?' she asked, gently pushing Carlo aside and going over to kiss Ricky warmly. Then she crouched down next to him to watch him work. Most of the bikes he sold he sourced from skips or from the city's rubbish tips, and then renovated them.

He nodded. 'It's a classic. An old Elan racing bike. The tyres are rotten, and it'll need new brakes, but they're classy bikes, Elans, lightweight, sturdy and well designed – Italian, of course!' he finished provocatively.

'The bike might be classy, but that doesn't stop you being a skip-rat!'

He rocked back on his heels and grinned at her. 'Hey, don't you mock my business model! There's nothing wrong with rescuing pre-loved stuff, giving it some TLC and a new lease of life.'

'Pre-loved? Hardly "loved" if it got dumped a skip!'

'Somebody loved this bike once, Charley, and by the time I'm finished with it someone will love it again. Trust me.'

'How could they not? It's Italian!' She leant over to kiss him again.

Ricky had no qualms about his scavenging business model, arguing that it was good for the environment, and good for his profit margin too. 'They don't come any cheaper than free' was his position – although his labour didn't come free, he was always swift to assert. Despite that, she reflected, he seemed to need to spend far less time running his shop than Charley did hers and, unlike her, he had nobody to help him – except Carlo, who he affectionately referred to as 'security' since the large lurcher could be relied on to guard the shop while Ricky nipped out for a coffee, or a pee, or to grab a sandwich from the deli.

Charley watched him contentedly for a moment, taking a vicarious enjoyment from the evident pleasure he took in his work, and the equally evident easy skill of his hands. She idly wondered how he managed to strip an entire bike without getting covered in oil. Despite kneeling on the ground and wrestling with a dirty old bike, Ricky's shirt and chinos were still spotless. She remembered watching Josh change the battery in his car, when he'd got absolutely plastered in oil, staining his T-shirt and jeans, smudging his cheek and even smeared in his hair. The memory slipped in, warm and tender, but she pushed it aside, uncomfortable at reminiscing over Josh when she was with Ricky.

'Hungry?' he asked, cutting into her thoughts.

'Very.'

Wiping his hands on a rag, Ricky rose to his feet and she followed him into the flat, Carlo close on their heels.

'Can I help?' She knew full well the answer would be 'no', but she still liked to offer and, as she expected, he shook his head.

Going through to the bedroom, she chucked her bag on the bed and then went back into the living room. Ricky's flat was smaller than hers, with just one bedroom, but it was open-plan, so it felt more spacious and she loved the way she could sit on the sofa and talk to him as he prepped supper in the kitchen area. Carlo immediately scrambled onto the sofa and curled up next to her.

'Push him away if he's too much,' said Ricky taking a bottle of Prosecco out of the fridge.

'He's fine.' Charley reached out to give the lurcher a good scratch behind his ears.

Ricky brought her over a glass of fizz and bent to kiss her lightly on the lips.

'Thank you,' she said after taking a slurp.

'For the kiss?' teased Ricky, going back to the kitchen.

'For the fizz! Although the kiss was nice too.'

He flicked her a loving look, a smile playing on his mouth, and she melted. She took another sip of her fizz. He always bought her Prosecco, knowing she preferred it to wine, although he always drank red.

'It's prawn linguine,' he reminded her, putting a pan of water onto boil. 'But don't panic, I'm putting way less garlic in this time!'

For a while she sat contentedly, relishing her Prosecco, scratching the soft pockets of fur behind Carlo's ears and watching Ricky in the kitchen until he glanced over to her and said, 'My mother called last night,' and she felt herself instantly tense.

'Oh, yes?' she said lightly.

'She wanted to tell me how much everyone loved you,' he said, holding her gaze and smiling proudly. 'In fact, she spent the entire phone call telling me how wonderful you are, she didn't even ask how I was! Apparently my aunt thinks you're beautiful, my father thinks I'm a lucky man, my sister says she hates you for your hair, and my mother adores you for making the effort to visit my grandmother who, by the way, thinks I don't deserve you.'

'She's right,' replied Charley with a straight face.

During their time in Tuscany, Charley had warmed to Ricky's grandmother most in his family, and Ricky seemed closer to her to anyone else, even his parents. Which was perhaps no surprise since, while Ricky's parents had been occupied with turning their small olive farm into a thriving business, he'd spent most of his childhood with his grandmother. Charley and Ricky had visited his nonna the day before they flew home and, to

Charley's amusement, her house was adorned with photos of Ricky, a good many of him as a little boy. To Ricky's obvious discomfort, his grandmother, with much gleeful rolling of eyes and dramatic gesticulation, had told Charley stories about his childhood scrapes. Of course they'd both had to rely on Ricky to interpret them and it had begun to strike Charley that Ricky's versions didn't seem to warrant, or reflect, the humorous delivery of the old woman's narrative, and she suspected she was getting some very edited highlights.

Narrowing her eyes at him, she'd said, 'Are you telling me the whole story?'

'Yes,' he'd vowed, with a feigned innocence that had sent Charley reaching for her phone.

'*Mi scusi*,' she'd said politely to his grandmother, and she had looked up the phrase which seemed to recur frequently in all the stories about him. '*Molto cattivo*,' she'd muttered as she typed. 'Aha!' She'd skewered Ricky with a meaningful look. 'Very naughty.' He had had the grace to look abashed and Charley, pointing at Ricky, had turned to his grandmother and said, '*Molto cattivo, sì?*'

Her entire face had lit up. '*Sì!*' she had replied with a conspiratorial twinkle in her eye and the two women had gleefully enjoyed the joke.

As they were driving back to his family home he had turned to her and said, 'Thank you for being so sweet to my grandmother. You were really kind to her.'

'Not at all. I thought she was lovely,' Charley had replied truthfully. 'I enjoyed meeting her. And especially getting the lowdown on you as a child!'

He'd smiled and turned his attention back to the road and Charley had relaxed into her seat, enjoying the warmth of the Tuscan sun and the stunning scenery sliding past the car window.

'My mother said to be sure to let you know you'd be welcome any time, for a holiday or whatever,' said Ricky, bringing her back to the present.

Or whatever? Charley wondered what that supposed to imply. 'How very generous of her,' she replied carefully. If Ricky detected the caution in her voice he didn't show it, merely turning back to his chopping board.

Meeting Josh's family had been altogether different. He hadn't introduced her to them formally, or en masse at all. She could vividly recall the first time she met Pam – it was a couple of days after she'd moved in with Josh. His mother had come round unexpectedly to drop something off, and had only stayed long enough for a quick coffee, which meant that Charley hadn't had time to feel nervous, since she hadn't even known the woman was coming. With hindsight, she realised how canny Pam had been, making that first encounter so casual and brief. She hadn't asked Charley a thing about herself, only about the holiday she and Josh had just had. When she'd left, all she'd said was, 'Lovely to meet you, Charley,' before adding airily, 'Come for lunch sometime, if you'd like to, when you've had time to settle in.'

It had been such a contrast to the ordeal of meeting Ricky's family, but that wasn't anyone's fault, she reminded herself, the circumstances had just been entirely different.

Ricky and Charley spent a chilled evening entwined on the sofa, watching a movie and when the film finished Charley went to fetch her toilet bag from her backpack, only to discover she'd left it at her place. In her mind's eye she could see it still sitting on the side of the bath in her flat. *Dammit!*

'There's a spare toothbrush in the bathroom cabinet,' Ricky told her.

'Oh, okay, thanks,' said Charley, going to help herself.

They stood side by side at the bathroom sink, and Ricky squirted a dollop of toothpaste onto his brush and then handed the tube to her before saying, 'You can leave some spare toiletries here if it makes it easier.'

Without waiting for her response he started brushing his teeth. For no reason, no reason at all, Charley felt her stomach tighten. She told herself it was a perfectly rational, sensible suggestion, and it would undoubtedly be simpler to leave a set of toiletries at Ricky's flat since she spent so much time there. So why did she feel a wave of disquiet wash over her as if, somehow, it was the first step towards moving in with him?

–

Later that night, after they'd made love, Ricky fell asleep but Charley lay awake, on edge. Eventually she slid upright, leant back on her pillow and looked at him. He wasn't drop-dead gorgeous, but he wasn't bad-looking. But then Josh hadn't been stunningly handsome either. Ricky's was a pleasant, gentle face, made lovely because his personality shone through it. His features were more sculpted than Josh's, and his dark curls lay against the pillow, so different from Josh's unruly blond mop. His dark lashes seemed so much longer than Josh's fair ones. Her eyes wandered down over his body. Watching his naked chest rising and falling softly with each breath, she felt a rush of love for him, but then the doubts came crowding in. *You are a lovely man, and I do love you. And I love being with you. But is that enough? Am I in love with you? Or am I just trying to convince myself I am?*

She didn't love him the same way she'd loved Josh; that was for sure. With Josh, there had been immediate chemistry. As a matter of fact, Ricky wasn't really her type. Strictly speaking, the very first time they'd met was when he'd picked her up out of the gutter after she'd tripped over while running for a bus. She'd thanked him, but hadn't given him a second glance. The first time she'd clapped eyes on Josh, on the other hand, she'd fallen for him instantly, hopelessly, and when he'd noticed her looking at him and had beamed at her, everyone and everything had seemed to disappear and she'd felt like they were the only two people in the entire world. Josh had only to catch her eye in a room full of people, or flash her his trademark broad grin, to make her pulse race and her heart tilt. Her entire, brief, marriage had felt like a honeymoon. She'd craved his company, wanting to spend every single moment of every day with him, clock-watching to see when he'd be home. And she'd known immediately, the moment she met Josh on that beach in Ibiza, that he was The One. The one she wanted to spend the rest of her life with. She'd flown home to Suffolk and dropped everything to move to Bristol, literally the other side of the country, to be with him. Would she do that for Ricky? If she was ruthlessly honest with herself, she didn't think she would.

—

'Pam, you sit there, between David and Theo. Phil, you're opposite Pam. I want the chair nearest the door... Zee and Mona, just fill in anywhere.' Toni merrily waved her hand towards the other chairs round the table. Pam's friends – all couples – casually opted for the nearest available seat. After decades of socialising together, her new singledom had somehow overturned the seating arrangements they used to adopt, where they'd all just piled round the table any old how. Now Pam's position at the table apparently needed to be 'managed'. It was meant kindly but only served to reinforce her acute awareness of being the only one on her own, spare and surplus to requirements, and the absent Geoff seemed to occupy the vacant chair, like the elephant in the room. It might have been her imagination, but nowadays the conversation felt stilted and strained. Beforehand, multiple conversations had bounced loudly around the room chaotically, with countless good-humoured interruptions, now they seemed awkward, and she struggled to contribute to them. This Saturday evening, the dinner-table talk kicked off with the subject of holidays, as a hairdresser might, on the grounds that it's usually safe territory.

'One guess where we're going this year,' said Mona flatly.

'France!' chorused everyone.

'Yes, *again*!' Mona groaned in mock despair.

'There's no point investing in a timeshare if we're not going to use the damn thing.' Her husband laughed, appealing to the group.

'But you say that every year!'

'Because it's true every year!'

'Well, we're having a modest staycation this year,' Toni informed everyone. 'Scotland.'

'Oh, how lovely,' said Pam, forcing herself to join in. 'It's beautiful up there.'

'If you can see it through the rain,' groaned Toni's husband.

'Phil's a little less keen than I am,' explained Toni, suppressing a smile. She rested her hand lightly on his shoulder as she stood behind him.

Automatically, unconsciously, Phil's hand came up to envelop hers. 'Yes, because you know what they say: *The rain in Spain falls mainly in... Scotland!*'

'Oh, ha, ha,' said Toni, waggling her hand free to give him an affectionate shove.

Pam felt a pang of jealousy, but crushed it, conscious she was seeing things through the skewed prism of her own loneliness. Before she and Geoff had split up, she hadn't noticed these loving gestures, looks and glances, and the banter and in-jokes between them. Even Zee and Theo – who couldn't exactly be described as being 'happily' married – exchanged the occasional knowing look or shared a wry smile. Now, acutely aware of them, they served to increase Pam's solitude and isolation.

Toni had turned to Pam and was asking, 'Have you got anything booked yet?'

'No, not this year,' she replied brightly, avoiding pointing out that she didn't actually have anyone to go with, knowing that her friends would all instantly offer to take her with them on their holidays. But she had underestimated their powers of perception, and perhaps their affection for her, too.

'Come with us!' offered Mona. 'There's plenty of room in the apartment, isn't there, David?'

'*Mais oui, bien sûr!*'

'Your French is really coming on,' Mona told him with a withering glance, and Pam laughed obligingly.

'Come to Scotland with us,' urged Toni.

'You'll need to bring your wellies, and a sou'wester and a mac,' Phil warned. 'And possibly a life jacket and small inflatable boat.'

Pam smiled at them all fondly before lying brazenly, 'Thanks, but I'm not sure I can get away this year. It'll be difficult for Charley in the shop on her own so I'd have to check with her.'

It was only the second half of the second sentence which was actually a lie. Pam had no intention of checking with Charley since she had no intention of going on holiday with any of them. It was bad enough feeling like a spare part all evening; she didn't fancy playing gooseberry for several days on end. Then she admonished herself for being churlish.

'Phil! Top up Pam's glass!' Toni ordered. Pam glanced down at her drink, mildly horrified to find she'd drained it so soon. Dutch courage, she supposed.

'No! Thank you, but I'm driving.' She covered her glass with her hand.

'You might have to hold back on the pud then,' advised Toni. 'I put *pints* of brandy in the syllabub!'

Pam groaned melodramatically, 'Oh no! I love your syllabub.'

'I'll put some in a tub for you to take home.'

'You should have let us give you a lift, Pam,' said Zee. 'In fact, why don't we drive you home anyway, you can pick up your car in the morning?'

Pam waved away the offer casually. 'No, I'll be fine, and anyhow, I think Charley wants me to help in the shop tomorrow morning.'

'On a Sunday?' queried Mona.

Pam quickly improvised. 'Stocktaking.' It was another downright lie and she was immediately swamped with remorse. But she didn't want to have to wait until Zee and Theo were ready to leave. She needed to be free to escape when she wanted to. Truth be told, Pam had almost chickened out of coming altogether. Geoff leaving her – and for a younger woman – had dealt her self-confidence such a savage body blow, she was still struggling to recover. She didn't need to be reminded that she was the only one in their friendship group who had failed at the life skill of marriage, the only one who had failed to keep her husband.

As the evening wore on, improbably slowly it seemed to Pam, she found it increasingly difficult to be jolly, and it was taking a monumental effort to remain focussed. A tension headache had crept from the back of her skull to her temples. As soon as it was polite to do so, she made her excuses and left.

'Please don't think me rude, but I don't like leaving my young students alone at home too late,' she said, deploying her pre-planned, get-out-of-jail-free card.

There was a flurry of hugs and air-kisses and Toni nipped off to get her the promised portion of syllabub so it was Zee who went to the front door with her.

'Are you okay?' her friend asked in a low voice full of concern.

'Yes! Absolutely!' But Zee's face remained unconvinced.

–

The house was in complete darkness when Pam pulled onto her drive, which wasn't exactly welcoming. *I must remember to leave some lights on if I'm going to get home late.* It wasn't so bad this time, since she knew her student lodgers were at home, but the thought of coming home alone to a dark, empty house in the future was not one she relished. Opening the front door, the complete silence that met her told her the boys had already taken themselves off to bed so she quietly headed into the kitchen. Switching on the lights revealed they'd left her the washing up from the supper she'd cooked them before going out herself. She sighed nostalgically. Half of her thought she ought to have been irritated that they'd left it for her, but they'd piled the dishes neatly on the side of the sink and it was a joy to come home to signs of human habitation, rather than to a pristine kitchen where everything was exactly as she'd left it. But as she put the portion of Toni's syllabub in the fridge, her sprits suddenly plummeted. Mentally, she'd flipped back fifty or so years, to when she was small, a child coming home from a birthday party with nothing but a slice of cake, and none of the proper prizes for winning any of the games. *Oh, pack it in, for crying out loud!* she told herself briskly. *Don't be so damned ungrateful, and look on the bright side; at least you're not missing out on Toni's syllabub.* Helping herself to a spoon, she tore the lid off the tub and tucked in.

Chapter Five

On Monday morning, Charley and Ricky cycled into work together with Carlo lolloping along beside them on a long lead. When they arrived at Cargo, the other shopkeepers were already unlocking doors, turning on lights and opening up for the day. A few early morning punters were making for the coffee shop and the deli.

'Morning, you two!' called out the florist, piling fresh flowers into the dozen or so cream-painted enamel buckets lined up in front of her unit.

'Morning, Del!' they chorused.

Hand in hand, and now wheeling their bikes, they passed the deli where Rita was putting out the sandwich board advertising her daily specials.

'Doing your favourite today, Ricardo!' she said. 'Buffalo mozzarella and pesto panini with baby plum tomatoes. Shall I hold one for you?'

Ricky turned to Charley. 'Will you want one?' She shook her head. 'Just the one please, Rita,' he called out and she waved in acknowledgement.

A few other people greeted them cheerily by name. The camaraderie of the place always buoyed Charley's spirits which, if she were honest with herself, were already flagging today. It was the start of half term, meaning Tara wouldn't be in and she'd be on her own every morning. It wasn't so much a daunting prospect as a dull one, because even when the footfall and the takings were down, when Tara was around at least they had fun.

She and Ricky reached her shop where, still holding hands, they stood for a lingering kiss, which would have been even more

44

lingering had it not been abruptly interrupted by Milo from the ice-cream parlour bellowing jokily at them, 'Oi, you two. Get a room!'

They broke off and Ricky good-naturedly made a rude sign at Milo who laughed and reciprocated. Bending close to Charley, Ricky whispered, 'Don't blame the man. He's just jealous!' before kissing her ear. 'Have a good day,' he said finally before heading off to the bike shop, Carlo at his heel.

'You too,' she replied.

She'd decided not to tell Pam that Tara would be off all week, guessing that the older woman would insist on coming in to work the mornings as well and, as Charley frequently reminded herself, her mother-in-law was already doing too much for her. It was an admirable decision, but she was soon regretting it. Perhaps optimistically, she'd earmarked the morning to compile a hundred and fifty gift bags for delivery that evening to a dozen or so venues across the city, but a steady stream of customers drifted through the shop all morning, putting paid to that plan. Worse, by late morning she was desperate for a pee and a coffee, in that order. Fortunately she was rescued by the unexpected arrival of Nisha, bearing a couple of take-away cups.

'Nishe, you absolute star!' beamed Charley and then, pausing only to garble, 'Please-can-you-hold-the-fort-so-I-can-nip-to-the-loo-before-there's-an-embarrassing-incident-we-will-never-forget,' she shot out.

When she got back, Nisha was happily recommending a juniper and Prosecco reed diffuser to a very earnest-looking young man.

'If it's a gift, I'd go with this one,' she was advising. 'It's a subtle fragrance, looks stylish, and since it's in a white bottle, it'll go in any room.'

Charley was amused by Nisha's spiel, but the young chap left happily enough, having purchased the diffuser.

'You didn't offer to gift wrap it for him, then!'

'Not without charging for the wrapping paper,' was Nisha's dry response.

Switching places, Charley slid behind the counter and took a grateful slurp of coffee. 'Hmmm, thanks for this. To what do I owe the unexpected pleasure of a visit from you in the middle of the working day?'

'I've just had a meeting with that PR company.'

'And?' prompted Charley, instantly agog.

'Oh. My. God. Their client list! Stellar or what? A-listers and beyond. It's *hugely* flattering to be asked to join them. I'm really tempted. I mean, I love being my own boss, you know I do, but ten years on and I'm still flat out 24/7. I know I *could* cut back some of my clients, but I hate turning down business.'

Charley empathised with that problem only too easily. Some days, especially mid-week, the shop saw precious few customers and she often wondered if it had been worth opening up at all, but she didn't dare risk cutting back the opening hours, or closing for half a day, knowing she'd lose customers.

Nisha took a delicate sip of her coffee. 'Obviously, we only discussed the headlines of a potential deal. Nothing concrete… possible job title, initial salary and commission, likely perks and so forth.' She swirled her coffee round pensively, and Charley didn't rush her. 'But it's a huge step – giving up my own business.'

'So how did you leave it?'

'They're going to work up the deal, put it all down in a contract, and send it through.'

'Well you know what they say,' said Charley. 'The devil's in the detail.'

'Too true.'

'When would you have to decide?'

Nisha shrugged. 'They said I can take as long as I like.'

'Well that must show how much they want you.'

'Maybe.'

The opening of the shop door prevented any further conversation.

'Morning!' said Charley brightly to a couple of young women as they walked in.

Slipping the lid back onto her coffee Nisha said, 'I'll keep you posted,' and left Charley to it.

–

Without Tara, Charley couldn't even nip out to get any lunch, so when Pam arrived for the afternoon, Charley asked her to hold the fort while she popped out to the deli.

'No Tara?' asked Pam astutely, immediately stepping in for Charley behind the till.

Dammit, thought Charley. 'Half term,' she explained.

'Why didn't you say? I could have come in.'

'There's no need, I just forgot to get any lunch.'

'If you'd called me I would have made you something.'

'I know you would.' Charley smiled, heading out of the door. 'That's why I didn't!'

The afternoon was even busier than the morning, at least in terms of footfall. Although while some had come in to buy, irritatingly, quite a few had all too obviously come to window-shop for things they were almost certainly going to buy online. One even had the audacity to whip out her phone and take a shot of a cotton pinny that had taken her fancy. It read: *If you can't stand the heat, open the fizz!* Then she stuffed it back on the shelf, not even bothering to re-fold it. Charley caught Pam's eye behind the customer's back.

'The cheek of it!' complained Pam once the woman had left.

'I know! But what can I do? I can't *make* them buy something!' Then, seeking a distraction from her irritation, she said, 'How was your weekend? Didn't you go to a dinner party? Zee's, was it?'

'No, Toni's, and it was… lovely,' Pam replied. But Charley had detected the slight beat before the word 'lovely' and the over-bright brittleness in her mother-in-law's tone.

It didn't surprise her. She could sympathise only too easily. After Josh had died Charley had drifted away from the friends they'd hung around with as a couple. They'd been Josh's friends anyhow, and she'd felt like she was tagging along to a club she no longer belonged to, and it had been painful to see the other couples sharing their loving looks and kisses, their in-jokes and playful banter.

'It's awkward going out with couples when you're on your own,' she said.

'Yes, isn't it? You feel like…' Pam was evidently at a loss as to how to express her thoughts.

'Like a fifth wheel,' Charley provided flatly.

Pam cocked her head appreciatively. 'Precisely! I've not heard that before. Is that a common phrase?'

Charley nodded and then Pam surprised her by saying. 'Well, that's reassuring.'

'Why?'

'Because if there's an idiom for something then it must mean a lot of people are in that same situation. So it makes me feel less… singled out. Single, yes. Singled out, no!'

'Well, that's one way of looking at it.' *Trust you to put a positive spin on things.* 'You know, now I come to think of it, when I go out with my mates these days, it's just us girls. Will and Baz never come.'

'Really? Why ever not?'

'Someone's got to babysit!'

'Ha! How very well trained.' Then, sounding distinctly wistful, Pam went on, 'As a rule my friends don't go out without their husbands in the evenings. We might meet up for a coffee now and again, of course, and very occasionally go for a pub lunch.'

Charley shrugged. 'Maybe it's a generation thing? Or just habit?'

'Are you implying we're all old and stuck in our ways?' exclaimed Pam, pretending to take offence.

'No!' protested Charley, 'but if you think about it, you've all been couples for—'

Pam raised a warning eyebrow. 'Don't even finish that sentence!'

'For some time,' said Charley tactfully. 'But why not have a women-only night now and then?'

The rest of the afternoon was rewardingly busy, but it meant that by closing time Charley still hadn't had time to assemble the gift bags she had to deliver that evening.

'How many have you got to do?' asked Pam as she was leaving.

'A hundred and fifty.'

Pam hovered in the doorway. 'I feel guilty leaving you that lot to do.'

'Don't! You do more than enough as it is. Go. GO!' ordered Charley, ushering her mother-in-law out of the door, then locking it behind her to stop any more customers drifting in since, apparently, the average shopper was incapable of reading the word 'Closed'.

She was clearing the large display table to make space to work when a light tapping on the window got her attention. It was Ricky, so she went over to open the door.

'Are you nearly done?'

'I wish!'

Eyeing the piles of empty gift bags on the table he said, 'D'you want a hand?'

She waved away his offer airily. 'No, it's fine. It won't take me long.'

He raised an eyebrow, as if asking her who she was trying to kid, but confined himself to saying mildly, 'Maybe not, but it'll take even less time if we do it together.'

'True,' she conceded gratefully.

They worked quickly and easily together but it was gone half seven by the time all the bags were all filled and collated, which meant it would be well after nine by the time Charley had finished the deliveries. She was trying not to think about it.

'I assume these have to go out tonight,' said Ricky.

'Yes, but I have to go and pick up the car first.' The prospect of cycling up the hill and then pitching out again to deliver the bags depressed her and she felt herself physically slump.

Ricky must have noticed because, taking pity on her, he said, 'My place is nearer. I'll cycle home, pick up my car and deliver the bags, you go home.'

'I can't ask you to do that!'

'You haven't asked me. I've offered.'

Charley shook her head. 'No... honestly. I ought to deliver them myself. They're my customers.'

'Okay, then, but I'll still get my car and drive you. It'll be quicker and save you cycling all the way back to yours.'

Charley caved and, sliding her arms round his neck, she kissed him.

'You are a lovely man,' she informed him, finally breaking away.

'And you are a very beautiful woman.'

–

It was just after nine when they made the last delivery so Charley proposed picking up pizzas and taking them back to hers.

'You're working too hard,' Ricky told her sternly as they ate, slumped on the sofa. 'I'm worried about you. Seriously,' he added as Charley looked up at him, frowning mildly in denial. 'You shouldn't be spending all your evenings doing deliveries.'

'Well there isn't any other time.'

'Maybe you should stop the gift bag side of the business? Or make it collection–only?'

Charley shook her head. 'I'd lose customers, and although it doesn't make a huge amount of money, it all helps.'

They continued eating in silence for a moment and then Charley yawned and slung her pizza slice back in the box. 'I'm done. I'm too tired to eat any more.'

Gathering up his half-eaten pizza, Ricky got up to leave. 'You need an early night.'

But Charley reached out to take his hand. 'Stay?' she asked, and when he hesitated she stood up, took the pizza box out of his hand and led him through to the bedroom. He started undressing her, slowly, teasingly and she pulled him down onto the bed, where the photo of Josh grinned down foolishly at them from the bedside table. *Dammit!* Ricky's visit had been impromptu, so she hadn't put the photo away beforehand.

She tried to ignore it, and to focus her attention on Ricky but it was impossible with Josh watching their every move. His trademark grin seemed to have developed a distinct leer. She couldn't even begin to imagine how awkward Ricky must be finding it, having your girlfriend's former husband staring at you from the bedside table, observing your technique and judging your performance. Talk about cramping your style.

'One second,' she whispered and, slipping free from his embrace, she leant over, grabbed the picture and laid it face down. Later, when she put it back upright, she would be wracked with remorse for treating Josh in that way.

Chapter Six

'Brownies,' announced Pam, putting a slightly battered and much-loved cake tin down on the kitchen table in front of Zee.

'Oooh, yes please!' Zee instantly prised off the lid and helped herself, releasing the warm, rich aroma of cocoa. 'Did you make them especially for me?'

'No, for the students.'

'You could have lied!'

'Would they taste any better if I had?'

'No. But it's the thought that counts!' claimed Zee and Pam grinned. 'Where are the lads, anyhow?'

'The aquarium. Honestly Zee, they're hardly ever here. Their life is one long social whirl. I had to send them off with a packed lunch and it's cheaper to make snacks than buy them.'

'And way more delicious,' mumbled Zee with her mouth full.

It was also much cheaper for Pam to have Zee round for coffee than to go out to a café, which was why the two women were sitting at the kitchen table, with fresh coffee brewing in the cafetière, instead of treating themselves in town.

'Shall I plunge?' asked Zee, reaching towards the coffee pot.

'Go ahead,' said Pam, and for a moment it was silent in the kitchen except for the faint *whoosh* of the plunger.

'You left Toni's very early the other night,' said Zee.

'Yes, I hope she wasn't offended.'

'No. More concerned. We all were.' Zee looked over to Pam meaningfully.

'I suppose I should call her and apologise. I keep underestimating how awkward it is seeing everyone, now I'm on my own,' admitted Pam, reaching over to pour the coffee.

'Perhaps we all have,' Zee responded gently.

Pam shook her head. 'It's my fault. Being the only single person at the table reminds me that my marriage has failed, and that makes me feel that *I've* failed.'

'Don't you dare blame yourself for something that's bloody Geoff's fault!' cried Zee, waggling her finger sternly at Pam before reaching over and taking her mug. 'It takes two to make a marriage,' she reminded her, 'and only one to break it.'

Pam sighed. 'But it still rubs it in that I'm on my own. Charley had a brilliant expression for it. "The fifth wheel"!'

'There were seven of us at dinner, Pam,' Zee pointed out teasingly. 'Your maths is appalling.'

'Always has been,' conceded Pam, nonetheless grateful to her friend for lightening the mood.

'Which is tougher,' asked Zee, 'being "the fifth wheel" or being the only wheel, as it were, when you're on your own?'

'Good question.' At least the discomfort of being "the fifth wheel" or whatever was only once in a while, whereas the bored, empty ache of being lonely was seven nights a week and all day Sunday.

'Anyhow, look on the bright side. At least we invite you because we actually want to see you. We only invite that bloody Barbara woman because we have to, otherwise we can't see Geoff.'

Ashamed as Pam was to admit it, the compliment boosted her no end. 'What's she actually like?'

'Ghastly,' replied Zee, rolling her eyes, although whether she was being loyal rather than truthful Pam had no idea. 'She's openly flirtatious with everyone, *not* just Geoff,' Zee stressed. 'If she doesn't stop batting her eyelashes at Phil, Toni will either lace her food with arsenic or impale her on a meat skewer. Possibly both.'

Pam chuckled and Zee continued. 'And talk about mutton dressed as lamb! Her tops are so low they leave nothing to the imagination. She dropped a stuffed olive down her cleavage one evening and, swear to God, it disappeared completely! Of course everyone was too polite to mention it.'

Although she very much doubted the story was true, and suspected that Zee was riffing on her theme purely to entertain her, the image still tickled Pam. 'Perhaps she was saving it for later!'

Childishly, she found herself wanting to ask Zee who they preferred inviting – her or Geoff. *Don't be so bloody petty*, she chided herself. *It's not a competition.*

Zee had dug into her bag for her phone and was busily screen-scrolling. 'We should find some fun things we can do together. Just you and me.'

'Like what?'

'Night classes?'

Pam pulled a face which prompted Zee to say, 'Don't give me that look! It's meant to be good for us at our age, learning something new. Okay, so, I'm on a list of evening classes in the Bristol area.' She pursed her lips as she scrolled. 'How about Ancient Greek?'

Pam stared at her incredulously.

Wilfully ignoring her friend's expression Zee went on, 'It says: "Have you always wanted to learn a dead language?"'

'No,' replied Pam.

'Good! Me neither! How about adults' ballet?'

'We're far too old!'

'Speak for yourself!'

'I speak as I find!'

'It's says it's for mixed ability,' Zee cajoled.

'Is there one for no ability?'

'No.'

'Gutting,' said Pam dryly.

Zee was scrolling down the page. 'Good grief! There's a class in acrylic nail extensions.'

'Seriously?' Pam was flabbergasted, and by the look on Zee's face she was too. 'Who knew you could do an evening class in how to do your nails?'

'Who even would?' More scrolling and then, 'Now this one is perfect,' claimed Zee. '"All about the menopause."'

'It's a bit bloody late for that!'

'Yeah, we could probably teach them a thing or two,' agreed Zee, still searching. 'Good grief, there's hundreds of courses. I'm still only on the As.'

'Oh dear God. Put your phone away! I am losing the will to live!'

Zee seemed reluctant to give up until Pam said, 'I probably can't afford to do evening classes anyhow.'

Reluctantly, Zee slipped her phone into her bag. 'Okay. Well, we'll just have to find some free stuff to do instead.'

Pam topped up her friend's coffee and then stood up and went to the fridge. 'You'll have to excuse me cooking. I've got to make the supper before I go to the shop and I want to get in early because Charley's on her own this week.'

Naturally her friend offered to help, so Pam told her she could peel some spuds.

Zee helped herself to a handful of potatoes from the vegetable rack. 'What are we making?'

'Shepherd's pie,' replied Pam, emptying a pack of minced lamb into a large pan, 'Because it's a thoroughly traditional British dinner and a cultural experience for my foreign students. Plus it's cheap and cheerful, with the emphasis on cheap!'

Fetching the peeler from the utensil drawer, Zee turned to Pam and said, 'I know it's not my place to say this...'

'But?' prompted Pam levelly, not even looking up.

'If you got a job instead of working for Charley for nothing, you'd have a bit more money to spend on yourself.'

The statement was undisputedly true, and it crossed Pam's mind every time her bank statement came in and informed her just how much money had gone out. Geoff was now living with Barbara and for the foreseeable future Pam had the house and, while there was no mortgage, the bills still had to be paid. Pride had prevented her taking any maintenance from Geoff. Pride and the overriding desire to sever all links with him completely. She didn't want to be beholden to him for anything. Taking paid work would obviously help her financial circumstances, but she'd committed herself to helping her daughter-in-law in the shop and she wasn't going to renege on that promise now. Plus, as she was honest enough to admit, in the back of her mind was the fear that since she hadn't worked for years – no, *decades* – she very much doubted anyone would actually want to pay to employ her.

'Charley needs me in the shop,' was all she said to Zee, and liberally sloshed Worcester sauce into the pan.

'Maybe, but you need to have your own life too.'

'How is my working with Charley getting in the way of that?'

'Well, if you can't afford to do night classes, for example.'

'But I don't particularly want to do an evening class.'

'Well, perhaps you should. You might meet someone.'

Pam put down her wooden spoon and shot Zee a pained look. 'I'm too old for all of that malarkey! Who'd want me?'

'Any number of men!' retorted Zee. 'You're attractive, fun to be with, smart and witty, and a strong, independently minded woman... plus you're a great cook. Seriously Pam, what's not to want?'

Buoyed by her friend's loyalty, suddenly in her mind's eye Pam pictured herself walking into an expensive, candle-lit restaurant with a man beside her. When they got to the table he courteously drew her chair back for her to sit down. Exactly who he was or what he looked like was a little sketchy, but she knew it wasn't Geoff, because her soon-to-be ex-husband was all alone at another table watching her, and looking downright demolished.

With an effort, she pulled herself back to reality. Zee was talking to her.

'I mean, obviously that's not the only reason to do a night class.'

'No, but it's not a bad one. I mean, at my age, how else *would* I meet anyone?'

Zee regarded her for a moment. 'Well, if you're really interested in meeting someone perhaps you should try internet dating.'

'Good God, no! I wouldn't know where to start! All that swiping left or right or whatever it is you're meant to do. It sounds hideous. Like some electronic cattle market.'

'Yes, as if you can decide whether or not you like someone just from a photo! I mean, where's the chemistry in that?'

'Or the romance? It was a lot more fun in our day,' concluded Pam wistfully. Then a thought struck her. 'Where did you meet Theo?'

'At a rock concert. Queen. Before they were big.'

'Oh my God, Zee! You are the pinnacle of cool!'

'And you and Geoff?'

'Blind date. Not so cool,' Pam confessed.

–

Driving down to the shop after Zee had gone, Pam caught herself pondering on the possibility, or more likely the impossibility, of actually meeting anyone new. *Well, you don't go to a lot of rock concerts these days*, she told herself, *night classes are beyond your budget, and nobody's going to fix you up on a blind date.* So, if she didn't want to be alone for the rest of her life perhaps she was going to have to bite the bullet and broach the terrifying territory of internet dating.

–

Charley was busy showing a customer Angie's artwork when Pam arrived at the shop so she slipped in quietly behind the till, not wanting to interrupt her.

'I actually wanted one of the bigger ones,' the customer was saying. 'You had some in last week.'

Leaning on the counter, Pam watched Charley shake her head apologetically and say, 'I'm sorry but we only have what's on display.'

'Haven't you got any more out the back?' The woman sounded aggrieved, accusatory even, and Pam bristled on Charley's behalf.

There is no 'out the back'! she thought, irked by the patently ridiculous suggestion that Charley was deliberately hiding or withholding stock from a customer.

'Sorry, no. This really is all we have available right now,' Charley explained politely.

'Well, when's the next delivery?' demanded the woman brusquely.

There's no need for that tone of voice! Pam bit back the desire to snap back on Charley's behalf. One of the few things she disliked about working in the shop was having to hold her tongue on the, mercifully rare, occasions when a customer was rude, especially to Charley.

'Er… I'm not actually sure,' said Charley. Her eyes flicked over to Pam who could hear the note of fluster in her voice.

'Well, I can't keep coming in on the off-chance!'

Charley's face flushed deep red and Pam's heart went out to her, but privately she conceded the woman had a point. Charley should know when delivery of a product was due. Going over to join them she said, 'We actually know the artist quite well. We could try to give her a call and find out.'

The customer turned to Pam. 'Do that.'

Please, corrected Pam mentally, but keeping a pleasant expression on her face said, 'I think my colleague has the number.'

Charley shot Pam a grateful look and took her phone out of her pocket. 'I'll try right now.'

'Thank you,' said Pam.

'Yes, thank you,' echoed the woman, in a noticeably more civil tone.

Thinking that Charley would prefer to call Angie without the customer eavesdropping, Pam attempted to distract her. 'Where were you planning to put the artwork?' she enquired.

'Oh, it's not for me. It's a leaving present for someone at work. I don't even know her that well, but I know she drinks Prosecco. In fact, that's pretty much all I know about her.'

Ah, thought Pam, beginning to feel sympathy for the poor woman, tasked with buying a gift for someone she barely knew.

'That's always a tricky chore,' she commiserated. Then, indicating one of the two smaller canvasses left on display, she confided, 'I've always liked that one.' The illustration showed a small bottle of fizz tucked into a chic make-up bag with the slogan: *Anything is possible with a little lippy and some bubbles!*

Charley had rung off and was coming over. 'The artist says she can deliver in two weeks.'

'Will that be in time for your colleague's leaving do?' Pam asked the customer.

Frowning anxiously, the woman said, 'Maybe. Just about.'

'Well, here's a thought...' said Pam tentatively. 'I know you wanted a single large piece, but would you like us to reserve these two smaller ones for you, as a pair, just in case it *doesn't* arrive in time?'

The woman looked a little wary, as if Pam were trying to palm her off with something she didn't want, so Pam added, 'Only as a fall-back? You don't even need to pay for them. We'll just reserve them for you.'

'Actually, yes. You're right.' The irritable expression on the woman's face began to evaporate. 'Having the pair would be better than not having anything at all.'

Behind the woman's back Charley silently mouthed, 'Thank you!' to Pam.

Once the woman had left, Pam tucked the two pieces of artwork behind the counter, and then she apologised to Charley. 'Sorry to put you on the spot like that.'

'No, it's fine. I should've thought to call Angie myself.'

'I hope she didn't think we were hassling her.'

Charley shook her head. 'No. You know Ange. Nothing fazes her. Although she did sound a bit frazzled.' She pulled a face. 'Honestly Pam, it sounded like World War Three had broken out at her place. Lily was screaming, Buster was barking, and the rest of them were yelling their heads off!'

'Half term,' nodded Pam sagely. Twenty years on she could still remember the mayhem of school holidays, with the kitchen table strewn with junk modelling paraphernalia, the garden full of duvet dens, pop-up tents and makeshift obstacle courses, and Luke and Josh rampaging round like pent-up wild things. She envied Angie, having a house full of children – all that chaotic fun, and all those spontaneous, loving cuddles.

'Apparently Will's had to go into school every day, so she's had all four of them on her own,' said Charley, bringing her back to the present.

'Good God, she must be exhausted!'

Charley nodded. 'I said I'd go round and give her a hand with them on Sunday.'

'Don't you usually spend Sundays with Ricky?'

'I don't have to see him *every* Sunday!'

Although it was said lightly, for some reason it rang a small alarm bell in Pam.

'No, of course you don't, darling.' *I just assumed you'd prefer to spend your only day off with Ricky rather than babysitting for Angie.* She found herself fighting the urge to ask Charley if everything was all right between the two of them. Then she reminded herself it was none of her business. Charley wasn't her daughter or, technically, even her daughter-in-law any more. So she said cheerily, 'But are you sure you want to spend your only day off wrangling four rumbustious childe-beests?'

'Yes! It'll be fun. Plus, if I look after the kids, Angie can do some more artwork.'

'Aha! I see there is method in your madness!'

–

It was a slow afternoon, with more browsers than buyers, and during one quiet spell, Pam took advantage of the empty shop to ask Charley's advice. She'd hummed and hawed about whether to confide in her, and it was taking all her resolve to pluck up the courage to do so.

'Um…' she started, not really knowing quite how to broach the subject.

'Yes?' prompted Charley.

'Have you ever...'

Charley raised an enquiring eyebrow. 'Have I ever what?'

'I mean, do you know how to...'

Leaning on the till table, Charley waited patiently.

'Actually, what do you know about this whole internet dating lark?'

Charley shot bolt upright. 'Oo-o-oh!' she sang, a mischievous glint in her eyes.

'Don't get all excited. I'm asking for a friend,' lied Pam shamelessly.

'Yeah, right,' snorted Charley. 'A friend.'

Pam felt a hot blush creeping into her cheeks. 'Yes. A friend,' she repeated firmly, determined to brazen it out.

'Well, I'm afraid you're going to have to tell this "friend",' Charley paused to gesture air quotes around the word, 'that I've never tried it so I'm truly sorry but I can't help her.'

'Oh, okay. Fine.' Pam felt as if a small bubble of tension had popped inside her, leaving her improbably deflated. 'Never mind. It was just a long shot,' she said casually, and then busied herself tidying the tealights.

'The thing is, Pam, I never needed to, did I?' Charley carried on in a more sober tone. 'Why would I? I wasn't looking for anyone after Josh. You know that.'

Pam knew only too well the truth of that statement. On the day she'd found out about Geoff's infidelity, blinded by panic, shame and despair, Pam had fled to Charley's flat and stayed with her until she'd decided what to do. It had taken her several months to recover enough to make any decisions at all, apart from wanting to be rid of her unfaithful husband as soon as possible. As the weeks passed, Pam had become deeply concerned to discover that although she herself had at least begun to be reconciled to Josh's death, her daughter-in-law was resistant to moving on. She still clung to her identity, her role as Josh's widow. '*You'll always be Josh's mother,*' she'd told Pam. '*But I can't be his wife any more.*

All I can be is his widow.' Even when Charley had met Ricky, she was adamant she wasn't interested in him, although it was obvious to Pam from the get-go that the pair were attracted to each other. Having seen them together these last months, Pam was even more confident she'd been right. Charley had lost that haunted look and recovered her sparkle. She was much more the bubbly young woman Josh had brought into their family, rather than the hollowed out, grieving widow left after he died. And Ricky clearly adored her.

'You know who you could ask?' Charley's voice cut into Pam's thoughts. She stopped fiddling with the tealights and looked up. 'Nisha. She's definitely tried internet dating.'

'Good grief, I can't possibly talk to Nisha about it.'

'No,' replied Charley impishly, 'but perhaps your "friend" could.'

Rumbled, thought Pam, ruefully, especially when Charley carried on.

'D'you know what, Pam? Out of all of my friends, Nisha is the one you most definitely *can* talk to about it – a) she'll completely understand and b) she is the soul of discretion.'

There was a brief pause before Pam said, 'Okay, thanks. But promise *you* won't tell anyone. Especially not Tara!'

'My lips are sealed,' promised Charley, making a zipping gesture across her mouth.

Chapter Seven

Early Sunday morning, Charley pitched up at Angie's with a bag of fresh jam doughnuts. She rang the bell, heard Angie call out, 'Charley's here!' and braced herself for the welcome bundling she'd get as soon as the door opened. Sure enough, three small children and a large boisterous Labrador hurled themselves at her.

'Hello, horrors!' Cheerfully, she pushed through the throng to embrace Angie, who took the doughnuts with one hand and promptly tumbled baby Lily into her arms with the other.

'These are for later!' Angie informed her gang firmly.

Somewhat hampered by her entourage clinging to her legs, and clasping Lily to her, Charley waded after her mate and into the kitchen.

'We're still having breakfast,' admitted Angie. 'Except Lily. She's had hers. Twice!'

Cradling Lily's soft little body, Charley gazed down at her lovingly. Lily contemplated her temporary carer for a moment, frowning earnestly then, perhaps suddenly recognising her, she gurgled delightedly, blew an endearing little bubble and Charley nearly dissolved onto the kitchen floor.

'We're with you after breakfast,' said Beth, Angie's eldest, as the children clambered back into their places round the table.

'Mummy's doing dwarwing,' three-year-old Finn informed her importantly.

'If that's okay?' Angie added hurriedly.

'Of course it is!' Then, turning to the kids, Charley foolishly asked, 'What shall we do?'

'Uh-oh! Rookie error!' Angie warned, with a sharp intake of breath.

'Football!' demanded five-year-old Elliot, immediately dropping his cereal spoon and rushing to get his ball.

'Nooooo!' wailed Beth. 'I want Charley to watch me on the trampoline!'

Finn was already climbing back onto his chair having fetched his shiny plastic cutlass. 'Piwats!' He brandished his weapon menacingly, just inches from Charley's face.

'Wooaah!' Charley lurched back out of range.

'Well, I'll leave you to it, shall I?' Angie beamed, clearing the table.

Charley was momentarily flummoxed. How on earth was she going to manage three spirited, hugely energetic kids, plus a baby, all determined to do different things? She turned in mute appeal to Angie for arbitration.

'I don't mind what anyone does, but I need the table!' insisted Angie.

Great help, thought Charley. Then, instinctively realising the worst thing to do would be to favour one child's preference over the other two, she said, 'Right! We can do all those later. But first…' She took a couple of beats, partly to tease but mostly to give herself time to frantically think of something. 'First… we are going to go dinosaur-hunting in the garden!'

'Dinosaurs!' bawled Elliot, instantly abandoning his football and leaping off his chair.

'Grrrrrr,' yelled Finn ferociously, clenching his little fists into claws like a Tyrannosaurus rex's front legs.

But Beth drenched Charley with a withering look. 'There aren't any dinosaurs in the garden.'

'How do you know?' challenged Charley, and instantly up-aged the game to engage the bright little seven-year-old. 'We're palaeontologists looking for fossils.'

Beth's eyes lit up. 'I'll get the trowel!'

'And the buckets and spades for the little ones!' called Angie as her daughter ran out of the kitchen.

Charley tucked Lily into her buggy, gave her a board book, and they followed the dinosaur hunters into the garden.

'Good luck!' called Angie over her shoulder, already sketching outlines onto her canvas.

–

A couple of hours later, after fossils had been found, goals had been scored, pirates made to walk the plank and Beth had scared Charley to death by doing backflips on the trampoline, Lily was getting fractious.

'She's prob'ly got a pooey bum,' Eliot told her sagely.

Nipping through the kitchen on her way to change Lily's nappy, Charley glanced over at the table to look at Angie's progress. Two large coupe glasses, filled with fizz and poised as if clinking together, dominated the canvass. A mass of bubbles floated up from the glasses and appeared to burst into stars. The slogan *Pour the Prosecco... It's my time to shine!* was sketched in pencil, framing the glasses.

'Oh, wow, Ange. That's fab!'

'Getting there,' said Angie self-deprecatingly, pausing to eye her work critically.

'I'm doing Lily's bum, so the others are out there, *alone!*' warned Charley.

'Oh, they'll be fine for a few minutes.'

'Finn's got his cutlass...'

Angie dropped her paintbrush immediately. 'I'm on my way!'

Upstairs in Lily's nursery, Charley swiftly changed the little girl's nappy and then, knowing that Angie was looking after the older children, she indulged herself with a five-minute cuddle. Closing her eyes, she inhaled the baby's sweet, milky smell and was immediately overwhelmed with an almost physical ache of longing. If Josh hadn't died they'd have had two or maybe even three kids by now, and she'd probably be hanging round with Angie and her mob every day, instead of trying to grab a few odd hours with them here and there. Taking Lily's podgy little hand, she held it against her mouth, adoring the softness of her skin against her lips. The baby's huge eyes watched her wonderingly, until Charley blew a raspberry on her palm. Instantly, Lily's face broke into a huge gummy grin, and her little body shook with an infectious chuckle. So Charley did it again.

–

By lunchtime, Angie had got to the stage where she needed to let the painting dry for a few hours. Will was still stuck at the school so the two women pulled together a scratch picnic, packed the food and the kids into the car, and headed to the playground for the afternoon. When they got there, Angie strapped Lily into her sling and she and Charley stood behind the swings, taking it in turns to push the bigger children.

'Thanks for this morning. I owe you,' said Angie.

'Are you kidding? I've had a ball! I wouldn't do it if I didn't love being with the kids. And you, of course.'

'Higher!' demanded Beth.

'Higher!' echoed the boys.

So Angie and Charley obliged, the kids squealing with pleasure.

'I know, but it's nigh on impossible to do any artwork with the kids around. I'm either feeding Lily, wiping bums, or trying to keep them out of A&E!' Angie joked. 'And if I couldn't do any art I'd spontaneously combust!'

Charley knew her friend was only half kidding. Angie was genuinely talented, and had given up a career as a graphic designer to have her kids. Until Charley had opened her shop, the only outlet for her mate's creativity had been painting the walls. Literally. Angie's kitchen was a field of sunflowers in full bloom while Jack's giant beanstalk wove itself along the wall of the hallway and up the stairs. Beth's bedroom was an underwater world, its dark blue walls teeming with fish, mermaids and a giant octopus. The boys slept between a vast pirate galleon on one wall, and a desert island on the other, with a flock of seagulls wheeling across the ceiling. Lily's room, now Charley's favourite, was painted duck-egg blue, with a family of pale grey elephants leading each other, trunk in tail, around the walls.

'I really do appreciate you giving up your Sunday,' Angie was saying. 'I know how full-on the shop is. You must get hardly any time to yourself. Or with Ricky.'

There was a beat before Charley said, a shade tersely, 'You're the second person who seems to think I should spend my Sundays with Ricky.'

Angie looked taken aback. 'That's not what I said. Or what I meant.'

'Sorry. I know. I'm just a bit... touchy about Ricky at the moment.'

Angie's face clouded over. 'Why? What's happened?'

'Nothing – except everyone seems to assume that we're... that it's permanent.'

Angie didn't say anything, and for a while the only sound was the creaking of the swings, the rustling of the leaves in the trees and the occasional chorus of 'Higher!' from the kids.

Eventually Angie prompted Charley. 'Everyone?'

'Yes! It was obvious when we were in Tuscany that his entire family were expecting us to get married. Why else would I have to be introduced to every single member of his extended family? Ricky seems to assume we're "forever", Tara's badgering me to let Monnie be a bridesmaid, and even Pam seems to think I should spend all my spare time with him.'

'Maybe she's just trying to let you know she's okay about you being with Ricky, after Josh?' When Charley didn't reply Angie went on gently, 'You know, after Josh, I think it's completely understandable that you might be...' She paused, as if choosing her words with care, '...cautious, or wary about making a commitment—'

'I'm not being cautious, or wary!'

'Seriously? You've been holding yourself back from the moment you met Ricky! You'd known him months, literally months, before you even lowered your guard enough to go out with him. And, credit where credit's due, he didn't even try to rush you. He waited for you to… catch up.'

Angie's challenge was light-hearted, nevertheless Charley sought cover in denial. 'Catch up? I have no idea what you're talking about. Ricky wasn't even remotely interested in me to start with.'

'Oh, right. So all those times he brought you coffee when you were first setting up the shop, or when he took in all your deliveries when you weren't open, or brought his lunch up so he could have it with you, he was just – what? Being nice?'

'He was just being… neighbourly. Helping another shop-keeper. That's just how he is. He still does that now.'

'What, he takes coffee to Del in the florist's, does he?'

'Well, no.'

'And helps her lug in delivery boxes?'

'Probably.' Charley's tone was becoming increasingly defensive.

'And he offers to get her lunch from the deli?'

Angie raised an eyebrow in query and Charley did her best to ignore it. Nonetheless, her mind flipped back to the early days of setting up the shop when – there was no denying it – Ricky had been hugely helpful and supportive, always there when she needed anything, and she'd relied on him for a good deal of advice – anything from choosing a till or how to get a card-reader, to where the cheapest parking was and the cleanest public loos.

She remembered the day she'd brought the furniture to shop. It was a pile of second-hand stuff from charity shops which she and Angie had painted up. There were so many bookcases, chairs and tables crammed into the car she couldn't even close the boot properly. Technically, she wasn't allowed to drive along the pedestrianised area and park outside her shop but there was no way she could carry the furniture from the multi-storey. So, heart in mouth, she'd taken the risk, hoping she wouldn't get a parking ticket, or worse, clamped, while she unloaded. No sooner had she opened the boot when a male voice had called out, 'Hey!' stopping her in her tracks. Her heart had sunk, expecting it to be a parking attendant, but it had been Ricky.

'Let me help,' he'd said, hurrying over, but she'd waved him off airily.

'Thanks but I can manage, honestly.'

'Did I say you couldn't!' he'd asked good-naturedly, coming across to her regardless, his eyes gently laughing at her.

'No,' she'd happily conceded, and had stood back while Ricky had swiftly deposited all the furniture in the shop in less than five minutes – a mere fraction of the time it had taken Charley to load it.

She'd thanked him, but he'd shrugged cheerfully and said, 'Give me a shout if you need me,' and headed back to the bike shop.

Later that day, after she'd spent hours arranging and then re-arranging the shop until she thought it looked okay, she'd been glad when he'd popped in and she'd been able to ask his opinion.

'Be honest,' she'd said. 'Does it say "shabby chic", or a "pile of old junk"?'

'Actually, just chic,' he'd replied. 'Not even a hint of shabby.' And then afterwards, he taken her to the deli to get some lunch.

They had rapidly fallen into an easy friendship, and she'd thought that was all that Ricky had wanted. It was certainly all that she had wanted until… well, until later when her feelings had evolved. But maybe Angie was right. Maybe she had misread those early signals from Ricky, and perhaps it was caution that had led her to misread her own feelings too.

Just then Finn interrupted them, breaking into her thoughts, asking to be lifted out of the toddler swing so he could go on the slide. So then all three of the kids ran off to the slide. Charley watched fondly as Beth helped her littlest brother climb up the steep metal steps, staying close behind him in case he fell.

'Thank you, sweetheart,' called out Angie, who, it seemed to Charley, missed nothing. Then she turned to Charley and queried, 'But you're still not sure?'

Charley shook her head. 'I love him, but I don't love him the way I loved Josh. I'm not head-over-heels in love with him, the way I was with Josh.'

'Give it time,' advised Angie. 'You've only been going out for a few months.'

'But the moment I met Josh I knew he was The One.'

'Okay, but it's not like that for everyone. You can't compare him to Josh.'

Why not? thought Charley.

'People fall in love in different ways,' Angie was saying. 'Look at Will and me. It wasn't love at first sight. Not by any means. We sort of drifted together. I liked him, and he was fun to be with, and then, one day he was making me a cuppa and he handed me the mug with the handle pointing towards me and, and I thought "I love the way he does that", and I suddenly realised I didn't just love the way he handed me my tea, I loved *him*. But we'd been going out for well over a year by then.'

'But that doesn't seem fair on Ricky, keeping him hanging around, *in case* I fall in love with him.'

Angie looked her in the eyes. 'Would you prefer to be with him, or prefer to be without him?'

Charley thought for a moment before she answered, honestly, 'With him.'

'Well then!' finished Angie.

But that's not enough, is it? And what if I only want to be him for the wrong reasons?

Chapter Eight

While Charley was getting Agony Aunt advice from Angie, Pam was getting a basic tutorial on the art of dating in the twenty-first century from Nisha. She had initially shied from turning to one of Charley's friends, but it had literally been decades since she'd dated anyone and she simply didn't feel bold enough to venture into the brave new world of internet dating without a guide. Since Pam firmly believed you shouldn't expect to get something for nothing, she'd offered Nisha lunch, so the two of them were sitting at the garden table, enjoying the early June sunshine, eating home-made caramelized red onion tart, with a green salad and fresh-baked sourdough rolls.

'I hope you didn't mind my asking your advice,' ventured Pam.

'Not a bit,' replied Nisha. 'It's daunting getting yourself out there after a long relationship.'

You're not kidding. Out of all of Charley's mates, Nisha was the only one she felt comfortable reaching out to. It was not the first time: after the shock revelation of Geoff's infidelity, Nisha had given Pam endearingly honest advice about getting a divorce, and had prevented her hurtling headlong into making hasty decisions she would have definitely come to regret.

'It's that whole issue about *why* your marriage failed,' Nisha was saying. 'When Jay went off with someone else, I thought there must be something wrong with me.'

Oh thank God! thought Pam. The younger woman had expressed, and thereby validated, the innermost fears that had haunted her since her separation. No matter how hard she tried to rationalise it, to tell herself it wasn't her fault that her soon-to-be ex-husband had left her for another woman, she couldn't stop herself thinking she was to blame. Technically, of course, she *was* to blame for ending their marriage since Geoff hadn't left her, she'd slung him out. Perhaps if she'd been more forgiving, more able to live with the humiliation, then her marriage could have continued. Perhaps. But it would have been utterly degrading and the notion was repulsive to her. Even now, a year on, Geoff's physical presence made her flesh crawl. In all honesty, she didn't know whether Jay had left Nisha, or whether Nisha had packed his bags for him – either way, she'd bet her bottom dollar Nisha wasn't to blame for the break-up.

Reaching out, she put her hand on Nisha's arm. 'There's nothing wrong with you, Nisha. You're a remarkable woman. Successful, compassionate and intelligent, and although I only know you a little, I like you a lot.'

Nisha looked up and smiled. 'Thank you.' Pam only hoped that Nisha actually believed her, however she doubted it, because the younger woman soon continued, 'But it really knocks your confidence. Every man I met either instantly asked why my marriage broke down, or immediately assumed I was to blame. Sometimes both!'

'More fool them. It's their loss.'

'Well, they've missed their chance,' Nisha rallied. 'I'm not looking for anyone any more. Too busy enjoying my freedom!'

'Are you not lonely?' asked Pam tentatively.

Nisha shook her head. 'I don't have time. I work pretty much 24/7. I'm far too busy to be lonely!'

Privately, Pam wondered whether Nisha worked flat out *because* she didn't have a partner or children, and if she were filling her time, and her life, with work.

'Besides,' Nisha carried on, 'there are many advantages to being single. I can do what I want, when I want, eat what I like, go to bed when I like. I don't have to clean up after anyone, or pander to their whims and wishes, and there are no arguments about money. Actually, there are no arguments, full stop!'

It all began to sound to Pam as if Nisha was trying just that little bit too hard to put a positive spin on her situation. But then again, she knew Nisha's marriage had been acrimonious to say the least, so maybe the younger woman was genuinely pleased to be on her own.

Noticing that Nisha's plate was empty, Pam said, 'Another piece of tart?'

'Thank you, but I've eaten too much as it is!'

'No room for a slice of lemon meringue pie, then?'

Nisha groaned. 'If I'd known there was pudding, I would have held back on the sourdough!'

'I'll cut you some to take home with you,' said Pam, heading for the kitchen with the plates.

'Thank you. And get your laptop!' she called after Pam as she disappeared into the house.

My laptop! Instantly, Pam was plunged into a jittery panic. When she'd first called Nisha, signing up for a dating site had seemed like a good idea. Now, however, faced with the reality of putting her details out there, and exposing herself to public appraisal, rejection, and possibly ridicule, she was suddenly getting very cold feet. Stoically reminding herself that the younger woman had given up her precious Sunday afternoon, Pam told herself she couldn't back out now.

When she got back to the table, Nisha had put up the parasol to shade the screen, so Pam put her computer down in front of her and, well aware of how much swifter the younger generations are at navigating the treacherous waters of the internet, willingly left her to it. It was a wise decision. Where Pam had been bewildered by the sheer array of dating sites available, Nisha rapidly found the top recommended site for over-fifties.

Pulling her chair round to sit next to her, Pam asked Nisha if she'd tried internet dating herself.

'A few times,' admitted the younger woman, 'but I was put off by only getting replies from men in their fifties and sixties. No offence, Pam!' she added, hurriedly, 'but that's a lot older than me.'

'None taken.'

'So... Are you a man or a woman?' Nisha read out the first question and clicked 'woman' box.

The next question was: 'Are you looking for a man or a woman?' Nisha turned questioningly to Pam.

'Er, a man,' Pam replied, mildly surprised that Nisha even felt the need to ask her.

Nisha shrugged lightly. 'I'm not taking anything for granted.'

Then the website asked for Pam's date of birth. Watching Nisha scroll through the long stream of years in the drop-down box made her feel positively ancient, verging on decrepit. Less than an hour later, Nisha had set her up account and her profile, except for uploading a photo.

'I don't think I even have a recent one,' Pam told her anxiously.

'Good! You can't just put up any old pic.' Whipping out her phone, Nisha said, 'Go and put on a flattering top and some snazzy earrings. You need to make an impression.'

An impression? Pam's brain short-circuited, temporarily rooting her to the spot. What kind of impression was she supposed to make, for crying out loud? And what the hell could she wear at her age that would be 'flattering'? Should she wear a scarf to hide the signs of aging on her throat? Or a polo neck? But it was high summer, she'd look ridiculous! And what did Nisha mean by 'snazzy earrings'? Should she wear dangly ones or would that make her look tarty? Her pearl studs, maybe? No, absolutely not, Geoff had given her those. She stood, hovering like a cat on a hot tin roof. 'I have no idea what to wear!' she wailed.

'Pam, you always look lovely. Just be yourself.'

Nisha took half a dozen shots when Pam finally came back down in her chosen outfit – a plain white shirt with a navy scarf and simple but elegant gold drop earrings – and they uploaded the one they both liked best, or rather, the one Pam felt the least embarrassed by. Showing Nisha to the door, Pam asked her not to tell Charley that she'd actually registered on a dating site.

Nisha frowned. 'There's nothing to be embarrassed about. Literally everyone uses them.'

'It's not that I'm embarrassed. I wouldn't do it if it made me feel ashamed. It's just that... well, if nobody actually wants to meet me it will be...' She searched for the word. 'Humiliating.'

'I very much doubt that will be the case,' Nisha reassured her, 'but I won't tell a soul.'

—

Pam didn't even confide in Zee – well, not until the 'like' notific-ations began pinging into her email, that is. Then she was thrown into a tail-spin about how to respond to them, and in some cases, whether to respond at all. She felt exposed and foolish. Was she even in her right mind, reaching out to total strangers like this? What if they were stalkers? Or weirdos? Or, since stalkers *were* weirdos, both? Was there some sort of litmus test she should apply to their replies which would reveal their genuineness, or their sanity even? And what about all those news stories about gullible older women being duped by unscrupulous gold diggers and chancers? Were there any recommended strategies to protect against them? She really didn't want to bother Nisha again, it made her feel too high-maintenance and needy. 'You really should be able to deal with this on your own,' she told herself briskly. 'You're a grown woman, for crying out loud!' At that moment, her email pinged a notification of another 'like', and she promptly called Zee.

Later in the week, after supper when her student lodgers were safely ensconced in their rooms with their phones and a plate of home-made double-chocolate-chip cookies, and unlikely to barge into the kitchen to raid the fridge, Pam felt confident she and Zee could vet the replies in privacy.

With trembling fingers, and her heart beating unnaturally and unnecessarily fast, she logged onto the site. Zee sat beside her at the kitchen table, openly curious, both of them keen to be able to put faces to the usernames in her inbox. It was not encouraging.

In fact, it was demoralising to the point of devastating. Real-istically, Pam wasn't expecting an array of dishy silver foxes but even so, the mug shots that confronted her almost made her want to weep.

'He must be at least eighty!' gasped Zee in astonishment. 'And so's he!' Quickly scrolling through the replies, it was immediately evident most of the men seemed way older than Pam. 'Most of these men have either aged incredibly badly, or they're about twenty years older than you!' Zee exclaimed indignantly. 'Why on earth would they think a woman in her sixties, her *early* sixties,' she corrected herself, 'would be interested in relationship with someone nearly old enough to be her father?'

'Nisha said she'd mostly been contacted by much older men too,' replied Pam morosely.

'Well that's bad enough at her age, but you've put that you're looking for a long term relationship. How can you have a long term relationship with someone who, let's face it, probably isn't actually going to be around that long!'

'Maybe they're not looking for a relationship. Maybe they're looking for... something else?' finished Pam, deliberately vaguely.

'Like what, casual sex?' spluttered Zee. 'At their age? Good God, it could be fatal!'

'Ageist! Anyhow, at least they'd die happy!' She was tickled to see Zee so outraged on her behalf.

'Yes, but imagine being the one who has to call the ambulance? The police would pitch up and you'd be logged as the cause of death!'

Pam burst out laughing, then almost choked when the kitchen door suddenly opened and one of her lodgers appeared. She slammed her laptop shut, as if she'd been caught watching porn, making Zee nearly jump out of chair. The young lad stood nervously in the doorway holding out his empty plate plaintively, looking for all the world like Oliver Twist.

'Please?' he said shyly. 'Is more cookies?'

There was a beat and then the sheer child-like innocence of his request, coming in such contrast to their ribald conversation, made both women explode with childish laughter.

'Of course, my lovely,' said Pam, getting the biscuit tin and handing it to him, and only just resisting the urge to ruffle his hair affectionately. 'See if the others want some too.'

'Okay. Thank-you-very-much,' he said, politely issuing his rote response and, taking the cookies, he gratefully fled the kitchen.

His interruption sobered the two friends.

'Maybe this dating lark isn't designed for the older woman,' sighed Pam. 'Either that or the older woman isn't designed for dating!'

'Absolute nonsense! You're still a very attractive woman, and you mustn't forget it.' Then, after a moment, she went on, 'But in all honesty, Pam, could you actually fancy someone in their eighties?'

'Morgan Freeman,' replied Pam instantly.

'Yes,' conceded Zee, 'and Harrison Ford.'

Pam nodded her agreement and countered, 'Tom Jones?'

'Definitely. Jack Nicholson?'

'No. But then, I've never fancied him.'

'Fair enough,' said Zee.

'We sound dreadful,' winced Pam. 'Atrociously judgemental. You'd think that by our age we'd have learned good relationships aren't about looks.'

Brought up short, Zee's face was a picture of contrition. 'Imagine how we'd feel if we thought men were making the same judgements about your picture.'

'I'd rather not,' replied Pam. 'Do you think you'd still fall for Theo if you met him today?' She didn't wait for a reply. She knew her friend had fallen out of love with her husband thirty years ago when he'd had an affair, and that they were only still together out of habit. It wasn't even for the sake of their children any more, both their daughters having flown the nest years ago. 'I wouldn't fancy Geoff,' she admitted. 'Even if he hadn't gone off with that bloody Barbara woman.'

'I bet Toni would still fall for Phil,' said Zee wistfully.

The image of Phil absent-mindedly taking hold of Toni's hand as it rested on his shoulder, slid into Pam's mind. *Lucky Toni*, she thought. *And lucky Phil.*

She opened up the laptop again. 'You know, it's very brave of these men to even put themselves on a dating site at their age. Let's try and judge them on their personalities, their life stories, rather than their looks or age.'

They spent the next few minutes being heroically generous, but despite that, there was only one man that seemed even remotely interesting to either of them.

'He looks pleasant,' Pam said tentatively, 'and he's actually younger than me. Fifty-eight.' For some reason she found that rather flattering.

'Message him,' urged Zee. 'Suggest a drink in a pub somewhere in town.'

A wave of anxiety swept over Pam, and she reeled back in her chair. 'That's a bit forward, isn't it?'

Zee raised an eyebrow. 'It's only a drink. You can always leave after the first one.'

'I don't know...'

'Wimp!' Zee regarded Pam soberly. 'Tell you what, how about Toni and I go to the pub at the same time?'

'For back-up?'

'Yes. If you like.' Then she shot a mischievous look at Pam. 'And to have a damn good nose!'

Chapter Nine

Bloody Tara! swore Charley. It was well after ten o'clock on the Friday morning and Tara had only just called in to say she wasn't coming in.

'Sorry, Monnie's got the dentist.'

Sorry? She hadn't sounded remotely apologetic. Charley had taken a deep, calming breath and tried not to let the irritation show in her voice, but she'd lined up half a dozen pitch meetings with pubs and hotels in an attempt to boost the party bag side of the business. So Tara baling on her, and with no notice, was a complete pain in the arse.

'D'you you think you'll be able to get in later?' asked Charley. It didn't take all morning to take a kid to the dentist, and there was no way that kid was ever going to need a filling. Tara was far too much of a helicopter parent for that.

'It won't be worth it. The appointment's not until quarter to eleven so by the time I've taken Monnie back to school it'll be nearly lunchtime.'

Charley did the maths in her head. *Actually, it probably won't be much later than eleven thirty*, she calculated, but she held her peace. 'Okay, well, thanks for letting me know. Have a good weekend,' she managed to add.

Her disappointment evidently reflected in her tone because Tara had finished, 'I'll make it up to you! Promise!'

Charley wasn't quite sure how. Nor was she sure how she was going to get to her appointments and hold the fort at the shop at the same time. Rescheduling would make a really bad impression, hardly demonstrating reliability. She sighed irritably. Either she was going to have to close the shop for the morning... or call Pam.

Less than twenty minutes later, a mildly flustered Pam rushed through the door. 'Sorry, darling. I got here as soon as I could but I couldn't find a parking space!'

'You're an angel! I don't know how to—' Charley started to say but Pam cut her off.

'You need to go!' She ushered Charley towards the door. 'Go!'

Pausing only to give Pam a swift thank-you hug, Charley grabbed her bag and her samples, and legged it.

The next couple of hours were disappointingly fruitless. Charley slogged round her pitch meetings, a positive expression glued to her face, but became increasingly discouraged. Only two of the pubs showed any interest. One said they liked the look of the bags and reckoned they'd go down well at the hen parties they *occasionally* hosted, but they'd need to raise it with the brewery head office. The other pub asked to keep a couple of sample bags to show the manager, which peeved Charley no end since she was pretty certain the woman she was talking to *was* the manager. She suspected the woman wasn't really interested and just wanted the freebies. The only real highlight was discovering that one of the dockside restaurants ran regular Prosecco events and they said they might be interested and would be in touch. Still, Charley got back to the shop in a low mood, feeling even more guilty for having asked Pam to drop everything and rescue her since she had nothing concrete to show for it.

'Well, that was a waste of time,' she muttered quietly to Pam as she joined her behind the counter. There were customers in the shop so she kept her voice low and slapped her professional face on and prepared to hold it, at least until the punters had left. Once the shop was empty again, she offloaded the frustration of her unproductive morning onto Pam.

'It doesn't sound a complete waste of effort,' Pam said encouragingly. 'That's still a couple of possible new venues. When you first started out you'd have been thrilled with that.'

'True,' said Charley, momentarily bolstered by Pam's optimism, then she grimaced. 'I'm just sorry I had to drag you in.'

'Well, that's not *your* fault.'

The unspoken criticism of Tara hung in the air and for some reason Charley felt compelled to defend her mate. 'She can't come in if she needs to take Monnie to the dentist.'

'No, but she should still turn up when she says she will, and not let you down at the last minute. And dentists are actually open in the afternoons,' finished Pam.

Good point, thought Charley, falling silent.

'By the way, Ricky was lovely while you were out,' Pam told her. 'He popped in on his way to the deli and when he saw I was on my own, he got me a coffee. And then I shamelessly took advantage of his good nature and asked him to get the box of flutes down off the dresser.'

'Oh, right,' Charley spoke lightly, but she felt her stomach knotting.

Her unease must have shown on her face because there was a beat and then Pam said, 'I hope you didn't mind my asking him?'

'No. Of course not,' she lied. She knew she was being insanely illogical, but every little gesture of kindness from Ricky seemed to bind them closer together, entangling her, and making their future together seem inevitable. If someone was unremittingly kind and loving towards you, and everyone around you, what possible reason could you have to end the relationship? How could you ever find the right moment to finish with them? Every day that passed made it harder and she felt as if she was sliding down a slope into a claustrophobic trap. She turned away, hoping her dismay didn't show on her face, and engrossed herself in checking the till roll, but the older woman knew her far too well.

Taking her by the shoulders, Pam turned her round to face her and Charley gave in.

'Oh Pam, I'm in a mess. I don't know what to do about Ricky. I don't love him the way I loved Josh. But everyone, *everyone*, seems to think we should be forever. Except me.'

'Of course you don't love him the same way you loved Josh,' replied Pam softly. 'He's not Josh. He's a different person, and you'll love him differently.'

'But I'm not *in love* with him, and I fell in love with Josh immediately.'

'You were *besotted* with Josh when you met him,' corrected Pam. 'You were young and blindly infatuated.'

Charley pulled away. 'No, we were in love!'

'Were you?'

'Yes! It was love at first sight. For both of us.'

'Can you fall in love with someone you don't really know?' questioned Pam mildly. 'I'm not sure you can. You know, I had a whirlwind romance, before I met Geoff. His name was Carl. I met him at a disco and I worshipped the platform shoes he walked on and, like you with Josh, I would have gone to the end of the world for him. But it didn't last. Nothing substantial grew out of it, thank God! He turned out to be a self-opinionated narcissist!' She rolled her eyes, presumably at her own gullibility, then continued more seriously, 'You were lucky, you and Josh. Your holiday romance *did* develop into something deeper, before the initial infatuation wore off.'

Charley reeled. She'd had no idea Pam had seen her relationship with Josh in that light. But no matter what Pam thought, she told herself, she knew she was right. She and Josh had been in love from the very beginning. They *had*.

'It takes time for people to fall in love, Charley,' Pam continued. 'Don't be too hasty to give up on you and Ricky just because your feelings, your emotions, are perhaps more...' she faltered momentarily, '...more mature than they were when you fell for Josh. You and Ricky are good together. Give it more time. Give love a chance to grow.'

'That's what Angie said,' replied Charley flatly.

'Were you hoping I'd give you a different response?' Sometimes Pam was too perceptive for Charley's comfort.

Deep down she had been hoping the older woman would advise her say that if Charley wasn't sure she loved Ricky then she should break it off. What she'd actually wanted, she realised, was for Pam to give her permission to end the relationship, and now she was disappointed that she hadn't. Just then, the shop door was flung open and a group of giggling women spilled in, so she didn't get to reply to her mother-in-law.

–

Halfway through the afternoon, very mindful that Pam had come in for the morning shift, Charley pressured her to leave early. 'You've done more than enough today. I can manage,' she said firmly and, indicating the empty shop, added, 'It's not like I'm rushed off my feet!'

With evident reluctance, Pam eventually left, assuaging Charley's guilt a little. Nevertheless, that evening, after she'd got in from work, Charley called Nisha to ask her advice about Tara.

'Is it a good time to call?' she asked, as she always did, since Nisha was almost always sleeves-up, head-down and knee-deep in some promotional campaign or other.

'It's a fine time. Perfect, in fact. I could do with a break. I'm wading through the contract that marketing company finally sent through.'

'Oh, excellent! And?' asked Charley eagerly, immediately setting aside her troubles in favour of hearing Nisha's epic news.

'Well… I'm not sure. They want access to my client list, which is fair enough. But there doesn't seem to be any guarantee that I'll get to keep running their campaigns.'

'Ah,' said Charley.

'It's taken me years to build my list. Years. I'm not sure I want to just give it away.'

'But didn't you say that the company represents some pretty stellar people anyhow? Maybe you'd get a share of those?'

'Maybe… But then again, maybe not. What if they just want my client list rather than me?'

'Then they'd be mad,' was Charley's loyal but genuine response.

'And what about my clients? I'm not sure I feel comfortable just handing over control of their marketing accounts to another company without asking them first. It's one thing to agree to something that's going to impact on you, but another if it's going to impact on other people.'

Charley could see Nisha's point, but for the life of her couldn't think of anything useful to say to help her resolve her dilemma. Fortunately, Nisha clearly wasn't expecting her to, since she concluded, 'So, like I said, I'm not sure. But anyway, how's things with you?'

'Ok-ay,' replied Charley hesitantly, 'but I wondered if I could ask your advice on something?'

'Fire away.'

'I'm not sure what to do about Tara. I had to ask Pam to rush in to cover for her today when she let me down at the last moment. I don't mind when it's just me she's messing around by not turning up when she says she will… Actually,' Charley corrected herself, 'I do mind,' and then, picking up on the term Nisha had just used, she added, 'but today it impacted on Pam too.'

'Well, I don't actually have staff,' Nisha reminded her. 'So this isn't my area of expertise, but it strikes me that since Tara's not formally contracted to you to work agreed hours, and is coming in on a purely voluntary basis, then you can't really expect her to come in if she needs to prioritise something else.'

'I know,' said Charley shortly. 'But she hardly gave me any warning. She's treating it like a hobby.'

'It *is* her hobby,' Nisha pointed out flatly, momentarily flooring Charley.

'But it's my *business*!' she protested. 'I'm trying to make a living out of this! And Pam doesn't…' she stopped herself from saying *piss me around* and changed it to, 'let me down, and I'm not paying her, either.'

'Well, that speaks volumes about Pam, doesn't it?' replied Nisha. 'And you know what Tara is like over Monnie. She comes first. Always has done, always will do. So it shouldn't come as a surprise to you if she puts her daughter before your shop. Sorry Charley, but unless you can *pay* someone to work, you can't ask them to do any more than they feel like doing. And to be brutally honest with you, you're enormously lucky to have two people willing to give up their spare time to help you get your business going, and you might want to bear that in mind.'

Ouch, flinched Charley, stung by Nisha's sharpness, but nonetheless she managed to thank her friend for her advice before ringing off. Slumping back on the sofa, she flung the phone irritably onto the seat next to her. This was the second time in one day she'd been wrong-footed when, having turned to someone for support, expecting them to agree with her, or at least empathise with her, they'd done the opposite.

Chapter Ten

Dressed in only her underwear, Pam stood in front of her full-length bedroom mirror, sick with anxiety and frozen with indecision. She'd changed her outfit half a dozen times already and her bed was strewn with discarded clothes, scarves and shoes. *This internet dating lark was a terrible idea.* In less than an hour she was meant to be having a drink with the man she'd met through the dating website. Dennis, his name was, or 'Dez', as he apparently preferred. So perhaps it wasn't surprising she was standing there almost paralysed by a double whammy of nerves and indecision.

'You're going to have to wear something,' she told herself, eyeing the clothes on the bed dispassionately. *Unless you phone him and tell him you've changed your mind*, pointed out her inner voice. It was tempting. Tremendously tempting. She'd massively underestimated what a terrifying ordeal actually going on a date with a complete stranger was going to be. *Just call him and cry off. Tell him you're sick*, wheedled the voice. Crossing the room, she picked up her phone from her bedside table. One quick call and all this totally unnecessary, self-imposed terror would disappear and she could sling all her clothes back in the wardrobe and resume her normal, quiet Saturday evening.

'Dammit!' Scrolling through her contacts, she realised she hadn't added his details, so she'd have to go downstairs and get his number from his email on her laptop. This minor hiccup was enough to bring her up short and make her challenge herself. 'If you back out this time, you'll never do this,' she warned herself out loud. 'Do you want to be alone for the rest of your life?' *No*, confessed her subconscious immediately. 'So give yourself a break. You haven't been on a date for forty years. No wonder you're petrified.' Perhaps she'd just forgotten what first dates were like? She cast her mind back to meeting Geoff, on a blind date set up by a mutual friend. Had she been scared then? No. Excited, yes, but not even remotely anxious. So why the panic now?

She regarded herself critically in the glass. Big knickers, generous and sensible bra, sagging breasts, body still slim but decidedly baggy round the middle. Her underwear wasn't even tight but small rolls of fat bulged around it, her flesh having lost its firmness. It wasn't bad for a sixty-three-year-old, she supposed, but the sight did nothing to boost her confidence.

'And that is why God invented clothes!' she declared brightly, determinedly pulling herself together. Whatever she wore would hide the multitude of sins currently confronting her in the mirror, so she may as well just scramble into something and be done with it. Rejecting anything formal or dressy in the fear that it might make her look like she was trying too hard, she pulled on a pair of light grey cropped trousers and a flowing turquoise top with a scoop neck, and yes, the lines on her neck gave her age away, but so what?

'I am what I am, and he can like it or lump it,' she told herself, before selecting a chunky colourful necklace in favour of a covering-up scarf.

Heading for the door, she halted in her tracks to give herself one last look in the mirror. 'You are a strong woman,' she reminded herself. 'You've lost a son, and dumped an unfaithful husband. You can cope with a bloody date.'

Yet as she drove into town, a clutch of niggling fears began to prey on her mind. What if Dez didn't show up? And if he did, how would she recognise him? Would he take one look at her and decided to beat a hasty retreat? Why on earth was she exposing herself to such potential humiliation? What kind of idiot was she?

'Well, it's too late now,' she told herself, and took a few deep, calming breaths, slowly breathing in for a count of four, then breathing out for six. They didn't work.

They'd arranged to meet for a drink at the Cottage Inn, one of the older pubs overlooking Bristol harbour used more by locals than students and tourists. She parked the car as a text pinged into her phone.

> I've bagged us a table outside. I'm wearing a black polo shirt and jeans. See you there. Dez

Well, at least he's prompt, thought Pam, and her earlier fear that he might not show up at all evaporated. As she approached the pub, he was immediately obvious to her: the chap sitting on his own with a nearly full pint of lager, apparently engrossed in reading something on his phone, and her irrational anxiety that she'd accost the wrong man vanished too. Plucking up her courage, she walked up to his table with what she hoped was an air of confidence. Toni and Zee, she noticed, were seated a short distance behind him. She studiously ignored them, but was uncomfortably aware that Zee would be in her eyeline all evening.

'Dez?' she queried.

He looked up. 'Yes. Pam?'

'Yes,' she replied, hoping she didn't sound too obviously nervous.

His face lit up, and Pam found herself wondering if he'd been anxious, too. Rising to his feet, he said, 'Lovely to meet you. Thank you for coming. Let me get you a drink.'

'No, you've already got one, I'll go,' she said, already taking a step towards the bar.

'No. Please. Let me,' he insisted and, having asked her what she wanted, he disappeared into the pub.

As soon as the coast was clear, Zee peered over and caught Pam's eye. 'Not bad!' she mouthed, adding a corny wink and Toni, whose back was to Pam, whipped round and gave her a thumbs-up. Pam closed her eyes melodramatically. That was all she needed. A judging panel.

Returning with her wine, Dez sat down opposite her. He was, Pam decided, pleasant-looking, if unremarkable. Plumper and shorter than she'd envisaged, with a round, clean-shaven face, receding fair hair which was some years from full baldness, he didn't exactly knock her socks off. But then Geoff hadn't either when they first met, she reminded herself. The fact that in appearance, Dez was a world away from her tall, bespectacled, dark-haired, soon-to-be ex-husband was, frankly, hugely in his favour.

There was the briefest of tense moments, where Pam found herself uncharacteristically tongue-tied but Dez broke the ice by saying, 'I hope you didn't mind me wanting to meet in person, rather than on Zoom or whatever. I mean, e-meetings are fine for work, but not for something like this, when you really want to get to know someone.'

'Not at all,' replied Pam warmly. She couldn't have agreed with him more and soon they were chatting easily about the impact of the internet on the modern world, both of them admitting they found it difficult to keep up with the rapid pace of developments.

'I'm not a Luddite,' said Pam, 'and I'm more than happy to embrace change. If only I could keep up with it long enough to get hold of it!'

Dez laughed, and from there the conversation slipped effortlessly onto Pam's attempts to upgrade her computer skills to be more use to Charley in her shop and then to her role in the growing business.

An hour or so later, she was wondering why she'd been so anxious about meeting him. There'd been no embarrassing silences or uncomfortable disagreements revealing them to be poles apart, and the only mildly awkward moment was when Dez had, predictably, asked why her marriage had ended. At least he'd had to courtesy to tack an 'I hope you don't mind my asking,' on the end of his query.

Taking a sip of her wine and mentally thanking Nisha for predicting that this would come up, Pam had replied, 'Of course not,' and given her prepared answer: 'My husband had an affair.' Which in her opinion said it all. Deliberately, she had decided not to go into details and that she would a) refuse to and b) deduct points if he'd pushed her to. But he hadn't.

'Well, I don't know the man,' Dez had replied carefully, 'and it's not my place to judge of course, but if you ask me, he sounds like an idiot!'

She'd laughed out loud and had then promptly caught sight of both Zee and Toni grinning at her like a pair of Cheshire cats. *I'll deal with you two later*, she'd decided.

The other, more difficult, question she'd been bracing herself to deal with was whether she had children. She'd avoided the question on the form. Technically, she only had one child now, Luke, but omitting Josh was too painful, and just wrong, so she'd left the section blank. She wasn't surprised when the question arose and she easily gave her usual, brief explanation about losing Josh, however she hadn't expected Dez to wordlessly reach across the table and momentarily place his hand over hers, and she was touched by the kindness of the gesture.

Spring had slipped into early summer and the mid-June sun had set by around nine thirty. The bar staff came round the outside tables handing out coloured glass lanterns, which was all very pretty against the darkening sky, but Pam was beginning to feel decidedly cold. Especially since a chilly breeze was coming in off the harbour. In all her stressing while dressing she hadn't thought to bring a warm woolly. She stuck it out until around ten, and then made her excuses and told Dez she ought to be getting back. The moment she'd said it she realised it might signal that she wasn't enjoying herself and wouldn't be interested in seeing him again, and she kicked herself.

Hurriedly, he downed the rest of his pint. 'Well, it's been lovely meeting you,' he said, getting up.

'You too,' she said, and then there was a pause during which Pam found herself willing him to ask her for another date.

'Perhaps we can meet up again?' he said cautiously.

'Yes, I'd like that,' she replied, and then she was improbably disappointed when he didn't go on to suggest a day and, like a lovelorn teenager frightened of rejection, she didn't want to push it herself.

They said their goodbyes and, only too aware that Toni and Zee would demand an immediate and full post mortem, she slipped into the Ladies', giving Dez time to leave before she joined them. How dreadful would that look, if he thought she'd posted a couple of stooges to spy on him? She left it long enough for the coast to clear before coming back out and slipping into the seat next to Zee.

'Well?' asked her friend, all agog for the details.

'How'd it go?' prompted Toni eagerly.

They quizzed her like a couple of teenagers, reminding her of the heightened melodrama and intense scrutiny of the after-date post mortems when she was young.

'It was… lovely!' she told them sheepishly.

'So, tell us all about him!' demanded Zee. 'Where does he live? What's his business? Has he got kids?'

'Actually, I don't know,' said Pam. Looking back, she realised she'd learned very little about Dez. 'He didn't tell me very much about himself.'

'I hope he's not hiding some dark and dodgy past!' joked Zee.

The idea amused Pam. 'I doubt it. He just seemed more interested in talking about me.' Which, now she came to think of it, was enormously flattering.

'I think that's quite classy,' decreed Toni.

'Or nosey,' countered Zee.

Pam shot her a look. 'A little harsh, methinks!' she said then carried on, 'But it was good fun. *He* was good fun.'

'There was certainly a lot of *hilarity*,' said Zee teasingly.

'Yes, a lot of *guffawing* and what-have-you!' added Toni.

Pam poked her tongue out at them. 'Anyhow, I think some of that was nerves,' she confessed.

'Well, it looked like you were having a good time,' Zee told her. 'You looked happier than I've seen you for a long time.'

'I was,' nodded Pam, 'and I know this is going to sound preposterous, but I felt… younger.'

'Did he mention the age gap?' asked Toni, raising an eyebrow.

'No! Of course not. He's far too much of a gentleman. And anyhow, I'm only five years older than him.'

'Cougar!' accused Toni.

'As if!' Pam thumped her friend playfully on the arm, then a chill breeze blew in from the water and she shivered. 'Come on, I forgot to bring a jumper and I'm freezing, let's go.'

· The women linked arms and walked three abreast along the path back towards the car park.

'Well done,' said Zee giving Pam's arm a squeeze. 'That took guts.'

Yes, thought Pam, momentarily proud of herself, *it bloody had*.

Chapter Eleven

Waking on Sunday morning in Ricky's bed, Charley reached out for him, expecting her hands to feel his smooth bare skin, but her fingers slid across an empty space, although the sheet was still warm. A faint smell of brewing coffee drifted through the open door. She stretched slowly, luxuriating in the pleasure of not having to get up and knowing that in a moment Ricky would bring coffee, and get back into bed. Sunlight poured through the thin, cream blinds suffusing the whole room with a soft light. She heard Carlo pad into the room and seconds later, a cold, damp whiskery nose nudged at her arm. She patted the bed and the grey lurcher lumbered up and settled down next to her, taking up more than his fair share of the bed – way more – so that when Ricky walked in a short while later, in his boxers and with a mug in each hand, he couldn't even get into bed.

'Off!' he said to the dog. 'That's my place!'

Instantly appealing to Charley, Carlo flattened his ears, raised his eyebrows and gave her a plaintive look from his soulful brown eyes.

'Nice try,' Ricky informed the hound, and handing Charley her coffee, 'but she doesn't want you any more than I do! Out!' Ricky pointed to the open doorway.

Carlo sighed exaggeratedly, then reluctantly sloped off the bed as if he were being cast out into the wilderness for ever.

'Poor Carlo. He hates it when he can't be with you,' said Charley. The lurcher was never more than a few feet away from Ricky, faithfully following him at heel whenever he so much as got up to leave a room.

Ricky shot her an amused look. 'There isn't room for all three of us,' he reasoned, standing beside the bed. 'You can have the dog, or you can have me.'

'You,' replied Charley, pulling back the quilt.

Later, they took Carlo for a long run on Clifton Downs, as they usually did on Sunday mornings. Holding hands, they walked along the gravelled track in an easy silence, the sharp tang of freshly cut grass floated on the warm summer air, while the dog ran around them joyously, in wide sweeping circles, a broad grin on his face. The sun warmed their backs and cast a single shadow of the pair of them on the ground in front of them. The Downs were weekend-busy, with dog-walkers and families out enjoying the sunshine. They passed a small group of dads having a kick-about with a dozen or so little kids, based around a mini pop-up goal. Charley could see Carlo eyeing up the ball, clearly keen to join in the fun.

'Leave it,' ordered Ricky firmly and, obediently, the dog gave the players a wide berth. But then one of the kids spectacularly mis-kicked the ball and it flew over and walloped into Ricky's back.

'God, I'm so sorry!' called out one of the dads.

'No worries!' replied Ricky, turning and reaching for the ball with his foot. Charley expected him to kick it back, but instead he proceeded to skilfully dribble the ball back towards the group.

'Tackle him!' yelled one of the dads playfully, and the biggest of the kids made a valiant effort, but Ricky neatly flicked the ball to one side and easily evaded him, and then he carried on until he was close enough to the pop-up goal to shoot. The ball flew into the back of net.

'Woo-hoo!' cried Charley, and Ricky raised his arms in mock triumph as the dads and kids broke into wild applause. *He'd make a great dad*, thought Charley, loving how the small boys were all looking up to him. She didn't even know if he wanted kids. She'd always avoided asking him. It was such a loaded question, but a brief fantasy of her and Ricky, complete with a couple of small children, slipped easily into her mind. They were here, on the Downs, and Ricky was running along behind a little girl on a bike, his hand on the saddle, keeping her balanced, while Charley walked behind them pushing a toddler on a trike. The fantasy was so clear, so real, that it took her an effort to pull herself out of it. Ricky, meanwhile, was solemnly shaking hands with the boy he'd outmanoeuvred and then, looking endearingly abashed, he came back to join her.

'Awesome goal!' said Charley.

'Well, there wasn't actually a goalie,' he pointed out, 'but thank you.' Then he leant down and kissed her.

'Well, I think you're being overly modest,' she told him as they walked on.

'Trust me, I'm not. Those lads would run rings round me in a match. In fact, Carlo could probably beat me in a full-on tackle.'

Josh had been a big football fan, glued to the sports channels at weekends and playing five-a-side on Wednesdays, but the game had always left Charley cold. She realised she didn't even know if Ricky even supported a team.

'Of course I do. I'm Italian!' he told her. 'It's practically the law. We play the best football in the world!'

'So who do you support then?' she asked, before adding hurriedly, 'And please don't be offended if I've never heard of them.'

'Italy,' he announced dryly.

Charley mock-grimaced and shook her head. 'Sorry, never heard of them.'

Ricky didn't even deign to reply.

–

They'd sort of effortlessly slipped into the routine of going out for a late brunch on Sundays after walking Carlo. Usually to a dog-friendly café where the lurcher would sprawl patiently under a table, sleeping off his morning run. The café was pretty full, and while Ricky queued to order their food from the counter, Charley grabbed a table, stowed Carlo underneath, and indulged herself with a little people-watching. A very young couple seated immediately opposite her – students, she reckoned – spent their time on their phones, barely talking to one other. Occasionally one or other would say something, or they'd screen-share something and then laugh. They seemed happy enough. Behind them, a middle-aged couple argued animatedly, but not acrimoniously, with each other, whilst behind them a much older couple sat at a table strewn with the Sunday papers, reading in companionable silence. Surrounded by couples, all enjoying each other's company in such varied ways, got Charley thinking that maybe Angie was right; perhaps she shouldn't compare the way she had loved Josh with the way she loved Ricky.

At the table immediately next to hers a frazzled young father was trying to persuade his toddler to eat a yoghurt. *Good luck with that*, Charley thought, watching the little lad clamp his lips tightly together and shake his head so furiously the wooden highchair wobbled. She watched him adoringly for a moment. He reminded her of Finn, except that Angie always let her kids feed themselves, which, she'd explained to Charley, not only taught them how to use a spoon and fork, but also cut down on food battles. Watching the stubborn toddler, Charley was itching to tell the father to back off, but it wasn't her business; the little one wasn't her child. She sighed and looked away. The various scenarios playing out around her led her to reflect on how different her Sundays had been with Josh. They'd never gone out for brunch. On Sundays, they'd wake up, make love, and have a lie-in. Eventually they'd get up and slob around the flat while Charley cooked Sunday lunch, usually roast chicken, Josh's favourite. Occasionally they'd go to Pam's for lunch and come back laden with Tupperware boxes of leftovers and slabs of her home-made cakes from tea. Carlo thumping his tail at her feet signalled Ricky's return. He slid nimbly sideways into his seat, balancing a tray laden with coffees, OJs and scrambled eggs on brown. Just at that precise moment, the little boy at the next table launched himself into a full-blown tantrum, violently thrashing his legs, kicking the tray out of Ricky's hands, and with a deafening crash, the entire contents hurtled onto the table.

'*Jason!*' bawled the father.

There was a split second of silence where everyone in the café turned round to look, and then poor little Jason burst into tears.

Charley leapt up to right the cups and glasses while Ricky turned to help the young dad. Flustered and apologising profusely, the poor man was struggling to unclip his now hysterical child from the highchair.

'It's not a problem,' Ricky assured him. 'It was an accident. Here, let me help.' And he gathered up the family's belongings and stashed them in the buggy, and then pushed it to the door, leaving the man with both hands free to carry his rigid, screaming child out of the café. Charley watched them, thinking how natural Ricky looked pushing the buggy.

'Don't have kids,' was the dad's passing shot as Ricky opened the door for him. Ricky just laughed and turned to Charley and threw her his warm, easy smile, and at once something clicked in her brain. She'd always wanted kids and had always assumed she'd have them, until Josh had died. But now, here she was, over thirty, her biological clock ruthlessly ticking the years away, and with them the chance of her becoming a mother. Secretly, Angie's last two pregnancies had really distressed Charley; the jealousy she'd felt had hurt, physically hurt. She didn't begrudge Angie her children, of course she didn't, but it didn't stop her being swamped by the immature feeling that it wasn't fair that her friend had four kids while Josh's death had left her not just widowed, but childless too. For the second time that morning, Charley had cast Ricky as a potential father and it occurred to her that staying with Ricky meant she could have children. Even as the thought solidified in her mind she chastised herself – it would be wrong-headed, and selfish, and absolutely no basis for a lasting relationship. She finished piling the crockery and glasses, and the sodden remains of the now *very* scrambled eggs, back on

97

the tray. One of the waiters had come over to finish clearing up the mess. 'Could we have the same again, please?' she asked him.

'Yes, of course.'

Ricky was taking his wallet out of his pocket.

'No, I'll get it this time.' Charley picked up her bag to get her purse.

'It's on the house,' the waiter told them. 'For being so understanding.'

Ricky shrugged the compliment off. 'These things happen.'

'Yes, but not everyone would have taken it the way you did. Some people would have been really difficult.'

Ricky merely smiled and calmly put his wallet away and sat back down opposite her.

'He's right,' said Charley, as the waiter went off to get their brunch order. 'Nobody else got up to help the poor bloke.' She indicated the rest of the customers who'd studiously ignored the man's plight and left him to it.

'Perhaps I have built-in sympathy for dads dealing with kids on their own,' said Ricky. 'I get so many of them coming into the bike shop.'

'Really? Why's that?'

'Oh, I don't know. Maybe because people think it's a kind of "dad thing" to sort out the bikes. Sometimes it's because the parents have split up and it's the dad's turn to have the kids for the weekend. There's a whole bunch of them that come in quite regularly.'

'Regularly? What on earth for?'

Ricky raised an eyebrow in mock offence. 'It might surprise you to know that some people are really into bikes! And they get their kids into biking too and jazz up their rides. They buy them bike bags, funky bells, flashing lights for the wheels—'

'Please tell me you don't sell them those ghastly glittery tassels!'

'No, I draw the line somewhere! But I do supply a fine line in snazzy handlebar grips. I'll put a sparkly rainbow pair on your bike if you like.'

'Over my dead body!'

Ricky laughed. 'They're a nice bunch, though. Some Saturdays I do so many running repairs it's like I'm holding a bike club – fixing bent forks, tightening brakes, mending punctures. And the kids are great. They always want to help. They love wielding spanners.'

Having seen Angie's kids mucking about with their plastic hard hats and toy tool boxes Charley could testify to the truth of that statement. She could just imagine little Finn on his knees in the bike shop solemnly handing Ricky a spanner and helping him fix the stabilizers on his little jungle bike.

'I bet you don't even charge them, do you?'

'Yes I do!'

Charley impaled him with a look.

'A little,' he confessed.

'Maybe you should run workshops? Get people to pay you to show them how to fix their bikes.'

Ricky laughed.

'I'm serious!' continued Charley. 'I mean, look at me, I couldn't even fix a puncture.'

'I'll show you. We can do it this afternoon, if you like?'

Charley could think of least a dozen things she'd prefer to do with Ricky. 'Maybe not. I can think of better things to do...' she hinted provocatively.

He laughed at her, holding her gaze, and smiling deeply into her eyes and she reflected that she did love him. She genuinely did. She just wasn't *in love* with him, but maybe, as everyone said, that kind of love might develop. Or perhaps having kids would trigger it? He'd be a wonderful dad, you only had to see him with children to know that. So maybe she'd fall in love with Ricky as a father, because of the way he was with their kids? Would that be such a terrible risk to take?

Chapter Twelve

'I am *so* sorry about last Friday,' gushed Tara, bursting into the shop shortly after nine on Monday morning, which was early for her – *very* early. She was juggling a fancy shop-bought coffee gateaux, two take-away coffees and a large bouquet of lilies, the last of which she thrust at Charley. 'I'm sure I told you about Monnie's appointment.' She pulled a face. 'Hope it wasn't too much of a problem.'

You didn't and it was. It briefly crossed Charley's mind to be honest and tell her Tara it had been a major inconvenience but, remembering her conversation with Nisha, she limited herself to saying, 'No, it was fine. Pam came in.'

'Oh, good old Pam!' said Tara, dumping the cake and the coffees on the counter. Barely pausing for breath, and handing Charley her coffee, Tara went on, 'You know what you should do – set up a shared calendar, then I can log all the days I can't get here in advance, *and* the dates of the school holidays. Then there won't be any problems.'

The suggestion jarred because it would mean she'd have to run *two* calendars and she had more than enough admin to do as it was, without running a double diary system.

But before she could voice her reluctance, Tara said, 'Actually, better idea, just give me access to the shop's calendar.'

'There isn't one,' Charley told her. 'I just use mine.'

'Well, there should be.' Tara's voice held more than a hint of rebuke. Helping herself to Charley's laptop, she said, 'I'll set one up now. I'll make it a shared one so I can access it too. Pam as well, if she likes.'

Charley accepted defeat. When Tara was on a mission, trying to stop her was like trying to halt a runaway train with a daisy chain. Less than five minutes later, Tara had created a new calendar and input all of Monnie's key dates.

'Now you just need to import your appointments, delivery dates, order deadlines et cetera,' Tara informed her, 'and from now on things will run more smoothly.'

Charley was left with the distinct impression that the problem with not knowing about Monnie's dental appointment had been her fault all along. However she didn't brood on the thought, reminding herself that no matter how brash and tactless her mate was, she always meant well and that, in any event, it was a lot more fun in the shop when Tara was in, and more profitable, too. The morning flew by, with a steady run of customers and Tara was on top form, chatting and joshing with them and somehow ensuring hardly any of them left the shop empty-handed. Charley left her to it, knowing she was best placed behind the till, just taking the money.

'Have you got any more of these Prosecco and fig scented candles?' she overheard a woman asking Tara. 'I wanted six but you've only got three.'

Knowing Tara wouldn't have a clue what spare stock the shop had, Charley called over, 'I'm really sorry, but that's all we have.'

'Oh never mind,' replied the woman, putting the candles back on the display.

'Did you need all six the same?' Tara instantly queried. 'Only we do have an extensive range of scented candles.'

Charley watched her mate hand the woman the nearest candle to her.

'This one's my favourite. Here, have a whiff,' she said, opening the lid.

Charley would have bet her last tenner Tara had absolutely no idea which candle she'd picked up, but that didn't seem to stop her charm offensive working, and two minutes later the woman left the shop happily clutching six different scented candles, plus a rhubarb and Prosecco fizzy bath bomb and a china cup and saucer bearing the slogan: *No milk in my Prosecco, thank you.*

'Nicely done,' said Charley, as soon as the shop door had closed behind her.

'I thank you!' replied Tara, bowing to an imaginary audience.

'You were born with gift of the gab, weren't you?'

'Yup,' beamed Tara. 'And if you've got it, flaunt it!'

Moments later she was flaunting it again. This time to a woman who'd come in to ask if the shop did party favours for weddings. Charley had long wanted to expand the gift bag side-line into weddings but hadn't yet managed to. She'd approached the Orangery, one of Bristol's most popular wedding venues, but although they'd liked her classy-looking gift bags, much to Charley's disappointment they already had a supplier. So she was about to reply, 'No, not yet,' when Tara piped up.

'Yes. We do a complete range of wedding favours,' she informed the customer, and Charley whipped round to face her, barely suppressing a gasp at her easy, barefaced lie. 'Is it your wedding?' Tara was asking the woman convivially.

'Yes.'

'Ooh congratulations!' babbled Tara. 'When's the big day?'

Bloody hell, Tara! thought Charley. Any minute now she'd be asking to see the ring!

'Oh it's not for months yet, but I'm just trying to make sure everything's lined up. So I wondered what the gift bags included and how much they were?'

Yes, so do I! thought Charley, shooting Tara a quizzical look.

Tara didn't even flinch. 'Wedding favours are such an important part of the celebration we think the bride should choose the contents personally,' she ad-libbed smoothly, 'so we have various products and prices. What's your budget?'

You are gobsmackingly shameless. Charley bit her lip and fought to keep a straight face. Although, as ever, she was impressed by Tara's ballsy, brazen approach. Personally, she was always wary of being too pushy with the customers, in case it put them off. To be frank, when she'd first met Tara she had found her a bit off-putting, too loud and gobby. It had been at a Zumba class not long after she'd first moved to Bristol, and it was through Tara that she'd met Nisha and Angie. Of the three of them, it was Angie who Charley had been more drawn to, and who she felt instinctively more comfortable with. But then, tragically, Tara's mum had died a few months after Josh and their shared experience of bereavement had thrown her and Tara closer. Losing her mum had changed Tara, softened her and taken the edge off her – well, marginally. Occasionally Tara's opinionated bluntness put stress fractures in their friendship, but now, watching her friend casually drumming up an order for one hundred and twenty wedding favours at twenty quid a pop, Charley reminded herself how lucky she was to have Tara as a friend – a woman who was as generous with her time as she was with her opinions.

As lunchtime approached, Tara offered to stay on until Pam got there in the afternoon. 'So you can have a proper lunch break for a change.'

Charley assumed she was still trying to make amends. 'Thanks but there's not much point,' she replied, since there wasn't anything she'd actually want to do with an hour off. The Cargo area was full of great eateries and quirky little shops, but she'd never been one for retail therapy and didn't fancy having a sit-down meal on her own, no matter how enticing the food was.

'Have lunch with Ricky.'

Charley shook her head. 'He can't take a lunch break. There's no one to look after the bike shop.'

'Well grab a sarnie and take it down to his shop,' persisted Tara.

When she'd first started going out with Ricky, Charley would have jumped at the chance of spending a lunchtime with him, but now it seemed faintly pointless. It wasn't as if they were two love-struck teenagers desperate to spend every snatched and stolen moment together. She'd spent all of yesterday with him, and last night, and the night before that. Besides, there was every chance he'd be too busy to even talk to her, so she'd just be hanging around looking self-conscious.

'He'll probably have customers,' she said and then watched as a small frown flitted across her friend's face.

'You two are okay, aren't you? You've not had a falling-out or anything?' she asked Charley bluntly.

'No, of course not.'

Tara didn't actually challenge her reply but it seemed to Charley she held her gaze just a shade longer than necessary before saying, 'Well, why don't you just grab a sarnie and nip down to the bike shop and see? You never know your luck. He might be free.'

Swallowing an irritable sigh, Charley did as she was told. She got a panini from the deli, on the grounds that she'd need to eat something anyway but, as she'd predicted, the bike shop was busy when she appeared in the doorway. Carlo lumbered over to greet her but Ricky could only glance up from the counter where he was showing a customer a range of bike locks. He frowned briefly with concern and, momentarily excusing himself to the punter, he broke off to say to her, 'Is everything all right?'

'Yes, yes. I was just wondering if you might be free for a quick lunch...' She trailed off feeling stupid, since it was obvious from the throng of customers that he wasn't.

'Oh, okay.' He looked mildly bemused before pulling an apologetic face and saying, 'Sorry, no.'

She'd intended to go back to the shop but suddenly feeling irked at how Tara had bullied her into making a minor fool of herself, she decided to wander down to the dockside, and find a bench to eat her lunch. The waterfront was always busy at lunchtime, flocked with office staff and shop workers all either stretching their legs or getting some fresh air and enjoying the colourful harbour-side scene. Charley sat herself down and prepared to join them. Glancing around, she noticed a few lone diners, like herself, eating picnic lunches in splendid isolation. Women, mostly, sitting primly with their legs tucked neatly together, eating home-made sandwiches from Tupperware tubs or tin foil parcels perched on their laps. The men, she noticed, mostly sat man-spreading, and tended to have shop-bought plastic-packed sarnies, or pies and pasties which they ate from bakers' paper bags. None of them looked as if they were particularly enjoying their lunches, or themselves, and she couldn't shake off the feeling that most of them seemed miserable. Of course they might have been perfectly happy, utterly relishing some much needed peace and quiet, but nevertheless, the image seemed to convey a collective sad loneliness. Realising the scene was dampening her mood, Charley stuffed her panini back into its wrapper and headed back to the shop. At least there she could have a laugh with Tara. Except that as soon as Charley reappeared, Tara reached for her jacket and handbag.

'I take it The Lovely Ricky was tied up then?'

Charley nodded.

'Well in that case I might as well go home then, since it's quiet.'

'Yes, of course.'

After Tara had gone, Charley leant on the till counter in the empty shop finishing her solitary lunch, and found herself wondering whether Tara's offer had been more about her wanting Charley and Ricky to spend time together than about giving Charley a break. Had Angie told Tara about her anxieties about Ricky? She doubted it. And Pam wouldn't have mentioned it, so maybe Tara just had an inkling something was wrong and was fishing. Well, she could fish away. Charley wasn't ready to share her anxieties with Tara, not quite yet. And anyhow, she knew her friend would only give her the same advice that Pam and Angie had said – only more forcibly.

Chapter Thirteen

Pam arrived in good time for the afternoon shift, as usual. She dumped her bag behind the counter and then calmly made a statement that knocked Charley for six.

'I'm sorry, could you just repeat that?' gasped Charley, once she'd regained the power of speech.

'I had a date,' repeated Pam nonchalantly.

'What? When? Where? Who with?' demanded Charley but, infuriatingly, just at that moment the door opened and a middle-aged couple walked in.

Sheer mischief sparkled in Pam's eyes. 'We have customers.'

'We have not finished this conversation!' hissed Charley hurriedly.

Pam assumed an enigmatic expression and strolled over to ask if the couple needed any help. Then she proceeded to show them round the entire shop, pointing out a few items here and there with what seemed to Charley to be exasperating and intentional leisureliness.

Charley didn't know how she managed to keep her cool. Curiosity seethed inside her on a rolling boil. *What the hell did Pam mean, she 'had a date'? And how could she be so bloody casual about it, for crying out loud!* In the end, after what felt like an hour but was in reality just a little over ten minutes, the couple left and, adding to Charley's frustration, without actually buying anything. Charley was just about to pounce on Pam, but no sooner had the door closed behind the first couple than another group of punters came in. Charley wanted to scream. Glancing at Pam, she could see her mother-in-law was suppressing a smile – or, rather, a smirk – clearly enjoying her daughter-in-law's frustration.

By the time the shop was empty, Charley's impatience was at fever pitch.

'So?' she demanded. 'Tell me everything!'

'You can have the edited highlights,' said Pam calmly, going on to give Charley a brief resume of her evening with Dez.

Charley kept interrupting, wanting more details. What did Pam wear? What had Dez worn? What did he drink? Did she have a picture of him?

'No! I didn't take a photo of him!'

'But there must be one on his profile. Where's your phone?' demanded Charley.

'My phone?'

'Didn't you download the app?'

'No, darling. I did it on the computer... with a little help from Nisha,' Pam confessed.

You kept that quiet, Nishe, thought Charley, *and so had Pam!* She thrust her laptop at her mother-in-law. 'Go on. Log onto the site and let's have a look at him.'

While Pam typed, Charley speculated on why the older woman hadn't confided in her. She hoped to God Pam had told *someone* she was going on a date. A sudden alarm bell rang inside her. Loudly.

'You didn't meet him all on your own, did you?' she asked.

'No, sweetheart. Zee and Toni were standing by at a nearby table.'

'Good,' said Charley. 'You can't be too careful. Honestly Pam, things aren't the way they were in your day and you have to think about safety all the time.' Gravely she listed a set of rules for safe dating, counting them off on her fingers. 'Never agree to meet anyone except in a public place. Always tell someone where you're going to be, and when you expect to be back. And don't take anyone back to your place unless there's someone else there – well, not to start with, until you get know him well enough.'

'Yes, Charley,' nodded Pam, deadpan.

'I'm serious, Pam!' Even to herself Charley sounded like a parent hectoring a teenager. 'I hate having to lecture you like this, but this is the modern world and you're a little bit out of touch, if you don't mind me saying so.' Since, judging by her expression, Pam appeared not to mind, Charley continued: 'Don't leave your drink while you nip off to the loo or whatever, anyone can spike it so don't let it out of your sight. And don't let anyone buy you a drink, or give you a drink unless you can actually see it being poured.'

Pam looked decidedly uncomfortable and Charley guessed she'd already made that beginner's error. 'Well, don't do it again!' she scolded.

'No, Charley,' promised Pam obediently.

Once Charley saw the photo of Dez she relaxed a little, realising she'd probably overreacted. He just seemed like an ordinary, decent-looking bloke and besides, she reminded herself, Pam wasn't an idiot.

'He's not bad looking!' she said approvingly.

The two of them stood side by side, leaning on the counter conspiratorially, looking at his picture.

'On a scale of one to ten, how attractive would you say he is?' asked Pam.

'At least a seven,' declared Charley.

'Well, that's not bad,' said Pam perkily.

'And you're an eleven.'

'I wish, darling. But boy, was I nervous! I nearly cried off at the last moment.' Then she looked Charley in the eye and added with endearing humility, 'Tell me honestly, am I ridiculous to be dating at my age? Am I making a fool of myself? He is a little younger than me…'

A wave of affection rose in Charley as she realised the courage it must have taken Pam to put herself on a dating site at all, and it hurt her to see her transparent lack of confidence. Putting an arm around her she said, 'Of course not. You're a fabulous woman. Wise, funny, attractive and good company, and you raised two wonderful sons, and you are without exception the best mother-in-law in the world – plus you're a brilliant cook! I'm proud of you. Seriously,' she added, since Pam was shaking her head self-deprecatingly. 'And I'm thrilled, *and impressed*, that you've already met someone.'

Pam slid her arm round Charley too and for a moment the two women stood side by side in a loving embrace, their heads leaning against each other's.

Then, after giving Pam a quick squeeze, Charley broke away and asked, 'When are you seeing him again?'

Pam pulled a face. 'I'm not sure. I'd like to, but he hasn't called me so...' She shrugged.

'You could call him.'

Pam looked horrified. 'Oh, I don't think so. I don't want him to think I'm chasing him!'

The arrival of more customers ended their conversation, at least for a while, since Charley was now determined to encourage Pam to not give up on the bloke, or rather on herself, too readily. In the event, she needn't have been concerned. A text pinged into Pam's phone shortly before closing time. Charley mentally crossed her fingers.

'It's from him!' Pam seemed to freeze, mild panic furrowing her forehead.

'And?' prompted Charley, hoping to God he was asking to see Pam again. She didn't like to think about how utterly demolished Pam would be if he didn't.

After rapidly scanning the text, Pam blurted out, 'He says thank you for a lovely evening and can he have my address so he can send me some flowers!'

'Oo-ooh,' sang Charley, relief flooding through her. 'He seems pretty keen!'

Pam flushed scarlet and busied herself tidying the dresser.

-

'Well, you kept that quiet, Nishe!' kidded Charley when she called her friend after work that evening.

'Kept what quiet?' Nisha's tone exuded total innocence.

'Don't try that with me! Pam's already spilled the beans and –
hold the front page – she's already had a date!'

'Go Pam!' whooped Nisha, tacitly admitted her involvement
by adding, 'She asked me not to say anything.'

'I'm joking,' said Charley. 'Who do you think suggested she
asked you to help her in the first place?'

'I did wonder, but I wasn't a hundred per cent sure,' admitted
Nisha. 'Anyhow, I'm glad you called. Are you free for a drink one
evening this week? I want to ask your advice about the buy-out
deal.'

'*My* advice?' questioned Charley, shocked and flattered.

'Yes. It's such a huge decision, I just need to talk it through.'

'Sure. I've got deliveries to do over the next couple of nights—'

'That's fine. I've got a deadline to hit too so, Thursday?'

'Perfect.'

–

Nisha had chosen a pub in the city centre and had already grabbed
one of pavement tables out the front by the time Charley arrived
on the Thursday evening. A bottle of wine rested in an ice bucket,
and as soon as she saw her friend approach, Nisha instantly poured
her a glass. Settling into the chair next to her, Charley thanked
her.

Nisha raised her glass. 'To Pam!' she toasted.

'To Pam!' echoed Charley cheerfully.

It turned out Nisha had deliberately chosen that pub because
it was directly opposite the offices of the PR company. Intrigued,
Charley swivelled in her chair for a good nose. The multi-storey
block was fairly new, a stunning style statement of stainless steel
and glass, with a palatial entrance foyer which positively oozed
elegance and money.

'Which floor are they on?' she asked.

'All of them,' replied Nisha coolly.

'Bloody hell!' When Nisha had said it was a top-notch
company she hadn't been joking.

'That's why I wanted to meet here, so the building reminds me what I'd be turning down.'

'So you've already decided then?' asked Charley, wondering why, if that were the case, Nisha wanted to talk to her at all. She felt vaguely disappointed, and her pride at being the person Nisha had chosen to turn to for advice popped like an overblown balloon.

'I think so. But I need to test my judgement,' Nisha clarified, boosting Charley's ego again. 'With someone whose opinion I value,' she added, sending Charley's ego off the scale.

'Go ahead.'

Nisha ran through the pros and cons of the deal, and then summed up her reservations with an intellectual precision that impressed the hell out of Charley.

'On the one hand, there are the pros,' she started and made a graceful sweeping gesture with her hand, indicating the classy construction opposite them. 'Posh offices, city centre location, prestigious company, global events, top-tier clients, and more money.'

'Very tempting,' said Charley.

'In some ways, yes,' agreed Nisha. 'But the cons, on the other hand are: one, they want access to my clients but without giving me any guarantee that I will end up running their accounts any more. Plus, I won't get to choose which accounts I *do* work on. So I lose all control of my business and my workload.

'Two, they're ruthless. Even if I do keep an existing client, they'll almost certainly impose new deals, charging more for doing less. I don't want to be forced into renegotiating deals with my old clients. And, worse, they'll jettison any of them if they don't think they'll bring in enough money. My clients have been loyal to me, and I want to be loyal to them.

'And three, we don't we share the same ethical values. I wouldn't choose to represent some of the companies and celebrities they take on – in fact, I wouldn't want to touch one or two of them with a bargepole. But for them, profit comes before everything. And I think that's the main problem: I'm not sure I want to be part of a company that puts profit before its clients, its staff, its ethics and its values. I want to keep control of what I do, who I chose to do it with, *or not*, and how I do it.

'So, bottom line, Charley. Am I making the wrong decision? Am I being completely up myself? Should I set all that aside, and grasp a fantastic, once-in-a-lifetime opportunity?'

Charley was completely flummoxed; she didn't feel at all in a position to offer Nisha any guidance until her mate cannily put the deal into perspective for her.

'Imagine if a *major* department store wanted to take over your shop. Somebody huge like, M&S or John Lewis or whoever. You could still call it *Charley's Prosecco Pop-Up*, but they wanted to dictate what you stocked, what you charged, when the shop had to open, including Sundays and evenings perhaps, and the deals you made with the gift bag side of the business or whatever, but they'd pay you far more than you earn now. Would that tempt you?'

'No,' replied Charley without a moment's hesitation. 'Because I wouldn't really be running my own business any more, would I?'

A look of satisfaction crept across Nisha's face. 'Precisely,' she said. 'See? I knew you'd get it!' She settled back in her seat, looking content. 'Thank you, Charley.'

'I don't think I really helped that much.'

'Yes, you did. One of the only drawbacks of being a sole trader is not having a business partner, someone to bounce ideas off, and challenge your judgements. So don't underestimate how useful it was having your perceptive insight this evening.'

Perceptive insight! thought Charley, thrilled to bits to garner such high praise from Nisha. *Go me!*

Nisha leant forward to top up their drinks. 'Dare I ask how things are with Tara in the shop?'

'Actually, a lot better,' said Charley. 'She seems a bit more committed. I think she's still feeling guilty for letting me down last week.'

'Long may it last!' said Nisha raising her glass.

'Too right!' Charley grinned and clinked her drink with Nisha's.

In reality, Charley knew Tara far too well to delude herself into thinking that her friend's remorse-fuelled keenness would last for ever. However, over the next couple of weeks or so it really did seem to Charley that Tara was making the effort to at least be more generous and flexible with her time. Of course she didn't actually arrive any earlier, but she did offer to work a little later some mornings. On one particular day, when a large delivery came in very late in the morning, Tara readily volunteered to stay well into the lunch hour to help unpack all the boxes, and she even took the cardboard to the recycling bins before she left. Truth be told however, Nisha's earlier assessment had been right: Tara still prioritised the needs of her daughter, and the demands of her domestic life, over helping out in the shop. Although she did now meticulously put notes into the shared calendar to warn Charley if she was going to have to come in late because she was waiting for a plumber or whatever, so at least Charley wasn't left in the lurch with no notice. All in all, Charley began to think things were looking up.

Chapter Fourteen

Are you vegetarian? texted Pam.

No, Dez texted in reply.

> Any foods you can't eat?

> No. None. See you Saturday.

'Oh, thank God!' said Pam out loud to the kitchen.

Over the last few years a plethora of dietary problems had plagued her friendship group, scuppering her best-loved dinner menus. Zee loathed fish and was allergic to shellfish, and Mona had become vegetarian years back so Pam had built up a wide repertoire of veggie risottos and pasta dishes. Then Toni's husband had developed IBS and they'd both gone gluten-free and so nowadays it was a real struggle finding a meal everyone could eat. So she was looking forward to some obstacle-free cooking. For the last couple of weekends, she and Dez had gone out together twice more for drinks but, not being a great drinker and resentful of continuing to shell out pub prices for wine when she was on a belt-tightening economy drive, Pam had planned a dinner at her place for their next date.

Zee had been a little alarmed. 'You hardly know him,' she'd warned. 'Is it safe to go back to your place, just the two of you?'

Pam was convinced her friend was worrying needlessly but to reassure her, she'd reminded Zee she still had her three lodgers. 'If anything happens, I'll scream!'

'Fat lot of good if they have their ear-phones in!' Zee had pointed out.

A small pile of cookery books littered the work surface in Pam's kitchen, their pages bristling with scraps of paper and Post-it notes flagging her tried and tested favourites. Flicking through them, she reminded herself that whatever she selected, she'd have to do five portions, and four of them generous ones, so she'd have to limit herself to something inexpensive. *Think posh on a budget*, she told herself. *Something cheap as chips – but definitely not chips!* Eventually she settled on chicken alfredo, boiled new potatoes and a couple of salads followed by Dutch apple tart. The timelessly classy pudding with its snazzy pattern of glazed apple slices was a veritable triumph of style over cost, she thought. Briefly she considered a starter, but rejected one on the grounds it might appear she was out to impress, and trying too hard.

–

Dez arrived promptly, bringing a bottle of white wine and a couple of tins of lager. Taking them, Pam thanked him and led the way into the kitchen.

'Lovely house,' he said, looking around appreciatively. 'How many bedrooms is it?'

'Er, four,' replied Pam, mildly surprised by the question.

'You must feel like you're rattling around in it a bit, now that you're on your own.'

'I would,' she agreed, 'except I've got three foreign students staying with me at the moment.'

'Oh. I assumed it was just the two of us.' Dez appeared mildly put out. 'I've only brought two beers.'

'That's not a problem, they don't drink. They're not old enough!'

'Phew!' said Dez jokily then he added, 'Mind if I have one now?'

'Of course not!' Pam felt suddenly rattled because she hadn't offered him one immediately. 'I'll get you a glass.'

'Don't bother. Save on the washing up.'

Taking the tin, he opened it and took a swig. Pam was mildly affronted. She didn't mind people swigging lager out of cans and bottles – the boys had done it all the time – but she'd laid the dining table specially, with her best runner and table mats and a vase of freshly cut roses from the garden, and the image of a can of lager gracing the table jarred on her. She told herself not to be so pernickety and judgemental.

Once supper was ready, she plated up and, calling the boys down, told them they could either eat in the kitchen or their rooms. She wasn't surprised when all three of them silently voted with their feet and, clutching their plates, shot out of the door.

Smiling to herself, she carried her and Dez's meals through to the dining room. Dez put the lager can down on the table and she tried not to wince.

'This looks good,' he said, rubbing his hands gleefully and sitting himself down.

Pam headed back to the kitchen to get the wine. 'Don't wait for me!' she sang gaily. When she got back she saw that he hadn't, which she took as a compliment to the chef.

'This is absolutely delicious!' he exclaimed, even before she'd sat down. She made a dismissive gesture but he went on, 'No, seriously, Pam. You're a marvellous cook!'

She positively beamed at him. She couldn't remember the last time Geoff had complimented her on her cooking, or on anything, really. Over the years, he'd just taken her culinary skills for granted. Truth be told, he'd taken *her* for granted too. And it wasn't the only compliment Dez gave her that evening, in fact he positively lavished them upon her. He praised the Dutch apple tart ('It looks professional!') and the coffee ('Mmm, smells so good, and so much better than instant!'). He congratulated her on her taste in décor and furnishings ('This is a really classy living room. I love these deep sofas'). He admired her looks ('It's not every woman who can carry off a haircut that short') and he was flatteringly attentive to her, topping up her wine glass when it was empty, offering to carry the plates into the kitchen and help load the dishwasher.

At the end of the evening, when she showed him out, he hovered at the front door uncertainly.

'Thank you for a lovely evening,' he said eventually.

'Thank you for coming.'

'I would offer to invite you back to my place,' he paused uncomfortably, 'but I've only got a studio flat the size of a shoebox. And in any event, I'm the world's worst cook, so it's probably just as well. There's every danger I'd give you food poisoning!'

Pam laughed and shrugged dismissively. 'Never mind, we can do this again here.'

'Yes. Please. I'd like to.'

Then, tentatively, Dez leant over and kissed her chastely on the cheek. 'I'm so glad we met,' he said softly.

Pam felt her cheeks flush hot. 'Me too.'

Closing the door behind him, she couldn't stop a broad grin from spreading across her face, and she realised her heart was fluttering wildly in her chest.

'Oh pull yourself together. You're behaving like a bloody teenager,' she told herself brusquely, and went off to finish tidying the kitchen.

–

Brushing her teeth, getting ready for bed, Pam's mind wandered back over the evening. Dez had been so… charming, flattering, and above all, kind. It was his kindness she appreciated the most, she realised, her toothbrush pausing in mid-scrub. Geoff's adulterous betrayal had been an act of such hurtful and uncaring selfishness, it had entirely crushed her. These past few months she'd been battling with depression, dragged down by the fear of being alone for the rest of her life, frightened by the prospect of a lonely old age. At sixty-three, she couldn't imagine anyone would ever want her, or care for her again, but now, having spent such a wonderful evening with Dez, she'd been proved wrong. Remembering his platonic, gentlemanly kiss made her glow. She caught sight of her face in the bathroom mirror. 'A little less smirking and a bit more scrubbing!' she ordered.

–

The following morning, she and Zee went for a long walk around the grounds of Ashton Court Estate. It was early July, and although the schools hadn't broken up for the summer yet, the park was already busy, so they veered towards the less well-beaten tracks. The sky was cloudless and the sun dazzling so Pam slipped on her sunglasses.

'Heavy night?' deadpanned Zee.

'No! Far from it. Most abstemious.'

'So how was dinner?'

'Actually, very nice.'

'*Nice?*' repeated Zee pointedly.

'Lovely,' corrected Pam. 'He brought wine, we dined, we talked, he stayed until around ten, and then he left. It was fun. And he's very *different* from Geoff,' she finished.

'Oh? In what way?'

'Well, he drinks lager rather than wine, appreciates my cooking, and he loads the dishwasher, for a start!'

'Someone's trained him well!'

Pam shook her head. 'He's never been married.'

Zee raised an eyebrow but said jokily, 'Oh. I wonder what that says about him.'

'Probably nothing, except the fact he hasn't found anyone he wanted to settle down with.' Although Zee had sounded teasing, Pam slightly bridled at her implied criticism. 'He's just a really decent bloke,' she continued. 'Kind, attentive, caring. He showered me with compliments all evening, and he's genuinely interested in what I say. So, like I said, *very* different from Geoff!'

'Sounds like he's from a completely different *planet* compared to Theo.'

Comparing the two men it dawned on Pam how much she and her husband had grown apart over their forty-year marriage. Talking rather than communicating, oblivious to each other's moods and needs, yoked together by a marriage licence and routine, they'd stayed together like a pair of old worn-out shoes. It hadn't been like that to start with and she wondered when it had changed. Long before Josh had died, that was for sure. Probably when the boys were born, she reflected, and when Geoff, like all fathers, had slipped from first place to second behind their children. Perhaps the relegation had caused him to look for someone else, someone who would put him back on a pedestal in prime position. It was an explanation, if not an excuse, but what had been unforgiveable, and had broken her, was his ultimate betrayal in carrying on his affair after Josh had died. It left her feeling they hadn't gone through the harrowing agony of losing their son together, as a couple. And it baffled her, deeply hurt her, that instead of wanting to protect his heartbroken family, he'd risked breaking up his marriage, by carrying on with another woman. He had dismissed their harrowing pain in favour of his own pleasure.

Halting in her tracks, she caught her friend's eye. 'Dez makes me feel wanted, Zee, valued and attractive, and I like him, which is odd because he's not really my "type". But I can see myself with him. I can, honestly.'

Zee tucked her arm through Pam's. 'Slow down, woman!' she said. 'You've only just met him!'

Pam laughed, mostly at herself, and the two of them walked on arm in arm.

'What does he do for a living?'

'He's setting up a driving school.'

'In Bristol?'

'I assume so.'

'So what did he do before that?'

'I'm not really sure. He's been working abroad a lot. Europe, the States…'

'Interesting… Doing what?'

Pam pulled a face. 'I'm not entirely sure. He did say. Logistics, I think.'

'What even is logistics?'

'I have absolutely no idea,' said Pam. 'But I wasn't going to admit that to him!'

'Very wise!' agreed Zee with a grin. 'And where does he live?'

'He has a studio flat in Redland, I think he said. But I might have made that up. Honestly, Zee, I can't remember. I must be having a senior moment.'

'Don't tell him that!'

'God, no! But I do remember him saying his place is tiny so we're better off at mine.'

'Yes, well if he's only got a flat it'd have to be a penthouse to compete with your place,' pointed out Zee. 'Actually, that must be difficult for him,' she continued thoughtfully. 'Nowadays, and at our time of life, we're all judged by the trappings of success. Our houses, the cars we drive, the holidays we take. When we were younger none of that seemed to matter.'

'That's because we didn't have anything! When I left home to marry Geoff all our furniture came from second-hand shops. Except the bed. His parents bought us that.'

'Luxury!' claimed Zee. 'Theo and I slept on a camp bed until we saved up enough to buy a double mattress.'

The two women fell silent for a while, nostalgically reminiscing about their early married lives. It had taken Pam and Geoff years – no, decades – to create the home she now had. Realistically, she knew her days there were numbered, and that once she and Geoff divorced they'd have to sell up and split the proceeds. The only way she could cope with that deeply distressing prospect was to determinedly enjoy the here and now, and live in the moment. Which brought her back to thinking about Dez.

Turning to her friend she confessed shyly, 'He kissed me.'

Zee pretended to look scandalised. 'You trollop!'

'It was very chaste. Just on the cheek.'

'How very gentlemanly. Also, rather romantic,' added Zee with a mischievous wink.

Pam felt herself blush.

Chapter Fifteen

Saturday evening, and Ricky had booked the restaurant. The expensive décor, the crisp white table clothes, and the sheer number of smartly attired waiting staff hovering in the wings warned Charley it was decidedly more expensive than the places they usually went to. The menu confirmed it, offering whole lobsters, oysters and types of wine she'd never even heard of. *How much for a dozen oysters? Bloody hell! Who could afford that?* She'd been ravenous when she sat down, but the prices had taken her breath away, swiftly followed by her appetite. Trying not to overreact, she glanced around at the other punters. They seemed to be taking the luxurious surroundings and the extortionate prices in their stride. Not surprising, she thought, judging by the clothes and jewellery on display.

'I'm not actually that hungry,' she said casually. 'I think I'll skip the starters.'

'Oh okay. I will too,' replied Ricky.

'Don't feel you have to,' she said hurriedly.

'No, it's fine,' he said, giving her his easy smile.

Briefly, she wondered if he'd been put off by the prices too, but on reflection she reckoned it was just as likely he was forgoing his starter to make her feel comfortable.

She ran her eye over the drinks menu and was dismayed to see they didn't have any Prosecco.

'Have a glass of champagne instead,' suggested Ricky.

She glanced at the cost. 'No, I'll just have a glass of house white.'

'But you hardly ever drink still wine. You much prefer sparkling.' His face was a picture of concern. Lowering his voice, he said, 'Would you rather go somewhere else?'

'No, of course not!' He looked so anxious she added, 'I'll happily have some champagne.'

'In that case, so will I,' he replied and, since Charley had never seen him drink any wine that wasn't red – well, except for champagne at his sister's wedding – she assumed that also was for her sake, so that she wouldn't feel she was the only one being extravagant.

When the waiter brought their champagne Ricky raised his flute to her, and they clinked glasses. Knowing how jaw-droppingly expensive her champagne was, Charley wondered if she could make it last the whole meal. Her first sip instantly told her that wasn't going to happen.

'Oh my God! This is delicious!' she raved. 'Careful, I could get used to this!'

Ricky didn't reply; he was too busy rootling around in his pocket.

'I have something for you,' he said, and held out a small, square jewellery box.

It was white and embellished with a thin gold band, the name of the jeweller's printed on the top, also in gold. Charley stared at the box in dismay and suddenly everything took on an entirely different meaning – the expensive restaurant, the champagne… Waves of nerves and nausea threatened to choke her. *Why the hell do men do this? Why propose in the middle of a bloody restaurant and risk a public humiliation – for everyone?* It was only too obvious how they must look. Surely the waiters and half the other diners must have noticed Ricky's gesture. *At least he hasn't gone down on one knee, but what the hell am I supposed to do?* Hoping to God her expression hadn't given anything away, she reached out to take the box. Mouth dry, hand trembling, she could barely look Ricky in the eye.

'Thank you,' she managed and then, taking a deep breath, she opened the lid.

A pair of pearl earrings gazed up at her. Innocuous, beautiful and bereft of all threat of a betrothal. Stifling the sudden desire to laugh manically in sheer relief, she channelled her releasing tension into gushing gratitude. Which was genuine, because she truly was enormously grateful – although more grateful because Ricky hadn't proposed than she was for the gift.

Not even wanting to think what the earrings had cost him, she stammered, 'They're gorgeous, Ricky, but you shouldn't have.'

'I wanted to treat you,' he said, his gentle brown eyes fixed on hers lovingly. Then his face clouded. 'You haven't already got some, have you?'

She immediately realised that in his typically sensitive way, he was anxious that Josh might have given her a pair.

'No. I don't have any pearls,' she replied. Josh had given her several pieces of jewellery over the years, but nothing valuable. All of it was cheap, junky stuff, which she loved and cherished, but most of it had cost less than a tenner. Still struggling to recover her composure, she said, 'I'll just nip to the Ladies' to put them on. I need a mirror,' and fled.

Later that night, back at Ricky's, she lay awake next to him, but sleep evaded her completely. Resigned to the knowledge that she was in for a miserable night, tense and restless with her mind going round and round in circles, she gave up. Sliding silently out of bed, she pulled on Ricky's towelling dressing gown and went to lie down on the sofa in the living room. Carlo instantly clambered up and, after having circled round a few times to find the comfiest position, eventually slumped down next to her. Automatically, she put her hand out to fondle his head and ears.

What the hell was that all about? Why had she practically hyperventilated when she thought Ricky had been about to propose? What the hell was the matter with her? He was a wonderful man, and she did love him, and she knew he loved her, but it was impossible to ignore the tidal wave of relief that had engulfed her when the box hadn't held an engagement ring. She didn't want to break up with him, truthfully she didn't, but was it fair to stay with him if she felt that way about marrying him? And, frankly, whether it was fair or not, what would be the point?

By the time dawn finally broke, and dreading having to not just face Ricky when her mind was in such turmoil, but also spend the whole of Sunday together, Charley had decided to feign a headache and bolt to her place even before breakfast. In her defence, having literally not slept a wink, she genuinely was feeling pretty groggy. Inevitably Ricky was wonderfully caring and understanding, making her feel even worse.

Back at her flat, drained and weary, she crawled under the duvet and there, cocooned and comforted by the security of her own bed, she slept until lunchtime. When she woke, still feeling grotty and in need of someone to talk to, she picked up her phone to call Angie, but Ricky had texted her.

> Hope you're feeling better. Let me know if you need anything. Love you x

Closing her eyes, she slumped hopelessly back onto the pillow. *Bloody hell. Bloody, bloody hell. Why did he have to be so bloody lovely?* Trying to compose a reply, she was ludicrously at a loss as to what to say. She gave up and sought sanctuary at Angie's.

Unusually, it was Will who answered the front door, cradling baby Lily in the crook of his left arm. 'Come in! Come in!' He embraced Charley warmly with his other arm, then led her through to the kitchen adding, 'Sorry, it's feeding time at the menagerie!'

Angie was dishing up a Sunday roast, her other three children already sitting round the table. Finn instantly climbed down and wrapped his arms round Charley's legs. She tweaked his nose affectionately.

'Have you eaten?' asked Angie cheerfully, and without waiting for Charley's reply, said, 'Will, get another plate, would you? And Beth, budge up, sweetie, make room for Charley to sit down.'

Charley's throat tightened, the loving family scene almost reducing her to tears. She shook her head, not trusting her voice to speak without breaking.

Angie's gravy jug arrested in mid-air and she focussed her attention on Charley. Moments later, Will had taken over pouring the gravy, and Charley was pouring her heart out to Angie in the living room.

'I have to finish with him. For his sake. I can't carry on like this.'

'Like what?' asked Angie gently. 'All he did was give you a pair of earrings.' She pulled away from Charley in order to regard her friend's ears. 'Are those the ones?' she asked.

Instinctively, Charley put her hand up to her ear. 'Yes,' she said absently, having only just realised she hadn't taken them off from the previous night.

'They're lovely,' said Angie appreciatively. 'Must've cost a bomb!'

'I know!' wailed Charley, 'And *he's* lovely too. But I don't think I want to marry him.'

'He hasn't even you asked to,' pointed out Angie mildly.

Charley sighed deeply. 'That's not the point. The point is that when I thought he was going to, just the thought of it sent me into a white-out panic.'

'Well I would've panicked if Will had asked me to marry him too soon,' replied Angie reasonably. 'We'd been going out for nearly two years before he popped the question. Don't you think you might be overreacting?'

Charley shook her head. 'No. Because I'm not sure that I love him enough. And if I have to even ask myself if I do, then I don't.' Her eyes welled up and she sniffed hard. 'I can't help it, I just don't,' she repeated sadly. 'And it's not fair to string him along. He's a wonderful man. The longer I leave it, the harder it will be to end it. The more people will expect us to stay together for ever, including him.' She fished in her jeans pocket for a tissue and blew her nose, before saying quietly, 'I have to end it now.'

'Must you? Why can't you give it a little more time?'

'Because I'm not in love with him, and I certainly don't love him as much as he loves me. And if I'm honest, I'm worried I only want to stay with him because...' She cut herself off, ashamed at what she was about to admit.

'Because what?'

'Because I want... all this!' she explained, waving her arm around, taking in the brightly coloured toys littering the living room floor, the photos of the children all around the walls, and the pop-up playhouse in the corner.

–

A short while later, fearing that if she stayed at her friend's any longer she'd be persuaded to change her mind – not by Angie, but seduced by the warm and loving environment of her family – she left and went back to her flat. Since she'd slept in her clothes she felt grubby and uncomfortable, and in need of a shower. Afterwards, standing in the bathroom, wrapped in a bath sheet with her wet hair turbaned, she regarded herself critically in the mirror. Under the harsh LED ceiling lights her face, without make-up, was pale with dark rings under her eyes. She looked every minute of her thirty-two years, and she felt even older.

If you do this, she warned herself silently, *you do know, this could be it. You might never find anyone else – or at least not in in time to have kids. Is that what you want? NO! No it's not!* pleaded her inner voice, until another, stronger voice kicked in. *Staying with Ricky just because you want a family, is wrong. Just wrong. And you bloody well know it.*

–

Feeling strangely calm, or rather numb, she dressed, dried her hair and pulled it loosely into a top knot, then she carefully put the earrings back in the white and gold box and drove to Ricky's. When she handed the box to him, he looked stunned. The look in his eyes as she explained why she was returning them tore at her inside. On the way over in the car she'd rehearsed what she wanted to say, so much so that, even to her ears, it now sounded glib and clichéd. Well-worn lines from every rom-com she'd ever watched fell from her lips. 'It's not you, it's me… I love you, but I'm just not in love with you… You deserve to find someone who loves you as much as you love them… I don't want to hurt you because I really care about you… I'm sorry, but it's better to end it now…'

He said nothing until her well-rehearsed piece came to an end and she'd literally run out of words. Then he looked her in the eyes and said simply, but with heart-breaking selflessness, 'I love you, Charley, and I want you to be happy. If I can't make you happy, then I hope, I really hope, you find someone who can.'

Charley fell apart. Tears scorched her cheeks and she couldn't even speak, her throat was so constricted.

He held the jewellery box out to her. 'Keep them as a gift, a memento,' he said. 'Please. You look beautiful in them.'

She shook her head. 'I can't,' was all she managed to get her voice to say, before turning on her heel and fleeing to her car.

Chapter Sixteen

'You're an idiot,' berated Tara.

Monday morning in the shop and Charley had arrived to open up, weary and puffy-eyed, after another sleepless night, much of it spent crying. She told Tara about splitting up with Ricky almost as soon as her friend had got in. Tara's response was predictable.

'Go down to the bike shop right now and tell him you've changed your mind. Tell him you want to try again.'

'But I don't,' replied Charley, shaking her head.

'Well you should! You're good together.'

'Yes well, being "good together" isn't enough, is it?'

'It is for most people!' claimed Tara, then added with her typical, yet astonishing, lack of tact, 'The problem with you, Charley, is that you and Josh never got past that honeymoon phase of marriage.'

Charley bit her tongue. She knew where Tara was going with this. Her mate had long held, and frequently expressed, the theory that Charley's brief marriage to Josh had given her unrealistic expectations about what married life was really like. For her part, although she'd never said it, and never would, Charley sometimes wondered if Tara and Baz had ever truly been in love. Having known what it was like to fall head over heels for someone, Charley wasn't prepared to settle for less. She couldn't. Turning away, Charley engrossed herself with needlessly tidying the nearest display. A tense silence filled the shop for a few minutes. When Tara broke it, she seemed to have decided to change tack.

Coming over to join Charley at the dresser, she said quietly and earnestly, 'You haven't given the relationship anywhere near long enough. Give it more time. You'll regret it if you don't. Trust me, you will.'

'That's what Angie said,' replied Charley, moving back to the till.

There was an awkward beat before Tara said, 'You told Angie, but you didn't tell me? Why didn't you call me?'

'I thought you'd be busy with Monnie,' lied Charley.

The truth was that Charley had been dreading telling Tara. She hadn't phoned her over the weekend, knowing only too well that her mate would barge straight round to her flat and try to bully her into changing her mind, and she simply hadn't had the energy to cope with Tara in full flow. At least in the shop she'd thought there'd be a chance that the presence of customers, or at least the working environment, would put a brake on Tara. But at nine thirty in the morning the shop was, perhaps not surprisingly, empty. Charley gazed out of the window, half in the desperate hope a punter would pitch up, but also to avoid having to look Tara in the eye.

'Well, whatever. But Angie's right,' said Tara. 'I didn't fall in love with Baz straight away. I didn't even really fancy him to start with. It was mum who encouraged me to stick with him. She fell for him at the get-go.'

'Kim loved him because he loved you,' Charley commented wisely.

'Possibly... probably,' Tara conceded. 'But my point is that sometimes other people see things that you don't. They see when someone is good for you, right for you. And I did fall in love with Baz, eventually. He sort of... grew on me.'

Unwanted body hair 'grows on you', thought Charley unkindly, *so do warts.* Tara and Baz's marriage had always appeared to her to be a muddling-along kind of marriage. Convenient, rather than romantic. Baz was a lovely bloke, but she couldn't have settled for him. After Josh, she could never accept a marriage as mundane, as run-of-the-mill as that, and she didn't see why Ricky should, either. Josh had been her world, her reason to live. She couldn't ever imagine Tara describing Baz in that way, and certainly not since she'd had Monnie, but more importantly, Charley doubted she would ever see Ricky that way either.

Suddenly wearied by having to defend herself, Charley sought to draw a line under the conversation, and the whole subject. 'I know you think I'm making a mistake—'

'Because you are!'

Ignoring her, Charley carried on, 'But I've spent a long time thinking this through. Weeks, in fact. Ever since we came back from Tuscany. And I've made up my mind and there really isn't anything you can say that will change it. So can we just drop it? Please.'

Tara visibly deflated and then said curtly, 'Okay, fine.' And to Charley's astonishment she left it at that. She didn't even try to have the last word.

—

When Charley broke the news to Pam that afternoon, her mother-in-law's response was in stark contrast to Tara's. She didn't tell Charley she was making a mistake, or try to encourage her to change her mind. Tellingly, nor did she tell Charley that she was doing the right thing and, since the older woman was usually such a vocal cheerleader for everything Charley did, her lack of approval was deafening. Pam's only concern seemed to be making sure Charley was all right. Wordlessly, she pulled Charley into a warm embrace and just held her.

'Don't be nice to me,' begged Charley. 'I'll fall apart.'

'Okay, sweetheart,' said Pam, reluctantly letting her go. Then, giving her a supportive little pat on the arm she said, 'You know where I am if you need me.'

Charley nodded tightly and turned away, fighting hard to get her emotions under control.

Business in the afternoon was depressingly slow, which didn't help boost Charley's mood and, worse, allowed her thoughts to stray to Ricky. She didn't seem to be able to stop images of him floating into her mind. Ricky bringing her a morning coffee in bed. The two of them laughing over a shared joke, or at some daft antic of Carlo's. Him cooking supper for them in his flat, holding out a wooden spoon for her to taste the sauce. And then Ricky undressing her, slowly, and sweetly making love to her. *Enough!* she told herself, and forced her mind to concentrate on drawing up the list of stock she needed to order. The afternoon dragged. Pam made small talk, telling her about a walk she'd had with her friend Zee the day before but Charley found it hard to focus on what the older woman was saying. She kept looking at the clock, hoping the afternoon would end and she could go home and… and do what, precisely? It wasn't the shop she wanted to avoid, she realised, but herself, and the dark, leaden dead weight squatting inside her. The sound of the shop door opening cut into her brooding. She looked up, grateful for the distraction, only for her stomach to knot. It was Ricky.

After politely greeting Pam, he came over to Charley and held out a plastic supermarket carrier. 'You left some things at my place,' he said quietly.

Tactfully, Pam slipped out of the shop, leaving them to it.

Charley took the bag.

'I thought I'd bring them here, rather than coming round to yours.'

'Yes, thank you. That was considerate,' said Charley, stashing the bag behind the till. Then the two of them stood looking at each other for what seemed to Charley to be an excruciatingly long time.

Eventually, Ricky said, 'I don't think I've left anything at yours.'

'No. I don't think you have, either.'

After a flat silence Ricky said, 'Well, I'd better get back to the bike shop, then.'

Charley nodded. 'Yes, you better had.' Instinctively she wanted to say sorry but she bit the word back, fearing it would only invite a painful conversation.

She watched him go, through the door, and back to the bike shop. He didn't turn round. As soon as he was out of sight, Charley sank onto her haunches behind the till, and made a tremendous effort not to disintegrate.

–

Nisha called her later that evening, Tara having taken it upon herself to break Charley's news to her, a breach of confidence that initially peeved Charley but which, after thinking about it, she decided she was grateful for. It was one less difficult task to have to face up to doing. Nisha offered to come round to Charley's with a bottle of pinot.

'I thought you might need some company.'

'Thanks, but I'm not good company this evening,' replied Charley, so Nisha didn't push it.

About half an hour later, Angie called to invite her round to her place. 'Come and have a bite of supper. It's only spag bol, but it'll save you having to cook anything if you're feeling rubbish.'

Charley was indeed feeling rubbish but she made the same excuse as she had with Nisha.

'Well, come another night, yes?' persisted Angie and Charley promised she would.

So Charley was left alone to contemplate her sorrows, the silence of the empty flat bouncing off the walls.

The next few days were emotionally gruelling for Charley, not helped by the fact that the other shopkeepers were initially unaware she and Ricky had split up. When they both inadvertently pitched up at the deli at the same time to get their morning coffee, Rita greeted them cheerfully from behind the counter.

'What can I get you two?'

There was an awkward moment until Charley indicated Ricky should order first. 'You were before me.'

'No, please, you go ahead,' he replied, stepping to one side.

You could have cut the atmosphere with a cheese knife and poor Rita clearly didn't know where to put herself. She brewed

Charley's cappuccino in a stilted silence, with the three of them avoiding each other's gaze. Charley couldn't grab her coffee and get away quickly enough.

It didn't get any easier once word of their separation got out, either. People didn't seem to know what to say, and the easy camaraderie Charley had so loved about the place appeared to evaporate. In her imagination, she felt everyone was disappointed, and especially in her, as if it were common knowledge that she had been the one to end things. She knew she was being irrational, Ricky simply wouldn't have been that indiscreet, but that didn't stop her paranoia. Soon she was avoiding everyone, giving up going to the deli completely, bringing in a flask of coffee and a packed lunch from home, but that only served to isolate her further, and even though her seclusion was self-imposed, she began to feel like a pariah. And every day, every single bloody day, she'd catch herself missing him. Something funny would happen in the shop and she'd think, 'I must tell Ricky', or she'd hear the shop door open and look up, momentarily wondering if it were him, bringing her a coffee or some Cargo gossip.

Then, one morning, with appalling timing, the gears jammed on her bike as she was cycling into work. *Bloody, bloody hell! Why? Why now!* she raged, resisting the childish urge the kick the damn thing. *You could have done that anytime over the last effing year!* Briefly, she toyed with idea of chaining the bike up to the nearest lamp-post and getting a mobile bike repair company to sort it out, but rejected the notion, accusing herself of being a wimp. She gritted her teeth, and wheeled the bike down to Ricky. *You're just another customer, with a broken bike*, she reminded herself as she pushed open the door to the bike shop.

Carlo rushed up to greet her like an old friend, snuffling at her hand excitedly and wagging his tail furiously. When Ricky came over to hold the door for her to wheel the bike in, she could barely bring herself to look into his eyes, not trusting herself to be able to hold it together.

'You can leave it with me, if that's easier,' he said, having given the bike a quick once-over.

Unsure whether he meant practically easier or emotionally, she merely nodded and thanked him. 'How much will it be?'

'Nothing,' he replied with a shrug. 'There's no parts and it'll only take me five minutes.'

Not wanting to be beholden to him she said, 'Let me just give you a fiver.'

A look of such deep hurt darkened his face she instantly wanted to bite her tongue off. 'I don't charge labour for mates, Charley, you know that,' he replied tensely.

She flushed, and swallowing the lump in her throat muttered, 'Yes of course. Thank you.'

Chapter Seventeen

Over the next month or so, Charley's isolation increased when the schools broke up for the summer, meaning Tara wouldn't be in for six weeks, leaving Charley alone in the shop in the mornings. Tara had studiously noted the dates in the shop diary, and had reminded Charley several times, mostly whilst eulogising over her numerous plans for Monnie.

'She's doing a surfing course with a friend in Wales, then we're going to Aquazone, and Longleat, shopping in Milton Keynes, which means a visit to Build-a-Bear of course! She's got pony club in August and I've bought her the biggest blow-up pool for the garden you've ever seen – it's literally big enough to swim in.'

'Are you doing anything with Baz?' Charley had asked dryly.

'Of course. Two weeks in Spain.'

'I don't begrudge her taking the time off,' Charley told Pam one afternoon. 'It's not like there's anyone else who can have Monnie.'

'Even if there was, Tara wouldn't want that,' remarked Pam astutely.

'No,' agreed Charley.

She knew Tara's childhood holidays had been grim and lonely, a latch-key kid home alone while her mum worked, and that her mate was determined her own daughter wouldn't suffer the same, but Tara's absence still left Charley running ragged trying to keep up. Stock-taking, ordering, dealing with deliveries and replenishing the displays took up every evening, whilst her Sundays were spent cleaning the shop and delivering gift bags all over Bristol.

The backlog of paperwork grew and the accounts, which she still hadn't started, loomed monstrously. Nisha had warned her to keep on top of them, to do them every month, but she kept letting them slide onto the backburner and was trying to forget about them altogether.

Naturally, Pam offered to work mornings as well, but Charley refused, adamant that Pam was already doing more than enough for her. It had become a matter of pride for Charley, and she realised she was treating the summer as some sort of test, needing to prove to herself she could cope. It was a relief that Pam wasn't taking a vacation, since she doubted she could have coped on her own all day, every day – not that she would have wanted Pam to know that.

'Promise me you're not missing out on a holiday just to stay and help me in the shop,' she demanded.

'Not at all. I've no-one to go on holiday with!' Pam replied.

Welcome to my world, thought Charley. She'd not been away for a summer holiday since Josh had died, and precisely for that same reason. The only break she'd had in five years was the week in Tuscany with Ricky back in the spring. She remembered Ricky saying his parents had invited them out again for a summer holiday, and she had to crush the pang of regret that she wouldn't be going.

Memories of Tuscany flooded back to her. With distance, the ordeal of meeting his entire family seemed less… traumatic. Surrounded by his family, Ricky had been so happy and relaxed, yet he'd been consistently attentive, protective even, towards her. Trapped in the endless round of family introductions his eyes would seek hers, checking she was okay and if he thought she was struggling he'd rescue her, and they'd slope off, just the two of them. It had been idyllic, Ricky driving them around Tuscany's narrow, winding roads, climbing up through the hills and villages, intent on showing her something special – a spectacular view, or a beautiful medieval town hidden way off the beaten track. One day they'd parked up and ducked into the peace and quiet of a tiny church. It had been so dark inside it had taken several moments for her eyes to adjust and when they had, she'd marvelled at the beauty of the paintings and sculptures around her, astonished to find such incredible work in so small a church.

'Are all the churches in Italy decorated as elaborately as this one?'

'Pretty much,' he'd replied casually.

'The churches in England are much plainer,' she'd told him. 'We just don't have all these gorgeously colourful pictures and statues. It's all white painted walls and dark, heavy wood. Although sometimes the stained glass windows are pretty.'

Her mind had flipped back to the small village church she and Josh had married in; the same church where his funeral had been held just four short years later. She knew precious little about the church, not even whether it was Norman or Saxon or whatever. As far as she could remember, the only vibrant colours in the entire place had come from the flower displays. Although to be honest, she couldn't be one hundred per cent sure of the accuracy of her memory. During her wedding she'd been too euphorically happy to take in her surroundings and as for Josh's funeral… everything had seemed bleak and grey, strained and colourless on that day. In fact, she could barely remember the agonising ordeal at all, and for some years afterwards she'd struggled to even step back inside a church, frightened that the memory of loss would overwhelm her.

On that day in Tuscany, however, she'd felt completely at ease. Perhaps it was because the church looked so different, and even smelled different, to an English country church. Of course she'd been there as a tourist rather than as a member of the congregation, although, perhaps not surprisingly since she'd been with Ricky, she'd excusably lost sight of that fact. She'd slipped her hand into his and he'd squeezed it lovingly. They'd stayed in the church for a long time and for most of that time they were the only two people there, but after a while a trickle of locals began to slip in, one by one, to light candles, or to pray, and Charley had begun to feel uncomfortably as if she were imposing, an intruder, so she'd signalled silently to Ricky and they'd slipped out as unobtrusively as they could.

On another day they'd gone to a market where they'd bought a picnic lunch of Fettunta bread, sun-ripened tomatoes and Raviggiolo cheese which was made, so he'd informed her, from local sheep's milk.

'This is my very favourite cheese,' he'd said and, breaking off a small piece of the fresh bread, he'd scooped a chunk of cheese onto it and offered it to her in his fingers.

'Is it very strong?' she'd asked warily. The only sheep's milk cheese she'd ever tried was Roquefort and she hadn't really liked it. She'd never been that keen on goat's cheese either, or any of those very ripe cream cheeses. Once, at a supper party, she'd been persuaded to try some Stinking Bishop and its strong, almost dirty, pungency had nearly made her throw up.

'No, I promise, it's sweet and fresh. I think you'll love it.' He'd held the bread closer to her mouth, urging her to taste it.

She'd taken a small bite, and then very quickly and eagerly a much larger one. 'Oh my God. It's delicious! More! I want more!'

Laughing, he'd generously plastered a slathering of cheese onto the bread and between them, they'd polished it off in a single sitting.

'Why haven't you given this to me before?' she'd demanded.

'Because I can't find it in England.'

She'd made a mental note to ask Rita from the deli to track some down for Ricky when they got back.

—

Reluctantly, she let the memories slip away. She'd never do any of that with Ricky again. Or with anyone, now she came to think of it. *Well, there was no point crying over spilt milk, sheep's or otherwise*, and she hauled herself back to the present.

Distracting herself by focussing on Pam's situation rather than hers, she said, 'You could always go on one of those Saga holidays. A cruise or something.'

The older woman visibly shuddered. 'I honestly can't think of anything worse! It makes me feel ancient just thinking about it.'

'You know what they say; you're only as old as you feel,' teased Charley.

At that precise moment, Pam was on her knees filling the lower shelves of the dresser. 'In that case, I think I'm currently knocking ninety!' she informed Charley.

—

As the summer passed, Charley grew increasingly low and exhausted. Rationally, she understood the two went hand in hand, each exacerbating the other, but that didn't mean she could escape the vicious circle. Working flat out, seven days a week, she slid numbly into a punishing routine that left her no time for herself, or to be herself, and things began to feel flat and pointless, as if she were treading water. Apart from Pam and the anonymous customers, she didn't see anyone. Tara was tied up with Monnie, and Angie had her hands full with her four, and ever since Nisha had turned down the PR firm she'd been throwing all her energies into her own business. Knowing Nisha, Charley wouldn't have minded betting she'd set her sights on building her company to rival the one she'd turned her back on.

Of course she saw Ricky. No matter how hard she tried to avoid him. Noticing that she was on her own during the mornings, Ricky had popped into the shop a couple of times and offered to get her a coffee when he got his. But she'd always declined and finally he'd taken the all too obvious hint and had given up asking. She knew her refusals made her look petty, and that he was just trying to stay friends, but being near him physically pained her. The only time she had given in and let him help her was when Jobsworth the delivery man had left some impossibly heavy boxes outside the shop, and neither she nor Pam could lift them. Not even together. *Bloody man!* she'd cursed inwardly.

Ricky had seen them struggling and had come over immediately. 'You're going to hurt yourselves,' he'd admonished.

Pam had stood back, but Charley had stubbornly persisted, 'No, I can manage,' and then had nearly killed herself trying to lug the topmost box off the pile, her legs almost buckling beneath her, and she was grateful when Ricky took it from her.

'Thank you,' she'd said when he'd dumped the last of the boxes in the shop.

'Yes, thank you very much!' echoed Pam.

'You're welcome,' he'd said, then turning to Charley, he'd added softly, 'There's no reason why we can't still...' There was a pause before he went on, 'Why I can't still help you now and again, with this sort of thing. It's no trouble to me. You only have to ask.'

Charley suspected he'd been going to say, 'There's no reason we can't be friends,' and she was relieved that he hadn't. She simply wasn't ready for that. Her emotions were still too raw, too ragged, to tuck neatly away and move on.

'Thank you,' was all she managed to say.

He gave them both a tight smile before heading back to his shop. Entirely unconsciously, Charley watched him go. She wasn't aware that her gaze was following him all the way back to his shop until she turned her attention back inside her own store and found Pam regarding her with a raised eyebrow.

'Darling...' started Pam gently.

Charley's held up her hand. 'I know what you're going to say,' she told her mother-in-law. 'But please don't.'

It'd had been tough enough making the decision in the first place, she thought bitterly, hard enough to be the one who had to end it. She wished everyone would just accept it as being the right thing to do, for both of them.

Chapter Eighteen

Pam's German students had flown home at the start of the summer holidays. In some ways she'd been sad to see them leave. Although they weren't the most scintillating company, she'd enjoyed the routine of having to cook for them every evening, if nothing else. Rather sweetly, and extremely shyly, as they'd stood by the front door with their bags all packed, waiting to be collected, they had presented her with a box of chocolates, and the poor boy who'd been designated to give it to her had even managed to utter a few words of thanks. Then the minibus had arrived to pick them up and, after the bustle of departure, Pam closed the front door behind them and emptiness descended like a low cloud. Now she'd be on her own until the next batch of students arrived at the beginning of the autumn term. She wondered again about getting a dog, but ultimately decided against it since she didn't think it would be fair to leave the poor hound alone every afternoon and all day on Saturdays while she was at the shop. *Actually, flip that thought*, she told herself briskly, *the reason you can't have a dog is because you have the shop to go to. So it's a positive thing, not a negative one.*

No matter how much of an optimistic spin Pam tried to put on things, it didn't stop her hating the loneliness, and the futile, pointless boredom of her evenings, so she invited Zee round for a mid-week supper, on her own, without Theo.

'It won't be anything special,' she'd warned.

Now she and Zee were sitting at either end of the sofa in the living room, with their feet on the coffee table, tucking into bowls of chilli.

'Why does this feel like such an illicit pleasure?' asked Pam.

After a moment's thought, Zee replied, 'Because it's all about us. We're not putting other people first, for a change.'

'Pathetic, isn't it?' said Pam dryly.

'Pitiful!' grinned Zee.

In their defence, both women had spent over four decades catering for and prioritising the myriad needs of their spouses and their children. It was hard habit to break. Even now, their conversation had drifted to the trials and tribulations of their loved ones, specifically their various offspring which, for Pam, included Charley.

'It's just painful watching her,' she said, 'like seeing some dreadful tragedy unfold in slow motion and being powerless to stop it. As if she's being wilfully self-destructive.'

Zee pulled a sympathetic face. ''Twas ever thus,' she commiserated. 'It's one of the toughest things about being a parent, isn't it? Your kids making foolish decisions and knowing you can't stop them because you're the last person on earth they'll listen to. I don't know which is worse: watching them being with someone you instinctively know is bad for them, and that it'll all end in tears, or seeing them let someone wonderful, who'd be really good for them, slip through their fingers, and knowing how much they'll regret it later.'

'She's not even my daughter,' Pam pointed out. 'There's only so much I feel I can say.'

The two women fell pensively silent for a while, until Zee said, 'Well, I guess you have to credit her with knowing her own mind. And looking on the bright side, at least she won't be moving to Italy.'

Pam pulled a face. 'Yes. I didn't relish that prospect, I will admit. Even if it was selfish.'

Zee dropped her fork noisily back in her bowl and looked over at her friend. 'Oh, for crying out loud, will you give yourself a break, woman! Of course it wasn't bloody selfish. I'd be gutted if one of my kids moved to another country. I wouldn't tell them that, obviously, and I wouldn't try to stop them, but I'd still be gutted.'

'But Charley's not one of mine,' Pam reminded her friend. 'I don't have a right to feel that.'

Zee's tone and face softened. 'Yes, you do,' she said, 'because you're scared that if you lose Charley you lose her connection with Josh.'

Pam took a gulp of wine to ward off the threatening tightening in her throat. 'I know Charley has to build a new life without Josh, and I want her to. I genuinely want her to be happy, and I know that Ricky is right for her, even if *she* doesn't,' she added despairingly. 'But if she moves to Italy I won't be able to be part of her life any more. And it'll feel like a door is closing on part of Josh's past life. She won't be here for Christmas, or his birthday, and the two of us won't talk about him anymore, or share her memories of him, and we'll never say, "Do you remember when Josh did this or that or… whatever?"' She swallowed hard and reached for her wine again.

Wordlessly, Zee put her empty bowl onto the table and shuffled up the sofa next to her friend. 'Life is all about phases, Pam, you know that. Children grow up, people grow apart and we have to accept things change. So yes, if Charley marries Ricky, or anyone, your role in her life will change, whether or not she moves away, but if your fear is that she'll lose touch with you, then I think you underestimate how much you mean to that young woman.'

It was a comforting thought. Maybe she was looking at things too bleakly, and bracing herself for the worst as a coping mechanism, on the grounds that forewarned is forearmed.

'Do you want pud?' asked Pam abruptly, changing the mood, as she scooped up the chilli bowls.

'Does the sun rise in the east?' enquired Zee witheringly.

Wordlessly, the two of them headed for the fridge.

—

'Key lime pie!' raved Zee, as Pam fished out a flan dish. 'Make mine a large one!'

'It was left over from supper with Dez,' Pam told her, cutting two generous portions.

'Lucky Dez!' commented Zee, taking her slice eagerly. 'How are things going with you two?' she added casually.

'Fine,' replied Pam airily.

'Only "fine"?'

'Actually rather well,' confessed Pam, trying not to sound like she was gloating.

She and Dez had fallen into the pattern of having supper at her place once or twice a week, and she loved the way their relationship had so easily, seamlessly, drifted from having 'dates' to something more regular and relaxed.

'When are we going to meet him?'

'Soon.'

'How soon?' persisted Zee eagerly. 'You've been with him for weeks!'

'Yes, and I still want to be with him weeks from now! Meeting you lot will be hugely daunting for him. I don't want to frighten him off!'

'It's only us! Bring him to supper at mine. I promise we won't eat him.'

Pam wavered. She had asked Dez if he'd like to meet her friends but he'd seemed reluctant.

'It's *you* I want to be with,' he'd replied. Then, taking her hand in his, he'd said sincerely, 'I don't want to share you, not yet.' So, flattered, she'd let herself be won over.

Zee, however, was not prepared to let it go so easily.

'If being trapped at a dinner table with us lot all evening is too intimidating – and to be fair to the man I can see why it might be,' she conceded cheerfully, 'let's make it drinks. Then you can leave whenever he's had enough.'

Put like that, Pam didn't feel she could refuse. 'Okay. Lovely.' She brushed aside the niggling fear rising inside her that Dez wouldn't like the suggestion. She'd just have to cross that bridge when she came to it. She couldn't carry on keeping the two halves of her life apart like this. Sooner or later he was going to have to meet her friends, and surely the sooner he did, the easier it would be?

As it turned out, she'd been right to be anxious.

'I just don't particularly like going out for drinks. I thought we'd be having dinner, just the two of us, like usual,' he said, a tad petulantly.

'We can have an early supper,' Pam promised, 'and go on to Zee's later.' He still looked disgruntled, so she said, 'We don't even have to stay very long if you don't want to. You'll like them,' she promised.

'But will they like me?' he replied, suddenly sounding vulnerable, and Pam's heart went out to him.

She caught his gaze and held it. '*I* like you,' she said. 'And I can't imagine for a moment that my friends won't too.'

There was a beat and then Dez asked, 'Will he be there?'

'Who?'

'Your ex-husband.'

'Over my dead body!' Pam burst out laughing, but the hurt in Dez's eyes made her stifle the laughter in her throat. She realised she'd been insensitive, stupid even. It hadn't crossed her mind that he'd be worried her friends would compare him to Geoff, nor that he and Geoff might actually meet each other. *No wonder he'd been reluctant to go to Zee's.*

The following Saturday, Pam duly prepared supper for six thirty, giving them plenty of time to enjoy their meal before heading off to Zee's around half eight. Setting the table in the dining room, Pam was in high spirits, and looking forward to introducing Dez to everyone. *Be honest, you just want to show him off!* Well, why not? He was a really nice bloke, not bad-looking, and *younger* than her. She knew it would all get back to Geoff and that thought alone was enough to put her on cloud nine. She was humming to herself when she went to answer the door.

–

He seemed nervous, downing the lagers he'd brought way more swiftly than he usually did and she momentarily felt remorseful. *Oh well, a little Dutch courage never did any harm*, she told herself, and offered him a glass of wine as well.

He shook his head. 'I'm driving,' he reminded her.

'I'll drive,' she told him. 'You can leave your car here.'

Slowly, he turned to look at her with what appeared to Pam to be a distinctly optimistic glint in his eye. To her horror, she realised he thought she was inviting him to stay the night, an invitation that, obviously, had enormous implications.

'I'll drive you home afterwards,' she added hurriedly. 'You can pick your car up in the morning.'

The optimism in his eyes didn't fade. It sort of hardened. 'I'm not sure how I'd get here on a Sunday,' he pointed out. 'Wouldn't it just be easier if I stayed over?' The suggestion seemed so reasonable, but it flustered Pam completely.

'No!' she blurted.

'I meant on the sofa,' he clarified hurriedly. 'Or in the spare room – or rather, in *one* of them, since your young lodgers have gone.'

'Still, no. I'd rather not,' finished Pam awkwardly. The thought of him staying the night, even in the spare room, filled her with apprehension. It was too soon, way too soon for that degree of familiarity, or anything else, surely.

There was a decidedly pregnant pause, eventually broken by Dez saying flatly, 'Oh. Okay, then.' And then he left it a beat before he added, 'I supposed I'll just have to get a cab back or something tomorrow morning.'

Yes, I suppose you will, thought Pam, determined not to yield.

By the time they'd left Pam's, Dez had already drunk two cans of lager and three large glasses of wine, which, Pam swiftly calculated with dismay, was probably almost a bottle. *It'll be fine*, she told herself, it wasn't like any of her friends were teetotal.

How wrong could she be? She endured about an hour and a half at Zee's before she simply she couldn't take any more. Dez turned out to be a larger than life, loquacious drunk, draping his arms round everyone, as if they were long-lost bosom buddies, as eager to be liked as a puppy. It wouldn't have been so bad if he'd managed to remember anyone's name. By ten o'clock she was desperate to leave, but it took her another forty minutes to persuade him to go with her and she was almost in tears by the time Theo and David had helped the almost paralytic Dez into her car.

'Darling, don't worry. It doesn't matter,' Zee told her, clearly highly amused. 'He's just pissed.'

'Don't tell Geoff!' Pam implored her.

'Of course not.'

—

Ferrying Dez back to his flat, Pam hoped to God he wasn't going to pass out. There was no way she'd be able to manhandle him out of the car if he did.

'Where are we going?' he suddenly piped up, looking out of the window.

'Your place,' Pam informed him.

'Not yours?'

'No.'

'Oh.' He sounded deeply disappointed.

They drove through the lamplit streets of Redland, substantial Edwardian houses on either side of the road. Pam could see, even in the muted glow of the streetlights, that many of them were sadly way past their glory days. They had her sympathy. She'd still not been to his place so she told him he'd have to direct her. He leant forward and peered through the front windscreen, as if he were trying to get his bearings.

'Next left!' he suddenly ordered, and after a few more turns he said, 'Just here will be fine,' so she pulled over.

He struggled with his seat belt, so she leant over and unclipped it for him and then got out to open the passenger door for him, suspecting even that basic mechanism would be beyond him too.

Staggering out of the car, he seemed to pull himself together. 'Would you like to come in?' he asked her. 'For a nightcap, or something...' he finished suggestively.

'Not tonight,' said Pam firmly.

'Well, thank you for a lovely evening,' he slurred, then added rather endearingly, 'I think I've drunk too much.'

'Just a bit,' replied Pam, and then he lurched off to what she could only hope was his front door. It seemed to be, since he managed to open it before almost falling inside.

—

Waking the following morning, a heavy weight immediately thumped into Pam's stomach as she remembered the excruciating shame of the night before. She'd have to call Zee and apologise. Sighing heavily, she slung her legs out of bed and opened the curtains, and immediately the weight in her stomach doubled. Dez's car was still on her drive and so sometime today he'd pitch up and she was going to have to... deal with him. It wasn't just the fact that he'd drunk too much and shown her up, it was more that the whole knotty problem of him 'staying the night' had arisen, completely unexpectedly, and had thrown her into a total panic.

Going into the kitchen to make herself a much-needed coffee, she saw from the wall clock that it wasn't even eight o'clock yet. She could give herself time to recover and marshal her thoughts before she called anyone.

As it turned out, Zee called her first.

'I'm so sorry, I can't apologise enough,' started Pam.

'There's no need,' Zee assured her. 'These things happen.'

'He was just incredibly nervous about meeting you all,' explained Pam. 'He's not normally like that, I assure you.'

'I don't imagine he is. I was only calling to make sure you got home okay.'

Fleetingly, Pam considered confiding in Zee over the whole thorny issue of Dez 'staying the night', but she felt too compromised by his behaviour, so she left it, then promptly regretted her decision as soon as she ended the call. The subject preyed on her mind ominously, making her feel mildly nauseous. After breakfast, still worrying over what the hell she should say to Dez, she took herself for a long walk, hoping the diversion and the physical activity would help. It didn't. Arriving home, she was still unsure what do to. However, as she turned into her drive she noticed his car had gone and hot, righteous indignation rose up inside her. *What a coward! And how rude, taking the car without even calling to apologise.* Belatedly, she noticed the bouquet of flowers leaning against the front door, and her fury dissolved. He'd left a profusely apologetic card, and she guessed he'd been too embarrassed to face her in person.

At the kitchen sink, scissors in hand, snipping the stalks before putting the carnations in a vase, it dawned on her the whole debacle was actually her fault. Dez had told her, several times, that he hadn't wanted to meet her friends yet, and she had known how anxious he was at the prospect of being compared to Geoff. She blamed herself for pressuring him into doing something he so obviously hadn't want to do.

Chapter Nineteen

Monday morning in the shop, the last week of August, Charley was *literally* counting the days until Tara would be back in. Only having the one pair of hands, she struggled to juggle everything that needed doing, but it was only having the one pair of eyes that was the real trouble. Gaggles of youngsters, no doubt bored at having been off all summer, had taken to hanging around Cargo and being what would politely be called a 'nuisance' but what Charley called *a complete pain in the arse*. The other shop-holders warned her bitterly it was an annual event. The ice-cream parlour and the deli had both banned teenagers from going in more than two at a time, and some of the shopkeepers had advised her they'd noticed a significant increase in shoplifting. Charley told herself it was only a petty problem, and that all shopkeepers had to factor in losing a certain amount of stock to theft, and that the kids were only young, only doing it for kicks and she shouldn't take it personally, but that didn't stop it pissing her off. She didn't know exactly how much she'd lost, but she was down several bath bombs and bottles of bubble bath, and a good many tealights, not to mention several packs of sweets and chocolates. Her shop, with its open displays and small items, was an easy target, especially when she was alone. *I bet nothing ever gets nicked from the bike shop.* You could hardly slip a racing bike under your hoody, and Carlo was on permanent security duty anyhow. She'd been tempted to ask if she could borrow the lurcher for a day or so, but rejected the idea on the grounds it would be overstepping the mark with Ricky. Gradually, tentatively, she and Ricky were finding their way back to a degree of friendship, and she didn't want to push things and spoil that.

Halfway through the morning, the shop door opened and a group of teenagers crowded in, insouciant, arrogant and rowdy. Girding her loins, Charley decided to be proactive. Locking the till and approaching them, she asked brightly, 'How can I help you, girls?' only just restraining herself from adding, *Are you shoplifting to order or purely on an opportunistic basis?*

There was a stunned silence – clearly they weren't used to a direct challenge – until one of the more brazen of the group said, 'We're just looking.'

'Okay, great!' said Charley, with an enthusiasm she truly didn't feel, and still holding her ground. Then the pack split up and Charley knew she was stuffed. Nevertheless, when she saw one of the girls pick up a bottle of bubble bath she called over, 'If you're interested in buying that, open it and have a sniff.' The girl stared at her with open hostility. Without batting an eyelid, Charley eyeballed her back and eventually the girl replaced the bottle on the shelf.

'Nah. It's okay,' she said, and then headed for the door, the others following her.

It felt like a minor victory to Charley, but her heart was pounding and, she reflected, she had no way of knowing if anything else had miraculously slipped into a pocket or two before the rest of the gang had sloped out. Feeling mildly shaken, she went back behind the till and, perhaps not surprisingly, was even more relieved than usual when Pam arrived for the afternoon a couple of hours later. Her mother-in-law was her usual cheerful self, but as the afternoon wore on, Charley thought she seemed a little distracted. So, once there was a brief lull and the shop was empty, Charley asked if she was okay.

A tiny flicker of a frown clouded Pam's face. 'Ye-es, but I wanted to ask your advice about something.'

'Go ahead, caller!' said Charley cheerfully, leaning on the counter. 'Ask me anything you like.'

'Do you think it's too soon for me to have sex with Dez?'

Charley gasped and nearly had a coronary. *Do. Not. Overreact,* she ordered herself and desperately tried not to show even a tiny fraction of the shockwave that had jolted her sideways.

'Well, do *you*?' she asked the older woman sincerely. 'That's the more important question.'

'In my day we didn't go leaping into bed with people so quickly,' replied Pam. 'Well, some people did, but Geoff and I didn't.'

Charley reeled. This was way too much information about her mother-in-law's sex life. But Pam was continuing.

'So on the one hand, it does seem a bit early in the relationship, but on the other hand I know I'm old-fashioned and definitely out of touch with modern sensibilities. I don't want to lose him by making him wait too long. I mean, how long do people wait these days?'

'Not very long, sometimes not at all,' Charley answered honestly, if not very helpfully, and inwardly hoping – desperately hoping – that Pam wouldn't ask her about her and Ricky or, even worse, her and Josh. She Ricky had known each other for months before they'd had sex, not least because they'd been friends before they started dating, but she'd ended up in bed with Josh the first night she'd met him. Not that she was going to admit that to Pam. Not in a million years.

'How long is "not very long"?' queried Pam, and to Charley she seemed achingly vulnerable and she tried to imagine how hopelessly lost Pam must feel, starting dating again *forty years* after she last went on a date. Bloody hell; that was a lifetime ago. No wonder the poor woman was struggling.

'Look, I'm not going to tell you how many weeks or whatever you should wait,' said Charley earnestly. 'My best advice to you is: don't do it unless you feel ready to. Even if you think you might lose him. You can't stay with anyone who expects you to have sex before you're ready to.'

Naturally it was at this precise moment that Ricky opened the shop door. Charley felt herself blush bright pink for some reason. It wasn't like he'd overheard them or anything.

'Am I interrupting?' he asked since both women had so instantly fallen completely silent.

'No,' said Pam.

'Yes,' said Charley, simultaneously.

Stopping abruptly in the doorway, Ricky looked from Charley to Pam and then back again. 'Oh, right,' he said flatly. 'I'll just leave this here then.' He propped a package against the door lintel. 'It was delivered to the bike shop by mistake.'

He turned to leave but Charley blurted out, 'Hang on, wait! I know what you're thinking and we weren't talking about you, honestly. We were talking about...' Pam shot her such a mortified look Charley momentarily floundered, '...something else entirely,' she concluded lamely.

'Right,' said Ricky, beating a hasty, embarrassed retreat.

Bugger! Charley cursed, since Ricky clearly hadn't believed her. Then she turned her attention back to Pam and bravely tried to wrap up the sex lesson. 'So, to sum up, don't have sex unless you want to and, just as importantly, don't *do* anything you don't want to do.'

'Like what?' Pam's eyes widened and she looked thoroughly alarmed.

Charley's heart sank to the soles of her shoes. The last person she ever expected to be having the Porn Chat with was her mother-in-law. She gritted her teeth and delivered a no-holds-barred explanation of the impact of porn on the sexual expectations of men, or rather *some* men, nowadays.

'Right... Oh, I see. Yes, well, I suppose the internet has a lot to answer for,' was Pam's measured response.

'And don't forget to use a condom,' was Charley's final piece of advice.

'I hardly need to at my age, darling!' The mere idea clearly highly amused Pam.

'Oh, please don't make me give you the safe sex talk too!' implored Charley.

Pam's hand flew to her cheek. 'Oh God, of course, STDs and so forth. I'd forgotten. One last question...'

'Shoot,' said Charley. She was way past caring that Pam would saying anything else excruciating.

'Should I leave Dez to get the condoms or should I? I mean, will it look like I was *expecting* to have sex if I've got some in?' she asked with loveable frankness.

'Always a tough call,' replied Charley, 'but personally I'd put safety first.'

'Thank you so much, darling. I hope you didn't mind my asking, but I've got absolutely nobody else to turn to,' finished Pam with a brave, self-effacing smile, as if she were trying to make light of it.

Pam's admission brought Charley up short, and her heart went out to her. 'I don't mind a bit,' she assured her gently, and honestly. 'In fact, I take it as a compliment.'

'Actually... can I ask a big favour?' said Pam.

As long as it's not buying you some condoms.

'Would you mind coming to M&S with me to help me buy some underwear?'

Oh thank God, thought Charley, rapidly recovering her composure. 'Not at all, when did you have in mind?'

'I think they're open until ten tonight,' replied Pam.

—

'Right!' said Charley. 'Let's do this!'

Straight after closing up, she and Pam had nipped into the big M&S in the centre of Bristol and were now standing in the lingerie department gazing at the bedazzling range of women's underwear in every shape, size and colour.

'I honestly can't remember the last time I bought myself new undies,' confided Pam.

'I don't even know where to start!'

Charley immediately picked up a skimpy scarlet thong. 'Something like this?' she asked with a perfectly straight face.

'Good grief!' Pam visibly winced. 'I've seen more substantial garden twine!'

Charley snorted with laughter and put the offending article back.

'Seriously, though, aren't they hideously uncomfortable?' asked Pam.

'I wouldn't know!' claimed Charley.

Pam replied with a raised eyebrow and, wilfully ignoring her, Charley moved on to a display of less provocative underwear.

'Joking apart, I don't want anything "sexy", obviously, but I don't want anything too frumpy. I want something that'll make me feel...'

'Comfortable?' supplied Charley.

'Confident.'

Charley completely understood. The last time she'd bought new underwear had been for her first date with Ricky. She certainly hadn't been expecting they'd end up in bed, it was more *dressing for every eventuality*, just in case. Like packing for a music festival in high summer and taking sun block, shorts and shades, as well as a brolly, waterproof coat and wellies.

It was she who'd asked Ricky out, now she came to think of it, and they'd gone out for a drink. As a first date it hadn't felt particularly momentous, but then they already knew each other pretty well and so they were at ease with one another. At closing time, he'd offered to see her home but they'd both cycled to the pub and the journey back to Charley's meant slogging up a steep hill. It had seemed so natural to her to end the night together that Charley had simply pointed out that Ricky's place was nearer – so they went back to his place. Hand in hand, they'd wheeled their bikes through the city, the streetlamps casting bright pools of light in the dark streets. She hadn't planned to spend the night with him, and she hadn't got the impression that Ricky had expected to either, it had just felt... right.

–

In the end, Pam chose two sets of lingerie, both with full-cup bras and *very* full-brief pants, modest cotton with just a hint of lace. Rejecting black as too sexy, and red as too tarty, she opted for navy and pale purple.

'What d'you think?' she asked anxiously. 'Not too young for me?'

'Absolutely not!' replied Charley. Casting her eye over them and choosing her words carefully she said, 'I like them, they're pretty. Feminine without being tarty.' Personally, she wouldn't have been seen dead in them.

Chapter Twenty

It was Saturday evening and, as had become the norm, Dez was coming to Pam's for dinner. After getting back from work, she hurriedly threw a basic coq au vin together and put a ciabatta mix into the bread-maker. The salad could wait. Coq au vin was a ridiculous choice for a hot August day, she knew that, but it was an inexpensive, presentable dish she could cook on automatic pilot and this evening she was way too distracted to be able to follow a recipe. She showered, washed and dried her hair and then stood, in her dressing gown, regarding her new underwear apprehensively. She'd laid both sets on the bed, where they seemed to regard her back, judgementally.

Just because you put your new undies on doesn't mean you have to sleep with Dez, she told herself. Which was true. But she knew already that she would. That morning she'd put fresh linen on the bed and cleaned the bathroom, putting a clean towel on the rail and a spare face flannel on the side of the sink with a new bar of soap. Actions which, when she came to think of it, weren't exactly romantic, and probably said more about her housekeeping than her sexual desires. To be honest, she wasn't actually longing to have sex with Dez – in fact, the idea terrified her. She hadn't slept with anyone other than Geoff for over four decades and the thought of undressing in front of someone else filled her with trepidation. Even just mentally taking things any further than that was intimidating and nerve-racking beyond belief. But she had no choice, not if she wanted a 'full relationship' as the dating site euphemistically termed it. And she thought she did. She wasn't only looking for 'companionship', someone to go to the movies with, or to join her on long walks. She had plenty of friends for the former and could probably borrow Carlo for the latter. She wanted more than that – a life partner. So, more than anything, tonight she just wanted to get the agonizing ordeal of the first time over and done with.

She chose the navy bra and pants, hoping the dark colour would be more flattering, and slipped into them, her fingers fumbling nervously with the bra fastenings. Then she regarded herself critically in the mirror. Well, she wasn't going to make it onto the billboards in the M&S lingerie department, that was for sure. But the new underwear was a distinct improvement on her existing selection. Scooping up the purple underwear set, she shoved it in her knicker drawer, and as she did so, she caught sight of the small, cellophane-covered package she'd stashed in there, and froze. She'd taken Charley's advice and bought some condoms. That in itself had been a nightmare. She'd never bought any before in her life, never had to, and she'd been thrown not just by the bewildering range, but by the nakedly sexual blatancy of the descriptions and options. *Ribbed for her pleasure, extra thin for his*, apparently. Then there were all the luxury brands offering… well, all manner of things, frankly. She'd scanned the options hastily and chosen the most innocuous-looking pack available, and had then randomly picked up a box of corn plasters and a jar of multi-vitamins on her way to the tills so that the condoms wouldn't be the only thing she presented at the checkout.

She shut the drawer and finished dressing, relieved to cover up the proof of her guilty agenda with a cool, flowing summery top and a pair of crops. Then she went downstairs to add the mushrooms to the chicken and rustle up a salad. It was such a hot evening she decided to set the patio table for supper. When she'd done that, everything was ready, and all she had to do was wait, increasingly anxiously, for Dez.

She was tense all through dinner, although Dez didn't seem to notice. Perhaps trying to compensate for his drunkenness at Zee's, he was particularly attentive and complimentary, bringing her chocolates (but having forgotten the wine). Perhaps wisely, Pam had decided to wait until they'd finished supper before inviting him to stay, but of course that just meant she grew progressively more stressed as the dreaded moment approached. Eventually *the dreaded moment* inevitably arrived and, equally inevitably, Dez accepted her stumbling invitation. Heart pounding with nerves rather than passion, she led him upstairs and into her bedroom. To her utmost relief it turned out she had worried needlessly. He was sweet, and so was the sex, and she needn't have bought the condoms either, he'd got some in his wallet.

–

The next morning, Pam woke and, fully expecting to find Dez in her bed, was surprised to find him gone. Sitting up, she realised she was still naked and pulled on her top from the previous night for decency, and only just in time, before the bedroom door opened and Dez came in with a mug of tea and the sugar bowl. He was already dressed.

'I didn't know if you took sugar,' he said.

'How lovely!' Pam slid back down under the duvet to luxuriate. 'I don't.' She took the tea from him.

He kissed her briefly and said, 'I'm going to have to nip off sharpish. You have a lie-in. Mind if I make myself a bacon butty before I go?'

'Er, no, of course not,' said Pam. She hadn't exactly envisaged what would happen 'the morning after the night before' but she was pretty sure that if she had, she wouldn't have expected it to start like this.

Vaguely disappointed for some reason she couldn't quite put her finger on, she sipped her tea and listened to the distant sound of Dez clunking around in the kitchen. She wondered if she ought to go down and offer to cook the bacon for him but thought better of it. *Start as you mean to go on!* she told herself, lying back against the pillow.

A few minutes later, he called up, 'Bye!'

'Oh, bye!' she called back, hurriedly putting her tea down on the bedside table and starting to clamber out of bed to see him out, but the front door slammed even before she'd stood up. Instantly, her lie-in lost its attraction. Hardly surprisingly, since in Pam's experience, lie-ins weren't enjoyable when you were the only one in the house. The whole point of them is luxuriating in bed while everyone else is up and doing the chores you'd normally be doing, like on Mother's Day for example. She threw the duvet off, stepped into her knickers and crops and went down to the kitchen to make herself some toast. Crossing the hall, she caught sight of herself in the long mirror by the front door. It was only then that the astonishing, amazing enormity of what she'd just done sank in, and she grinned at herself and then promptly blushed scarlet. Which was ludicrous, when she came to think of it. It wasn't as if it she'd been a virgin.

'Can you come over?'

'What, now?' asked Zee down the phone.

'Only if you're free,' replied Pam lightly.

'What's happened?' Zee's tone was edged with concern.

Pam tried to sound nonchalant. 'Oh, it's nothing to be alarmed about.'

There was a tiny beat before Zee said, 'I'm on my way.'

The two old friends sat at the wooden patio table in Pam's garden, under the shade of the large green parasol. Although it was only just after ten o'clock it was already too hot for coffee so Pam had made a jug of iced tea. She poured some into a long glass and handed it to Zee, trying to suppress the broad grin threatening to hijack her entire face.

'Stop looking so smug! You remind me of that godawful T-shirt people used to wear! The one that said *Smile if you had it last night*.'

'Josh had one! I'd forgotten. It was ghastly,' agreed Pam, rolling her eyes.

Zee put her glass down on the table and turned to her friend, a light frown furrowing her forehead. 'Wasn't it a bit sudden? A bit soon?' she ventured tentatively.

Pam wasn't surprised by Zee's question. In fact, she would have been amazed if she hadn't asked it. She shook her head. 'I don't think so. We've known each other some weeks now, and besides, people don't wait so long nowadays. It's the modern way.'

'But is it *your* way?' persisted Zee carefully.

Pam shrugged. 'I really like him and, well, why wait? I mean, God, Zee, the agonies we went through when we were younger. All that "keeping yourself" for that special person and worrying about getting a reputation for being a slut. What *really* was that all about?'

'Good question. It just led to a lot of frustrated groping and some dreadfully disappointing honeymoons as far as I can make out.'

Pam laughed. 'And we're neither of us teenagers. Neither of us getting any younger. So again, why wait? What precisely would we be waiting for?' When Zee didn't seem to have an answer Pam joked, 'And anyhow, I hadn't had sex for months!'

'I haven't had sex for years but I'm not complaining!' countered Zee. Her tone was flippant but she looked away, and not before Pam caught the look in her eyes.

'Oh, Zee,' she said softly. Her friend's admission hadn't surprised her. There was little left in Zee and Theo's marriage except convenience.

'It's not the sex I miss. It's the affection,' Zee confided with heart-wrenching openness. Pam couldn't imagine what that must feel like, a marriage without any physical contact. She and Geoff had enjoyed regular, good sex right up until they separated. Even, she thought bitterly, during those last five years when he was having an affair, having his cake and nibbling his bit on the side too.

'I can't remember the last time Theo touched me. Or kissed me,' Zee continued. 'In fact, I reckon the average nun probably has more fun than me!' she quipped, evidently trying to lighten the mood.

Pam shot Zee an amused look, to reward her for her bravery if nothing else. For years, Pam had known how unhappy Zee was, but it wasn't until she'd left Geoff that it occurred to her that Zee could, perhaps even should, leave Theo. Ironically, it also made her more cautious to suggest it, knowing how bloody tough it was, tough and lonely. More to the point, she feared her advice might be misconstrued, and that people might suspect an ulterior motive since if Zee left her husband, Pam wouldn't be the only solo one in the group.

'What's Dez's place like?' asked Zee, deftly changing the subject.

'I still haven't been there,' replied Pam.

'Didn't you drive him home the other night?'

'Yes, but I didn't go in. It was late, it was dark… He was pissed!'

'So, you still only ever come here?'

'Well, yes,' said Pam, wondering where Zee was going with this.

'It just seems a bit odd.'

'Why? He's only got a small flat.'

'You could still go there for a drink,' persisted Zee. 'Maybe you should invite yourself there. Have a nose!'

'What do you think I'm going to find, Zee? Corpses under the carpet?'

Zee shot her a withering look and didn't reply.

Later, after Zee had gone, her observation began to prey on Pam's mind. Dez did always come to hers, and she always cooked for him. Granted, he brought his own beers, and sometimes a bottle of wine or some chocolates, but it was all still a bit… one-sided. The perceptiveness of Zee's questions began to make Pam feel slightly uncomfortable and it felt as if her friend had slightly rained on her parade. Maybe not a full downpour, more of a drizzle really, setting off a small – very small – alarm bell in the back of her mind. So small she decided to ignore it.

Chapter Twenty-One

'Tara! I am sooooo glad to see you!'

It was nine-thirty on the first day after the school summer holidays and Tara had just walked through the shop door. Charley would have flung her arms round her if it hadn't been for the fact that her mate was, as usual, burdened with gifts, juggling two coffees, a box of pastries, a large carrier bag, plus her handbag.

'Are you talking to me or to your breakfast?' Tara handed Charley the coffees with a grin.

'Both! But I am more pleased to see you. Well, marginally,' Charley said, prising the lid off her cup.

Tara held the carrier out to Charley. 'From Spain!'

'Ooooh, thank you! Please tell me it's a straw donkey in a sombrero?'

'It would have been if Monnie'd had her way!'

Charley pulled a pair of cotton espadrilles out of the bag. They were white, adorned with bright red cherries and dark green leaves. 'Oh my God, they're gorgeous!' she said, instantly kicking off her sandals to put them on.

'I bought Pam a flamenco fan. Hope she won't think it's a bit naff.'

'Of course she won't. She'll be chuffed to bits you got her anything. And how was Spain?'

'Hot. As in, lying on a tiled floor trying not to expire.'

Charley grimaced sympathetically.

Her friend hadn't been in the shop more than a minute before Charley was wondering how she'd managed to cope without her. Above all, she'd missed her company, her banter, her sense of fun.

The shop came to life when Tara walked in, but then any room brightened when Tara walked in. Spontaneously, Charley went over to give her friend a hug. 'I've really missed you,' she said.

'I've missed you too,' responded Tara.

Liar, thought Charley, then immediately downgraded that to the more affectionate and less judgemental *fibber*. She knew that Tara's every waking moment throughout the entire holiday would have been spent devoted to giving Monnie fun. Unfortunately, time wasn't the only thing Tara had lavished on Monnie. Apparently, she'd maxed out the credit card and Baz was livid. Charley was well used to Tara's rants on the theme of her husband's miserliness, which were heated, colourful and totally untrue. Baz wasn't tight-fisted, he merely thought Tara spent too much on their daughter. Privately, Charley agreed with him. Babysitting Monnie was like spending the evening in a toy store. The little girl could barely get into her bed, it was so cluttered with fluffy animals and teddy bears which, given that it was a king-sized double, was saying something. Charley honestly reckoned that Monnie had more toys and games than all of Angie's kids put together. Adding to the outlay was the fact that Tara never bought Monnie anything second-hand. In Charley's opinion, Baz was remarkably tolerant to the expenditure, but probably only because he knew that his wife was in some way compensating for her own poverty-blighted childhood and didn't want Monnie to go without in the way she had. Even so, it had long been a source of marital friction between the two of them. All the while Tara had worked part-time and had had her own income, the details of her spending on Monnie had escaped Baz. However, now that Tara had given up paid employment to help Charley in the shop, every single penny she spent came out of her and Baz's joint account, so it would have been hard for him to miss precisely how much was spent on their daughter.

Charley had to wait for the full, blow-by-blow account of Tara's spat – or rather, spats – with Baz, because a steady trickle of customers drifted into shop for the next hour or so, meaning that a steady trickle of money drifted into the shop too. It always seemed busier when Tara was in, mainly because she kept the customers talking so they stayed in the store longer. She *claimed* it was a good business tactic on the grounds that a shop with customers in it is more appealing than one without, but Charley suspected the real reason was that Tara couldn't resist a good gossip.

It was almost the end of the morning before the shop emptied and Tara could return to her theme. 'He's saying that from now on we have to agree on a budget and stick to it!' she fumed. Which seemed completely reasonable to Charley, but clearly not to Tara. 'How's that supposed to work? Am I meant to calculate, in minute detail, everything Monnie and I want to do and buy in advance? Can you imagine it? *Sorry Monnie, you can't have an ice-cream, because we didn't put it in the budget. No Monnie, we can't go to the funfair because we didn't know there was going to be one and so we didn't include it in our long-term holiday expenditure projection!*'

Charley laughed.

'It's ridiculous!' Tara continued, buoyed by Charley's laughter. 'The whole point of holidays is that they're meant to be fun. *Spontaneous* fun!'

'*Apart* from that, did you have a good holiday?' said Charley.

'Yes,' Tara conceded.

'Good!' replied Charley, giving her a grin, which lasted all of thirty seconds before Tara dropped a bombshell that wiped it clean off her face.

'But the thing is, Charley, I can't go on with Baz controlling my spending like that. Controlling *me* like that. I need to have my own money coming in.' She looked at Charley pointedly.

'Oh, right.'

'When I invested in the shop,' Tara continued. *When you and Baz invested*, corrected Charley mentally. 'It was on the basis that I'd have a share of the profits once the shop got going,' Tara reminded her.

Small butterflies of panic butted the walls of Charley's stomach. Yes, that had been the arrangement when Tara and Baz had given her the three grand, but the shop still wasn't doing that well, barely making enough for Charley to get by on.

'I know,' replied Charley awkwardly. 'I'm just not in a position to pay you anything yet.'

'Okay,' said Tara, and Charley felt herself let out the breath she hadn't realised she'd been holding, but her mate wasn't done. 'So when *do* you think you'll be in a position to do that?'

'I honestly don't know.' Charley shrugged apologetically.

'Really?' queried Tara in a tone that very much implied she should know.

'Tara, the shop's not been open a year yet. Surely you didn't expect it to be making a huge profit already?'

'No, maybe not, but I do expect you to know when it will.'

Tara left it at that, but there was as distinct awkwardness between the two friends for the rest of the morning and Charley doubted she'd heard the last of it.

Just before lunchtime Tara left and Charley was relieved to see her go. Pam's arrival in the afternoon did little to raise her spirits, only serving to remind her that she wasn't paying Pam either. A double whammy of guilt and failure began gnawing away at her. The only high point in the day was when Angie popped in, with baby Lily in the buggy, bringing in a few pieces of artwork she'd managed to do over the holidays.

Charley immediately dropped what she was doing to embrace Angie enthusiastically and then she crouched down in front of Lily in her buggy.

'Hello my little poppet pie!' Lily wriggled irritably in her straps and Charley turned to look up at Angie. 'Shall I get her out?'

Angie sighed heavily. 'Sorry, Charley, but it's probably not a good idea. She's not having a good day and she'll only scream the place down when I have to put her back.'

Charley pulled a sympathetic face at the baby and gently stroked her cheek. 'Poor little munchkin. Are you having a difficult day?' In response, Lily stuck her bottom lip out and started up a fretful whimpering, so Charley rose to her feet, not wanting to make it worse.

Angie had fished a batch of canvasses out of their wrappings.

'Sorry there's not much,' she apologised. 'Lily's *still* teething and it's a nightmare trying to get anything done.' As if on cue, or perhaps hearing her name, the baby increased her fractious fidgeting, so Angie rocked the buggy, attempting to soothe her.

'No worries,' replied Charley, enthusiastically flicking through the half a dozen or so canvasses with Pam looking over her shoulder. 'These are fabulous, Ange!'

'Thank you,' replied Angie. Then Lily turned up the volume and she leant down to stroke her little one's forehead. 'It's all right, sweetie.'

'I love that one,' enthused Pam, pointing to a painting of a cork popping out of a Prosecco bottle, in a foaming sea of bubbles, with the slogan *Life should be bursting with fun!* scrawled across the top. 'You've really captured the moment!' she told Angie, who flushed deeply.

Charley took the pictures and immediately went over to display them on the back wall. Lily turned up the volume another notch.

Angie winced. 'Sorry, Charley. I had hoped she'd go off and we could have a quick catch-up. I haven't seen you all summer.'

'I've been too busy,' explained Charley but with more than twinge of guilt.

At which point Lily turned the volume up to a full scream, and the three women could barely hear themselves think, let alone talk, so Pam offered to push the baby around outside for a while, to give Angie a break. Wheeling the buggy through the doorway, she promised to return with some tea, baby permitting.

'I can't stay long,' Angie warned Charley. 'I have to pick Finn up from playgroup and then get the others from school.'

Once Angie had caught Charley up on her family's summer, she asked Charley how the shop was going.

'Not well enough.' Taking a deep breath, Charley confided in Angie the gist of her conversation with Tara.

'Blimey, Charley, you'd need the turnover of the average Primark to cover the cost of Monnie's summer holiday treats!'

said Angie, and Charley managed a small smile. 'Do you want to take a cut from the artwork? Would that help?'

'No!' Charley was mortally offended that Angie would even think she was angling to renegotiate their deal 'That's not why I mentioned it.' Now she wished she hadn't brought it up at all.

Wisely, she decided not to mention it to Pam that afternoon but later, when she got home, she called Nisha for advice, as one professional to another – only to wish she hadn't.

'It's not unreasonable for Tara to ask when she might get a cut of the profits,' was Nisha's opinion. 'You should be able to project that from the accounts.'

Charley winced; she hadn't even started them yet, but she wasn't going to admit that. Oblivious to the fact that she'd inadvertently hit a nerve, Nisha went on, 'You can't expect Tara to go on working for nothing ad infinitum. She's not a volunteer in a charity shop, she's your business partner.'

Charley flipped.

'She's hardly what I'd call a "business partner",' she snapped. 'She only drops in for a few hours a day, and leaves everything pretty much to me. And she hasn't even been in all summer! So she can hardly blame me if the shop isn't making a big fat profit she can take a share of!'

She knew she sounded petulant, and she hated herself, especially for taking it out on Nisha, but she was tired and at the end of her tether.

'If you feel like that then you need to tackle her on it,' said Nisha calmly. When Charley didn't respond, she went on. 'If the shop isn't doing well enough to give Tara a decent profit share then you need to develop a growth strategy to enable it to do so.'

I have absolutely no idea how to do that! And when am I supposed to find the time? despaired Charley. Overwhelmed, and feeling completely out of her depth, she fought to keep the anguish out of her voice. 'Could you help me with that?'

There was a lengthy pause and then Nisha replied, 'If it was just your shop I would, Charley, readily, but Tara and Pam are your business partners so you should ask them, not me. Get everyone together and draw up a development plan. Tara has an MBA,' she reminded Charley, 'Ask her to pull together a draft proposal. Sorry, Charley. I know that's not what you wanted to hear. But you can't run a shop, or any business, on free labour forever.'

Biting back her disappointment, Charley thanked Nisha, then rang off, more despondent than ever.

Chapter Twenty-Two

Spreading a generous dollop of blueberry compote onto the top of a cheesecake, Pam was unexpectedly interrupted by the doorbell. Irritably, she plonked the palette knife onto the work surface and headed to the front door.

'Dez! I wasn't expecting you.'

'I know. Surprise!' he said with mock jollity, hovering expectantly at the threshold. Since he was holding a small bunch of flowers and the usual four-pack of beers, Pam assumed he was expecting to be invited in. Which was a bit of a problem, because she was just about to go out.

'Can I come in?' he prompted.

Pulling herself together, Pam stood back to let him inside. 'Yes of course,' but as he followed her through to the kitchen she said over her shoulder, 'I'm afraid you can't stay long, though. I'm out this evening.'

'Oh.' He sounded surprised. 'I brought you these,' he went on, thrusting the bunch of asters at her.

'Lovely,' said Pam a shade tersely, but automatically taking the flowers and going to put them in a vase. 'But I'm off to Mona's. She's having an Abba evening!'

'Sounds fun,' replied Dez. 'I'd be up for that.'

'You'd hate it! She's got a karaoke machine and we do all the Abba hits, and I mean *all*.' It wasn't even Pam's thing, really. She'd never been into Abba and couldn't for the life of her see what all the fuss was about. But Mona was a massive fan and so was Zee; she and Toni just joined in for the pure fun of singing along. The menfolk predictably escaped to the sanctuary of the kitchen, although Phil was sometimes known to do a mean Benny – or was it Björn? She honestly had no idea.

Dez pulled a face. 'Can't you cry off?'

I could, but I don't want to, she thought, irked by the assumption that she would immediately drop everything just because it suited Dez.

'I'd rather not,' she said. 'It'd be very last minute, *and* I'm taking the pudding.' She indicated the half-finished cheesecake on the surface and hoped it would scotch any further debate.

Dez's face fell. 'I just really wanted to see you.'

'We're seeing each other on Saturday,' she reminded him. 'Drinks at yours. Or had you forgotten?'

'No but, about that… Something's come up and I've got to go to Birmingham.'

'Oh?' Pam was surprised rather than disappointed.

'Sorry, but it's business.'

'That's rather short notice, isn't it? I hope it's nothing serious.'

'No, no, everything's fine. I've got to meet someone about getting the cars sorted for the driving school.' He shrugged apologetically. 'It's the whole dual control thing, it's much more complicated than buying normal cars, and a lot more expensive,' he added despondently. Pam could well see that it might be. 'So I was just really hoping that I could see you tonight,' he continued, 'but obviously I don't want make you choose between your friends and me…' He finished pointedly, leaving the notion suspended in an uncomfortable silence between them.

Pam felt herself weakening. There'd be other karaoke sessions at Mona's, and if she were honest, halfway through an *entire* evening of Abba she was usually wishing Sweden had never won the bloody Eurovision Song Contest in 1974, or whenever it was. Plus, now that she came to think of it, Dez being away at the weekend was actually rather a boon since her new student lodgers were arriving on the Sunday, and it would be easier all round if she were on her own to focus on them.

'I haven't got anything special in for supper,' she said vaguely. *Or anything very much at all.* Now that she wasn't having to feed a hungry troop of teenagers every night, Pam was economising as much as possible on the food shop.

'I'm not expecting a feast,' said Dez hurriedly. 'I'd be happy with beans on toast. Oh, and a slice of that cheesecake!' he added, giving the pudding an appreciative nod.

Pam caved and called Mona. Hearing herself explain why she couldn't go, she knew she sounded pitifully weak and unconvincing, but of course Mona was too tactful to comment. She rang off and went back into the kitchen. She finished coating the cheesecake, and then dug around in the fridge to see what she could rustle up for a store-cupboard supper. Dez had taken himself through to the living room and put the TV on, taking his four-pack of beers with him. Finding half a dozen eggs and a lump of cheddar, she settled on a cheese soufflé. She put the oven on, greased the soufflé dish, grated the cheese and made a binding sauce. By the time she was separating the whites from the yolks she was regretting giving in to Dez, angry with herself, and wishing she'd stuck to her guns and gone to Mona's.

As she was laying the table in the dining room for supper, Dez wandered in.

'Anything I can do to help?'

It's a bit late now, thought Pam, setting the cutlery next to the plates, faintly irritated that he'd not offered before. *It's your own fault*, she chided herself. *You could have asked him to help, so don't play the martyr now.*

'I'm pretty much done,' she told him.

'Mmm, something smells delicious!' he said, settling himself down at the table.

'Cheese soufflé,' she replied, heading off to the kitchen.

'Fantastic! Oh, by the way,' she heard him call after her, 'we're nearly out of Scotch.'

We're nearly out of Scotch? What's with the '*we*'? It's my damn Scotch! The thought niggled as she took the soufflé out of the oven. Then she reminded herself that, technically, the whisky was Geoff's. It had been his Christmas present from his brother, the year before they'd split up. It was, she seemed to recall, a particularly decent malt. It had come in a posh gift box and Geoff had made quite a fuss when he'd unwrapped it. She was surprised he hadn't taken it with him, but then he'd probably had other more urgent things to pack, like underpants and socks... and *condoms*, no doubt, she added bitterly. Her marriage had ended abruptly, without warning, in a pub car park and she hadn't even been in the house to witness him pack his belongings. She was neither surprised nor remotely sympathetic to discover that he'd left some of his things behind, not least because she hadn't been there to dutifully go round afterwards checking for him, as she'd always done when they'd packed to go on holiday.

On the one hand, she supposed she should be angry that Dez had been helping himself to the Scotch, and so freely that he'd drained the bottle. On the other hand, she couldn't deny her childish delight that her new lover had drunk all of her soon-to-be ex-husband's whisky. And the fact that it was a bloody expensive bottle only tickled her even more.

—

The following morning, while Pam made breakfast, Dez rather laboriously unloaded the dishwasher from the night before as she'd, rather pointedly, asked him to do. He wasn't an enormous help, professing not to know where any of the crockery went. He'll learn, she told herself briskly. After breakfast, much to her surprise, Dez showed no signs of leaving as he usually did, but settled himself at the kitchen table, helping himself to more tea. She hoped he wasn't expecting to hang around all day, but mid-morning came and he was still happily ensconced, by now in the living room, drinking coffee.

'Um, what are your plans today?' she asked him. 'Only I have to leave for the shop at lunchtime.'

'Okay, I'll slope off when you do.'

Right, thought Pam wishing she could think of a tactful way to ask him to 'slope off' sooner than that. Now-ish even. She couldn't, so he was still there when she went up to her room to get ready to go to the shop. Putting her shoes on, she heard the doorbell.

'I'll get it!' called up Dez.

'No, I will!' Pam shouted firmly. But by the time she was halfway down the stairs, Dez had already opened the front door.

'Can I help you?' she heard him say.

'Who the hell are you?' demanded a man's voice. It was Geoff's.

'Who the hell are *you*?' countered Dez, and Pam could see him physically squaring up to Geoff in the doorway.

'Geoff!' cried Pam, arriving at the door, completely flustered, and trying to intervene between the two men. 'What are you doing here?'

Geoff attempted to push his way into the house, but Dez deliberately blocked his path.

'Pam?' appealed Geoff, peering over Dez's shoulder. Which wasn't hard, since Geoff towered over him.

Oh this is ridiculous. 'Dez, this is Geoff, my...' She faltered because she'd literally just been about to describe him as 'my soon-to-be ex-husband', which she knew would only inflame the situation.

'Husband,' Geoff supplied proprietorially, inflaming it nicely.

Dez whipped round to look at Pam, accusingly. Which was fair enough, she thought. It was grossly misleading for Geoff to claim to still be her husband, even though, of course legally he was. Rather than attempting to clarifying things, Pam opted to introduce Dez instead.

'Geoff, this is Dez, my...' *My what?* panicked a voice inside. *My friend? My boyfriend?*

'Partner,' supplied Dez, and Pam wanted to scream.

–

Geoff, it transpired, needed his passport which he hadn't thought to take with him. Pam left him on the doorstep while she went to look for it, leaving the two men eyeballing each other. She hoped to God it wasn't going to end in fisticuffs.

'Could you give us a minute?' she said to Dez, returning with the passport.

Reluctantly he nodded, and with no further word to Geoff, took himself off to the kitchen.

'You could have phoned beforehand,' Pam said curtly, handing the passport over.

'I didn't think I needed to,' replied Geoff, similarly brusque.

'Why?' she challenged, infuriated. 'Because you think I'll always be in? Or because you assume I'll always be here alone?'

'Well, I won't make that mistake again,' he retorted.

'Good!'

Then her soon-to-be ex-husband turned his back on her and left. Neither of them said 'Goodbye.' Pam barely controlled the urge to slam the door behind him.

How dare he get on his high horse about me seeing someone? she seethed, leaning against the door and trying to regain her self-control. *How bloody dare he!* He'd been unfaithful to her, not the other way round. It was up to her, completely up to her, if she chose to have a man in her house, at any time day or night, and none of his damn business. Or anyone else's, come to think of it. So what if Dez had overstated things a little by describing himself as her 'partner'? But, come to think of it, it wouldn't hurt Geoff to think that Dez was her new partner. In fact it would bloody well serve him right to think that she *had* found someone to replace him, the way he'd found someone to replace her. She composed herself, then headed into the kitchen to soothe Dez's ruffled feathers, wish him luck in Birmingham, and to fix up another date for him to come round when he got back.

Chapter Twenty-Three

Things were a little strained in the shop between Tara and Charley throughout the rest of the week. Despite Nisha's advice, Charley was reluctant to ask Tara to draw up a development plan. She recoiled from asking her mate to do even more for her for nothing, and had already mentally added it to her own To Do list, once she'd finished the accounts. Additionally, at the back of her mind was the disagreeable suspicion that having to ask Tara to help would be a tacit admission that she couldn't run her own business. Mercifully, Tara didn't mention money again, so Charley didn't either, on the grounds that it was easier to let sleeping dogs lie. Unfortunately, the dogs were rudely kicked awake on the following Friday morning when Charley asked Tara if she'd mind the shop while Charley whizzed round a few venues delivering gift bags.

'It shouldn't take me more than an hour or so,' she promised. 'I've got to drop off a dozen at the Snug, ten at the Vaults, another dozen at that new bar at the top of Park Street, twenty at the wine bar next to Watershed, and thirty-five to the Avalon, but I'll probably do those this evening.'

'Are you driving?'

'No, I'm on the bike. Parking costs a fortune!'

'So you're going to spend what, an hour and half delivering fifty party bags?'

The inferred criticism set Charley's hackles rising. 'Yes. If it's a problem I'll do it this evening,' she offered coolly.

'It's not that,' said Tara. 'But why are you wasting so much time delivering such small numbers of bags? It's not cost-effective.

You should make them order a hundred at a time. *Minimum,*' she finished, stressing the last word.

Charley tried to keep her rising temper under control. 'They won't.'

'Then you'll have to tell them you won't deliver. They'll have to collect from the shop.'

'And risk losing my customers?' Charley was outraged. It had taken her months to build up this side of the business and it was only now slowly beginning to gain momentum.

'What's the profit margin on the bags?' demanded Tara. When Charley didn't answer Tara prompted, 'A pound a bag?'

I wish, thought Charley. 'Probably nearer fifty pence,' she admitted reluctantly.

'That's ridiculous!' spluttered Tara and Charley felt her face flush hot, but her friend ploughed on regardless. 'You should be aiming for a forty per cent profit margin *minimum*. You need to cut back on anything making less than that.'

'But that'd mean losing the entire gift bag side-line just when it's starting to really take off.'

'Yes. If it's not cost-effective, drop it.'

'I'm not doing that.' Charley felt fiercely protective towards her customers, recalling Nisha's loyalty towards her clients when they were discussing her buy-out deal. It had been a key factor in her decision-making. 'I'm not letting my customers down like that. And besides,' she pointed out, 'the shop has to make more money. You know that. The party bags might not me making as much profit as you'd like them to, but every little helps.'

Tara sighed heavily – patronisingly, to Charley's mind. 'You're missing the point, Charley. The problem with you is that you don't think in a business-like way. It's not about how much profit *I* think things should make. It's about how much they need to make for the shop to run successfully, and profitably. And have you even factored in the cost of your time?'

Charley bit her lip. She hadn't. And in fact, she had no idea what she should be charging for her time. The whole point of the party bag business was that it was a side-line. Anyhow, it was her time she was giving up, not Tara's, and she was more than prepared to sacrifice her time to make the shop a success.

'Forget it,' said Charley brusquely, putting the box of gift bags back behind the till. 'I'll take them round tonight.'

'Oh Charley, don't be like that!' groaned Tara. 'That's just cutting off your nose to spite your face. Do the deliveries now. I'll hold the fort.' When Charley still hovered Tara shooed her out. 'Go!'

Feeling she'd been dismissed, like a junior colleague, Charley picked up the box again, and set off on her bike. *How is she so staggeringly bossy and opinionated? It's my business, not hers*, she reminded herself. And what if Tara had invested three grand? That was a *fraction* of what Charley had put in, given that she'd ploughed all her savings and her redundancy money into the venture. And less than Pam had. After Tara's outburst this morning, despite Nisha's advice, she felt even less inclined to ask her 'business partner' to help draw up any sort of growth plan, fearing her party bag side-line would be axed at a stroke.

Not surprisingly, cycling round the city for a good hour de-stressed Charley and she'd calmed down considerably by the time she got back to the shop. It was surprisingly busy but Tara seemed to be handling everything smoothly, so Charley slid behind the till ready to take the payments. It was nearly lunch time when the last punter left and Charley was hoping Tara would go without raising the issue of the shop's profitability, or rather its non-profitability, again.

Fat chance. But to her relief, Tara adopted a more placatory tone than before. Perhaps she realised she'd overstepped the mark, thought Charley. Again, fat chance.

'About the profit margins, don't take it personally, Charley, please. This isn't about you. It's purely about the shop. I want to help you make it more profitable.'

Charley's heart hit her boots. *Here we go again.*

'I invested in this shop because I believe in it, and I believe in you too,' Tara was continuing earnestly. *Could've fooled me,* thought Charley, but she kept schtum. 'I want it to be a success because I like working with you. It's fun! But if the shop can't pay me – and not a wage, just a profit share,' Tara stressed hurriedly, 'then, even though I really, really don't want to do it, I'm going to have to pack in working here and get a job instead.'

And having dropped that shattering announcement, Tara left. Charley wasn't sure if it was a statement of fact or a threat; either way, her spirits nosedived. They sank even further when the door opened a short while later and Ricky walked in, with Carlo at his heel but, unusually, on a lead. She forced herself to greet Ricky brightly, but he was just about the last person she wanted to see. She simply wasn't feeling resilient enough.

'Charley, I'm sorry to have to trouble you, but I have a family emergency.'

He looked so serious she felt a twinge of fear. 'What's happened? Are you okay?'

He nodded. 'Yes. But my grandmother has been taken ill. She's in hospital. My mother has asked me to fly back to Italy.'

'Oh, no. What's wrong with her?' Charley was genuinely anxious about the kindly elderly woman.

'She's had a stroke.' The pain in Ricky's eyes cut Charley deep inside.

'Oh Ricky, I'm so sorry.' Without thinking, she reached out and pulled him into her arms, and then she stiffened, alarmed and caught off guard by the sheer physical pleasure of being close to him. Hurriedly she pulled away, embarrassed, shying from meeting his gaze, sensing his discomfort too.

There was a brief silence until Ricky broke it. 'Do you think Pam would have Carlo for me while I'm gone?'

'Yes of course she will, and if she can't, I will,' she promised.

'Thank you. You're… very kind.'

For a moment Charley thought he was going to lean over and kiss her. The atmosphere felt distinctly charged, and she found she was holding her breath, but he didn't and the tension evaporated.

'How long will you be gone?' she asked.

'I don't know. Will that be a problem?'

'No, of course not! What are you going to do about the bike shop?'

He shrugged. 'I'll just have to close it while I'm gone.'

Knowing how much that might damage his business she said, 'I wish I could offer to look after it for you.'

He smiled down at her, his slow, soft smile. 'Thank you, but you've got too much on your plate already.'

Handing Carlo's lead to her, together with the keys to his flat, he ordered Carlo to sit and stay. Then he crouched down and ruffled the lurcher fondly between the ears. 'Be good for Charley,' he said, then he rose and with one last glance at Charley, he left.

Charley watched him go, unfeasibly overwhelmed by a sense of loss.

—

When Pam got to the shop half an hour or so later, she immediately offered to look after Carlo, since she'd looked after the dog before. 'He's no trouble,' she told Charley, 'I liked having him around, the great galumphing lump!'

'Actually, I think I'd like to take him back to mine,' Charley said.

'Oh, okay,' replied Pam, sounding a little disappointed. 'Good idea,' she added, and when Charley looked at her quizzically, the older woman explained, 'He's good company,' and Charley felt a little selfish, keeping the dog for herself.

For a while, Carlo sat patiently by the shop window looking out, obviously waiting for Ricky to return. After about an hour, he slumped down, put his chin on his paws and sighed melodramatically. He stayed like that for the rest of the afternoon. Every now and again he'd let out a small whine and waggle his eyebrows gloomily.

—

Having unexpectedly acquired Carlo, Charley was now presented with the small problem of how to get home since, as usual, she'd cycled in. She opted to leave her bike chained up at the shop and walk back, giving the lurcher some exercise. When they got back to the flat, she put him in the car and went round to Ricky's place to pick up the dog's things. It felt weird letting herself into his flat and being there without him, almost as if she were trespassing, or spying on him in some way. A faint hint of his body cologne hung in the air, earthy and musky. She walked into the bedroom. It was tidy and the bed was made. The only signs of his recent habitation were the faint dents in the duvet where she assumed he'd packed his case, and a half-full water tumbler on the night stand. She picked the glass up and took it through to the kitchen area meaning to put it into the dishwasher, but the machine was empty. So she washed it up and left it to drain on the side. She had to resist the urge to wander round the apartment, picking up his belongings, and running her hands over the furniture, a sudden wave of nostalgia and longing sweeping over her. She fed Carlo and while the dog was eating, she piled the bag of dog food and a few of his chew toys into his basket, gathered the lot up and took it to the car. Then she went back for Carlo. She clipped his lead on, scooped up his water and food bowls and turned to leave.

'Come on boy, let's go,' she said. Carlo promptly sat down. 'Carlo, come!' she ordered. The lurcher only responded by hanging his head and regarding her balefully. 'Oh, don't do this to me! Please!' What the hell was she going to do? She couldn't drag him to the car, he was way too heavy. Equally, there was no way she was going to be able to pick him up. Out of the corner of her eye, she saw one of Ricky's jackets on a hook by the door. In what she thought was an inspired moment she slipped it on and held her arm out for the lurcher to sniff. 'Come, on,' she coaxed.

If a dog could have rolled his eyes, Carlo would have done so. Instead, he gave her a decidedly withering look, as if to say, *you can't fool me*, but to her relief he reluctantly stood up and plodded after her, disdainful protest in every step. His indignation was comical.

She wasn't finding Carlo quite so amusing when the lurcher spent half the night outside her bedroom whining. The only reason he only spent *half* the night like that was because she gave up in the small hours and let him into her room. He clambered onto her bed, curled up against her, and did the soulful sighing routine.

'Poor Carlo.' She scratched his rough nose sympathetically. 'Don't worry, he's not gone forever.'

Chapter Twenty-Four

You are an absolute sweetie! decided Pam, regarding the young girl standing in front of her. Her name was Freya, as she had just informed Pam, and she was one of the two young foreign students Pam would be hosting for the next few weeks. Both the teenagers wore ripped jeans, T-shirts and trainers, and distinctly nervous expressions. The rep from the language school had only just dropped them off and Pam had taken the girls through to the kitchen to welcome them with home-made cranberry cookies. Her new temporary lodgers always arrived on a Sunday, which suited Pam perfectly, giving her time to devote to getting them settled in and trying to make them feel at home as best she could. The freshly baked cookies were her way of trying to bypass the inevitable language barrier, but even so she knew not to expect more than a word or so out of her visitors on their first day. So Freya had taken her completely by surprise. Whilst the other girl, Sofia, had barely spoken a word, not even to thank her when she'd taken a cookie, Freya had taken a deep breath and carefully recited what was obviously a prepared introduction speech, in a Danish accent.

'Hello. I am Freya. I am fifteen years old. I live in Copenhagen with my mother and father and my two brothers. I am very happy to come to England. Thank you for letting me stay in your home.' She'd stopped and then beamed at Pam.

'You are very welcome.' Pam smiled at her warmly and, glancing over to include her other guest, added, 'You both are.' Sofia merely nodded.

'Come and see your rooms,' said Pam, heading for the door.

Silently, the two girls picked up their bags and followed her upstairs. She put Freya in Josh's old room, and Sofia in Luke's. The first day with new lodgers was always the hardest, Pam had discovered, both for her and for them. She was conscious of how daunting it must be to arrive in the home of a total stranger who didn't even speak a word of your language. Most of the youngsters barely managed to utter a word, apart from a few 'thank-yous' and 'yes pleases', so it wasn't surprising Pam had found Freya's effort so endearing.

Having shown them the wardrobes and chests of drawers they could use, and pointed out where the bathroom was, she left them to settle in, and went back down to start cooking supper – pizza, the staple diet of teenagers across the globe. Not sure of their tastes, she was preparing several small ones, including some veggie and vegan ones just in case.

Neither of the girls had come back downstairs so, once the food was ready, Pam called them down. A few minutes later, sitting in the dining room and happily tucking into pizza, Sofia was engrossed with her phone screen, but Freya's phone was nowhere in sight and, to Pam's surprise, the youngster started talking to her.

'Do you have children?' she asked Pam slowly.

Oh dear. Bad luck, Freya! What a question to choose to start with, thought Pam. As always, she answered simply and honestly and hoped the teenager wouldn't be too discomforted by her reply. 'Yes. I had two sons, Josh and Luke, but Josh died.'

A slight frown slid across Freya's young features, and she didn't respond immediately, as if she were checking in her own mind that she'd understood properly.

'That is very sad,' she said eventually.

'It was a few years ago,' Pam told her, smiling reassuringly.

'It is still very sad,' said Freya. 'My grandfather died. We all cried very much.'

Pam commiserated with her and then moved the subject to less emotional territory and asked Freya about school. Between them they managed to keep a simple conversation going all throughout supper. Once or twice, Pam tried to draw Sofia in by asking her a question, but the poor girl looked like a rabbit caught in the stare of a stoat, so Pam took pity on her and left her alone. As soon as they'd finished eating, Sofia fled to her bedroom, but Freya helped Pam carry the dishes through to the kitchen and then calmly started stacking the dishwasher.

'You don't have to do that,' Pam told her, mildly astonished.

'At home I help,' shrugged Freya and carried on.

'Well, it is very kind of you.'

Watching the girl efficiently loading the plates Pam wondered just how much more Freya was going to offer do to help, and how much she should let her, especially if Sofia didn't volunteer. Her thoughts were interrupted by the doorbell. She wasn't expecting anyone so, mildly irritated, she went to open the door.

'Dez! I wasn't expecting you. I thought you were in Birmingham for the weekend?'

'Yes. Just got back. I was just passing so I thought I'd drop in,' he said, walking in. 'Mmmm, something smells good! Any left?' He winked and then headed straight for the kitchen. Letting out a small, vexed sigh, Pam followed him.

'Oh, hello. Who are you?' said Dez, in a surprised tone, as he encountered Freya, who was finishing up at the dishwasher.

The youngster politely abandoned what she was doing and turned to face him. 'Hello. I am Freya.'

Half expecting the poor girl to launch into a re-run of her introductory speech, Pam interrupted. 'Freya is one my student lodgers,' she explained. 'I did tell you they were coming.'

'Oh, was that today?' He frowned, briefly. 'Sorry.' Then, turning to Pam's young lodger, he added cheerfully, 'Hello, Freya!'

Freya hovered uncomfortably but her eyes flicked to Pam's in a silent SOS. So, after thanking her for helping, Pam asked her if she'd like to join Sofia upstairs, and the girl gratefully fled. The leftover pizza slices were still on the side and since Dez could hardly miss them, Pam felt obliged to offer him some.

Handing him the plate, she said, 'I'm afraid you can't stay long. I have to look after my guests, get them settled in.'

'You go ahead, I won't get in the way,' he promised, mumbling with his mouth full, as he sat himself down at the kitchen table. 'I'll eat this and then keep a low profile in the living room.'

Pam bridled. *Was she going to have to spell it out to him?* 'I'm sorry, but it really isn't convenient for you to be here this evening.'

'Why's that?' he challenged. Wordlessly, Pam raised an eyebrow at him. 'Sorry, Pam. I'm not trying to be awkward, but it's a big house, and I presume they've got their own rooms. It's not like we're all going to have to cram onto one sofa in a tiny living room like we'd have to at my place!'

Keeping her tone mild, Pam replied, 'The students get full use of the whole house, Dez. That's part of the arrangement with the language school. I'm meant to spend their evenings with them, talking to them, making sure they're okay and helping them learn English.'

'What, every night?'

'Well, yes. But it's only this first evening that I don't want you to be here. Actually, the first few days,' she corrected herself. 'Although,' she added, now that she came to think of it, 'I'm not happy with the idea of you staying the night while I have young girls in the house.'

'Oh? Why not?' Dez's voice rose sharply, an edge to his tone, and the hand holding his pizza froze halfway to his mouth. 'What exactly are you implying?'

'Nothing!' exclaimed Pam defensively, feeling vaguely sick as she realised how badly what she'd just said could be misconstrued.

'Don't you trust me or something?' he demanded, going red in the face. 'D'you think I'm going to sneak into their rooms in the middle of the night and molest them?'

'No, of course not!' Pam felt her face flush. Obviously she hadn't meant to imply that Dez would behave in a predatory manner. 'I just... I just don't think it sets a good example...' she stammered. Catching the furious expression on his face, she cursed herself for handling things so badly. She wished she'd had a chance to clarify in her own mind why she wasn't comfortable with him staying over when she was *in loco parentis* for two young girls. In her defence, he'd totally caught her on the hop by arriving uninvited.

Throwing his pizza back onto the plate, he demanded peevishly, 'How long are they going to be here?'

'A month.'

'So basically our relationship is off for a month? Is that what you're saying?'

'No, of course not. You can still come here, and we can go to your place if we want to… make love.'

'It's not about the sex, Pam,' he snapped. 'I'm not that desperate. It's about putting them before me!'

He pushed back from the table, standing up so violently the chair toppled over onto the floor.

'I thought we had something. I thought you genuinely liked me. But if a couple of foreign kids mean more to you than I do, than *we* do, then…'

He stormed out of the kitchen, brushing roughly past Pam as he did so.

She rushed after him. 'You're being completely unreasonable!'

He whipped round to face her. 'You're the one being completely unreasonable. Ludicrously over-protective. They're not bloody children, for God's sake.'

'Keep your voice down!' she ordered, worried that his shouting would upset the girls. 'And actually, they *are* children. They're only fifteen.'

He didn't seem to have an answer to that so, still glaring at her thunderously, he left, slamming the front door so savagely the hall windows rattled.

Pam sank back against the door, stunned by the sudden escalation of a perfectly normal situation into a frightening, major row. *What the hell just happened, and how?* She went back to the kitchen and picked up the chair, but as she did so, she realised her hands were trembling. A few seconds later, her whole body was shaking in delayed shock. She leant on the work surface to steady herself, trying to calm herself sufficiently to go upstairs and check that Freya and Sofia were all right. They must have heard the commotion, and she just hoped to God they hadn't understood what Dez had actually said. A few moments later, once she'd recovered her composure, she went upstairs and found both girls sitting together on the bed in Luke's room. They looked at her, silent and wide-eyed when she opened the door.

'I'm sorry about that shouting,' she started. 'My… friend got angry about something. Please don't worry. It won't happen again.'

She kept her sentences short and simple, in the hope that both of them would be able to understand and, since they both looked relieved, she assumed they had.

Then Freya brought a lump to Pam's throat when, with a look of genuine concern in her young blue eyes, she asked, 'Are you all right?'

Pam wanted to scoop her up and hug her.

Later, last thing that night when she was on her way up to bed, Pam thought she heard muffled crying coming from Josh's room so, knocking lightly, she popped her head round the door. Freya's tearstained face turned to look at her. The girl lay curled in a foetal position, her eyes red-rimmed and sore, and Pam guessed she'd been crying for some time with her face buried in the pillow, to muffle her sobs. Involuntarily, Pam's mind flashed back five years, to seeing Charley hunched in the same position, on the same bed, in raw agony of mourning for Josh.

Traumatised and devastated, her daughter-in-law had bolted to Pam's where she'd gone to ground in Josh's old bedroom like a wounded animal in its cave, instinctively knowing that Pam, and only Pam, could understand her aching loss. Charley's own parents, particularly her mother, had found it hard to accept the rejection of the love and care they wanted to give their daughter in her bereavement, and her mother had resented Pam's role in

Charley's life ever since. The flashback of the grieving Charley brought a sudden, unexpected wave of anguish coursing into Pam, and she had to remind herself that Freya wasn't a young widow drowning in harrowing loss, but a teenager who was simply homesick.

'Oh, sweetheart.' Pam sat down next to her on the bed. 'Is this your first time away from home?'

Freya gulped and nodded, then she wiped her nose on the cuff of her PJs, as if she was ashamed of having been caught crying.

Gently, Pam pushed a strand of damp hair off the young girl's forehead. 'It's okay to be sad,' she told her. 'It hurts when we miss the people we love.' Her kindness instantly brought on fresh floods of tears from Freya. 'I'll get some tissues,' said Pam, and went off to fetch the loo roll.

When she got back, Freya had sat up and was taking a few juddering breaths, trying to calm herself. Pam handed her a damp flannel to wipe her face, and the roll of tissue to blow her nose, then she made Freya promise to come and find her if she woke upset in the night.

'Don't lie here all alone and sad.'

'You are kind,' Freya told her. 'You are like my grandmother,' she added, leaning over and giving Pam a hug.

–

Lying in bed later that night, the row with Dez circled round in Pam's head restlessly like a wasp caught in a bottle trap. Perhaps she *was* being unreasonable? After all, the girls were going to be with her for several weeks so she couldn't expect him not to resent her putting their sex life on hold for the entire duration of their stay. She groaned inwardly, recalling how badly she'd bungled it and, even worse, how she'd implied she couldn't trust him around young girls. Which was an appalling suggestion. *Seriously? Could you have messed this up more if you'd tried?* No wonder he'd taken offence and flown off the handle. She'd have to call him and apologise, although the prospect made her wary, fearful that he might try to exploit her guilty conscience to make her change her mind. Finally, she gave up on sleep, sat up, flicked on the light and picked up her book, infinitely preferring to escape to the sanctuary of someone else's life and immerse herself in their problems and dilemmas, rather than have to think about her own.

Chapter Twenty-Five

Charley had decided to take Carlo to work during the day as Ricky did, rather than leaving him alone in her flat. Every morning, as they neared the shop, the poor dog started straining on the leash, trying to pull her down to the bike shop, obviously hoping to find his beloved Ricky.

'He's not there, lovely,' Charley told him, but every day she duly walked him down to the bike shop so the dog could see for himself. They both peered through the window and, to Charley, the shop seemed dead and lifeless without its owner's presence. The daily ritual usually put a dampener on the morning and they were both miserable when they returned to her shop to open up, but for the rest of the day the lurcher either sat or lay in the window on Ricky-watch.

'Did he do that when Ricky and I were in Italy?' Charley had asked Pam.

'Yup!' Then, perhaps noticing that Charley looked genuinely concerned, Pam added, 'It's pure melodrama, trust me!'

It turned out having a raffish-looking lurcher in the window was a fantastic marketing ploy since a lot of customers drifted in wanting to pet the dog, and then most of them felt compelled to buy a 'little something' on their way out, presumably because they'd have felt it rude not to.

'We might have to get him on permanent loan,' observed Charley.

-

Throughout the week several Cargo shopkeepers dropped by to ask about Ricky which, thought Charley, was a touching testament to how well-liked he was. She promised to keep them posted. After work, she spent every evening battling with the accounts, determined to figure out how, when, or even if, she could give Tara a share of the profits.

Initially, she wasn't really sure where to start – unsure, for example, whether to treat the gift bag side-line separately, and how to log the products she had to give away to promote that part of the business. Tara might have an MBA but Charley had never had any business training and although she'd downloaded an accounts spreadsheet template, she felt painfully as if she were re-inventing the wheel. It was sorely tempting to call Nisha and ask her advice, but she couldn't keep asking her friends for favours; she'd taken that hint from her last phone call with Nisha, if nothing else. Her progress was painfully slow, but she doggedly ploughed on, usually dropping into bed just after midnight when she literally couldn't think straight. While Charley spent her evenings stoically slogging through Excel sheets, Carlo spent them missing Ricky. He moped and pined, and when Charley fed him he only ate a token amount, and she got the distinct impression he was only doing that to be polite. He took to forlornly following Charley around like a shadow, even when she went to the loo. She hadn't realised how disconcerting it was trying to pee while a huge pair of brown eyes gazed at you intently. Nor had she realised how unsettling it would be just having him around, a constant reminder of Ricky. She told herself she wasn't actually missing Ricky, it was just that she obviously associated him with Carlo. Her mind, however, kept filling with memories of her and Ricky together. The way he'd discreetly touch her elbow or the small of her back when they were out together in public, his easy smile... and she dwelt on their idyllic Sunday mornings, making love and then taking Carlo for a free run on the Downs, and having brunch out afterwards. Sundays without him seemed... empty.

Suddenly craving scrambled eggs, she instantly abandoned the accounts in favour of making herself some. Pushing the eggy mix round the frying pan, she was reminded of Ricky cooking supper for them both in his flat, and how he deftly cracked eggs one-handed when he made carbonara.

Josh had done barely any of the cooking during their marriage. She could probably count on the fingers of one hand the number of times Josh had taken on the responsibility of cooking an entire meal. He would always help peel the spuds, if she asked him to, and he happily carved the meat, but cooking just wasn't his thing. Ricky had made point of finding out what Charley liked eating, and had planned their meals around her favourite foods, adjusting his cooking to meet her taste, like not putting too much garlic in the prawn linguine, she remembered, smiling to herself.

The eggs were nearly done, so she buttered the toast and then slid the eggs on top. Shoving her laptop clear, she sat at the table to eat, idly musing on how very different Josh and Ricky were from each other. Josh had lived with an almost permanent broad grin on his face, laughing out loud at anything daft and silly, sometimes at rather than with people if she were honest, whereas Ricky's sense of humour was dryer and he was more likely to share a wry smile than a burst of laughter when something amused him. He was, she realised with surprise, kinder than Josh, more considerate. She thought about the time she'd stumbled into the gutter and Ricky had stopped and got off his bike to help her. If that had been Josh, he would have helped her too, but he would probably have found it funny and told her how comical she'd looked. Even now she could remember the look of concern in Ricky's eyes, and there hadn't been a trace of amusement in them. They were so different in other ways, too. Ricky was tidy, his flat immaculate, while Josh preferred a more shambolic living style – which, in some ways, was more relaxing of course, although she couldn't imagine having to scoop up Ricky's discarded boxers and socks to put them in the wash the way she'd had to with Josh. And if Ricky were here now, she mused, he'd have insisted on making her scrambled eggs so that she could have carried on with her accounts, whereas Josh... actually, could Josh even make scrambled eggs? She doubted it. She'd certainly never seen him try. Although, in his defence, she reminded herself, he made a mean cheese and ham toastie.

A pang of guilt brought her up short, and she reproached herself for having been disloyal to Josh by comparing him with Ricky. Then she realised she seemed to have made a mental shift. Whereas previously she had compared Ricky to Josh, now the comparison was reversed; she was comparing Josh to Ricky. The understanding threw her. It was as if her world view had skewed and shifted so that Josh had slipped from his position at the heart of everything, and Ricky had somehow slid into his place. Having finished her eggs, she rinsed the plate and put it in the dishwasher and then forced herself back to do battle with her accounts, wilfully forcing the disquieting revelation from her mind.

–

Early on the Thursday evening, Ricky texted her to say her that his grandmother was worse and had been taken into intensive care.

She sat for a few moments, carefully considering how to respond. Clearly it would be inappropriate, and glib, to say *I hope she gets better soon* since, sadly, there was every likelihood the elderly lady would not. The phrase *I'm so sorry* also seemed unsuitable. They were the words written in the sympathy cards she'd received when Josh died, and would imply Ricky's grandmother was already dead, or written off and disregarded. It's odd, reflected Charley, how words that are meant to comfort can wound when used carelessly. Eventually she typed, *I am sorry to hear that. Please let her know I am thinking of her, if you can, and give my best wishes to your family*, and sent it.

Then, for no good reason at all, Charley felt herself well up, her throat tightening, her face contorting with grief. *Stop it!* she ordered herself, harshly. *This isn't your loss. You hardly know his family*. But she knew how close they were, and could imagine how they would be worrying and bracing themselves, fearing the worst. She hoped Ricky was okay. Picturing him and all of his family gathered round the large table in the sun-filled kitchen, she felt unexpectedly grateful that she had been to his family home and had met them all, enabling her to clearly visualise him there, comforting his mother, rallying round everyone, making coffee or putting a meal on the table, distracting himself with activity. Sensing her unhappiness, Carlo ambled over and rested his rough head on her leg.

'Poor Ricky,' she sighed, stroking the lurcher's head.

At supper time she put Carlo's food down for him, but he turned his nose up and left it. Regarding the unappetising, dry chunks of kibble she couldn't blame him. Concerned by how little he was eating, she nipped out to the local supermarket to get something that might tempt him, returning with a sachet of Gourmet Chicken and Duck for Adult Dogs. Judging by the picture it looked more like a posh pâté than dog food. It certainly cost enough.

He sniffed at it, then completely ignored it, so she put a handful of his kibble in a tub on the floor as well, but he wasn't tempted by that either. Kneeling down on the floor, she tried to encourage him, picking up the food in her fingers and offering it to him like a treat. He merely looked away so she eventually gave up and sat cross-legged on the floor next to him. Resting his nose on his paws, he let out a huge, heartbreakingly sad sigh.

'I know,' she sympathised. 'I miss him too.'

–

It was almost quarter to nine when Charley, with Carlo plodding along beside her on a lead, arrived at the shop the following morning, far later than usual. To her surprise – actually, her *amazement* – for the first time ever, Tara was there before her.

'And what time d'you call this?' Tara tapped an imaginary watch with mock severity.

'I had to walk Carlo!' Charley defended herself good-humouredly and unlocked the door. Since the lurcher needed a good walk before work, she'd decided to cut herself some slack, just while Ricky was away, and come in later to open up.

'I can't expect him to spend all day indoors if he hasn't had the chance to… empty himself,' she said delicately. 'And from both tanks, as it were.'

Tara groaned theatrically. 'Spare me the details,' she grimaced, 'And remind me never to get a dog!'

'Why are you in so early?' Charley asked her, flicking on the lights. 'Not that I'm complaining.'

'That,' said Tara, going to switch on the till and the credit card reader, 'is because I've had a brilliant idea. Let's do a massive promo event. You know, like we did when we opened.'

Charley's heart sank to her espadrilles. When she'd first set up the shop, Nisha, with her marketing hat firmly crammed on her head, had tried to persuade her into staging an opening launch. Charley had steadfastly refused, preferring to open the store when she was ready, and start trading slowly and let it build. However the fates had conspired to outmanoeuvre her. Once a year, Charley ran a fundraiser, a Prosecco Night, in memory of Tara's mum. Last year, just two weeks before the event, the venue they had originally booked had been forced to cancel. In a moment of insanity, which she had regretted for every single minute of the following fourteen days, Charley had tentatively proposed hosting the fundraiser in the shop – the only snag being that the shop hadn't even opened yet. Nisha had leapt on the idea, immediately deciding that Charley should combine the fundraiser with a grand shop opening, persuasively arguing that it would look unprofessional not to. So Charley had caved. They'd distrib-uted hundreds of leaflets offering a glass of Prosecco to anyone who spent more than a tenner, and the shop was mobbed. It had been an enormous success but equally, an enormous amount of work. Right now, Charley had so much on her plate with the shop, the gift bags, dog-sitting, not to mention the bloody accounts and a development plan, that the thought of taking on anything else literally made her want to weep. Tara, on the other hand, was enthusiastically building promotional castles in the sky.

'Angie can do some special pieces of artwork and sign them so we can charge a premium, Pam can bake those fabulous Prosecco and white chocolate cupcakes she made last time, and we can have a bit of a sale and get rid of stock that isn't shifting. There's boxes up there,' she indicated the top of the dresser unit, 'crammed with stuff we're never going to sell full price. Let's mark it down, flog it off, and re-stock with more popular lines.' Warming still further to her theme she carried on, 'If we do it before the end of September, while the weather's still mild, we can spill out onto tables outside and make it even bigger than last time! Genius, or what?'

Bloody hell Tara, you have absolutely no idea how much super-human effort I'm already putting in just to get through each day, do you? Pulling her best I-don't-want-to-be-a-spoilsport face Charley said, 'It's a good idea Tara, but I'm really sorry, I'm fire-fighting as it is. I just can't take on anything else. Maybe we could do it next year?'

'I sodding *knew* you'd say that!' exploded Tara. Then she floored Charley by saying, 'Well, Nisha thinks it's a good idea.'

'You went behind my back and talked to Nisha?' Charley didn't even try to keep the fury off her face.

'Yes. Because I knew you'd wouldn't be up for it. And anyhow, I didn't "go behind your back" as you so dramatically put it. I only gave her a call. And she's all for it. She's happy to get the Prosecco, like last time, and take care of all the marketing and social media et cetera…'

Charley was dangerously close to spontaneous combustion. 'You had no right to do that without asking me first.'

Tara seemed genuinely taken aback. 'I was only floating an idea with her.'

'An idea that involves *my* shop.'

'Yes, but I work here too. I'm your business partner,' Tara reminded Charley pointedly.

Charley was speechless. Which was probably just as well, otherwise she would have undoubtedly said some things she would have deeply regretted. A whole lot of things, actually. Fortunately, for both of them, some customers came into the shop at that moment, so they had to park their argument.

When they could resume it, Tara offered to run the event herself. 'I can do it with Nisha, and Pam if she's free. You don't even have to turn up.'

'Tara, I can't possibly *not* turn up for an event held in my own shop. How unprofessional would that look?'

Tara eyeballed her for a moment, but Charley didn't flinch. 'So that's a "No" to the promo event, then, is it?'

'Yes,' replied Charley, tight-lipped.

It was a long, uncomfortable morning and Charley was grateful when it was over. She was still seething when Pam got in, and the poor woman got the full onslaught of Charley's fury almost before she'd even taken her jacket off. Charley slammed round the shop, furiously tidying stacks of chocolates bars, needlessly rearranging bottles of bubble bath and plumping Prosecco-themed cushions with far more vigour than was necessary.

'She has no idea how much I already have to do, just to keep up. And how dare she call Nisha without talking to me first? How dare she!'

'Yes. I think that *is* overstepping the mark,' said the older woman guardedly.

'By about a mile!'

'Darling, you don't have to run a promotional event just because Tara and Nisha think it's a good idea,' pointed out Pam evenly.

'Well, do *you* think it's a good idea?'

Pam pondered for a moment then replied, 'Well, if it's as successful as the launch then it'd be great, obviously. And I'll happily make a mountain of cupcakes and help out on the night if you want me to, but you shouldn't take it on if you can't manage it. You can only do so much.'

'Precisely!' Charley tactically, if dishonestly, refrained from admitting that Tara had offered to run the event without her.

'And I cannot tell you the number of times I've told Tara how much I'm struggling to cope with everything as it is. But, you know Tara, she never lets reality get in the way of what she wants to do.'

'Yes. She can be a little...'

'Bossy? Pushy? Opinionated?'

'Assertive,' finished the older woman, with commendable tact.

'And then she has the barefaced cheek to defend herself on the grounds that she's my "business partner",' said Charley, adding air quotes and wilfully stoking her indignation.

Pam, objective as ever, paused before saying, 'Well, technically she is.'

'Technically,' echoed Charley. 'But then so are you.'

'Yes, I am,' replied Pam levelly, which brought Charley up short, rather belatedly grasping that she wasn't being exactly professional slagging off Tara to Pam. In her old job she wouldn't have dreamt of criticising one colleague to another. The only difference here was that Tara was her mate and Pam was her mother-in-law, which in many ways, she realised, made it worse. *Bloody hell!* Why did working with friends and relatives make things so much more complicated?

'I'm sorry. I shouldn't dump on you like this. It puts you in a difficult position with Tara,' she said. Then another thought struck her and she added, 'And I'd hate you to think I talked to Tara about you like this.'

'So would I!' replied Pam.

The afternoon passed quietly, punctuated by a few customers coming in and some heavy sighs from Carlo, who still sat glued to the window, looking for his adored Ricky. The lurcher was still off his food and pining listlessly. Not wanting to alarm Ricky by calling him for advice, Charley turned to Pam.

'When Ricky and I were in Tuscany, did Carlo eat properly?'

'Yes. He wolfed his meals down, and even brought his empty bowl to me in the hope that I'd feed him twice!'

Which wasn't the reassurance Charley was hoping for.

'If he's not eating, maybe he's missing Ricky more than he did last time?' ventured Pam.

'Why would he do that?'

Her mother-in-law shrugged, 'Perhaps he's picking up on how much you're missing Ricky.'

'I am not missing Ricky,' denied Charley, her cheeks flushing as the weight of that lie slid home.

Later, at home, Charley put a quick call in to Nisha. And this time she didn't bother to check if it was a good time to call. Nor did she ask her advice.

'Nisha, about Tara's idea for a promo event. I'm sorry but I've decided against it.'

'Why? You'll make a lot of money, and it'll be great publicity.'

Oh, don't you start on me as well. 'I'm sure it will, but I just don't have the time to organise it,' she finished, hoping that would be the end of it.

'Get Tara to run it.'

Charley forced herself to take a deep, calming breath, while her mind raced to find a response that wouldn't drag her into any further discussion. 'Perhaps I will, but another time,' she replied firmly.

After she'd rung off, she checked her messages to see if there was one from Ricky which she might somehow have not heard pinging in, or any missed calls from him, and then she was disappointed when there weren't. Briefly it crossed her mind to text him, to ask him how his grandmother was, then she hated herself for sinking so low as to even consider using that as a ruse, since he would undoubtedly have texted her if there was any news. She'd just have to sit tight and wait for him to contact her. Which wasn't a problem, she reminded herself.

Chapter Twenty-Six

The following morning was a Saturday so Charley got up extra early to give herself time to walk Carlo and arrive at the shop in good time to set up for the day. Thoroughly bored of plodding round the streets, she decided to take him for a quick run on the Downs, reckoning he'd get twice as much exercise in half the time. Despite the painfully early hour, a good many joggers and dog-walkers were already out, some combining the two and running with a dog lead tied round their waists. It all looked horrendously keen to Charley.

'You can run, but I'm sticking with walking,' she informed the lurcher. Unclipping his lead she let him go, expecting him to lope around her in wide circles as he usually did when Ricky was there. Carlo had a different idea. He shot off, in a straight line, streaking across the grass and heading back towards the city. *Bloody hell!*

'Carlo! *Carlo!*' she yelled, but the dog ignored her, wilfully deaf to her increasingly desperate bawling. *Bloody, bloody, hell!* She raced off after him, still bellowing his name. Heads turned and a few people tried to grab Carlo as he passed them, but they had no chance of catching him. To Charley's horror, the dog was almost at the road and she could see cars coming in both directions.

'*Carlo!*' she screamed. There was a cacophony of squealing tyres as multiple cars slammed on the brakes. Miraculously, the lurcher emerged on the other side of the road, unscathed, and still racing onwards. Raising her hands in apology and gratitude to the drivers for not killing Ricky's precious hound, she dodged between the cars, in hot pursuit. Ten minutes later, she was out of breath and the dog was out of sight. *Bloody, bloody, bloody hell!* What on earth was she going to do? She couldn't even think clearly, her mind too bombarded with sickening images of Carlo getting hit by a car or a bus. Snatching her phone from her back pocket, she called Angie.

She garbled a panic-fuelled, incoherent account of the situation ending with a plaintive, 'I don't know what to do!'

'Go back to the car, drive around looking for him. You'll cover more ground that way,' Angie advised rationally. 'Let me sort out the kids and then I'll come and help.'

Still out of breath, Charley walk-ran back to the car and started cruising round the streets nearest the Downs. She felt physically sick. If anything happened to Carlo she'd never forgive herself. And neither would Ricky. Should she call him and let him know? What good would that do? It wouldn't achieve anything except worry him. Twenty minutes later, she'd driven around about half of the streets in Clifton and the Whiteladies Road area abutting the Downs but there was still no sign of the dog. Her phone rang and she hurriedly pulled over and grabbed it, thinking it would be Angie.

'Charley, darling, it's Pam.' Charley had been so convinced it would be Angie it took her a moment to focus on what her mother-in-law was saying. 'I'm so sorry to do this to you at the last minute but I'm not going to be able to get into the shop today. Freya, one of my young lodgers, isn't at all well. She's running a very high temperature and I just can't leave her.'

In her panic about losing Carlo, Charley had forgotten all about opening the shop. Whilst she wanted to reassure Pam and tell her not to worry about getting in to work, she was desperate to get her off the line in case Angie tried to ring her.

'It's not a problem, Pam. Don't worry, honestly. I can manage,' she said abruptly.

'I'm so sorry…' Pam persisted.

'No. It's fine.' Then, realising her brisk tone might imply she was annoyed, she added, 'Sorry Pam, I'm just in the middle of something. But thanks for letting me know. And I hope she's okay.'

She ended the call and glanced at the time on the screen. Nearly eight thirty. There was no way she could get in to open up in time; she didn't even have the keys with her. They were in her handbag back at her flat. And besides, she had to find Carlo. She bit her lip and thought about her options – or rather, her only option. She'd have to call Tara. It wasn't a pleasing prospect, given how frosty things were between them just now, plus Tara never worked weekends; her time with Monnie was sacrosanct. Charley was going to have to beg. She'd also have to make a grovelling apology and maybe even cave in on the promo event if necessary. Biting the bullet, she dialled her number. She barely had time to finish explaining her predicament before Tara interrupted her.

'Does Pam have a key to the shop?'

'Yes.'

'I'll pick it up and go straight in. Should just about make it by nine.'

'Tara, you're a star—' started Charley, her gratitude only just outweighing her amazement.

'Have you called the police?' Tara cut in.

'No, why? They're not going to look for a missing dog.'

'No. But if he causes an accident, they'll know who to call. You don't want them calling Ricky, do you?'

Charley's mouth went dry. 'How will they know to call Ricky?'

'Carlo will be chipped and Ricky's number is probably on his collar tag.'

Charley gulped at the idea of Ricky getting a call from the police about his dog.

'And Charley, call 101 not 999!' was Tara's parting advice before ringing off.

You might be bossy, pushy and opinionated, but you're also a bloody good mate and brilliant in a crisis. She rang 101, navigated the automated menu, and then hung on, waiting for her call to move up the queue and be answered. She waited ten minutes, all the while imagining Carlo involved in a dire accident, until she simply couldn't cope with the sheer frustration and impotence of sitting there not actually doing anything to find him. She put the phone on speaker, plonked it on the passenger seat and carried on driving round looking for Carlo, trying to crush the rising panic inside her. A few minutes later, Angie called, so she gave up on the police to take the call. Angie had scoured the whole of the Redland district on the other side of Whiteladies Road but hadn't seen hide nor hair of Carlo. They divided the inner city up between them and spent the next hour or so criss-crossing the streets, fruitlessly searching for him. Eventually, admitting defeat, Charley rang Angie to call off the hunt.

'Do you think he's found his way back to the bike shop?' Angie didn't sound at all optimistic.

'Tara would have called if he had. Someone would have seen him and let her know, surely.'

'What about Ricky's flat?'

'I don't think he'd know the way back, and it's miles.'

Nevertheless, they both drove down to Ricky's place in Bedminster, where they found an exhausted Carlo, lying flat out on the doorstep. Charley sank to her knees in relief, flung her arms round the dog and hauled him into an ungainly hairy hug. Carlo thumped his tail but still looked at her sorrowfully.

'He's not here, boy,' she told him sadly.

–

It was almost lunchtime by the time Charley got into the shop, full of gratitude towards Tara, to the point where she was even beginning to feel guilty about scotching her proposal for the promo event. Whatever her mate's flaws, Tara was big-hearted and supportive, and Charley knew the idea would have been driven by the best motives. Maybe she'd been too up herself? Too angered by Tara going behind her back to Nisha. Why not let Tara run the event? The woman was a human dynamo and it was only a one-off marketing venture, for goodness' sake. Charley could probably pretty much leave it to her, although she drew the line at not turning up.

'I owe you big time,' said Charley arriving at the shop, with Carlo firmly on his leash, and spontaneously giving Tara a hug. 'Seriously, thank you so much.'

'Where was the little sod?' asked Tara, nodding at Carlo who'd settled at his watch post in the window.

'He'd taken himself to Ricky's.'

Tara smacked her forehead in exasperation. 'Why didn't we think of that to start with!'

'I know,' said Charley, shaking her head at her own stupidity.

'Anyhow. No harm done. He's safe, thank God, and you don't even have to 'fess up to Ricky.'

'Thank God,' echoed Charley.

She was fully expecting Tara to shoot off sharpish to spend the rest of the day with Monnie, but Tara astounded her for the second time in one morning by suggesting she fetch them both some lunch from the deli.

'Baz is expecting to look after her all day, so I may as well let him. Anyhow, being in here was actually way more fun than watching Monnie ride round and round at pony club.'

Business was brisk and they had to grab snatches of lunch between customers so it wasn't until halfway through the afternoon that there was a chance to catch up. Charley was still toying with how to broach the subject of the promotional event without losing face, while Tara gave her a rundown of her morning's activities.

'The wine bar called wanting a twenty-five more party bags.'

'Oh, fantastic!'

'I told them there was now a minimum order of a hundred bags, unless they wanted to pay a delivery fee.'

You did what? Indignation surged up inside Charley, until Tara took the wind out of its sails by saying, 'They were fine with it. So if you let me know which products you put in theirs I'll order everything.'

'Oh, right,' said Charley flatly, not just outmanoeuvred by Tara, but totally deflated.

Especially when Tara continued, 'The thing is, it makes good business sense. If the venues have bought a hundred bags then it's in their interests to shift them. They won't want them hanging round gathering dust, all of which is great marketing for the shop, of course. Although it would be even better if you actually had the shop's name on the bags, not just the "Charley's" logo.' The implied criticism hit home and Charley struggled not to leap to her own defence. 'There's no reason we can't impose a minimum order with everyone,' Tara finished blithely.

'The pubs won't order a hundred bags at a time,' Charley told her, shaking her head. Thinking about the pub she'd worked in before she set up the shop, she explained, 'They won't have the space to store them, for a start.'

'Do you know that for a fact or are you speculating?'

'Well no, but—'

'Well, we'll just have to see, won't we?' replied Tara, glibly dismissing both Charley's objection and her professional insight. 'I'm telling you, Charley, this is the way forward with the party bags. The *only* way forward,' she persisted, putting her hand up to silence Charley's protest. 'It's all about economies of scale. It's basic business sense. If the pubs don't want the minimum order, we drop them.'

'How can losing customers be good for business?' challenged Charley.

Tara let out a sigh, which Charley took personally, before she explained rapidly, but in a painstaking tone, 'Look, profit is total sales minus total costs, right? The total costs are the variable costs plus fixed costs. The variable costs are what we put in the bag, and the fixed costs are the cost of delivery – regardless of how many bags you deliver. So to make a profit, total contribution has to exceed total costs. So, factoring in...'

Charley zoned out. She'd tried to follow Tara but was defeated by what seemed to her to be the deliberate opaqueness of her business-speak. She only refocussed when Tara asked her a direct question.

'Would you deliver one bag?'

'No, of course not.'

'Precisely. You have to know how many bags you need to deliver to make it profitable. So, unless you know that figure…?' Tara raised a challenging eyebrow. Charley gave her brief shake of her head. 'Then I'm saying let's go for one hundred. Okay?'

'Fine,' said Charley, completely defeated, knowing she couldn't even begin to muster an argument to counter Tara's decision.

'You know, this is a brilliant little shop, Charley. I'm absolutely convinced that if we just roll up our sleeves and focus on improving the profit margins we can make a real go of it!' Which seemed to Charley to be an insufferably pompous insult.

Working with Tara was like being on a rollercoaster. One minute she felt she was getting a handle on working with her and that everything would be fine, and the next minute Tara did something that made her want to retreat to a darkened room and resort to primal screaming.

Later, brooding on their exchange, Charley felt as if she'd somehow lost an important battle, outgunned and outclassed by a more knowledgeable opponent. Worryingly, she hadn't really understood what Tara was saying, and the bottom line was that the conclusion still didn't make sense to her. How could it be good business practice to deliberately lose customers? She rebuked herself for harbouring the probably unfair suspicion that Tara had made her explanation deliberately complicated. Nevertheless, it had left her feeling stupid, out of her depth as if she were playing a game whose rules she didn't fully understand.

Chapter Twenty-Seven

The following morning Charley decided to call Ricky and 'fess up, despite her mates' wiser counsels.

'What the eye doesn't see the heart doesn't grieve over,' was Tara's opinion.

Angie felt Charley should wait and tell Ricky when he returned. 'Put yourself in his place. Would you want to know? He'll only worry it might happen again.'

'It won't!' Charley had retorted. 'I can promise you that.' Although even to her ears a promise from Carlo himself would have probably sounded more convincing.

In the end she'd decided to own up, partly because deceiving him, even by omission, made her feel uncomfortable, and partly because, selfishly, she wanted the closure of being forgiven. But mostly, had she been honest enough to admit it to herself, it was because she was craving to hear his voice. So, checking the time difference between the UK and Italy, she called him just after breakfast. He picked up almost immediately.

'Hi.'

That was all he said. Just one word, and she was overcome by a physical longing to be with him. She could see him in her mind's eye, his dark hair flopping onto his forehead, his trademark easy smile wrinkling the corners of his eyes, and she could almost smell his cologne, mingling as it always did with the scent of freshly laundered linen from his shirt.

'Hi,' she echoed.

'Is everything okay?' he asked, clearly wondering why she'd called him so early on a Sunday morning. 'What's happened?'

She had just been about to ask him how his grandmother was, but the anxiety in his voice led her to reassure him instead.

'Yes, of course,' she replied hurriedly which, whilst it wasn't the whole truth, wasn't a full-blown lie. 'Everything's fine. Well, it is now...' she added, more honestly, and went on to tell him about losing Carlo. 'It's my fault,' she finished, 'I shouldn't have let him off the lead.'

'It's not your fault, Charley, it's mine. I should have thought to warn you not to, but it didn't occur to me he'd run off. He's never done it before. You must have been worried sick.'

God, how are you so lovely? I tell you I nearly got your bloody dog run over and all you can think about is how tough it was for me.

'Well, yes, I was worried, but only because I was terrified he'd be hit by a car and I knew how devastated you'd be. Me too,' she finished truthfully.

'But he wasn't, Charley. It happened, but he's fine, so don't beat yourself up.'

'Thank you,' she said quietly. Changing her tone she said jokily, 'Of course he's missing you dreadfully. He does a lot of pathetic sighing and mournful gazing out of the window at the shop waiting for you to return. Honestly, he's so melodramatic!' Then she continued more soberly, 'He's not really eating properly...'

'He's probably sulking. He'll eat if he gets really hungry. If you're worried you could try feeding him at my place. That's if it's not too much of a hassle,' he finished hastily.

'No, not at all. It's a good idea. I will.' Charley left a beat or two before going on to ask Ricky about his grandmother.

'The doctors tell us she's still stable, but she's slowly worsening. They don't think she has long now.'

Charley's heart went out to him. 'That must be so hard for everyone.'

'She's sedated, so I'm not sure how much she realises what's going on. It's my mother's who's struggling.' She could hear the weariness in his voice. 'She's with her day and night and doesn't want to leave her.'

Charley was reminded of Tara's ordeal, how she had struggled to get through her mum's last days. It had been traumatic and devastating and towards the end, as Kim's gruelling battle with cancer drew to a close, Tara had just wanted it to be over. For herself as much as for her mum. She remembered how ashamed Tara had felt even admitting that, even to Charley. One thing bereavement had taught Charley was not to beat around the bush when it came to talking about death, not to tiptoe around, hiding behind euphemisms, too frightened to call it by its name.

'This is a dreadful time for you and your family, Ricky,' she said gently. 'Waiting for someone to die is gruelling. It's probably harder for those left behind than it is for the dying. And although it might make you feel guilty to admit it, it will be a relief for everyone when she dies, not just for your grandmother. And it's not wrong, or selfish to want the waiting to be over.'

There was silence down the phone. Charley hoped to God she hadn't offended him by speaking so bluntly, and that he didn't think her insensitive or uncaring. It was so difficult when she couldn't see his face, couldn't see the impact her words were having on him. After a while she prompted him.

'Are you still there?'

'Yes.'

'Are you okay?'

'Yes.' Then there was a beat before he said, 'I'm fine. And thank you, Charley.'

'You know where I am if you need to talk. Anytime. And I mean that.'

'Yes, thank you,' he repeated.

'Give my best wishes to your family. Tell them I'm thinking of them.'

She put her phone down on the kitchen work surface feeling bereft, and wishing she could be there for him and his family. In her experience, only the bereaved can really comfort the bereaved. The cavernous, aching void of loss is simply beyond imagining for the uninitiated. More than anything, she wanted to be with him.

Carlo's breakfast lay, mostly uneaten, in his bowl at her feet, while Carlo himself lounged on the floor nearby, morose and moping. Making a snap decision, she picked up the dog's bowl and food bag and stuffed them into a plastic carrier. Going into her bedroom, she packed her overnight rucksack with everything she'd need for work on Monday. Then she slung it over her shoulder, clipped Carlo's lead on him, gathered up the dog's basket and his food and took them both round to Ricky's. Letting herself in, she halted momentarily in the hallway to take in the essence of Ricky that seemed to hang in the air. It wasn't just the faint smell of him, it was more as if it were the imprint of his existence. Ricky's presence haunted his flat in much the same way the ghost of Josh, even five years after he'd died, still hung in the air at hers.

Being back in Ricky's flat had an immediate effect on Carlo. As soon as she put his food bowl on the floor he shoved his nose into it and, quite literally, wolfed his breakfast down. After which, with an air of self-importance that amused Charley, the lurcher did a quick tour of the flat. She watched him, unsure if he was looking for Ricky, or just checking the place over. He scratched lightly on the back door, asking to be let out, and did a swift circuit of the garden before trotting back in happily, tail up, ears up, big daft grin on his face. Then, his security duties apparently completed, he leapt onto the sofa, and curled up contentedly.

'Happy now?' she asked him. He regarded her from under his shaggy eyebrows and whacked his tail on the sofa cushion. 'And now you're just gloating,' she told him.

–

She took her overnight bag through to the bedroom and was about to dump it down on the duvet when it struck her that it might be taking a liberty assuming she could sleep in his bed. Perhaps she should borrow the quilt and bunk down on the sofa instead? She hesitated, trying to imagine what Ricky's response would be if she asked him if it would be okay, then she smiled as a clear image of him floated into her mind telling her not to be so ridiculous. Of course he wouldn't mind.

–

The rest of the day slipped into a typical Charley-and-Ricky kind of Sunday, albeit without Ricky. Keeping the hound on his lead, she took them both for a long walk around the Downs, and then she went to her and Ricky's favourite café for brunch, where Carlo stretched out contentedly under the table while she ate scrambled eggs on brown. Then the two of them spent the afternoon lounging on the sofa back at Ricky's flat. Charley knew she should be catching up on the accounts but she whiled away the afternoon scrolling through photos of Ricky on her phone and then watching a rom-com while Carlo snoozed and snored. She felt sublimely content. Which was odd, because the last time she'd been in Ricky's flat, only a few days ago to collect Carlo's kit and caboodle, she'd felt almost like a trespasser, whereas now she felt totally at home. Even raiding his fridge for a store-cupboard supper left her guilt-free.

She decided to stay at Ricky's until he came back, telling herself it was purely in the interests of the lurcher and definitely not because she also was enjoying being there. It was only when she went to bed that something felt wrong. Slipping into Ricky's bed alone triggered a sense of loss, the empty space beside her reminding her he wasn't there, and wasn't in her life any more. She turned face the other way and was grateful when Carlo slunk onto the bed and lay with his back against hers.

'Don't tell Ricky,' she told him.

–

Charley slept like a log and shortly after dawn she drifted into an extraordinarily vivid dream. She was standing on the Rialto Bridge, holding hands with Josh, as she had done on their honeymoon. Except that when she turned to look at him it wasn't Josh, it was Ricky. And then all of a sudden Ricky was running and pulling her along the bridge behind him, except she was floating up above him, as if she were a party balloon on a string. And every now and again he'd turn round, look up at her and laugh. And then she was laughing too and somehow she knew they were heading for a hotel, except she knew they were going in the wrong direction because the hotel was behind them, but it was all right because when they got to the hotel it was a church. And then quite suddenly she started falling and Ricky put out his arms to catch her – but just at that point her alarm went off and woke her up. The dream had been so vivid she reached out, expecting to find Ricky next to her. Discovering he wasn't, she rolled onto her back, disappointed.

Daylight was already pouring through the blinds and it gradually dawned on her that it was a Monday and she'd better get up. She padded barefoot through the living room to the kitchen area, Carlo following her optimistically, hoping for his breakfast. She flicked the kettle on and fed him while she waited for it to boil. Then she reached for the Italian ground coffee – ground, because Ricky refused to give instant houseroom – and opening the packet, she inhaled the rich, slightly bitter aroma deeply. *Mmmm, I love his coffee!* And then it hit her.

Of course she loved his coffee… and she loved his flat, and his bed, and his sofa, and she loved his eyes, and his mouth, and the way his hair flopped over his forehead, and the way he looked at her and the touch of his hand. She loved his smell, his smile, his accent, even his bloody dog – no, *especially* his bloody dog… She loved all of this, and all of him, because she *was* in love with him. He was… not The One, she reminded herself, because Josh was The One. No, Josh *had been* The One. Ricky was The One now. The One *after* The One.

She glanced at the clock on the cooker. It said six forty, which meant it would be seven forty in Tuscany. Was it too early to call him? Maybe. Marginally. She'd grab a quick shower and call him after that. Standing in the shower, enjoying the hot water tingling on her skin, she rehearsed what she'd say to him. *I'm an idiot, and you are a wonderful, wonderful man. I was wrong. I do love you… no, I am* in love with you. *I'm really sorry if I hurt you. Can we try again? Please?* There was so much she wanted to say to him.

Towelling herself dry, she heard her phone ringing on the side in the kitchen. Wrapping the towel round her, she dashed through. It was Ricky. She snatched up the phone, her heart pounding.

'Hi,' she said, 'I was just going to ring you.'

'Oh?' he queried, but without giving her the chance to reply he said, 'My grandmother just died, Charley. She's gone.'

Charley felt the world pause for a second, and then a rush of compassion swept over her, brushing aside what she'd so desperately wanted to say to him and leaving her feeling utterly bereft on his behalf. She sat down hard on a kitchen stool. 'Oh, I'm so sorry, Ricky. So sorry. Please give my condolences to your family.'

'Yes of course,' he said, then continued flatly, 'I need to stay on until the funeral. Would you mind having Carlo a little longer? I'm not sure when it will be. Sorry.' He sounded done in.

'Of course I will. You don't even need to ask. And you certainly don't need to apologise.'

'Thank you,' he said, then, after a beat he asked, 'Why were you going to call me?'

This is so not the time, said a voice inside her, so she merely said, 'It doesn't matter. It can wait until you get back. Take care.'

Chapter Twenty-Eight

'So wait, you *literally* woke up and smelled the coffee?' said Tara.

Charley nodded sheepishly. 'Yup!'

'About sodding time!' said Tara, rolling her eyes. 'I *told* you. But you just wouldn't listen to your Auntie Tara, would you?'

It was just after they'd opened up the shop on the Monday morning, Tara having again pitched up bright and early.

'Please don't say anything to anyone else, not yet,' begged Charley, not wanting her news getting round Cargo before she even spoken to Ricky.

'I won't tell a soul,' Tara promised. Then a few minutes later she added casually, 'Have you told Angie?'

'No, not yet. Nobody knows, except you. Not even Ricky!'

'Oh, right,' Tara said, and Charley thought she detected a slight hint of gloating in her friend's tone. She'd always suspected Tara was a little jealous of her friendship with Angie, which she put down to Tara having been an only child, unused to having to share attention and affection, making her over-protective of her friendship with Charley. Bearing that in mind, Charley nonetheless made a mental note to call Angie later that evening, after work, to let her know.

Tara nipped out to get them both some breakfast, and Charley set about refilling the displays and thinking she was glad she'd confided in Tara first. Working with her best mate was... challenging, to say the least, and putting a strain on their friendship, but Ricky's loss had reminded her why she and Tara had grown so close, how much they'd been through together, and why she would never want to lose her as a mate. She just had to figure out how to work with Tara, the same way she'd had to manage working with difficult colleagues in the past. And what if Tara was opinionated and pushy? That was Tara, just the way she was. They could work it out; they were both adults, for crying out loud, and the fact that her mate had so willingly bailed her out on Saturday, and at such short notice, made Charley optimistic they could easily put their working relationship onto a better footing.

If only. Almost as soon as Tara returned with their breakfast, she opened her mouth, and instantly put Charley's back up.

'About the promo evening,' she started. 'I've had a thought.'

Charley slapped on her professional face and merely replied, 'Oh yes?'

'Well, we don't have to do it if you really don't want to…' *Too right, I don't*, thought Charley. 'But there's still piles of dead stock that's just not shifting, so we do need to have a sale.'

A sale? Do we actually 'need to' or do you just think we should? Pulling herself up for being negative and forcing herself not to overreact, she tried to objectively apply the litmus test of whether Tara was overstepping the mark, or manoeuvring her into doing something she had neither the time nor the inclination to do. 'What were you thinking?'

'I'm glad you asked me that!' grinned Tara. Delving into her bag, she brought out a bundle of garish, plastic bunting in neon orange, green and pink.

Inwardly, Charley shied like a horse startled by a fluorescent traffic cone but, astonishingly, she managed to keep her expression impassive.

'I've brought some of Monnie's party bunting and I'm going to loop it across the window, and I made these…' Digging into her bag again she brought out some home-made, A4-sized *SALE* signs, printed on a startling range of Day-Glo coloured paper. 'We can plaster these all over the glass and then fill the window with marked down items. So what d'you think?' beamed Tara, clearly expecting Charley to be thrilled to bits.

Charley was momentarily speechless, although her thoughts were crystal clear: *over my dead body.* When she'd set up the shop, Angie had put an enormous amount of effort into helping Charley create a signature style. Every item of furniture, the shelves, the tables, and even the wicker chairs, were painted matt white, and all the decals and slogans decorating the walls and window were in either black or gold. Even the gift bags reflected the theme, plain white with a minimal scattering of small gold stars and the words *A Gift for You* written in a simple, gold font. Put simply, the style statement of the shop pronounced '*classy, shabby chic*'. The style statement of Tara's planned sale window screeched '*ghastly, crappy tat*'.

'Well?' Tara persisted, brandishing the bunting enthusiastically and Charley felt she detected a hint of challenge in her tone. She couldn't keep turning down Tara's suggestions, she realised, even if the thought of reducing her tasteful shop window into a lurid bargain-bucket store made her cringe. Taking a deep breath and rapidly making the calculation of likely income versus damage to shop's image and, more importantly, the cost to her friendship with Tara if she refused, she queried carefully, 'How long were you thinking the sale would last?'

'One week. This time next week, everything back at full price.'

'And the window back to normal?' double-checked Charley.

'Yep!'

'Okay,' said Charley and, with a verve and enthusiasm she really, really didn't feel, cried, 'Let's do this!' She only hoped Angie didn't drop into the shop – she'd have a coronary. Either that or she'd kill Tara, very probably strangling her with her own bunting.

When Tara bought into an idea, she was like a whirling tornado. So straight away she was up and down off the chairs getting boxes down from the top of the dresser and hoiking out the spare stock stashed behind the counter and under the display tables. Then she proceeded to ruthlessly, and tactlessly, rummage through them. Charley tried very hard not to take Tara's comments personally. It wasn't easy.

'We're never going to sell all of these,' she announced, dumping a stack of tea towels onto the floor.

'I think we might have ordered too many of those from the outset,' explained Charley.

'Just a few!' quipped Tara before ripping open a box full of Prosecco-flavoured truffles. 'The sell-by date on these is pretty short. Blimey! How many packs of these have we got?'

'We had a bit of a run on them so I ordered a load more and then suddenly none of them shifted.'

'Even so... Did you check the sell-by dates when they were delivered?'

It hadn't even occurred to Charley to do that and she made a mental note to do so in future. Fortunately, Tara hadn't bothered to wait for a reply, merely adding the truffles to the pile on the floor.

'And why have we got all these Prosecco peel-off face packs? I mean, who wants to put Prosecco on their face? What a waste!'

Her joke brought a smile to Charley's face, but nonetheless she felt the need to defend herself. 'I had to get a load in to make up some party bags for the Avalon and then they suddenly wanted something else in the bags instead.'

'You should have told them it was too sodding late to change their minds.'

Charley bit her tongue. Tara had hated working at the Avalon before she quit her job to help in the shop, and Charley decided to put her mate's sharpness down to her feelings towards her previous employer.

'And we can shift all this lot too,' said Tara, brusquely consigning half a box of tealight holders to the growing sale pile.

'Actually, they do sell rather well, it's just that I'd forgotten to put any more out.'

'Yeah? Well I've never really liked them so let's get rid of them.'

Taking a deep breath, Charley decided to leave Tara to her savage cull.

In a little over an hour, the window – and therefore the signature look of the shop – had been completely transformed.

Standing outside, Charley gazed silently at the sale display in utter dismay, which deepened when Del from the florist's called over to her.

'Blimey Charley! That's a bit in-your-face, isn't it? Does it glow in the dark!'

'Very probably,' replied Charley. Still, it was only for a few days, she reminded herself.

Towards the end of the morning Pam called Charley to say she wasn't going to be able to get in at all that afternoon, and very probably not for the next few days since her young guest was still ill. Charley assured her mother-in-law not to worry, and that she could cope. When she rang off, Tara immediately offered to stay a little later every day until Pam could get in. Charley had to swallow down her surprise.

'As long as I leave by quarter to three, I should just make it to school pick-up on time.'

'Don't make yourself late for Monnie.'

Tara shrugged lightly. 'Oh, she'll be fine. Plenty of parents hang around for a natter after school, they'll keep an eye on her. And anyway, there's always a teacher on duty making sure none of the kids wander off, or get abducted by aliens!'

'Well, okay, if you're sure… Thanks.'

Charley knew she should be grateful, but it had belatedly begun to dawn on her that the more time Tara spent in the shop, the more it seemed to strain their relationship. Which was pretty bloody obvious, really. The supreme irony was that whilst she had been irritated beyond measure when Tara had treated the shop like a hobby, swanning in when she felt like it and leaving Charley to do the bulk of the work and decision-making, she was actually finding the newly motivated, full-on, hands-on Tara even more infuriating. It wasn't only their clash of personalities; she was worn down by Tara's seemingly constantly criticisms, telling her they ought to be doing something differently, or that they weren't doing enough.

Charley's self-confidence in her ability to run her own business had always been egg-shell thin, and it had taken all of her friends, plus Pam, to persuade her she was capable of running a shop in the first place, and her self-doubt was never far from the surface. The more Tara involved herself in the business, the more Charley felt her failings were being exposed. Loath as she was to admit it, she was gutted at how successful the sale was turning out to be. She tried telling herself not to be so bloody childish, but increasingly she was finding it hard to be objective towards any of Tara's ideas and opinions and had to fight her knee-jerk reaction to oppose anything she proposed, simply because of the implicit personal criticism of the way she was running the shop.

By mid-week, Charley was counting the days until Pam would return – or she would have been, had she known when that might be. She took her phone out of her pocket, intending to text her mother-in-law for an update and noticed she'd missed a text from Ricky.

> The funeral is tomorrow. I'll be back at the weekend.

He'd be back at the weekend. Charley's spirits soared and she immediately texted him a reply.

> Hope the funeral goes okay. Give my love to your family. Let me know your ETA at the airport and I'll pick you up. Safe trip home.

'Three days,' she told Carlo, giving the lurcher a loving scratch behind his ears. 'Four at the most!' The dog got to his feet, wagging his tail jauntily, looking for all the world as if he'd understood every word she'd said. Which was ridiculously fanciful, obviously. She put it down to him being able to detect her cheerful mood, which had made everything seem better – even Tara's sale window.

Chapter Twenty-Nine

As it turned out, Pam didn't manage to get into the shop until the very end of the week. She was too tied up looking after her poorly young lodger. The previous Saturday Freya had woken with a roaring temperature, aching throat and glands the size of bantams' eggs, and was very weak and tearful. Having had two sons and with two grandchildren, Pam was well used to looking after sick children, but it was inevitably more worrying when they weren't your own. She didn't even risk giving Freya any paracetamol without permission, so she'd called the language school and the rep had come out almost immediately. They'd both decided it would be better for Sofia to lodge with another family, in case whatever Freya had was infectious, and the rep arranged for a doctor to call in. In the meantime, Pam sponged Freya's burning face and limbs with cooling flannels, plied her with liquids and sat with her, reassuring her and keeping her company.

Poor kid, thought Pam, gazing down at Freya, imagining how tough it must be, feeling ill in a stranger's bedroom, far from home. Freya lay with her eyes closed, her damp hair plastered against her forehead, small and vulnerable, looking more like a primary school-girl than a teenager, and breathing hot, shallow breaths. *They always look so much younger when they're ill*, mused Pam. When Freya dozed off, she slipped quietly downstairs to put off Dez who was meant to be coming for dinner that evening. After his previous outburst he had texted and called Pam several times to apologise, and had followed up by sending flowers.

'It was all my fault,' he'd told her earnestly. 'I realised afterwards that I'd completely misinterpreted what you meant and overre-acted. My only defence is that I was so mortified, so offended that you, of all people, would think I wasn't completely trustworthy, it just upset me terribly.'

Then, he'd humbly asked if she could forgive him and let him have a second chance. Pam was prepared to build bridges, but she wasn't prepared to capitulate on the issue of him spending the night whilst the girls were staying with her, and had been pleasantly surprised when he hadn't even tried to persuade her otherwise. That didn't stop her tensing as she picked up her phone to tell him he wouldn't be able to come round this evening, and bracing herself for a potential quarrel.

'Oh, poor girl,' was his response, much to her surprise. 'And poor you, having to look after her.'

'Oh, it goes with the territory,' she replied dismissively, 'and she's such a sweet kid I don't mind. I just feel sorry for her.'

'If you're stuck in the house, is there anything you need?'

She was about to ask him if he'd get her some groceries and a bottle of blackcurrant squash, to help keep Freya hydrated, but stopped herself, wary of giving him an excuse to come round and get his foot in the door – or rather, his boots under the table.

'Thanks, that's very good of you, but I've got everything we need,' she said firmly, and then hated herself for being suspicious and cynical. *You're probably being very unjust. He was only trying to help.*

Since there were a few things she really did need for Freya, she called Zee and asked her if she could pop into the supermarket and pick her up a couple of things.

'Of course!'

'Not much at all,' Pam told her, 'just some blackcurrant squash... Oh, and some eggs and, actually, come to think of it, I'm nearly out of bread... and some tinned peaches, a couple of bananas, some plain yoghurt for smoothies... a bottle of lemon juice and a pot of honey...' The list went on until Zee interrupted her in mock exasperation.

'For God's sake woman, text me a list!'

Throughout the weekend Pam had looked after her young charge with the same care and affection she would have shown one of her own. She whizzed up fruit smoothies, mashed bananas and cooked vegetable soups in an attempt to get some food into her. When Freya's PJs were soaked through with sweat she helped her change into a dry pair, and she stripped the bed so the fresh, clean linen would be cooling and comfortable. She even looked out one of the boys' Harry Potter books and read aloud to her, although how much Freya followed the story as she slipped in and out of her restless sleep, Pam had no idea, but she doubted it would be a problem, assuming that half the kids in the world knew the stories inside-out. She made gallons of hot honey and lemon, as she had when the boys were poorly, knowing the homely remedy would soothe the girl's throat as well as get some fluid and energy into her.

'Thank you. You are very kind,' croaked Freya feebly, sipping the mixture. Talking was clearly painful for her, and Pam's throat almost ached in sympathy.

'It's no trouble,' said Pam kindly. 'Do you want anything else?'

Freya's face crumpled. 'My mother,' she admitted in a small voice, and tears spilled from her eyes and down her flushed cheeks.

'Oh sweetheart,' said Pam, sitting down on the bed next to her and pulling her into an embrace, holding the youngster while she wept. Then Pam got a cold cloth and gently wiped her face.

'You are like my grandmother,' Freya told her with a sniff.

It was the second time the young girl had made that comparison, realised Pam, taking it as a huge compliment.

—

It transpired that Freya had tonsillitis and was prescribed antibiotics, but by the Monday she was still very unwell, so her mother flew over from Copenhagen. Pam was infinitely relieved, not for herself, but for Freya and for her mum. Hard as it was for the youngster to be sick and away from home, Pam guessed her mother was finding it even tougher. She remembered when Josh had broken his leg on a school residential trip. Even though everyone had assured her he was okay – the teachers, the medics and Josh himself – it was only when she saw him hopping clumsily off the coach at the end of the trip, with a plaster on his leg and a broad grin on his face, that she'd finally ceased worrying.

Freya's mother, Hanne, had booked herself into a nearby Airbnb but, after much cajoling, Pam persuaded her stay in Luke's room instead. Freya perked up considerably with the arrival of her mum, as did Pam, who instinctively warmed to Hanne, getting the immediate impression of a very open, friendly, grounded sort of woman. Motherly not 'smotherly', was her assessment. Hanne dressed casually and looked very much like an older, rounded version of her daughter, with the same pale blue eyes, although distinctly more stylish, decided Pam, since the woman's knees didn't poke through rips in her trousers. By the Wednesday morning there was a marked improvement in Freya. At Pam's suggestion, they settled her on the sofa in the living room for a change of scene and left her happily channel-hopping, while they took themselves into the kitchen for a coffee. While Pam put the kettle on, Hanne automatically fetched the mugs and Pam was reminded of how markedly helpful Freya had been even on her first evening.

'She's a lovely girl,' she told Hanne. 'She's been so helpful. I'd be very proud of her if she was mine.'

'Thank you,' said Hanne, with a modest smile. 'I am proud of her.'

Pam had been surprised, and relieved, at how fluent Hanne's English was. She complimented her on it. 'Are you an English teacher, or a translator?'

Hanne smiled and shook her head. 'No. Everyone in Denmark can speak English.'

A fact which left Pam feeling humbled and rather inadequate. 'I don't speak any other languages,' she confessed sheepishly.

'Do not try to learn Danish!' Hanne warned her cheerfully. 'It is much too difficult!'

Over their coffee, the two women bonded in the time-honoured way, through sharing stories about their children, particularly the scrapes they had got into and the number of trips to A&E. Luke, Pam informed Hanne, had held the family record for the overall number of visits (six) but Josh had held the record for the number of stitches (fourteen) and the number of broken bones (three).

After a pause, Hanne leant closer to Pam and said gently, 'Freya told me about Josh.' Her eyes sought Pam's. 'I am very sorry.'

Pam took a deep, controlling breath and then a quick slug of her coffee. What was it about receiving sympathy from another mother that affected her so deeply? She supposed it was because she knew they were trying to empathise with the pain of her loss.

She nodded briefly and said, 'Thank you,' and then went on, 'Freya was very sweet to me about it. Very mature.'

'She understands. My father died and Freya was very sad. They did a lot together.'

'And your mother? How is she coping?'

A small sigh escaped Hanne and she took a moment before she answered. 'He was very ill, so she had time to prepare. When he died she was…' She paused and Pam guessed she was searching for the right word.

'Relieved?' she ventured and Hanne nodded. 'She must miss him very much,' said Pam gently.

'Of course. We all do,' replied Hanne sadly, and then she changed her tone and went on, 'But my mother is very busy. She is writing a cookery book. And she is learning Tai Chi and she swims in the sea every day. Even in the winter.'

Pam shuddered dramatically. 'Brave woman! Does she live by the sea?'

'In Copenhagen. We have the beach.'

'A beach! With sand?' Pam was astonished. The only image of Copenhagen in her mind's eye was the colourful buildings in the harbour, which always reminded her of the brightly painted houses in the Hotwells district of Bristol. But a sandy beach? Who knew?

Hanne was continuing proudly, 'She is very fit. She cycles everywhere. And she is always doing something. She helps in a workshop where they repair things and she is mending a boat with a friend. And it is a very big boat,' laughed Hanne, 'so it will take them a long time!'

'She sounds remarkable.'

'She is.'

Remembering how Freya had likened her to her grandmother, Pam felt flattered and warmed even more to the youngster.

Until Hanne said, 'She is seventy-eight,' and Pam was horrified. *Seventy-eight! That's nearly eighty! Genuinely elderly. Seriously? Freya thinks I'm like an elderly woman?* It was crushing.

'My mother says she does more now than when she was married. She has more time.' Hanne told her, and then went on to politely ask Pam what she did with her time.

Not very much compared to your mother. 'I work in my daughter-in-law's shop.'

Hanne nodded encouragingly, as if she expected Pam to continue. 'And that's about it,' concluded Pam, feeling humbled and inadequate for the second time in one coffee break.

–

By the end of the week Freya was well enough to fly home. Pam gave them a lift to the airport and walked in with them to the departure area. To her surprise, the teen spontaneously threw her arms round her before politely reciting what Pam guessed was another little prepared speech.

'Thank you for letting me stay in your home. And thank you for looking after me. You arc very kind. I will not forget you.'

'You're most welcome, sweetheart,' smiled Pam, genuinely touched.

'Come and visit us in Copenhagen,' invited Hanne warmly. 'We have a small Airbnb apartment. We wouldn't charge you,' she finished hurriedly.

'How very kind of you.' Pam carefully avoided implying that she might take up the offer, since she very much doubted she would.

Hanne embraced Pam, and then Freya gave her another hug. As Pam watched them walk off, heading for their gate, a lump caught in her throat. *Oh, don't be so ridiculous. Pull yourself together. You barely know them. It's only because you hate goodbyes.* It was Josh's sudden death, in a car accident on an icy road, that had triggered Pam's struggle with farewells. The unexpected, traumatic loss had created a fragility in her, an irrational fear that whenever somebody went away it might be the last time she'd ever see them. The simple act of saying goodbye was now freighted with emotional baggage.

Even so, she was genuinely sad her guests had gone, and far more so than she'd thought she would be. Freya was an absolute poppet, and as for Hanne, well, having another adult around had been wonderful, and it had served to remind Pam what she was missing now that she was on her own. *You've got Dez*, she reminded herself but somehow the thought didn't comfort her as much as she thought it should, and she reflected that she had actually enjoyed the company of Hanne, another woman, far more than she did being with Dez. The thought brought her up short, and she chastised herself for being disloyal and unfair to Dez. It wasn't his fault he was a man.

Chapter Thirty

When she'd arrived back at her house after dropping Hanne and Freya at the airport, Pam was immediately struck by the thick, dull silence that greeted her. The house had somehow come alive with the three of them there, but now it felt empty, and so did she. Briefly, she considered whether Sofia would like to come back, but decided it wouldn't be fair since the girl was better off where she was, in a house with other young students, which was obviously more fun for her. Pam wandered round stripping the guest beds and loading the washing machine in a bid to fill the house with activity if nothing else. Then she texted Dez and invited him for supper.

He texted back, almost immediately.

> When? Tonight?

Flattered by his enthusiasm she texted back.

> Fine.

Then, since there was over an hour before she'd have to leave for Charley's shop, she threw her energies into planning a menu and making a shopping list. Given how understanding he'd been about Freya's illness she decided to treat him, to push the boat out and cook something special, and damn the expense.

Flicking as much through her mental recipe log as her cookery books she opted for baked camembert with honey and rosemary, and garlic bread to start with, followed by butterflied sea bass with zesty lemon dressing, new boiled potatoes and a salad, and then mocha chocolate pots. Then, remembering that Dez liked meat more than fish, and didn't seem to be a big fan of soft cheeses, she instantly changed her mind and opted for a very traditional and simple Parma ham and melon starter, followed by steak in garlic butter, with potatoes dauphinoise and a salad – no, with broccoli, since he preferred hot vegetables. She stuck with the chocolate pots for pudding though – there were limits to the culinary sacrifices she would make for him! The prospect of cooking, and then eating, some of her much-loved dishes raised her spirits and she swung breezily into Charley's shop just after two o'clock that afternoon. She'd texted her daughter-in-law to let her know she was on her way but even so, the younger woman's face lit up when she walked through the door.

'I am so sorry, I couldn't get earlier this week—' started Pam, then she broke off in surprise at seeing Tara still in the shop.

'It was fine,' said Charley, embracing her warmly. 'Tara's been staying late.'

'Oh! How very good of you,' said Pam turning to Tara and trying to keep the astonishment out of her voice. 'I was so worried about leaving Charley in the lurch.'

Tara shrugged it off. 'It was no problem. In fact it's been fun!' Then reaching for her bag and coat she added, 'But since you're here, I may as well nip off. It'll give me time to pick up a treat for Monnie on the way to school.' On her way out she looked back over her shoulder at the door, 'Back to normal next week, then, Charley?'

'Fine. And thanks again!' Charley called as the door swung shut.

It didn't escape Pam that having Tara's additional help might have been a double-edged sword for Charley. 'I hope it didn't put you out, having to ask Tara to cover for me?' she said anxiously.

'I didn't have to. She offered.'

'Oh!' said Pam, this time not bothering to conceal her surprise.

'Yes, she's been very committed, all week,' said Charley and Pam detected a note of mild despair in her tone. 'We've had a *sale*,' she said meaningfully, indicating the window.

'Ah,' said Pam, taking in the lurid display. 'Tara's idea, I take it.'

'Yup. And her bunting,' replied Charley somewhat needlessly.

Pam grimaced. 'Well I am sorry, and especially for giving you such short notice.'

'Good!' replied Charley, suddenly chippering up. 'Because I need to beg a favour.'

'Anything!'

'Again, good! I wanted to ask if you could look after the shop on your own tomorrow, while I get Ricky from the airport.'

'Of course I will,' said Pam, secretly delighted to hear that Charley had offered to collect Ricky, yet trying hard not to let it show on her face, or to read too much into the gesture. However, given the light shining in Charley's eyes and the elation on her face, she felt safe to at least mentally cross her fingers.

Especially when Charley began confidingly, 'The thing is...'

At which point a customer walked in, cutting Charley off.

Champing at the bit to hear what 'the thing' was going to be, Pam started unnecessarily tidying the tea towels, then the aprons, then the oven gloves and countless other items until, after spending the best part of ten minutes buying a couple of packs of sweets and a scented candle, the customer finally left and Charley could continue.

'The thing is,' she started again, and Pam held her breath and hoped against hope that her daughter-in-law had finally seen sense and realised that one of the loveliest men she would ever meet, and who absolutely adored her, was the man she was meant to spend the rest of her life with.

When Charley somewhat sheepishly admitted that she had, Pam raised her hands to the heavens in mock irony and exclaimed, 'Hallelujah!'

'Although I haven't actually told him yet,' confessed Charley. 'I was going to tell him at the airport when I pick him up. Which is why...' she paused briefly. 'Why I was wondering if it would be all right with you if I didn't come back to the shop afterwards?'

'Of course, darling,' said Pam trying to keep her face expressionless, despite secretly assuming that the two of them would undoubtedly want to leap into bed to make up for lost time. 'I'm sure you'll have a lot to talk about,' she said, deadpan, and much to her delight, her daughter-in-law blushed bright pink.

'Seriously, darling,' said Pam after a few moments, giving the glow in Charley's cheeks time to subside, 'I couldn't be happier for you.' *And I know Josh would be happy for you too*, she thought, but with admirable sensitivity, refrained from bringing Josh into the frame.

Most Friday evenings Pam stayed on after closing to help Charley prepare for Saturday. This evening, however, she was eager to get away as soon as the last customer had left.

'I feel dreadful nipping off when I've hardly been in all week, but I'm cooking supper for Dez and I need to get to the supermarket beforehand,' she explained.

'No, that's fine,' Charley said, then went on to ask casually, but with a mischievous glint in her eye, 'How are things going between you?'

The all too evident air quotes around the word 'things' made it Pam's turn to blush pink. 'Fine,' she said airily. 'Actually, more than fine. I really like him.'

'Fantastic!' enthused Charley, and Pam was touched to see she seemed genuinely pleased for her. 'When am I going to meet him?'

'Um...' Pam adopted a pensive look as if she were running through her mental calendar. After Dez's drunken exhibition at Zee's, she was wary of introducing him to anyone else. 'I'm not really sure.'

'Well, why don't we all go out for supper one night, you and Dez, and Ricky and me? A double date!'

God no! Instinctively Pam wanted to protect Dez from having to meet Charley and Ricky in a public venue, or maybe it herself she was trying to protect. Either way, she sought cover in comedy.

'I know I'm out of touch with modern dating, darling but, can I just ask, is it considered absolutely normal for a daughter-in-law and her boyfriend to go on a double date with the daughter-in-law's mother-in-law and the daughter-in-law's mother-in-law's boyfriend? Only it all sounds desperately complicated to me!'

'Hmm. Maybe let's not!' agreed Charley, with a mock grimace, much to Pam's relief.

–

A short while later, wincing at the cost, Pam pinged her credit card at the supermarket checkout. She'd splashed out a bit *too* much, having bought a bottle of red for Dez to go with the steak, as well as a four-pack of beers and a small bottle of dessert wine as a special treat. Oh well, it was too late now, she thought, packing everything into the motley collection of bags-for-life she kept stashed in her handbag.

'Have a good evening,' said the checkout man politely – or more probably, automatically.

'Thank you! I'm certainly planning to,' she replied. 'You too,' she added over her shoulder as she left, although thinking about it, the poor chap was probably going spend it stuck behind the till.

Getting back to the house, she put some music on, loudly, to banish the silence, and started preparing the dauphinoise potatoes. Once all the food was prepped, she went through to set the dining room table. She fished out her best white tablecloth and, employing her time-honoured technique, she held two corners and deftly flicked it out, watching it flutter down to neatly cover the table. She ran her hands over it, smoothing out the creases, and then dressed the table with candles, the cloth napkins which only came out at Christmas or birthdays, and a small vase of assorted late blooms she'd hunted down in the garden. Giving the table a final once-over she decided, 'Not bad. In fact, downright classy!' It was late September, and although it was still light outside, by the time Dez arrived it would be dusk, and dark enough for candles.

She went back into the kitchen to finish cooking, excitement and anticipation simmering inside her.

–

'Wow!' breathed Dez in the dining room doorway when she led him through to the candle-lit room. 'This looks stunning!'

'Thank you!' beamed Pam.

'And so do you,' he said, taking hold of her before leaning over and kissing her warmly.

Cheeks glowing, he went to bring in the starters, and realised she was looking forward to sharing not just the meal, but the rest of the night together too, and was unabashed when a frisson of anticipation shivered inside her.

–

It was just after she'd brought the steaks through that the evening began to turn sour. He asked her for money.

'Just a loan,' he added hastily. 'For a deposit on the dual control cars.'

Momentarily thrown, Pam didn't immediately reply.

So Dez continued. 'I've tried to source them second-hand, but there's nothing decent out there. And I can't start a driving school without cars, can I?' he explained jokily. 'I've raised most of the money, but I'm twenty grand short.'

'Twenty grand!' erupted Pam. *I'd struggle to lend him twenty quid, especially after shelling out for the dinner.*

'I'd pay you back within a few months, once the school is up and running,' he promised.

'I'm sorry,' stammered Pam, 'but I can't possibly lend you that sort of money. I just haven't got it.'

'Don't be ridiculous,' he scoffed, 'you've got all this!' He swept his arm round grandly to indicate the house and, presumably, its contents.

Mildly resenting the need to explain, Pam outlined her financial situation to Dez. 'Only half the house is mine, and everything's tied up until Geoff and I are divorced. At which point I'll have to sell up and buy a flat or something. And right now I'm struggling to make ends meet. Why do you think I take in lodgers?' she asked him. Then, suddenly struck by how preposterous it was that Dez should think she was a wealthy woman, she started laughing, as much from nerves as amusement.

Dez slammed his right fist down on the table so violently the cutlery leapt up off the surface. Startled, Pam jumped, her hand instinctively flying to her throat, instantly, frighteningly aware that she was alone in the house, apart from Dez.

'Don't you dare laugh at me,' he shouted.

She forced herself to stay calm, and not reveal the fear rising inside her. Trying to picture Dez as a tantrum-throwing toddler, she thumped both of her fists on the table, just as violently as he had, then replied coolly, but in a tone sharp enough to cut glass, 'Don't you raise your voice to me at my table.'

He seemed momentarily confounded. Clearly he hadn't expected her to come back at him like this.

'Then don't take me for a fool, Pam. With this amount of equity you can easily raise twenty grand. And you know it.'

Pam had absolutely no idea whether that was true or not. Nor did she care.

'Get out,' she ordered, willing her voice not to tremble, and keeping her fists clenched to shop her hands shaking.

He didn't move, merely sat there eyeballing her, as if he were wondering whether he could gamble on pushing it, or whether he'd completely blown it.

She made it perfectly clear to him. Rising to her feet, slowly, magnificently, and with enormous self-control she said with icy calm, 'Get out of my house *now*, or I will call the police.'

He tried one more roll of the dice. 'If I go,' he threatened. 'I won't come back. That's it, we'll be done.'

'We're done, full stop,' she informed him.

He stood up and turned to go, then, with flash of childish petulance, he snatched the still half-full bottle of red wine off the table and stormed out. Moments later, she heard the front door slam and through the dining room window she watched him climb into his car and drive off, the wheels furiously spewing up the gravel on the driveway.

She rushed to the front door, but only to slip the latch down behind him. Then she locked the back door in the kitchen and the French doors in the living room, and then she raced round the whole house, fastening all the windows, even the upstairs ones. It was only then that the fear properly kicked in. Her legs trembled so violently she had to cling onto the bannister rail to get back down the stairs, and her hands shook so much she could barely hold the phone steady enough to call Zee. Her old friend promptly dropped everything and rushed over.

—

'Has he got a key?' was Zee's immediate concern. Pam shook her head, so Zee said brightly, 'Well, at least you won't have to change the locks!'

Pam managed a wry smile at her friend's attempt to lighten her mood but her shoulders slumped as she said in a small voice, 'I've been a bloody fool, haven't I?'

Zee pulled a noncommittal face. 'You won't be the first one to be taken in by a gold-digger, and you won't be the last,' she told her philosophically.

While waiting for Zee to arrive, Pam had cleared away the supper things and tided the table in the dining room, shoving the tablecloth and napkins into the washing machine. The candlesticks and flowers had seemed to mock her, so she'd closed the door on them. She'd kept her wine glass and she and Zee were now settled on the sofa in the living room, a bottle of white wine on the coffee table in front of them. Zee topped up Pam's glass, which was emptying more quickly than usual.

After a while Pam confessed sorrowfully, and with painful honesty, 'I think I knew all along he had some ulterior motive for being interested in me.'

Zee regarded her sympathetically, but didn't reply, her silence inviting Pam to open up.

'But I ignored the warning bells. I stuck it out for the wrong reasons, because I didn't want to be alone.'

'That's not a crime,' said Zee gently.

'And because I wanted to get back at Geoff, wanted to show him that I could get someone too.'

'That's even more understandable.'

'Except he didn't really want me at all, did he? Just my money.'

'Well, more fool him,' said Zee. Pam gave her close friend a warm look, comforted by her loyalty until, with perfect comic timing, Zee added, 'Because you haven't damn well got any!'

Pam managed a laugh and Zee filled both of their glasses again.

'Are you driving?' warned Pam, eyeing Zee's drink.

Zee shook her head. 'I thought I'd stay the night. Bunk down in one of the boys' rooms,' she said casually.

Zee had never stayed over before, none of her friends had. Pam was moved, and grateful. She hadn't savoured the thought of being alone.

'Don't be too hard on yourself, Pam. The man's a... a total shit.'

An audible gasp escaped Pam, who was shocked to hear such an extreme expletive from her old friend.

'He's probably tried it on with a lot of other women too. These people are very credible.'

Although Pam knew Zee was trying to make her feel better, somehow lumping her together with other gullible women made her feel even more stupid. It bruised her pride to think she wasn't smart enough to see through a cheap conman plying one of the oldest tricks in the book. 'Don't tell anyone,' she pleaded. 'I don't want it getting back to Geoff.'

'I won't,' promised Zee. 'But it wouldn't, anyway. We're all still too damn angry with him to give him that satisfaction.'

There was a beat before Pam said in a quiet voice, 'The thing is, Zee, he didn't fool me. I fooled myself.'

'Maybe,' Zee shrugged lightly, 'but we all do that. We all kid ourselves things are how we want them to be rather than how they really are.' Pam wondered if Zee was referring to her own marriage. 'Ah well, there's no fool like an old fool,' finished Zee teasingly.

'How very dare you! Fool, yes, old, no!'

Then Pam remembered the chocolate mocha pots and the bottle of dessert wine chilling in the fridge. The two old friends demolished the puddings and then sat drinking into the small hours, and when the wine ran out, they hit the gin. Which turned out to be a very, very bad idea.

Chapter Thirty-One

By rights, Charley should have been a complete wreck. She'd barely slept the night before, knowing it was the last night she'd be spending in Ricky's bed on her own. In an effort to drop off, she'd tried counting sheep, but had ended up counting the hours until his plane touched down and she could be with him. When dawn broke, she was deep in a fantasy where she was standing waiting for him at the arrivals gate, his faithful hound by her side. She had no idea whether or not dogs were allowed in the airport, probably not, but she wasn't going to let that get in the way of the romantic vision. In her mind's eye, she saw him arriving at the passport control desk, his eyes already scanning the crowds of waiting people, looking for her. He'd find her, their eyes would meet and his whole face would light up with a beaming, joyous grin.

'Charley!' he'd bellow, pushing people aside in his haste to get to her.

'Ricky!' she'd reply breathlessly, and they'd run into each other's arms. 'Can we try again?' she'd beseech him.

'I thought you were never going to ask, my darling!' he'd cry, sweeping her off her feet and kissing her lingeringly.

Then the fantasy had been rudely interrupted by Carlo nudging her bare arm with his cold, wet nose. He'd sensed she was awake and was reminding her about his breakfast.

On the dot of nine Charley flipped the sign on the shop door from 'Closed' to 'Open'. Carlo had already settled himself in the window, looking for all the world as if he were one of the 'Final Day of Sale' bargains. Wincing at the garish bunting still blighting the style statement of the shop's exterior, Charley made a mental note to come in on Sunday and rip it all down. A few early customers wandered in, bought a few sale items and had a nose around the rest of the shop. Ricky's plane wasn't due to land until mid-morning which would give her plenty of time to make sure Pam was ensconced happily, with everything sorted for her to manage on her own for the rest of the day. Charley had been tracking Ricky's flight on her phone, and knew it had taken off and was due to land at Bristol on schedule.

'He is literally on his way!' she told Carlo, excitement already bubbling inside her.

By nine thirty Pam still hadn't come in and Charley was beginning to be concerned that something had happened. Her mother-in-law was a stickler for time-keeping, and never late for anything. *Maybe the traffic was bad, or she couldn't find a parking space? Another fifteen minutes, then I'll give her a call.*

A little over ten minutes later Pam arrived, apologising profusely for being late. Despite the fact that it was an over-cast, grey, autumn day, she was wearing sunglasses and appeared decidedly fragile.

How typical of her mother-in-law to selflessly drag herself into the shop even when she was obviously ill. Charley wondered if she should send her straight home and text Ricky to tell him to get a cab. It would put an end to her momentous plans for the day, but that wasn't Pam's fault, she reminded herself.

'Are you okay?' she asked. 'Have you got a migraine or something?'

Clearly struggling, Pam steadied herself against the counter and said in a quiet monotone, 'I have the mother and father of all hangovers and it would be a kindness if you would just let me die now.'

'Oh! Right,' said Charley, completely taken aback. In all the years she'd known Pam, and despite everything her mother-in-law had been through in that time, Charley had never, ever seen Pam hungover, or even, now she came to think of it, drunk.

The surprise in Charley's voice prompted Pam to defend herself. 'There are mitigating circumstances,' she explained in a strained voice. Although whether it was the 'mitigating circumstances' or the excess of alcohol that was causing her pain, Charley wasn't sure. Probably both, she guessed.

'What's happened?'

'I have finished with Dez,' Pam spoke slowly, and with evident effort.

'Oh no! I'm so sorry—' started Charley.

Her mother-in-law put up her hand to silence her. 'Don't be. He is a despicable liar, an unscrupulous conman, a pathetic loser of a gold-digger and an all-round, complete and utter bastard. Plus, he drinks lager out of a can at the dinner table.'

'Oh!' Charley was at a loss for words.

'I have had a narrow escape.'

Very probably, thought Charley but then, as the full implications of what Pam was saying sank in, she realised how devastated and demoralised her mother-in-law must be feeling. 'Oh Pam, what a—'

'Shit?'

'*What a terrible thing to have happened*, is what I was going to say,' said Charley. 'But yes, "shit" probably covers it.'

'Zee's word, not mine,' clarified Pam. Then, weakly, she made a dismissive gesture with her hand. 'I don't deserve too much sympathy. Both Dez and the hangover are self-inflicted wounds.'

Charley was torn. Whilst she was full of compassion for Pam, Ricky's plane would be landing in half an hour and it would take her thirty minutes to get to the airport. Casting her eye over Pam, she tried to gauge if she was even in a fit state to run the shop. Saturdays needed high energy, and right now the poor woman didn't look like she'd make it through the next ten minutes. Perhaps heartlessly, but understandingly, Charley decided that she bloody well wasn't going to abandon her reunion with Ricky, just because of her mother-in-law's self-imposed plight.

'You need coffee, carbs and a lot of water.' Grabbing her handbag she headed for the deli. As it turned out, it was an act of mercy she was going to bitterly regret.

Rita greeted her warmly. 'Hey Charley. The usual?'

Charley nodded. 'Please, and two bottles of water.'

Rita set about making her coffees and bagging up a couple of croissants, but when she handed Charley the coffees she leant over confidingly and said in a low voice, 'Did you know Ricky's given notice on the bike shop?'

Charley felt like she'd been hit by a brick. The deli seemed to spin round and she had to mentally double-check what she'd just heard. 'W-what?' she stammered.

Rita nodded. 'Del told me.'

Charley's world toppled off its axis. Ricky was selling up? And he hadn't even told her? She muttered something incomprehensible, thanked Rita for the coffees and croissants, and completely forgetting the water, fled.

There were a few customers in the shop when she got back, but Pam had removed her dark glasses and seemed to be managing, just about. Numbly Charley put the cups and the pastries on the till table. Her immediate thought was to text Ricky and ask him to get a cab. She couldn't face him. She just couldn't. Then she realised he'd have to pick Carlo up and she didn't want to have an excruciatingly painful scene in the shop.

A throng of customers at the till prevented her from telling Pam what she'd heard from Rita so she waved vaguely in her mother-in-law's direction, put Carlo on his lead and headed to her car. Driving to the airport she was so distracted and distraught she nearly crashed the car, twice.

Once she got to the airport, she parked and, leaving Carlo in the car, headed to arrivals. The sight of Ricky coming towards her, sporting his trademark easy smile, as if everything was all right, sent her emotions boiling over.

'Why didn't you tell me you've given notice on the bike shop?' she demanded, without even waiting for him to say 'Hi'.

'Because I haven't,' he replied blandly.

'Oh.'

For the second time that morning, Charley's world span round her, but this time, it toppled back onto its axis. Her heart began to lift until, clearly deeply embarrassed, Ricky went on to confess that he had in fact decided to give up his shop and move back to Italy.

Charley reeled as if she'd been slapped. 'Back to Italy,' she repeated flatly.

'Yes.'

Back to Italy. She couldn't trust herself to speak. Turning on her heel she strode back to the car.

'Charley, let me explain!' Grabbing his case, he hurried after her.

'Tell me in the car,' she said over her shoulder, not even slowing down.

When they got to the car, Carlo was ecstatic at Ricky's return, clambering all over him and yelping excitedly, so much so that Charley couldn't even drive off safely.

Eventually, with a great deal of firm persuasion, Ricky finally managed to settle the lurcher in the well of the front seat between his legs and she could reverse out of the parking space.

Driving back to Ricky's flat, Charley listened dully to his explanations, hardly taking in what he was saying, battling back her despair and willing herself to concentrate on the road sufficiently to not plough them both into the back of a truck.

'My parents aren't getting any younger,' he was saying, 'and now that my sister's married and moved away, my family need me. There's nothing keeping me in the UK. I can run a bike shop in Tuscany just as well as here.'

It sounded like a well-rehearsed speech to Charley, and it cut her like a knife to imagine him practising it, getting it word-perfect, before he delivered it to her. His plans, it turned out, were not to give notice on the shop immediately, but to keep it going and try to sell his business as a thriving enterprise rather than selling off the stock at no doubt knock-down prices.

'When were you planning on telling me?' she asked.

He shot her a sideways look from the passenger seat. 'I'm telling you now, Charley. As soon as I could, when I got back. I didn't think it was something I could tell you over the phone. I wanted to be able to explain.'

'Yes, I see,' she heard herself say. And she supposed she could see. It was a typically considerate gesture on his part. Besides, she reminded herself, he's been dealing with a family bereavement and he's only just got back from a funeral. Given that, she could hardly expect him to make it his priority to tell her about his future plans, but nonetheless she still felt side-lined, as if she didn't matter.

'So how come Rita seemed to know before me? And Del?'

'They didn't,' he replied with a shrug. 'They must have heard a rumour. Some gossip. But you're the first person I've told, Charley. I promise.'

He turned away and she didn't know what to say. They drove back to his flat in a strained silence, giving Charley the opportunity to re-run his words in her head. *There's nothing keeping me in the UK*, he'd said. Well, if that were the case, then it was clearly pointless asking him if they could try again. It would just be futile and humiliating.

Gradually the agonising realisation that she'd been deluding herself sank in. Clearly Ricky had already moved on, and no matter what they'd had together, it was all history now.

Arriving at his flat, she pulled over to the kerb, but left the engine running. He clambered out of the car, followed by Carlo, and lugged his case out of the boot. Charley stayed sitting behind the wheel from where, lowering the window, she handed him his keys.

'Are you coming in?' he asked.

She shook her head, desperate to get away before she broke down completely. 'I've got to get back to the shop.'

'But I have a thank-you gift for you, for looking after Carlo...'

'Give it to me in the shop.'

He crouched down next to the driver's door so his face was level with hers through the window. 'Charley, please come in. Let's not leave things like this.'

She shook her head, then swallowed hard and added as lightly as she could, as if it were an afterthought, 'Oh, by the way, I've left some of my things at your place. I'll pick them up another time.'

'Of course, any time,' he said, and when she started to close the window, he stood up and stepped back from the car.

Charley drove off. In her rear view mirror she could see him standing on the pavement, watching her, with Carlo, as ever, faithfully sitting beside him at heel. With commendable effort she managed to keep herself under control until she got back to the shop. Pam's concerned expression at seeing her there flipped her over the edge and she promptly burst into tears, which was awkward, since there were a good many customers.

'Go and get yourself a cup of tea,' Pam ordered kindly, and Charley bolted. Not to the deli, she couldn't face Rita. She got herself a take-away tea from a kiosk and sat on a bench over-looking the docks. Crying her eyes out, sipping tea and watching the vibrant harbourside life going on around her she wondered, not for the first time in her life, how other people's lives manage to blithely continue all around you when yours has just completely fallen apart. Finishing the tea, she binned the cup and took herself back to the shop. It was still busy, and she welcomed the distraction as much as the custom. When the shop emptied for a few moments towards the end of the afternoon, she confided everything to Pam.

The older woman let her finish, without interrupting before she said, 'Did you tell him how *you* feel? About wanting to try again?'

Shaking her head, Charley said, 'It's too late.' She sighed wearily, too drained to be tearful.

'No, it isn't, Charley,' persisted Pam.

'It is!' snapped Charley. Then she immediately hated herself for taking out her disappointment on Pam. Apologetically softening her tone she continued, 'I can't make him choose between his family and me.'

Pam put her hands loosely on Charley's shoulders and held her gaze. 'Charley, *everyone* has to choose between their life partner and their family at some stage or another. It was the decision you made when you left home and moved half way across the country to be with Josh. You chose Josh over your family. I chose Geoff over mine. That's an essential part of… leaving home, becoming your own person. But that's Ricky's choice to make. Not yours to make on his behalf.'

'Yes, but I've *seen* Ricky with his family, remember? So I know how much they mean to him, and how much he means to them.'

'But he doesn't know how much he means to *you*, Charley. And he never will if you don't tell him.'

Charley shook her head sadly. 'He's not going to choose me, Pam. He said, and I quote, "There's nothing for me in the UK", so clearly I'm not enough to make him want to stay.' Turning away, she focussed her attention on tallying up the till, trying to ignore the sense of profound, heart-breaking loss for the second time in her life.

Chapter Thirty-Two

Back at her flat later that evening, Charley wandered into the kitchen, dumped her bag on the table and opened the fridge. She supposed she ought to eat something. Having spent much of the week at Ricky's, and anticipating she'd be there for the weekend too, she found her fridge was even more pathetically empty than usual. She leant heavily against the fridge door. This was so not how she'd expected this evening to pan out. In her mind's eye she'd imagined, or rather *fantasised* as it turned out, that she and Ricky would be celebrating, going out to dinner together somewhere special. She'd envisaged candles and champagne, attentive waiters, delicious food… and Ricky… the feel of his skin on hers as he reached across the table to take her hand in his, his warm caressing smile and the gaze of his brown eyes, soft with love. She pulled herself up briskly. *Now you're just torturing yourself.* Even so, whatever she'd pictured, it wasn't a lonely, scrappy meal of leftovers in her kitchen with a mug of tea. Actually, not even a cup of tea since she didn't have any milk.

She knew she ought to go to the supermarket, but she just couldn't be arsed to drag herself there. Slamming the fridge shut, she picked up bag and her keys, and longing for company and a shoulder to cry on, slunk round to Angie's.

'I thought you'd be with Ricky,' said Angie, as she opened the front door, her brood clustered behind her in her wake as usual.

'So did I,' replied Charley, flatly. 'But he's going to back to Italy. Permanently.'

Angie's face fell. 'Oh Charley!' She moved forward to embrace her friend, but Charley put her hand out to stop her.

'Don't!' she warned. 'I will completely fall apart.'

'I know,' said Angie gently, encircling her with both arms. Charley promptly fell apart.

'Why is Charley crying?' asked Finn loudly.

'Because she's sad,' Angie told him. Then, shooing the kids towards the kitchen, she said, 'Tell Daddy he's in charge, I'm with upstairs with Charley,' and she led the way up to her bedroom where Charley flung herself on the bed and sobbed her heart out.

A few moments later, Will came upstairs with two mugs of tea. Finn slid in cautiously behind his dad. Silently, the little boy sidled up to Charley and pressed his bedraggled and much beloved fluffy dinosaur into her hands. She took it and hugged it to her, finding it improbably comforting.

'Thank you, Finnie,' she managed between sobs.

'Good boy, Finn,' said his mother, running her hand over her small son's head lovingly.

Angie didn't try to persuade Charley to go to Ricky and ask if they could try again. But then, instinctively, Charley had known she wouldn't. If she'd wanted someone to do that she would have pitched up at Tara's instead. Where Tara was opinionated and forceful, Angie was pensive and cautious in the advice she gave, more likely to let you draw your own conclusions than impose her judgements on you. Intuitively, Charley had chosen to turn to the friend who was more likely to tell her what she wanted to hear − or rather, who wouldn't tell her what she *didn't* want to hear. When she was all out of tears, thirsty, and in desperate need of another mug of tea, they went back downstairs. Going into the kitchen, she noticed Angie's artwork on the kitchen table, where she'd evidently abandoned it to look after her mate.

'I'm sorry, Ange, I've distracted you,' she said, but her friend merely shrugged dismissively. 'Do you want me to stick around this evening so you can get some done?' offered Charley.

'No, don't be daft. It's too late to start anything now, anyhow. Lily needs a feed and putting to bed, and then we're into the full baths, drinks, teeth-cleaning, stories and bedtime palaver, after which we will all collapse with a well-earned glass of wine!' she promised.

While Angie dealt with baby Lily, Charley foolishly volunteered to supervise Eliot and Finn in the bath. Gleefully, the little horrors ruthlessly exploited her inexperience, staging a full-scale water battle, drenching her and the entire bathroom with their Super Soakers. She fought back heroically with a water-spouting plastic whale, but she was outnumbered and outgunned. No doubt hearing the hysterical pandemonium, their big sister Beth put her head around the bathroom door and, taking in the sodden state of the room pronounced ominously, 'Uh-oh! You're going to be in big trouble!'

Charley and the boys exchanged horrified looks.

Will whisked his mischievous sons off to dry them and put them in their PJs while Charley cleared up the bathroom. Then she went into Beth's room to read her a bedtime story, and the two of them snuggled up under the quilt taking it in turns reading *Fantastic Mr Fox*.

Eventually, all the kids were settled for the night and Charley went downstairs to join Angie and Will. Understandably finding the prospect of leaving such a lively, full house and going home to a barren, empty flat unbearable, she asked Angie if she could stay the night. She'd never done it before. Angie didn't even have a spare room.

'Of course, but you'll have to kip on the sofa.'

Charley would have slept in Buster's basket rather than go home.

–

She couldn't hide at Angie's for ever, and in any case, being in the chaotically happy family home wasn't making it any easier for her, so shortly after breakfast the next morning Charley went back to her place. The oppressive silence of her flat reminded her of the emptiness, physical and emotional, that had consumed her after Josh had died. From now on, every evening and all day Sunday it would be just her, unless she gate-crashed one of her mate's weekends or went round to Pam's for Sunday lunch. Telling herself to snap out of it and not to be so bloody maudlin and self-pitying, she went into the living room to put the TV on, just for the company. As she crossed the floor, her foot kicked one of Carlo's chew toys which she'd obviously missed. She picked it up and gazed at it for a few moments, then sank heavily onto the sofa, hugging it to her. She was even missing the bloody dog. There and then she made a rash decision – one she was going to regret, as it turned out, and quite a bit.

Less than two hours later she'd wilfully let herself fall head over heels for a lovable-looking rogue with a sheepish grin and lopsided ears.

'*Can you give Bubbles his forever home?*' asked the strapline over the dog's photo on the rescue centre webpage. *Yes, I absolutely can,* decided Charley pretty much on the spot.

> Bubbles is an eighteen-month-old cockerpoo who lives up to his name – he's loves to play and is a lot of fun. He is good with dogs and children, completely housetrained, is very good on the lead and has excellent recall so he can be exercised off lead. He could live with another dog. He is very affectionate and likes a lot of cuddles and attention.

Frankly, Bubbles, what is there not *to love about you?* thought Charley, regarding the dog's cute face adoringly. *Well, apart from your name.* If she hadn't already believed in love at first sight, seeing Bubbles' photo would have convinced her.

Clicking on 'Next Steps' she discovered there was an application form to complete, so she made herself a mug of coffee and sat down to fill it in. It was eight pages long and by the time she was halfway through, Charley reckoned it was probably easier to adopt a child than a dog. She clicked away stoically. 'Yes, I have car and a garden and yes, I own my own home. No, I don't have a cat and no, I'm not planning on changing my job or moving home any time in the next three months…' Finally she finished it, submitted the form and an automatic reply told her the rescue centre would be in touch.

—

Ten days later, after a further phone interrogation, plus sending photographic evidence of her 'dog-proof' garden, she finally passed the application process, and was invited to meet Bubbles to see if they were compatible. So she'd begged Pam to look after the shop for a couple of hours and set off to the Four Paws Dog Rescue Centre, taking Angie with her for advice since, apart from Ricky, she was the only person she knew who actually owned a dog. Charley had originally proposed going after school, so that Angie could bring her whole gang. 'It'll be fun!' she'd promised.

Wisely, Angie had vetoed the idea, on the grounds that she didn't want a second dog and there was only so much pester-power a parent could take. So they'd gone just after lunch, with Lily.

The second the kennel staff opened his crate, Bubbles hurled himself enthusiastically at Charley and since she had crouched down to greet him, he nearly knocked her over. The caramel-coloured fluffball wriggled frantically with desperate affection in Charley's arms, and let slip a small excited puddle while she cuddled him.

'What sort of dog is this?' asked Angie sceptically.

'I think he's a cockerpoo, or maybe a labradoodle,' replied the kennel worker. 'Or he might be a shnoodle, come to think of it.'

Charley and Angie exchanged amused looks.

'Are you sure it's not a cock-a-doodle-poo? Or a labra-doodley-don't?' enquired Charley with a straight face. She didn't dare risk catching Angie's eye, knowing they'd both lose it completely, and focused her attention on the dog. He gazed back at her with imploring brown eyes and Charley completely melted.

'Actually, who cares? I absolutely adore him.'

'And I think it's reciprocated,' smiled the woman. 'Okay, so, as you know, we do ask for a £200 contribution. He's had his first jab, but he'll need a booster in a week and then once a year. And you'll have to worm and de-flea him every two months. Have you got a lead and a basket, and a dog bowl and some food?' She didn't even stop for a reply before adding, 'We have everything you'll need in our shop, including toys and treats!'

Charley turned to Angie, suddenly aghast at the mounting cost.

'It's too late to back out now,' Angie told her, looking at the soulful brown eyes staring at them pleadingly. 'One of us is going to have to take him, and it's not going to be me.'

'Lucky Bubbles,' the woman added winningly, and beamed at them.

'Bubbles?' queried Angie flatly. Charley visibly winced, picturing herself having to call the ridiculous name out loud on the Downs.

'Can I change his name?' she asked.

'I wouldn't,' replied the woman. 'He has excellent recall and you'll only confuse him.'

'Bad luck,' said Angie.

A few moments later, at the car, Angie strapped Lily into her booster chair in the back, and Charley settled Bubbles on her lap in the passenger seat. As they drove to her flat, the cockerpoo looked out of the window but every so often he would turn to lick Charley on the chin and she'd give his scruffy little body a hug.

'Oh, you're adorable!' she told him. She turned to Angie. 'Isn't he?'

'Cute, yes. Adorable? Possibly, but only time will tell,' replied Angie sagely, thoroughly alarming Charley.

The first thing she did when Angie dropped them off was let the dog out into the garden. Leaning against the French doors she watched the cockerpoo snuffle excitedly around his new domain, his tail wagging furiously. His evident delight was infectious, and she couldn't help smiling, but moments later her amusement rapidly disappeared when Bubbles starting frantically digging up the lawn.

'No!' wailed Charley. Turf and mud scuffed everywhere as the dog pounded away with his front paws. '*No!*' she bawled, but the cockerpoo ignored her, intent on his work, so she went over and clapped her hands loudly at him. 'No. Bad boy!' she shouted. Startled, Bubbles abandoned his digging, then he shot her an impish look and darted in through the open French doors and leapt onto the sofa, where he sat pleased as punch and with a daft grin on his scruffy face, having trodden mud all over the fabric.

'Oi! Off there, muddy paws!' ordered Charley, racing in after him. Bubbles stayed where he was, flattened his ears and did his soulful eye routine.

'I mean it! *Off!*' She bellowed sternly and reluctantly the cockerpoo sloped onto the floor looking very hard done by and then promptly rolled onto his back to ask for a belly rub.

Charley sighed and obliged, despite despairingly beginning to wonder what she'd let herself in for. Angie's dog didn't behave like this, and of course Carlo was impeccably trained.

'You are a right bloody handful!' she informed him affection-ately.

She stayed with the dog for an hour or so before settling him in the kitchen in his new basket, and putting a bowl of water down. Then she gave him a rubber chew to keep him occupied while she nipped back to the shop to help Pam close up for the day. 'It's only for an hour or so,' she promised. She had planned to take him to the shop with her, but the rescue centre had advised her to let the dog get established into his new home before introducing him to too many new environments and people, so that had scuppered that notion.

'Be a good boy. I'll be home just after six.' *You do know he can't tell the time?* asked a withering voice in her head. She felt mean shutting him into the kitchen but she wasn't going to take any chances with the carpet in the living room. Which was just as well, because when she got back, whilst there weren't any puddles or other 'accidents' on the floor, the cockerpoo had taken all the cushions off the kitchen chairs and ripped them to shreds. Bite-sized chunks of polyfoam littered the entire floor. God only knew how much damage he would have done to the sofa. She stared at the damage askance, then slowly she turned her gaze on Bubbles, who sat in his basket, cheekily cocking his head at her and wagging his tail, clearly proud of his achievements. Cursing under her breath, she kicked him out into the garden while she swept the mess into a bin bag. Naturally, when she went to let him back in again, he was enthusiastically digging another hole in the lawn.

She rang Angie. 'What the hell am I going to do? I can't possibly take him into the shop if he's going to be this destructive!'

'Calm down! You've only just got him. There are bound to be a few teething troubles to begin with. Tell you what, why don't I pop round with Buster every day for a bit? They can have a doggy play date and wear themselves out in the garden.'

'I can't ask you to do that!'

'Yes you can. I have to walk Buster anyhow. And in the meantime, put everything chewable out of reach and then take him for a long, long walk. It'll do you both good.'

Charley trudged round and round the streets for an hour and a half in an attempt to tire the dog out. On the lead, Bubbles trotted obediently by her side, perfectly at heel, every so often looking up at her as if to say, 'Well, this is fun!' They passed quite a few other dog walkers, many of whom, she noticed, were practically having their arms torn out of their sockets, their dogs were pulling so hard. 'Good boy, Bubbles,' she said loudly, trying very hard not to gloat. Getting back to the flat, she fed him, then herself, and then they both sat together on the sofa in a companionable silence while Charley read, holding the book in one hand and running the dog's silky ears through her fingers with the other hand.

'We can make this work, can't we?' In response, Bubbles waggled his eyebrows at her. Adorably.

The comforting, tactile pleasure instantly reminded her of petting Carlo, and from there her thoughts strayed to Ricky. She wondered how he was spending his evening, what he was doing now. Probably crashed out on the sofa with the huge lurcher curled up next to him, a mirror image of her and Bubbles.

'You'd like Carlo,' Charley told the cockerpoo, 'He's very...' She hunted for the right words to describe the lurcher. 'Cool, stylish and loveable.' Then she realised she'd unintentionally summed up Ricky instead. 'Oh well, they say dogs are like their owners,' she told herself defensively. Which, now she came to think of it, made her a scruffy, badly behaved lunatic. At bedtime she put Bubbles in his basket and, wisely, shut the kitchen door. Ten minutes later she opened it again. She just couldn't take the heart-rending howls coming from the kitchen and nor, she suspected, could her upstairs neighbours. She let him cuddle up to her on the bed.

'If you snore, you're going back to the dogs' home.'

Chapter Thirty-Three

'Would you mind very much if I didn't come?' ventured Pam, hating herself for even asking.

'Yes!' cried Zee. 'Very much!'

Which was fair enough since Zee was arranging a pub lunch with their close friends to celebrate her birthday.

'I'm sure Charley can manage without you for just one lunch-time,' Zee had contended. Which was so obviously true that Pam was forced to be open with her old friend and admit she'd rather not go, much to Zee's exasperation.

'You cannot go into hiding, Pam.'

'I'm not!'

'You are.'

Pam cringed, knowing her friend was right. After the fiasco over Dez, she had pretty much gone to ground, too humiliated to face anyone other than Zee and Charley.

'It's only going to be me, Mona and Toni,' coaxed Zee.

Pam could feel her defences lowering. *You'll have to face them sometime*, she reminded herself. Taking a deep mental breath, she eventually agreed.

'Brilliant! I'll pick you up.' Pam guessed her mate didn't trust her not to bottle out on the day.

–

As Zee pulled into the pub car park, Pam let out a melodramatic groan and sank her face into her hands.

'Oh my God! I've just remembered the last time we all had a pub lunch together! It was the day I left Geoff.'

'Good grief, was it? We really have to get out more!'

Prior to her separation, the four friends had often treated themselves to a pub lunch, until one fateful day when, after changing venues at the last minute, they had stumbled on Geoff having lunch with his mistress, or 'That Bloody Woman' as they'd immediately dubbed her. It was the look of pure guilt written all over his face, much like a small boy caught with his hand in the biscuit tin, that had given the game away and, without even waiting for an explanation, Pam had turned on her heel and walked out of the pub, shame and humiliation burning inside her. If she'd just hung on another thirty seconds she'd have witnessed the glorious moment when Zee had hurled the contents of a water jug over the woman and called her an exceptionally rude name, before dashing out after Pam.

Geoff had chased after Pam to the car park, catching up with her as she'd reached the sanctuary of Zee's car where, to her horror, she'd realised the doors were locked. Frantically rattling the handle, she'd looked around despairingly for Zee. In the few moments before Zee had emerged, Pam had been forced into a humiliating exchange with Geoff. She'd demanded to know how long his affair had been going on. When he shamefacedly admitted it had been five years she was devastated. How could she not have known, or at the very least suspected something? Her fury had evaporated, ousted by her assumption of her own gullibility and stupidity. In a matter of seconds she was betrayed and then robbed of every vestige of her self-esteem.

Well, here were are again, thought Pam, plucking up her courage as she and Zee walked across the gravelled car park. *Another pub lunch, another impending humiliation.* Then she told herself off for being self-pitying. *This time, you are the architect of your own destruction.*

Mona and Toni had already bagged a table by the window. They waved enthusiastically to Pam and Zee, then rose to their feet to embrace the others warmly.

'We must get back into the habit of doing this more often!' enthused Mona, as they all sat down.

Pam nodded but inwardly winced at the potential cost.

'Just every other month or so,' added Toni hurriedly, looking directly at Pam, and it belatedly occurred to her that since her mates fully understood she could ill afford the treat, this occasional pleasure had become another casualty of her separation.

'Absolutely,' she agreed. 'I've missed this.'

They ordered and, while they waited for the food to arrive, they chatted animatedly, catching up on everyone's news. As usual, there was a lot to cover: their children and grandchildren, their holidays, their various household crises involving central heating boilers, washing machines, Wi-Fi problems, and the ongoing saga of Toni's struggle with the damp in the downstairs loo. And, equally as usual, there was a lot of interrupting, noisy laughter, affectionate teasing and banter, typical of friendships thriving on the spice of life.

Nobody mentioned Dez and although initially Pam was grateful, in her own mind he began to loom large, until she began to sense that, like the absent Geoff at their dinner parties, Dez had become the elephant in the room.

'I know you're all being incredibly tactful, but can we just talk about me making a complete and utter fool of myself with Dez, and get it over and done with?'

'You didn't make a fool of yourself,' Zee was swift to assure her.

'If you'd given him money, *that* would have made you a fool,' agreed Toni.

'How were you to know what he was really like?' said Mona.

'You don't think I might have missed a few teeny, tiny clues?' asked Pam sarcastically. 'Like never being invited to his place, or Dez drinking all the booze in the house, or throwing a tantrum when he didn't get his own way? Not to mention him getting horrendously pissed at your place, Zee!'

There was a beat before Zee conceded with a grin, 'Yes, all right. You were a bit of a fool.'

'But you know what they say,' said Mona. 'When a man knows he's made a mistake, he doesn't need you to tell him.'

'And when a woman knows she's made a mistake, she needs a gin and tonic!' quipped Toni.

'I'll drink to that!' Pam raised her drink. 'To old friends.'

'And old fools,' added Zee mercilessly, bringing a wry smile to Pam's face.

'You know what you need?' said Mona, turning to Pam when they'd all put their glasses back down. 'A break. A little holiday. Something to bookmark the end of the Dez episode, and put it behind you.'

Pam was just about to make various oblique excuses as to why she didn't need a holiday she couldn't afford when Zee spoke up, uncannily as if she'd read Pam's mind.

'Go to Copenhagen! Hanne said she wouldn't even charge you stay in their Airbnb.'

'Now that's an opportunity too good to miss,' declared Mona.

'There's still the flights,' Pam pointed out.

'Get a budget flight,' said Toni. 'Cheap as chips if you don't mind going at some godforsaken hour.'

Copenhagen, with its brightly painted buildings along the harbour, drifted into Pam's mind enticingly. She wouldn't mind travelling in the middle of the damn night if it made it affordable. And Mona was right; it was an opportunity too good to miss. The only fly in this otherwise extremely appealing ointment was the thought of going by herself. The prospect of travelling alone, or pretty much doing anything on her own, thoroughly depressed her. A montage of scenarios loomed in her mind: sitting alone on the plane, or eating a solitary meal in a restaurant, and tramping round the city with nobody to share the pleasure and the experience.

She shook her head. 'It wouldn't be much fun on my own.'

Immediately three hands shot up in the air and a chorus of 'Take me!', 'No, me!', 'Choose me!' erupted.

'It was my suggestion!' claimed Zee with mock petulance. 'And, if you take me, since you're providing the accommodation, I'll pay for the flights,' she finished in an act of brazen corruption.

'Absolutely not!' Although even as Pam refused the generous gesture, an image of her and Zee exploring Copenhagen together slid into her mind, colourful, entertaining, and above all, fun.

Oh bugger the cost! YOLO, she reminded herself and turning to Zee she said, 'I'll go if you will… but I'm paying for my flight.'

'You're on! And we'll argue about the flight later!'

In the car on the way back to Pam's, Zee badgered her until she texted Hanne to get the ball rolling. Even before they'd arrived at the house, Hanne had pinged back a link to the Airbnb with instructions to book themselves in for a long as they liked, and as soon as they could, while the autumn weather was still warm. *It is empty at the moment*, she had finished coaxingly, catapulting them both into a fit of intense excitement.

—

It was nearly three by the time Pam got to Charley's shop, later than she'd anticipated, but her daughter-in-law brushed aside her apologies.

'Did you have a good time?' quizzed Charley cheerfully.

'Yes, it was lovely. We went to the pub by the suspension bridge and…' She trailed off, because Charley obviously wasn't listening. Her attention had been drawn to something going on outside. Pam's eyes followed Charley's gaze through the shop window, and alighted on Ricky. He was walking along, Carlo at heel, and chatting animatedly to a young woman. A very attractive young woman, realised Pam with a sinking heart. Immediately, her eyes flicked back to Charley in concern.

Wordlessly, her daughter-in-law turned slowly to face her, and the look of shocked anguish and undisguised pain in her eyes sliced into Pam like a scalpel. Rapidly but forensically reassessing what they'd both actually seen, rather than what Charley clearly thought she had seen, Pam clocked that the pair hadn't been holding hands, or walking particularly close to one another. In fact, there was nothing to indicate there was anything going on between Ricky and the woman.

'Don't jump to conclusions,' she warned. 'She might just be a friend, or even a customer.' It was evident from Charley's face that she didn't believe either scenario, and Pam wasn't overly convinced herself. Then, to her dismay, it was as if a set of shutters slammed down across Charley's face, and she turned her back to the window.

'I don't really care who she is. It's none of my business what he does.'

Pam, on the other hand, watched Ricky as he led the woman to the deli where he courteously opened the door for her. The woman beamed up at him, sickeningly coquettishly in Pam's opinion, and although Ricky gave her one of his trademark ready smiles in return, Pam noticed he didn't touch her, he didn't put his hand on her elbow, or in the small of her back, as she had so often seen him do with Charley. So maybe there was nothing in it, and Charley had misread the scene. She very much hoped so.

Clearly wanting to change the subject, her daughter-in-law chirpily asked Pam if she'd had a good time at lunch, apparently oblivious to the fact that she'd already asked her.

'Yes, it was *lovely*,' repeated Pam without batting an eyelid. 'We all agreed we need to do it more often – if you can spare me, that is,' she finished hastily.

'Of course,' nodded Charley.

'On that note…' said Pam, and hesitated so long that Charley looked at her enquiringly and prompted her.

'Yes?'

'Could you spare me for a few days if I go to Copenhagen?'

Far from looking anxious, as Pam had feared she might, in which case she would have instantly abandoned the idea, Charley's whole face lit up.

'Copenhagen? Yes! You absolutely *must* go!'

'Are you sure? I know how much of a struggle it is on your own.'

'It won't be a problem, I've got Tara. When were you thinking of going?'

'Not really sure. Maybe in the next couple of weeks, unless that's too short notice.'

'No, that'll be absolutely fine.'

Chapter Thirty-Four

The unwanted image of Ricky with the young, attractive woman kept forcing itself into Charley's mind, re-running itself like some over-used meme. The following morning, determining to put it – and Ricky – out of her mind, she concentrated on stocktaking and studiously avoided looking out of the window. When Tara came in Charley was more than usually grateful, for the distraction if nothing else, until her mate delivered her Thought for the Day.

'We need to rearrange everything in the shop.'

'Do we? Why?' The layout of the shop seemed to be working fine to Charley. She'd applied a great deal of thought and impeccable logic to the displays – all the sweets, confectionary and edible items were stacked onto the large table in the middle, linens and fabric items were piled onto the dresser with the glass and china, the smaller tables housed tealights, bath products and other sundries, and Angie's artwork hung on the back wall.

'It'll be a massive job!'

'We need to ring the changes,' said Tara dismissing Charley's objection. 'If the customers look in and see the same old layout, the same old displays, and the same old stuff it doesn't draw them in. I mean, look around, it's been like this for months. Even I'm bored of it!' Tara may have meant it as a joke, but Charley bridled. 'I'll do it,' Tara added hastily, thereby nipping in the bud any objection Charley could make in terms of the time it would take.

Surprisingly, Charley found herself warming to the idea. If only so that they could move the till counter so that she didn't have to look out of the bloody window.

'Where were you thinking of putting everything?' she asked warily, remembering what an enormous task stocking the shelves had been in the first place.

Her friend shrugged. 'It doesn't matter, as long as everything is clearly displayed and *nothing* is in the same place where it started.'

'Okay. Fine, let's do it,' agreed Charley.

A look of mild astonishment flicked onto Tara's face, but she quickly banished it and said, 'Great!'

The two women rapidly set to work, having quickly decided the best approach was to swap entire displays around, rather than randomly shifting everything individually, although Charley stuck to her guns about moving the counter.

'What we really need are some new products, some new lines,' said Tara, neatly stacking a pile of cotton pinnies onto a table, with the rest of the linens. 'That's the only real way to boost interest. There'll be a lot of new products out there we don't even know about. We can't afford to sit on our heels, Charley. Do you want to me to look into it?'

Not really, thought Charley but she couldn't see how she could justifiably object, so she heard herself agree. They were halfway through the refurbishing and Tara nipped out to get them coffee to boost their flagging spirits. However, when she came back she brought news that sent Charley's spirits plummeting.

'I've just bumped into Ricky in the deli. He's with another sodding woman!' she announced furiously, displaying both a commendable loyalty towards Charley and an astounding lack of tact.

Charley tried to focus on what she was doing and not to overreact, or better still, not to react at all. *Another woman?* she wondered. *Or was it the same woman she'd already seen him with?* Frankly, it made no difference either way. Determinedly crushing her dismay, she kept her tone level and unemotional. 'Young woman? Tall, slim, blonde, with long hair, sun-shades perched on top of her head, probably wearing a print dress and a denim jacket just a shade too large, cleverly designed to make her look vulnerable, cute and sexy at the same time?' she asked, probably revealing more about herself than the woman.

'Yup, that's the one.'

Charley turned away and busied herself thumping cushions. 'I saw her with him yesterday.'

'Well, he didn't waste any time,' fumed Tara.

'Why should he?' replied Charley mildly, her light tone belying her misery. 'He's a free agent. I'm happy for him if he's found someone.'

The look of sheer incredulity on her mate's face indicated Tara didn't believe her for one second but, unusually for Tara, she didn't challenge Charley, limiting herself to muttering, 'Well I'm bloody not.'

Mechanically, Charley spent the next hour or so swapping products round, happy to follow Tara's lead, but in her head she was miles away, or rather months away, lost in her memories of when she and Ricky had been together. His birthday, when she'd surprised him with breakfast in bed and tickets to the Foodies Festival. She'd got the tickets secretly, on a whim, instinctively guessing he'd love to go. His face had lit up when he'd opened the envelope and she'd been chuffed to bits. And then the weekend of the Tour de France when she'd sworn blind that watching the entire highlights with him was absolutely her idea of a *perfect* Sunday. It hadn't been a complete lie; spending the day entwined with him on the sofa had been wonderful. Then her mind drifted to more routine, regular times with him, other Sundays, date nights, picnics on the beach and long walks with Carlo. The trouble was that the bloody woman kept forcing herself into the scenes so that it was her and not Charley walking across the Downs with Ricky, and her lounging on Ricky's sofa, with Carlo's head on her lap, while Ricky cooked them supper, and it was her sliding into Ricky's bed... *Oh pack it in, for crying out loud, don't do this*, Charley rebuked herself harshly, banishing the images from her mind. But the damage was already done and she was left bleakly wondering how she'd managed to screw things up so badly.

Shortly afterwards, a customer came in and went over to browse Angie's artwork on the back wall. She picked up a large canvas and eyed it critically. The painting portrayed a huge, stylized question mark, made from bubbles, erupting from the top of a Prosecco bottle with the slogan, *Whatever the question, Prosecco is the answer!*

'They're painted by a local artist,' Tara told the woman enthusiastically.

'I do like it…' replied the woman, but her tone was lukewarm.

'So do a lot of people,' said Tara effusively, 'but we have exclusive rights to sell the artist's work so you can *only* get it here.'

That last statement seemed to re-kindle the woman's interest. 'The thing is, I'm opening a restaurant, and I'd need ten pictures but you've only got four.'

'That's not a problem. When do you need them by?'

'Friday week.'

'We can easily get another six in by then.'

'Or the week after,' Charley called over hurriedly from the till, alarmed by Tara's casual promise.

Tara flashed her a sharp look behind the customer's back.

'Well, in that case, can I take these four and order the rest?'

'Certainly,' said Tara, and she started taking the artwork down while the customer went over to pay Charley at the till.

'Do you need me to pay for the others now?' the woman asked Charley.

'No, when you pick them up will be fine,' replied Charley, ignoring a second peevish look from Tara.

The restaurant owner had barely closed the door behind her when Tara blurted out exasperatedly, 'Charley! You should have taken the money up front!'

'But I didn't want to take the money and commit Angie to doing six pieces of artwork before asking her if she can actually deliver that much by next Friday,' replied Charley reasonably.

'But *now* there's no guarantee the women will come back in and buy it even if Angie does,' pointed out Tara, and once she'd had a moment to think it through, Charley had to concede she'd made a blunder.

'And while we're on that subject,' Tara went on, 'we need to start setting Angie deadlines. It's not professional to have her dropping off bits of artwork every now and again, when, or *if*, she feels like it.'

Charley leapt to Angie's defence. 'Tara! This is our mate we're talking about. You know, the one with the four kids!'

'What's that got to do with it?' countered Tara hotly. 'I can hardly explain that to a customer. What am I supposed to say? *"Sorry, I have no idea when the next delivery of artwork will be because our mate Angie's got four kids so she's very busy wiping noses, changing dirty nappies and doing the school run"?*'

'No, of course not, but Angie is genuinely busy "wiping noses, changing dirty nappies and doing the school run" and we can't expect her to drop everything and prioritise making a huge volume of artwork for the shop just because a customer comes in out of the blue and puts in a massive order.'

Tara groaned but adopting a jokey tone said, 'Charley, we're meant to be running a sodding business, not a bring-and-buy stall! If we're going to sell something we need a reliable supply line, regular deliveries and agreed deadlines. She's treating it like a hobby!' Which, coming from her, rendered Charley literally speechless.

'I'll give her a call,' said Tara, going to get her phone from her handbag.

'No, I will. Later.' *When you're not around to eavesdrop and butt in.*

Tara eyeballed her and for one brief moment Charley thought she was going to override her but, to her relief, Tara backed down. 'Fine.'

Charley left it at that, but the atmosphere between them remained strained until Tara left to pick up Monnie. As soon as the shop was clear of customers, Charley called Angie.

'I can't possibly do six pieces of art by the end of next week!' exclaimed her panic-stricken friend. 'Is Tara insane?'

'No, she just doesn't have four kids,' replied Charley. Then, since Angie sounded like she was hyperventilating at the end of the phone, Charley continued reassuringly, 'Don't panic, I know you can't, and I warned the customer it might have to be the week after.'

'Honestly Charley, I'm not even sure I can promise to deliver them by then,' said Angie anxiously. 'It's parents' evenings at the school so Will's not around, the kids have got a rash of birthday parties to go to over the weekend, Finn's picked up a grotty, snotty cold from nursery and Beth's got a football tournament.'

'Just do what you can,' Charley said soothingly, 'and seriously Ange, don't worry. It won't be the end of the world if you can't.'

–

Saturday got off to a really lousy start. Arriving at work just a little after eight thirty, Charley happened to glance down towards Ricky's shop, where he was opening up for the day and the damn blonde woman was with him. Charley immediately looked away, not wanting to process what she was seeing. Either the woman was a very early riser or... *Don't even finish that thought.* Pam had warned her not to jump to conclusions but, seriously? This early in the morning, what other conclusion could she come to? Unlocking the shop door, she fled inside to the sanctuary of her own space, her heart thumping in her chest. Obviously it was none of her business what Ricky did, but did he have to be so bloody blatant about it? How did he think it was supposed to make her feel? If things were reversed, and he'd finished with her, would she so flagrantly flaunt a new boyfriend right under his nose? She had no right to be jealous, none at all, she reminded herself, but somehow that didn't make it any less painful to watch. The incident threatened to put her in an irritable mood all day, until Pam arrived, bubbling over with excitement.

'We have booked the flights!' she announced eagerly. 'This time next week, I will be in Copenhagen!'

Her entire face beamed, and her daughter-in-law couldn't help but be infused with her child-like joy.

'Do you want to see the pictures of the Airbnb?' gushed Pam, taking her phone out of her handbag. 'Just very quickly, before we open,' she stressed, but already having opened the app and frenetically scrolling.

'Of course I do! Hand it over,' demanded Charley eagerly, before skimming through the pictures of the apartment. 'OMG! It's fabulous! It's like something out of a magazine. It's so...'

'Chic... stylish... cool?' offered Pam. 'Scandi?'

'Yes! All of the above,' agreed Charley. 'I have flat envy!' she wailed. Privately, she also envied Pam going on holiday, then she chastised herself for being self-centred. Her mother-in-law, she reminded herself, needed and deserved this break, and she shouldn't begrudge her a moment of it.

'I hope you have a wonderful time,' she said, genuinely meaning it, and embracing the older woman warmly.

Midway through the morning a delivery arrived, which somewhat threw Charley since she didn't remember having ordered anything.

'Hang on,' she said to the delivery man while she double-checked the address on the boxes, but the labels clearly stated *Charley's Prosecco Pop-Up*.

'Oh, good grief!' gasped Pam, a few moments later, unpacking a couple of Prosecco flutes. 'These are a little...'

'Ghastly?'

'I was going to go with "gaudy" but I think your description is closer to the mark,' admitted Pam.

The two women regarded the garish flutes with dismay. They were shocking pink with the word 'FIZZ' emblazoned on them in silver, and looked like they were made out of plastic. There was an entire box of them. Charley flicked one with her finger and, much to her surprise, it gave off a tell-tale 'ping'.

'Oh, they're glass!' exclaimed Pam.

'Apparently,' said Charley flicking the flute again, harder.

'Careful, you'll break it, darling.'

'With a bit of luck,' replied Charley dryly.

'I take it you didn't order them.'

'No. I guess Tara did,' sighed Charley looking at the rest of the unpacked boxes, dreading to think what other tasteless monstrosities were awaiting discovery.

'Did you know she was going to order them?'

'She did mention sorting some new stock,' replied Charley, with deliberate vagueness. 'But I didn't know she was actually going to order any.'

'What happened to the *rule of three* law?' asked Pam pointedly.

Good question! thought Charley but she didn't reply.

When they'd first set up the shop, Tara had been so assertive about what the shop should stock, even when the others disagreed with her, that Charley had instituted the 'rule of three' law, whereby all three of them had to agree to stock an item. Now, to Charley's annoyance, it looked like Tara had flouted that rule and was striking out unilaterally.

She palmed her forehead in despair. 'What the hell am I going to do about Tara?'

Her mother-in-law carried on unpacking the flutes in silence, implicitly inviting Charley to expand further.

'She's ordered piles of stuff without even consulting me, and she's demanding I set Angie deadlines for her artwork...'

Pam immediately froze and raised an eyebrow.

'I haven't,' Charley assured her hurriedly. 'And she constantly, *constantly* criticises the way I'm running the shop.'

Putting down a couple of the shocking-pink flutes onto a nearby table, the older woman turned to look her in the eye. 'Charley, you've known Tara for years. In all honesty, darling, what did you *think* working with her was going to be like?'

I thought it was going to be fun, wailed Charley's inner voice. She'd been childishly naïve. Even Pam, who'd only known Tara a few months, had predicted how things would turn out.

Charley sighed bitterly. 'I just didn't realise it was going to be this difficult.'

'You're just going to have to discuss it with her,' Pam said firmly.

Charley bit her lip. She hated confrontation at the best of times, but tackling Tara head-on about anything was to be avoided at all costs. Confrontation was Tara's forte. She was a master of the ancient craft of unarmed verbal conflict. Utterly ruthless and completely fearless, she unerringly went for the jugular. Charley knew there would be blood on the carpet, and all of it would be hers.

'I know you don't want to, Charley, but if you don't want us to sell things like this, then you'll have to tackle Tara about it.'

Inwardly, Charley flinched. Nowadays, tension between her and Tara always seemed to be simmering on a rolling boil. An outright conflict with her might just be enough to tip them both over the edge, and end their friendship altogether.

'I just don't want to make it even more difficult to work with her,' Charley tried to reason. 'She's one of my closest friends…' Pam's expression made it all too evident that the older woman knew she was wimping out. 'Why don't I wait and see if this stuff actually sells?' finished Charley, bottling it completely.

Her mother-in-law didn't reply.

They ploughed on through the rest of the delivery. To be fair to Tara, there were only a few items Charley and Pam would have vetoed outright: the lurid pink and silver flutes, cheap party sashes reading *Pour Me A Proseco*, ('So cheap they couldn't afford to spell-check them,' observed Charley), sparkly hen-party tiaras proclaiming the wearer to be a *Prosecco Queen*; and last and worst of all, men's boxer shorts bearing the slogan, *Pop my Prosecco and watch me get fizzical*.

'Please tell me we don't have to sell these?' Pam picked up a pair disdainfully between her thumb and forefinger.

'Not if they were the last Prosecco-themed product on the planet!' Charley plucked the underpants out of Pam's grasp and stuffed them back in the box.

At the end of the day, Charley headed home, looking forward to putting a difficult day to bed, and having a therapeutic cuddle with Bubbles. She opened the front door to find the cockerpoo eagerly waiting for her in the hall, his tail wagging away nineteen to the dozen. The remains of a ripped-up letter lay on the doormat.

'Did you do that?' Charley asked him sternly. The dog's ears went back, his tail tucked between his legs, and he slunk up the hall and put himself into his bed in the kitchen.

'I'm taking that as a "Yes",' she called after him, gathering up the pieces of paper and then following him into the kitchen where she pieced the soggy, half chewed remnants together on the table. It turned out to be a note from the upstairs neighbours complaining that her dog had howled the house down for hours and informing her that if she didn't do something about it they would report her to Environmental Health.

Bloody, bloody hell! What a perfect end to an all-round rubbish day. She turned to the cockerpoo. 'You are a complete nightmare,' she informed him. He did the flattened ears routine again and looked up at her with pitiful brown eyes. She wilted. It wasn't his fault, she reminded herself, but even so what the hell was she going to do now? Angie had seemed so certain that bringing Buster round every morning and letting the dogs chase each other silly round the garden was going to settle Bubbles for the rest of the day. But clearly the doggy play-dates weren't working. The only solution was to bite the bullet and take him to work with her – and if that didn't work out? Well, she'd have to cross that bridge when she came to it. Carlo spent all day in the bike shop, it'd probably be fine, she told herself. She made a mental note to go upstairs and apologise later, and promise she'd got the problem under control. The last thing she needed was neighbours with Environmental Health on speed-dial. Bubbles was impeccably behaved all day Sunday and she began to think taking him into the shop would indeed be the solution. With hindsight however, she discovered she'd been naively lulled into a false sense of optimism.

Chapter Thirty-Five

Very briefly, in a moment of mild insanity on the Monday morning, Charley considered cycling into the shop with Bubbles on a loose lead running along beside her, as Ricky did with Carlo. However, a vivid catastrophe fantasy involving other dogs, a cat, several cars and an ambulance, wisely made her decide to walk instead. She set off optimistically, determined to thoroughly enjoy the journey. It was a dry, autumn day, with a slight breeze, and Bubbles trotted along obediently at heel. He was a joy to walk and she found herself hoping Ricky would see her arriving at Cargo with her well-behaved dog. Not that she particularly wanted to see Ricky, she reminded herself sharply.

As it happened, she didn't see Ricky on her way in, which was probably just as well, because the moment she unlocked the shop door Bubbles went ballistic. He shot inside, ripping the lead out of her hand, and raced around shop like a demented demon, frantically jumping up and sniffing at everything.

'Bubbles stop! Calm down! Come here! HERE!' Desperately she tried to make a grab for his leash as it snaked tantalisingly past her, but just missed it. Leaping up to investigate one of the side tables, the dog knocked the entire display over, sending tealight holders, scented candles and countless other objects crashing to the floor.

Bloody dog! she cursed, then, 'Drop it! *Drop it!*' she bawled as Bubbles snatched up a pack of Prosecco-themed cocktail straws and charged round the shop with it, pleased as punch with his trophy.

Eventually she caught him and, tying his lead to the leg of the biggest table and hoping to God he wouldn't be able to pull that

273

over, she righted the small table and collected up all the stock. Fortunately nothing was damaged, except her confidence in her plan to have the dog in the shop.

To be fair to Bubbles, he had calmed down considerably by the time Tara got in, but the wild excitement of someone new set him off again and he hurled himself at her, as if she was a long-lost friend.

'Get down, you sodding great dollop!' she ordered, pushing him off crossly. 'I hope he's not going to do that to the customers.'

So do I, thought Charley but all she said was, 'He'll be fine once he gets used to being here.' If all else failed she'd tie his lead to her thigh if she had to.

Tara shot her a withering look as if to say, *Who are you trying to kid?* which, uncharitably and probably unfairly, Charley put down to jealousy. Tara had been distinctly put out when she'd learned that Charley had taken Angie to the dogs' home instead of her.

'Monnie would have loved to go with you,' she'd complained. 'You know how much she loves animals.'

'I would have asked you but I needed Angie's advice,' Charley had replied defensively. 'She's got a dog so I thought she'd know what to look for.'

Tara had left it at that, but Charley was sure the grievance still rankled.

As the morning progressed Bubbles did calm down but, embarrassingly, all the customers got the full-on, long-lost friend greeting.

'You're going to have to leave him at home,' Tara told her.

'I can't. He howls the place down and the neighbours have complained.'

'Good job you got Angie's advice then,' was Tara's sarcastic riposte, and Charley bit her tongue. 'In that case you're going to have to get him under control!'

Easier said than done, thought Charley.

Things went from bad to worse when Ricky strolled by with Carlo. It was Charley's bad luck that just at that precise moment a customer was leaving, and so the door was open. Seizing the moment, Bubbles shot through the doorway and launched himself playfully at the lurcher.

Charley raced after him, 'Bubbles! Come here!' she ordered firmly, desperately trying to convey in her voice that this was absolutely not the kind of behaviour her dog usually indulged in. 'Come here!' she yelled more loudly since Bubbles had apparently gone completely deaf.

Poor Carlo was trying to behave himself, but the cockerpoo was jumping all over him like a maniac. Eventually, Ricky managed to grasp his lead and haul him off the poor lurcher.

'Is this yours?' he asked Charley.

She wanted the ground to swallow her up, her previous fantasy bursting like a bubble. 'Yes,' she cringed.

Calmly telling Carlo to sit and stay outside the shop, Ricky hauled the still manically bouncing Bubbles inside. 'Lively little fella,' he commented mildly.

Charley held her hand out for the lead. 'Yes, he is a bit. Thank you.' Inwardly dying of embarrassment, she added by way of explanation, 'He's a rescue dog and it's his first time in the shop.'

'He's a sodding nightmare, and it'll probably be his last,' muttered Tara loudly and Charley shot her a furious look. 'Well, he is!' Tara promptly turned to Ricky and infuriated Charley still further by asking, 'Any ideas on how to control a hyperactive hound? Apart from nailing him to the floor?'

Ricky pulled a face. 'That's the trouble with adopting a dog; you don't really know what you're getting. It took Carlo a long time to settle.'

'Oh, I'd forgotten Carlo was a rescue dog,' said Charley.

'Well, you've done a great job with him,' Tara told Ricky, rather pointedly it seemed to Charley.

'To be fair, he was a bit different from... Bubbles, is it?' checked Ricky. Charley nodded. 'In fact he was the complete opposite, very nervous, and wary of strangers.'

'Yes, I don't think we've got the same problem with Rent-a-Mugger,' said Tara dryly, since the cockerpoo was now up on his back legs, straining at his leash, to get to Ricky.

'Seriously, have you got any useful tips?' asked Charley, gently hauling the dog backwards and then discreetly trying to push his backside into a sit.

Ricky glanced behind the till counter. 'It might help if you bring his bed,' he advised her. 'That'll show him he's meant to settle. It's what I did with Carlo.' He shot Charley a wry smile. 'I'm not promising it'll work with that one, but it's worth a try.'

Charley kicked herself. *Why hadn't she thought of that?* 'Good idea. Yes, I'll do that. Well, thanks for your help,' she said, hoping Ricky would take the hint and leave, before Bubbles disgraced himself further.

Although Ricky turned to go, it was Tara who didn't seem to get the hint, delaying him by asking him if there was any news about selling his business. Charley could have happily strangled her.

'Actually, yes. I think I've found a buyer.'

A lead weight seemed to wallop into Charley's stomach. 'Already?'

The palpable dismay in her voice led both Tara and Ricky to turn to her, so she added hurriedly, 'That's fantastic news. I was just surprised it's happened so quickly.'

Tara shot her a withering look, which Charley ignored.

'Yes, me too,' agreed Ricky.

There was an awkward silence, during which Ricky's eyes never left Charley's, until Tara reminded him that his faithful lurcher was still obediently sitting outside, at which point, with some reluctance, Ricky turned to leave. 'Good luck with the dog,' he said to Charley.

'Thanks, and good luck with the buyer,' she responded. When he'd gone she studiously avoided looking at Tara, determined not to prompt any unwanted discussion about Ricky.

Since Charley couldn't lug a dog's bed into work with her every day she nipped out to buy Bubbles another one for the shop. 'If you had pocket money I'd be making you pay for this,' she told him, as she positioned it under the counter. The cockerpoo sniffed his new bed, clambered onto it, circled round busily half a dozen times and then plonked himself down with what seemed to Charley to be a satisfied sigh. Ricky, it turned out, had been right. Happily curled up in his new bed, the dog went to sleep.

The following afternoon, Ricky dropped into the shop, bearing a small carrier bag. Bubbles immediately leaped out of his bed, tail wagging nineteen-to-the-dozen.

'This is for him,' said Ricky, handing the bag to Charley with one hand, and stroking the cockerpoo's head fondly with the other.

'Oh,' said Charley awkwardly. Her discomfort worsened when Pam loudly professed a sudden desire for tea and with glaring unsubtlety nipped out to get some, leaving Charley and Ricky alone together in the shop.

Opening the bag, 'helped' by Bubbles standing on his hind legs and trying to snuffle out the contents with his nose, Charley took out a complicated-looking dog toy.

'You put a treat in it,' explained Ricky, 'and the dog has to work out how to get it out.'

'Thank you,' said Charley. 'It's very thoughtful of you. Really. And I do appreciate it.'

Ricky stood self-consciously for a moment, as if he had something else to say. So Charley waited and a lengthy silence grew between them.

Eventually Ricky said, 'It should keep him happily occupied for hours. Well, that's what it says on the pack...'

'Let's hope so. I'm sure he'll love it. And thanks again.'

'I'd best get back to the bike shop,' he said, still not making any attempt to leave.

'Yes, of course,' agreed Charley, and finally, with one last ruffle of the cockerpoo's ears, Ricky left.

After he'd gone, Charley stood gazing numbly at the dog toy in her hand, overwhelmed by a confusion of conflicting messages. Why did he have to be so nice to her on the one hand, whilst on the other hand heartlessly parade his new girlfriend under her nose? Either way, it hurt.

—

Pam returned a few minutes later, with the tea.

'There was no need for you to scoot off like that,' Charley told her.

'I was just getting us some tea!' Pam feigned an air of aggrieved innocence as if butter wouldn't melt in her mouth. Since it was so profoundly untrue, Charley didn't even deign to reply.

By the end of the week, even Tara had to admit Bubbles was settling down, and she'd taken to bringing in dog treats in the mornings, as well as coffee and pastries for her and Charley. The tension had also settled between the two friends, which was a huge relief for Charley, not least because the group were all having drinks at her place that evening, and whilst she always tried to adhere to the rule that *what happens at work, stays at work*, Tara did not. Looking on the bright side, however, Tara seemed to have got over her jealousy towards Angie, and the fun and banter had returned to their working relationship, so Charley was looking forward to seeing everyone. Well, she was... until lunchtime.

The restaurant owner who'd come in the previous week and ordered six of Angie's paintings arrived, expecting them to have been delivered. When she discovered they hadn't been, and that neither Tara nor Charley seemed to have any idea when they were expecting them, she erupted, venting spleen on Tara, volubly and publicly, in front of a shop full of people.

'You promised me they would be here by the end of this week!' she exclaimed at the top of her voice. Heads turned as customers sought to discover what the barney was about. Charley wondered if she should intervene and take the flack; it was her shop, after all. Bubbles slunk into his basket, frightened by the woman's strident tone.

'I do apologise,' said Tara with impressive calm. 'I was told they would be here. I'll chase up the artist and find out what's happened.' Then, turning to Charley, she said imperiously, 'Give her a ring please and find out when we can expect the outstanding artwork.'

Sympathetic as she was that her mate was getting a humiliating and very public shredding, Tara's high-handed tone instantly incensed Charley and she would have loved to ignore Tara's request but, mindful of how unprofessional that would look, she took her phone out, only for the woman to stop her.

'No! It's too late for that. You should have done that already!'

'Perhaps if we call the artist—' Tara started, but the woman cut her off rudely.

'I only bought the other four because you promised you could get me the rest on time. So you either lied, or you're incompetent.' Tara's face flushed livid, and Charley held her breath anticipating a volcanic outburst, but the woman had already turned her back on Tara and was striding towards the door.

'Either way I don't want the other ones,' she snapped. 'I'll bring them back. And I shall expect a full refund!'

Instinctively, Charley decided it was best to pretend that the entire embarrassing scene hadn't happened, and to discuss it with Tara later when the shop was empty, so she carried on serving the remaining customers as calmly as she could. The moment the last one had left the shop, Tara exploded at Charley.

'I *told* you to give Angie a deadline,' she ranted, 'and now look what's happened! Listen Charley, if you want run the shop like a… like a car boot sale that's up to you, but I'm not up for being yelled at and being made to look like an a complete sodding idiot in a shop full of people!'

'You were the one who over-committed Angie in the first place,' Charley reminded her. 'I warned you she might not be able to deliver that much artwork in time.'

'She hasn't delivered any!'

'She's obviously been too busy!'

Tara folded her arms and eyeballed Charley. 'I knew you'd take her side.'

'I'm not *taking sides*!'

'Yes, you are. You've sided with Angie throughout this whole artwork problem.' *What artwork problem?* thought Charley. 'And you don't even sodding well realise it,' Tara continued furiously. 'All along, I've tried to get her to be more professional, to get *both* of you to be more professional, actually, and you've constantly undermined me.'

Charley opened her mouth to protest, but at that precise moment Pam walked in. By the openly wary expression on her face it was clear she realised she'd interrupted something, but then it wouldn't have taken a genius to work that out. Tara, arms crossed, was glaring at Charley, who was regarding her coolly, mouth pressed in a thin line, and the tension in the shop was almost physical.

After a beat Tara said, 'Right, well, since Pam's here, I may as well go,' and, pausing only to nod at Pam, she picked up her bag and left.

Pam raised a querying eyebrow at Charley.

'Don't even ask,' replied Charley, closing her eyes. So, tactfully, Pam didn't.

Although later, clearly having had time to brood on the issue, she asked Charley if she wanted her to cancel her trip to Copenhagen.

'Absolutely not!' Charley was deeply moved that the older woman was prepared to abandon her holiday, and at the very last moment, if she was needed in the shop. 'You go, and have a wonderful time.'

But for the rest of the afternoon Charley was distracted, fretting about what the bloody hell she should do about Tara. Obviously she'd have to try to resolve things before Monday since she didn't want to risk a public quarrel in the shop and she knew it would be wise give her mate time to cool off, so she made a mental note to call her on Sunday, or better still, go round to her house with a peace offering. Which seemed like the perfect plan, until she remembered that everyone was coming round for drinks at hers that evening.

What if Tara has a go at Angie? She'll annihilate her.

Chapter Thirty-Six

Walking home with Bubbles, Charley heard a message ping into her phone. It was from Tara. With admirable honesty she'd put,

> Not in the mood for drinks. See you on Monday. PS Please send me the A/Cs

Charley's initial reaction was relief. Then she read the text again. *The accounts?* She still hadn't got the books up to date, so now she was going to have to spend the entire weekend doing them. She raised her eyes heavenwards in despair. *Bloody, bloody hell.* Trudging on, she determined not to let the thought spoil her evening with Angie and Nisha. Making a detour via the mini supermarket, she picked up some Prosecco and crisps since of course Tara wouldn't be bringing her usual supplies. When the others arrived, Charley made Tara's excuses for not coming, yet deliberately avoiding going into any detail.

'Is something wrong with Monnie?' asked Nisha, as Charley poured the fizz.

'I don't think so,' she replied vaguely. 'She didn't say...'

Nisha raised a querying eyebrow, which Charley ignored, but nevertheless she was taken aback when Angie said apologetically, 'She's probably pissed off with me for letting you down about the artwork.'

'Wait, what?' said Charley, her drink pausing halfway to her mouth.

'She called me,' explained Angie.

Charley plonked her glass noisily back down onto the table. *Bloody Tara!* she thought. *Way out of order, again!*

'I am sorry, Charley, really I am. I know I've landed you in it, but there's nothing I can do about it.'

'Angie, it's fine…' Charley tried to reassure her, but her mate ignored her and ploughed on.

'It's Will. He keeps promising to get back early enough to look after the kids, but things keep "cropping up" at school and he never does.'

'It's really not a problem—' started Charley.

'It is to me!' cried Angie hotly, and Charley was alarmed to see tears welling up in her friend's eyes.

Nisha shared a concerned look with Charley, who slid over to sit next to Angie.

'What's happened, Ange?' she quizzed gently.

It turned out that Tara's phone call had triggered an enormous and bitter row between Angie and her husband over Will not prioritising her artwork. In all the years she'd known the couple Charley had never heard of them having any significant disagreements. In her eyes, they were the perfect couple. Demonstrably affectionate towards each other, obviously deeply in love despite the numerous and exhausting demands of their four small children, and seemingly happy and content. So what the hell had Tara said that had set the cat amongst the pigeons?

'Tara said I had to start treating my artwork more professionally, deliver regularly, set deadlines and stick to them, and I get it, I can see why the shop needs that, I really do, but I literally can't paint and look after the kids at the same time, and so I tackled Will about it but he got on his high horse and said he's the breadwinner and he can't put my "hobby" over his work,' spat Angie.

Oh, Will! thought Charley irritably, and she heard a slight intake of breath from Nisha.

'I'm not some sort of amateur crafter, for crying out loud!' ranted Angie. 'I have a degree in art! And when I met him I gave up my entire career to raise our kids. All I'm asking is that he gives up one evening, one *effing* evening a week, so I can pursue my art.' Then, seeing the distress on both Nisha and Charley's faces, Angie's fury subsided and she visibly crumpled, her tears spilling over and down her cheeks. 'I'm sorry! Lily's still teething and whinges if I put her down for even a second, they've all had a disgusting tummy bug with projectile vomiting and diarrhoea so I've been up all night changing beds and washing sheets, I can't keep on top of the housework, the kitchen looks like it's been struck by a tornado, and I haven't had a decent night's sleep for about seven bloody years…'

Charley put her arm around her mate and pulled her into a comforting squeeze. 'Oh, Angie, what a nightmare. I'll come round at the weekend and give you a hand.'

'No, it's fine. I can cope, you know I can,' replied Angie, sniffing hard and shaking her head. 'And anyhow, you've got enough on your plate as it is. It's just I can't guarantee to hit any deadlines. My life's just not like that. Not anymore.'

'Angie, don't worry about the artwork, I'll explain all that to Tara,' said Charley.

'I already did! She tells me I should stand up to Will, Will tells me to stand up to Tara, and I'm too damn knackered to stand up to anybody!' Tears of exhaustion trickled down Angie's face. 'Ignore me,' she said, wiping her eyes with her sleeve, 'I'm just over-tired, over-emotional and overreacting.'

'What can I get you, Ange?' asked Nisha practically, getting to her feet, 'Mug of tea? Glass of water? More wine?'

'Yes please,' nodded Angie.

'Right then, all three,' said Nisha after a beat, then headed to the kitchen.

By this time, a slightly frantic Bubbles was trying to clamber onto Angie's lap, presumably wanting to comfort her. Charley went to push him off, but Angie scooped him up and cuddled him so, reminded of Finn consoling her with his fluffy dinosaur, Charley let the cockerpoo be.

'I think the best thing is if I give up trying to do it altogether,' concluded Angie miserably.

'Is that what you want?' challenged Charley. 'You love your painting.'

'I know, but I can't meet Tara's terms,' she said sadly.

'Tara's terms?' Charley tried to keep her voice and her rising fury under control as Nisha walked back in with a tray bearing a mug of tea, a glass of water and the wine bottle. 'Sorry, what exactly are Tara's terms?'

A small frown crossed Angie's brow, as if she was surprised that Charley didn't know. 'Two pictures every week, and not just a pile ad hoc whenever I can.'

I am going to bloody kill that Tara, thought Charley.

Crying had given Angie a headache, so she left early. Nisha offered to slope off too, but Charley pleaded with her to stay. 'I hardly ever get to see you, you're so busy all the time.'

Inevitably the conversation drifted round to the shop, and specifically to Tara.

'I gather you didn't know about the deadlines she'd given Angie,' said Nisha dryly.

'No, I bloody didn't! She went behind my back and didn't even mention it. Presumably because she knew I wouldn't agree to it.'

'So what are you going to do about that?'

Charley took a deep breath and let it out before saying, 'Well, I'm going to have to have a little chat with her about it, aren't I?'

'That's putting it mildly.'

You can say that again. Having a little chat with Tara was akin to trying to engage a grizzly bear in polite conversation. The outcome was likely to be the same, with Tara ending up ripping Charley's head off. It wasn't an appealing prospect. 'But I'm not going to let her push Angie around.'

'Well, that's a good starting point,' agreed Nisha, giving Charley the distinct impression that her friend didn't have much confidence in Charley winning any head-to-head battle with Tara. Which, truth be told, was pretty much what Charley thought too.

With Pam now in Copenhagen, Charley was on her own in the shop on Saturday with just Bubbles for company. She coped with the workload, but in reality it was more being on her own that depressed her, not having anyone to talk to or being able to share and enjoy the little episodes and incidents of the day with anyone. Seeing Ricky with his new girlfriend again didn't improve her mood either. They were becoming a regular item, she observed gloomily. Watching them walking past the window, presumably on their way to the deli, Charley took a long, hard look at the woman. She was wearing a full-length floral skirt, slit up to the thigh, and a low cut, body-hugging T-shirt with a military-style jacket draped over it. It was a style Charley particularly disliked, carefully calculated to combine a fragile femininity with sexy toughness, and she instantly loathed the woman for adopting it. Just at that moment, Ricky glanced over and caught Charley looking at them. Cheeks burning, she hurriedly looked away, engrossing herself with tidying the till table, trying to pretend she hadn't been staring, daggers drawn, at his girlfriend. It was a good try, but she knew she hadn't got away with it, and she spent the next few hours beating herself up about it, so when Ricky dropped into the shop later that afternoon, she braced herself.

'I'm sorry I didn't have time to introduce you to Erica earlier,' he said lightly.

Why on earth would I want to meet your new girlfriend? thought Charley incredulously. Feigning as much disinterest as was humanly possible, she confined herself to querying in a mild tone, 'Erica?'

'Yes. I thought you might have noticed her with me... this morning,' he prompted.

'Oh, yes, I did see you with someone,' said Charley vaguely.

'Apparently she was a little pushed for time today, otherwise I would have brought her in to say hi.'

Seriously? Charley was at least one hundred per cent sure that out of everyone in the entire world, *Erica*, with her flowery prints, oversized jackets and naff sunglasses was absolutely the last person she'd want to say 'Hi' to. She was still pondering the insanity of Ricky's suggestion when he proceeded to floor her completely.

'She's interested in buying the business,' he said.

For a couple of beats all Charley could do was gape wordlessly at Ricky. 'Buying the business?' she repeated flatly.

'Yes,' he nodded. 'She's a keen cyclist and she's been looking for an opportunity in the cycle trade for a while.'

A veritable flood of sweet relief gushed into Charley, and her spirits soared. Erica was interested in the business, not in Ricky. 'That's fantastic!' she enthused eagerly. Improbably eagerly.

Ricky looked mildly taken aback by her wild enthusiasm but ignoring it, replied, 'Yes, it is. To be honest, I didn't think I'd find a buyer so soon.'

'Well, yes, perhaps it is quite quick but in all honesty I can see why. I don't want to knock the second-hand bike trade, but you've got to admit most used-bike shops look decidedly grungy and a bit down-at-heel, and they sell a mixed jumble of any old bikes. But your shop has a real style statement. All that retro sixties chic. Plus you've built a reputation for selling high quality, cool and stylish vintage bikes. Blimey, even I'd buy a second-hand bike from you if I hadn't done so already!'

'What I sell are good old-fashioned, second-hand, well-made bikes, that are worth investing in,' he replied, with what Charley thought was typical modesty.

'Don't sell yourself short, Ricky. Your shop is the epitome of chic. It was what made me determined to give this place a classy look. I'm not surprised it's been snapped up.'

They chatted for a little longer until Ricky made his excuses to get back to Carlo, who he'd left on security detail. After he'd gone, Charley felt cheered for the rest of the day, not just in the knowledge that he and Erica were not an item after all, but because for the first time for many weeks she and Ricky had been able to have an enjoyable, easy conversation, much as they had done in the past. Although later that night it belatedly struck her, like a dead weight, that her relief was ill-founded since if Erica was buying his business, that meant Ricky was one step nearer to leaving for Italy. For good. Either way, for Charley, the bitter truth was that the arrival of Erica was a lose-lose situation.

No doubt she would have brooded on the thoroughly dismal thought, had she had the time, but the urgent need to get the accounts up to date for Tara absorbed her totally. She slogged away at them all Saturday evening, and long into the night, and for the whole of Sunday. They were more or less presentable by around nine thirty that evening. Adding a note apologising for sending them so late in the day, she forwarded the Excel sheets to Tara, hoping to God she hadn't made too many glaring blunders. Then she dropped into bed, exhausted, with columns of figures dancing endlessly in front of her eyes.

Chapter Thirty-Seven

At an eye-wateringly early hour on the Saturday, Pam and Zee had taken the bus to Bristol airport. Clambering off at the terminal, hauling their cabin bags behind them, Pam still couldn't quite believe she was actually on her way to Copenhagen. She had never, in forty years of marriage, taken a holiday without either her husband or her sons. It felt weird somehow, like a guilty pleasure. Zee, it seemed, was feeling the same.

'I keep looking round for Theo!'

'Don't tell me you're missing him!'

'Good grief, no. I just can't believe I've escaped.'

It was a feeling neither of them could quite shake off until the plane landed and they'd gone through customs at the other end.

'Well, there's no going back now!' Pam dug out the instructions Hanne had sent for catching the Metro to the Airbnb. 'The nearest stop is Nørreport.'

Zee scanned the route map on the wall. 'Dead easy. We don't even have to change lines.'

Less than half an hour later they'd collected the key from a nearby convenience store and were climbing up the stairs to the top floor apartment.

After three steep flights carrying their cases, both women were out of breath.

'How many more?' gasped Zee, stopping for a breather on the landing.

'Only two,' Pam informed her stoically.

'I wish Hanne had warned us about the stairs,' groaned Zee.

'She did. I just didn't warn you!' confessed Pam with a grin, picking up her bag and pressing on, overtaking Zee.

'It had better damn well be worth it,' muttered Zee, following her.

It was. The small, open-plan apartment, decked out in minimalist Danish style, would have been reward enough, but it was the panoramic view of the city from the floor-to-ceiling windows which rendered them speechless as well as breathless.

'Blimey. How the other half live!' kidded Zee.

They decided to spend the rest of the day wandering around and getting their bearings. The apartment block was in what seemed to be an older part of the city, in a quiet, narrow road lined on both sides with mature trees. A deep red, climbing rose grew up from a gap in the paving slabs, and framed the outside of the door. Looking around, Pam noticed a number of other buildings had roses either growing up them, or in large tubs.

'What's with all the roses?' queried Pam.

'Maybe they're the national flower of Denmark?' reasoned Zee. She fished her phone out of her handbag and they both stood still while she typed.

'Nope. That, apparently is the Marguerite daisy,' Zee informed her friend.

'Bang goes that theory!'

'And their national fruit is the strawberry.'

'Seriously? Who has a national fruit?'

'The healthy Danes!' replied Zee.

'Well, you learn something new every day,' said Pam as they both set off again.

After a long afternoon of traipsing idly around the streets, going wherever the mood took them, strolling through a park, and popping into a few shops, they were pretty much all-in by the time they made their way back to the apartment. Which was a shame, because they still had to tackle the dreaded five flights to the flat.

'It's not the strawberries that makes the Danish so healthy,' panted Zee. 'It's all these damn stairs!'

'Nearly there!' lied Pam encouragingly as they approached the third flight.

When they finally made it to the apartment they both kicked off their shoes and collapsed onto the sofa.

'I can't face doing that more than a couple of times a day,' said Zee.

'Me neither,' agreed Pam then she cursed out loud. 'Dammit! You know what we should have done? Picked up something for dinner.'

'Oh good grief. I haven't got the energy to go the shops, or to cook,' groaned Zee. 'Tell you what, let's eat out. As a treat.'

Pam pulled a face. 'I might be on holiday, but my budget isn't.'

'Just this once. On me, as a thank you? Since you wouldn't let me pay for the flight,' pleaded Zee.

Reluctantly, Pam agreed and once they'd regained enough energy, they set off to find a restaurant, but when they saw the prices on the menus displayed outside Pam vetoed the notion on the spot. 'Good God. That is literally more than I spend on food in a month.'

Zee had gone quite pale, so Pam slipped an arm through hers. 'Come on, let's find a supermarket!'

They picked up the ingredients for a veggie pasta at a late night store and spent the evening happily plotting and planning the week's outings, focussing on things to do which were free, and determined not to let a lack of funds spoilt their enjoyment. The table in the apartment was strewn with guidebooks, most of them in English, and the two friends pored over them excitedly.

'Walking costs nothing,' said Zee, 'so we can explore the city and the harbour.'

'And the Little Mermaid.'

'Absolutely! She's a must-see. There are lots of parks… there's lakes… and the Botanical Gardens are free.'

'Oh, and there's a beach!' said Pam, remembering her conversation with Hanne. 'And of course we're going to meet up with Freya's family…'

'We will not be bored!' declared Zee.

–

What struck the two women most over the next few days as they cheerfully worked their way through their See for Free list was how pleasurable it was not having to accommodate the endless and often conflicting interests of their respective husbands and children.

'Theo always insisted we go to at least one museum,' Zee groaned. 'Which would have been fine for a couple of hours or so, but he invariably wanted to stay all day. So I'd end up trying to keep two bored and fractious little girls entertained for about six hours while he trawled around at a snail's pace minutely examining every single exhibit. Nightmare,' she finished, rolling her eyes.

'Geoff used to disappear,' said Pam. 'He'd just slope off, leaving me with the boys. I vividly remember going to the Science Museum when they were quite small, and within two minutes of arriving he'd vanished into thin air, God only knows where. Josh and Luke immediately shot off in different directions, yelling, "Mum, Mum, come and look at this!" and I spent the next two hours trying not to lose them as well. I can laugh about it now, but it wasn't funny at the time.'

Enjoying Copenhagen on a budget turned out to be relatively easy, until Pam entered the famous Torvehallerne food market. It suddenly became a monumental challenge keeping her purse in her handbag. 'I could live here,' she sighed happily.

'Copenhagen?'

'No, Torvehallerne.' She gazed around, mesmerised by the myriad stalls crammed with meats and cheeses, chocolates, wines and oils, fresh seafood and piles of fruit and veg. She inhaled deeply, relishing the sharp, tangy smell of the cheeses and the salty fish, and the heady, sweet aroma of ripe fruit. 'We *have* to have a Smørrebrød for lunch!' she said, dragging a more than willing Zee over to the open sandwich stall. She opted for the rare roast beef with remoulade and pickle, took one mouthful. 'Mmm, heaven on a plate,' she mumbled.

—

The week flew by and on their last full day in Copenhagen they'd arranged to have lunch with Freya's family. Hanne's mother, Gitte, was to collect them at the apartment and take them to a dockside restaurant for lunch where they would all meet up. Pam winced at the likely cost, but determined to grin and bear it.

'YOLO,' she told Zee, who frowned at her questioningly. 'You only live once.'

'Too true.'

Freya's grandmother turned out to be as lively and animated as Pam had envisaged her and, to their embarrassment, she appeared to have taken the five flights up to the apartment in her stride. The family resemblance to Freya and Hanne was striking. Her long grey hair was tied back in a loose plait, and she beamed at Pam through an older version of Freya's pale blue eyes. She wore dark blue trousers, boat shoes, and a short, navy pea-coat.

'You will need a warm coat,' she informed them. 'We are going in my friend's boat.'

'Oh, have you finished repairing it?' enquired Pam, a little confused since she thought Hanne had told her repairing the boat was going to be a long project.

It was Gitte's turn to look momentarily confused. 'Ah, different boat!' she said finally, her face clearing, and the three woman laughed companionably and then made their way to the harbour.

If you'd asked her afterwards what sort of boat Pam had imagined they'd be going in, she wouldn't have been able to answer. Obviously she wasn't expecting a Viking longboat, that would have been preposterous, but she certainly wasn't expecting a speedboat. There was someone already aboard and Gitte called out a greeting in Danish.

'This is Katrine,' Gitte said when a woman turned to welcome them. Pam was completely thrown. For some totally illogical reason, she had expected Gitte's friend to be a man. Instead, she was confronted by a tall, slim woman, probably in her late sixties, with the bronzed, weather-beaten face of someone who spends a lot of her time in the fresh air, mucking about in boats.

'Hello, hello!' Katrine came over to help Pam and Zee clamber onto the boat. Then she indicated they should sit in the two seats at the rear of the deck, while she and Gitte went to stand by the ship's wheel.

Turning round, Katrine gave them a mischievous grin. 'Okay?' she asked.

'Yes,' said Zee.

'Absolutely,' nodded Pam.

Katrine turned back and yanked the throttle. The boat roared away, throwing both Zee and Pam violently backwards against the seats.

'Woo-hoo!' yelled Pam.

'It's like being in a James Bond movie!' Zee shouted.

'*You Only Live Twice!*' they chorused, and promptly collapsed into giggles. Gitte turned round and grinned at them impishly.

White spray surged high on both sides as the boat raced across the water, leaping and juddering as it hit the bow waves of other boats. It was exhilarating and, with the wind ruffling her hair and briny water on her lips, Pam thought she'd never felt so alive.

'That was amazing!' gasped Pam, giddy with excitement, when they slowed to moor up ten minutes or so later by an open-air dockside restaurant. Freya was already seated at a table with Hanne, waving frantically at her.

Sitting outdoors, in the autumn cool, Pam was grateful Gitte had told them to bring warm coats and that the venue had thoughtfully provided woollen blankets. Snugly bundled up, she ate the best seafood she'd ever eaten in her life. When it came to the bill, she and Zee tried to insist on at least paying their share of it, but Hanne looked scandalised and simply wouldn't let them. Pam made a mental note to buy some choice goodies from Torvehallerne and leave them in the apartment as a thank-you.

Walking back to the apartment from the harbour, after Gitte and Katrine had dropped them off, Pam slipped her arm though Zee's. 'That was one of the best days of my life,' she told her friend sincerely.

'Mine too,' agreed Zee. 'Why don't we live like this?' she groaned enviously.

Pam suddenly stopped in her tracks. 'Yes, why don't we?' she asked, but in all seriousness and with a note of challenge in her voice. 'Copenhagen isn't that different from Bristol. There are boats, dockside restaurants, free places to go, and there must be dozens of things to do that we don't even know about.' She started walking again, and warming to her theme, carried on. 'There are new people to meet, different foods to try, exhibitions we never bother to go to.'

'We could go to London! Cheap day return,' added Zee hurriedly.

'It's not about the money, it doesn't have to cost a fortune,' Pam continued. 'The only reason other people get more out of life is because they demand it, Zee. They make it happen. Look at Gitte. She's been on her own for over a decade and she's squeezing every last drop of living out of her allotted time on this earth. I've got this all wrong, Zee. I don't need to find a life partner. What I need to find is a life!'

Chapter Thirty-Eight

Charley had been dreading having her 'little chat' with Tara, but she was determined to stick up for Angie and not let Tara ride roughshod over her. Since she'd sent over the accounts on the Sunday evening, Charley hoped that might have placated Tara a little. As it happened, the gesture backfired spectacularly. When Tara arrived at the shop on Monday morning, Charley was busy dealing with customers, but her mate's curt tone when she said '*Good morning*,' and the way her entire body stiffly radiated anger as she walked in warned Charley to brace herself.

Barely waiting for the door to close behind the last of the customers, Tara launched off. 'So I looked at the accounts,' she said tightly.

And? thought Charley, bewildered. Surely the fact that they weren't as professional as they might have been wasn't enough to provoke Tara's scorching wrath.

'And I discovered that Angie gets all the money from her artwork. You don't even take a cut.'

'No. She's a mate,' said Charley, still wondering what had set Tara off. 'She offered me a cut, but I turned it down. I don't want to make money out of a friend.'

There was a beat and then Tara said tersely, 'Would you class me as "a friend"?'

'Yes, of course! Tara, what is this about?'

'It's about the fact that since you've been trading, Angie's made over six hundred quid from her artwork, some of which I've actually sodding well sold for her, while I've been working five mornings a week, *and* I invested three grand to help you buy stock, and I've had nothing back except for a few boxes of chocolates and some bubble bath.'

Oh, shit, thought Charley. *Shit, shit, shit.* Put that way, she could see why Tara would feel exploited and consider she'd treated Angie better than her. Charley's brain raced to find a defence, but Tara didn't give her time.

'And even though I *told* you I needed an income or I'd have to get a job elsewhere, you still didn't pay me anything.'

'I know. And I'm sorry, and I've said so countless times, but as I explained, the shop isn't making enough to pay you. I'm only just scraping by – you can see that from the accounts.'

'I'm not sodding surprised you're not making any profit!' fumed Tara. 'The deal with Angie brings you in nothing, and the whole gift bag venture was barely breaking even until I stepped in. And you refused point blank to let me and Nisha run a promo night – which, by the way, would have brought in a couple of thousand, minimum, in one sodding evening.'

Charley bit her lip, tactically letting Tara vent rather than interrupt her in full flood.

'I've tried to come up with ways to improve turnover and profitability but you've consistently fought me,' Tara went on. 'You're running this shop like it's some glorified hobby, Charley.'

The injustice of Tara's assessment set resentment boiling in Charley. *A hobby? How dare she!* 'I'm working flat out to make a success of this business!' she said hotly. 'I *literally* could not put any more hours and effort in.'

'That's not the point, Charley! You can't make a success of a business just by working hard. You have to run it professionally, in a business-like way. Face it. If you carry on like this, it's never going to make enough money to pay me any profit share, or even pay me and Baz back.'

Charley reeled, speechless, as Tara ploughed on.

'I've got a sodding MBA, Charley. I know what I'm talking about, but you've consistently dismissed all the help I've tried to give you. Except my free labour,' she ended bitterly.

'I'm sorry,' was all Charley could manage to stammer. Tara's litany of accusations and criticisms had completely taken the wind out of her sails, not least because most of them were true.

Silently, her friend locked eyes with her and then shook her head slowly, and Charley was mortified to see it was hurt in Tara's eyes, not anger.

'I really wanted this to shop work – for both of us, Charley,' continued Tara sadly. 'I thought working with my best mate was going to be my dream job. But it's not. And actually, I'm not even sure I am your best mate. I think that gig, and the money that goes with it, is Angie's.'

'Oh, Tara, please don't say that,' implored Charley. But Tara was already scooping up her coat and bag. She shot Charley one agonisingly unhappy look, tears glittering in her eyes, and walked out.

'Tara! *Tara!*' Charley rushed after her, but after a few paces she stopped. Heads were already turning amongst the other shop-holders and pedestrians, and she didn't want to make a scene in public, nor could she leave the shop unattended. Bubbles wasn't exactly a deterrent; he'd let anyone nick anything and probably lick them to death while they were at it. She trailed back inside and the enormity of what had just happened flattened her like a runaway truck. The shop, which had seemed such a great adventure, so full of promise, now felt like a ludicrous vanity project which was not only not making enough money, but had now cost her one of her best friends.

Numbly, she took up her position behind the counter and leant on it in acute misery. 'I have really screwed up, Bubbles,' she said, addressing herself as much as the dog. No doubt picking up on her dejected tone, the cockerpoo put his ears back and thumped his tail anxiously.

Later that afternoon, she texted Tara. She'd tried calling her several times, but her calls were rejected.

> Tara, I'm really sorry. Please let's not fall out like this. Let's meet and talk. Please x

She didn't get a reply.

–

The following morning, Tara didn't come to work, which didn't exactly surprise Charley. What did surprise her was getting a text at lunch time saying she wouldn't be in at all for the rest of the week. Charley was used to her mate's stormy outbursts, and they usually blew over quickly, but she knew better than to try to force the pace so she texted back immediately.

> Okay. Thanks for letting me know. Catch up soon. Love x

–

The week dragged by, a frustrating mix of being either rushed off her feet or standing alone and bored in an empty shop. There was plenty to do, more than enough, but Charley was struggling to motivate herself. She hated working in the shop on her own, but most of all she hated herself for handling things so badly with Tara. When she'd called Nisha for advice, her friend had sympathised but bluntly told Charley she didn't blame Tara for being angry. Her candid advice was a) give Tara time to cool off, b) apologise and c) renegotiate Angie's art deal.

If the week had got off to a bad start, the end of it was even worse. Charley's least favourite delivery man, Jobsworth, appeared on Friday morning with a sack truck laden with boxes. As usual, she wasted time trying to persuade him to bring them into the shop and as usual, he steadfastly refused. So, propping the door open, she lugged the boxes inside, one at a time, and wished there was somebody, anybody, to help her, while he stood back watching her struggle disinterestedly.

'That bloody man is a complete pain in the arse, Bubbles,' she exclaimed breathlessly, dumping the last box onto the till table. Obviously she wasn't expecting a reply, but nevertheless she glanced down to where she'd left the cockerpoo, happily settled in his bed... and froze. The basket was empty. He must have slipped out behind her back while the door was propped open. Her hand flew to her mouth. 'Oh no, *no*!' She darted out of the door.

'Bubbles! Bubbles!' she yelled, looking frantically around, but there was no sign of him. What the hell was she going to do? She had absolutely no idea which way he'd gone. Her mouth went dry and she felt sick. Then Rita came to the door of the deli.

'He went that way!' she called over, pointing left.

'Thank you!' yelled Charley, inwardly thanking God the dog hadn't run the other way, towards the main road.

Quickly, she nipped into the shop to grab the keys to lock up before rushing off after him, but by the time she emerged it was to see Ricky, with Bubbles on Carlo's lead, walking up towards her from the bike shop. She wanted to throw her arms round him, but confined herself to thanking him profusely. Then, dropping to her knees, she hugged Bubbles instead and ruffled his ears.

'You little sod!' she exclaimed. Looking up at Ricky, she asked, 'Where did you find him?'

'He came into the bike shop, looking for Carlo.'

She could hardly bear to imagine the chaos that might have caused. 'Oh God! I'm so sorry!' She rose to her feet and led the way into her shop where she unclipped Carlo's lead and handed it to Ricky.

'It's not a problem for me,' he said, 'but I don't think you should let him make a habit of nipping out on his own. If he'd run the other way he'd could be on the main road by now.'

Charley closed her eyes, not even wanting to contemplate the potentially horrific outcome if that had been the case. All at once, the relief of discovering Bubbles was safe, together with the emotional fall-out from her horrible exchange with Tara, and the exhaustion of coping in the shop on her own all week caught up with Charley. Momentarily overcome, she quickly turned away, but not before she felt her face crumple.

'Hey, what's happened?' Ricky asked her gently.

Furiously, she flapped a dismissive hand at him. 'Nothing. I'm just having a moment. Ignore me,' she pleaded, desperately trying to hold it together.

'Is there anything I can do to help?' he asked, putting his hand on her arm, and instantly causing her a nearly total meltdown.

Please don't be nice to me, she begged silently, *it's just making everything so much worse.* 'I'm fine. Honestly.' She made a dive for her handbag and rootled frantically round inside for a tissue.

He waited patiently until she'd recovered and turned back to face him. Then, urgently needing to change the subject, she asked brightly, 'So, any news on the buy-out?'

'Yes. She's put an offer in.'

'That's excellent news!' exclaimed Charley, plastering a chirpy expression onto her face and hoping it looked a lot more genuine than it felt.

'There's still a few things to sort out,' he went on. 'But it's not a bad offer and it'll mean I can set myself up in Italy.'

'Excellent,' repeated Charley, incapable of finding any more words, and nodding like an automaton.

'And of course it means I don't have to give four months' notice, because she'll take on the tenancy of the shop on. So...' He paused, then shrugged lightly and said, 'It could be all sorted within a month or so. Unless something happens to stop it...' He trailed off, with his eyes on Charley.

A month? The muscles in her face tightened, threatening to distort it into an expression of dismay. Charley forced her face to hold onto that chirpy look while every fibre of her body wanted to scream at him, *Don't go. Please, don't go.* She swallowed hard. 'That soon?' she managed to say.

He nodded. Then, since he'd left Carlo in charge of the bike shop, he hurried back.

Leaning forward, she dropped her head onto her arms on the counter as the bottom of her world fell away from under her feet. A month. Without even needing to look at a calendar she knew that would be, almost to the day, when she and Ricky would have been, *should* have been, celebrating their first year together. But instead, he'd be gone and she'd probably never see him again. *Don't. Don't do this*, she ordered herself brusquely. Then, hearing the shop door opening, she stood upright, turned to the doorway, flicked on her professional face, and greeted the incoming customers with a cheery, 'Hi there!'

–

She had no idea how she got through that week. It was a gruelling marathon, emotionally and physically, and by closing time on the Saturday she was on her knees. Finally getting home she fed Bubbles, took him for a quick toilet walk, and then ran herself a hot bath. The warmth of the water nearly sent her to sleep, so she hauled herself out, pulled on a towelling dressing gown, and dropped into bed, not even bothering to pull on her nightclothes. Bubbles leapt onto the bed and snuggled down next to her. She fondled his soft ears, and then she caught sight of Josh, grinning at her from the photo on the bedside table.

'What did I do so wrong,' she asked the cockerpoo, 'that the bloody fates have conspired to make me lose both of the men I loved?' She lay there feeling numb and empty, too weary to cry.

Chapter Thirty-Nine

On the plane back from Copenhagen, Pam and Zee spent the flight eagerly making plans and writing lists.

'How about one of those house-swap holidays?' suggested Zee.

'Good thought! I have no idea how you go about it, but definitely put it on the list.'

'Camping? That's cheap and cheerful.'

'Oh good grief, spare me! Cheap, yes, cheerful, no. I always need the loo in the middle of the night and there's nothing cheerful about trudging across a field in your PJs in the dark trying not to tread in a cowpat or rick your ankle in a rabbit hole! Plus the loos are always full of spiders!'

'True,' admitted Zee with a slight shiver. 'Glamping, then?'

'Oooh, yes, in a yurt!' Pam mentally conjured up a lavishly furnished bell tent with a four poster bed, Persian carpets and a wood burning stove.

'I can see you in a yurt.'

'So can I,' enthused Pam, adding richly decorated floor cushions, a sumptuous meal laid on a low wooden table and a bottle of wine in an ice bucket.

'Although I don't think they have toilets. Plenty of room for a bucket, though!' teased Zee, instantly popping Pam's glamorous fantasy.

By the time the plane landed at Bristol they'd compiled an encouragingly lengthy To Do list and they both were looking forward to working their way down it over the coming weeks and months.

An hour so later, opening her front door, Pam braced herself for the inevitable wave of oppressive silence and emptiness to engulf her. But, stepping inside, she was immediately struck by its absence. What greeted her instead was a companionable silence, the kind you share with an old friend and although she dismissed it as a fanciful notion, it felt as if the house itself was welcoming her back. Going into the living room, she cast her eye over the furniture, comforted by its familiar, solid presence then, sinking down onto the sofa, she put her feet up and gave herself a few moments to enjoy the profound pleasure of being home.

–

The following morning, after a leisurely breakfast, she showered and dressed. On the spur of the moment, she decided that a long walk with Charley and that bubbly idiot of a cockerpoo of hers would be fun. Never wanting to arrive unannounced or at an inconvenient moment, she picked up the phone, then she faltered, fearing she might be gate-crashing her daughter-in-law's only day off. *She can always say 'no'*, she told herself, and dialled her number. Then, having been assured that Charley would 'absolutely love' her go round, she gathered up the souvenir gift she'd bought her daughter-in-law in Copenhagen and headed over. Driving along, she eagerly ran over in her mind everything she had to tell Charley about her holiday, wondering whether to start with the highlights or whether to relate everything chronologically, leaving the best, the boat trip, 'til last.

At soon as Charley opened the front door, Bubbles hurled himself at Pam to give her an ecstatic welcome, whimpering in pleasure and bouncing up at her joyously.

'Your tail will fall off it you wag it that much!' Pam warned him.

'I'm more worried he's going to pee himself in excitement!' said Charley. 'Come in if you can get in!' she laughed, trying to pull the energetic mutt out of the way. 'Off! Get down, you great lump!' she yelled, then, giving up, she reached over him to give Pam a warm hug.

'How was Copenhagen?' she asked as Pam followed her inside.

'Wonderful. Amazing. In fact, life-changing!' Barely pausing for breath, Pam launched into a full and comprehensive account of her trip, waxing lyrical for the best part of an hour, while Charley made coffee, listened attentively, and then made more coffee, until Pam realised she'd bombarded her daughter-in-law continuously, barely giving the poor young woman a chance to get a word in edgeways.

'Enough of me!' she cried. 'In fact, more than enough! How's everything with *you*?' she asked, stressing the last word.

Charley sighed and looked heavenwards as if not knowing quite where to start. 'Well... pretty much everything is going horribly, horribly wrong.' She looked so utterly dejected that Pam's buoyant mood instantly evaporated. 'Tara's walked out of the shop and isn't talking to me because Angie's been getting all the money from her artwork, whereas I haven't paid Tara a penny for all the months she's been working with me...' *Oh dear*, thought Pam. 'So Tara thinks I'm treating Angie better than her and, bottom line, she thinks I'm better mates with Angie than I am with her.' *She's probably right there.* Charley carried on, 'Nisha says I should renegotiate the deal with Angie, which will upset Angie and probably stop her doing her art altogether.' *Now that would be a shame.* 'The bloody dog is a nightmare in the shop and actually ran off to go and play with Carlo so Ricky had to bring him back, which was excruciatingly embarrassing. Plus, it meant Ricky gave me an update on selling his business and it looks like he's sold it already and he will probably be gone in a month,' finished Charley.

'A month?' queried Pam, suddenly sitting forward.

'Yes. And I'm not ready for that... I'm just so not ready for that,' admitted Charley in a strained voice, seeming close to tears.

'Oh, sweetheart,' said Pam. Then, in an attempt to prevent Charley from going into a full meltdown, which wasn't going to help solve anything, she lightened her tone. 'So, just a few hiccups to sort out, then?'

Charley managed a small smile. 'Just a few.'

Pam was silent for couple of moments, marshalling her thoughts and deciding in which order to tackle Charley's disasters.

'Very few things are irredeemable, Charley,' she started sagely. 'Let's start with the shop. Why don't you ask Angie if you can have a cut of the sale price of her artwork? I'm sure she'll understand and, if my memory serves me right, I think she even offered to give you one right at the beginning.'

Charley nodded. 'She did, and she offered again a few weeks back.'

'So why are you reluctant to take it?' Her daughter-in-law didn't reply, so Pam ventured, 'Is it pride? Having to admit you made a mistake when you arranged the deal?'

'No. I just don't want to make money out of a mate!' replied Charley.

'But isn't that just what you're doing with Tara?' said Pam carefully.

'Yes, but no…' protested Charley. 'When I opened the shop Tara said she'd be happy to work for nothing. For fun. And besides, she doesn't need the money. She and Baz are pretty comfortably off. Even when she worked at the Avalon it was only very part-time and the pay was pitiful.'

Pam felt she could detect not just a flaw in Charley's logic, but a flaw in her perception and understanding of the relative needs of her friends.

'Why does that mean Tara doesn't need to be paid?' she queried. 'And why do you assume Angie needs paying more than Tara does?'

'For two reasons,' argued Charley, counting them off on her fingers. 'One, she's got four kids, and two, Will treats her artwork like it's just a hobby, so she needs to be paid to give it… status, and so she has a reason to prioritise doing her paintings over looking after the kids. She needs her work to be *valued*.'

'I can understand that, but Tara needs her work to be valued too,' Pam pointed out gently. 'We all need our work to be valued, surely?' Then she fell silent as she watched a look of sinking realisation followed by remorse slide onto Charley's face.

'Bloody, bloody hell. I have so messed up.' Charley sank her head into her hands. 'And now I'm going to lose Tara as a mate.'

'I honestly don't think you will, darling. Your friendship means a lot to Tara, and she won't want to jeopardise it any more than you do. But she does need to feel that you value her, and her role in the shop.'

Charley's face shot up to look at Pam. 'I do... I want to... but she constantly criticises me, and she keeps trying to... to take over, make changes and run things her way. And it's *my* bloody shop!' she finished hotly.

Ah, so that's the root of the problem, thought Pam. It was undeniably true that Tara had a tendency to dominate things and to boss people around, it was in her nature. But what was also true was that the woman had a heart of gold, the best of intentions, good business sense, a great sales technique and an MBA.

'Let me ask you something,' said Pam. 'Do you think the things Tara has suggested and the changes she wants to make will improve the way you're running the shop at the moment?' When Charley didn't answer she prompted, 'Will they make you more money? Will the shop be more successful?' She waited patiently through an uncomfortable silence, during which Charley evaded her gaze. 'Be honest,' she prompted again.

Charley slumped back in her seat and Pam could almost see her home truths hitting their marks.

'Yes,' admitted Charley finally.

'Then I refer you to my earlier note about valuing her role in the shop,' said Pam. 'Forgive me for saying so, my darling, but you would be a complete idiot not to take advantage of Tara's considerable business knowledge and her outstanding selling skills.'

'I *am* an idiot.'

Pam shook her head. 'No, you're not. But you have to sit down, the two of you, and figure out how to work together, in partnership, rather than in some sort of competition.'

'She'll walk all over me,' groaned Charley.

'Probably,' agreed Pam. 'So ask Nisha to mediate the meeting.'

Charley perked up instantly at the suggestion. 'And I think you should be there as well,' she told Pam. 'You're a business partner too.'

'Is that so that I can help you outvote Tara?'

'No!' cried Charley. Pam shot her a look. 'Well, yes,' she accepted sheepishly.

'Don't bank on it,' Pam warned her with a grin. 'If Tara has a good idea, I'll very probably get behind it.' Then, looking fondly down at Bubbles sprawled at her feet, she added fondly, 'And as for the "bloody dog being a nightmare in the shop", I suspect he's probably just bored, stuck there all day.'

'There's nothing I can do about that! I can't leave him at home and I really don't want to take him back to the rescue centre.'

'I know, so why don't you drop Bubbles at my house in the mornings and I'll bring him in with me at lunch time? That way I can give him a really good, long walk and a run around the garden and knacker him out so he'll spend most of the afternoons sleeping. On Saturdays, of course, he'll have to be in the shop all day, but perhaps we could both nip out in the quiet spells and take him for a walk round the block.'

Charley was already shaking her head. 'I can't ask you to take on Bubbles as well as everything else you do for me. He's my responsibility.'

'Oh, don't be such a pig-headed martyr!' exclaimed Pam.

Charley blinked at her, apparently speechless at her outburst. It wasn't surprising. Pam rarely challenged anyone so directly, and especially not her daughter-in-law. 'I *want* to look after Bubbles. It's a win-win for me! I get the daft sod's company and an excuse for getting lots of exercise, but without the food and vet bills.'

'If that's what you really want…'

'It is,' insisted Pam.

So Charley caved.

When it came to Ricky, Pam only had one, firm piece of advice. One that would brook no argument or invite any debate.

'The reason you're not ready for Ricky to leave in a month is that you will *never* be ready for him to leave you. Tell him how you feel, now, before it's too late.'

Charley looked as if she were about to protest but Pam held up her hand to stop her. 'You didn't choose to lose Josh, darling, but you *are* choosing to lose Ricky.'

Chapter Forty

Pam's final words echoed in Charley's ears long after her mother-in-law had left, and she spent the rest of the weekend racked with uncertainty. Was she 'choosing' to lose Ricky? She honestly didn't think that decision was hers to make, yet Pam seemed to think it was so easy.

'Tell him how you feel,' she'd said, and apparently that would sort it all out; Ricky would abandon his plans, and his family, and give everything up for her. If only. Life isn't a rom-com, and the route to 'happily ever after' isn't that straightforward. Sometimes, as Charley knew only too well, the road ended abruptly, at a cliff edge, leaving you confronting a sheer drop into an empty chasm. If she did call Ricky, how would the conversation *really* pan out? She tried to imagine it, building a fantasy reunion in her mind's eye, but she couldn't write a convincing script, couldn't even work out what they would say to each other. Besides, there was one glaring mistake in Pam's assessment of the situation. She hadn't factored in what Ricky wanted. It didn't seem to Charley that Ricky was even remotely interested in rekindling their relationship. Quite the reverse in fact; it was patently obvious he'd already moved on. You only had to see how enthusiastically he was pursuing his plans to sell Erica his business. If he'd given Charley any indication of wanting to try again, or even to be with her, just once, well, then it might be different.

On Monday morning, she dropped Bubbles at Pam's for the morning, and then headed into work. She was in a low mood, not having slept well, fretting over trying to sort things out with Tara.

'I am so not looking forward to this,' she muttered as she unlocked the door to the shop. 'Obviously the best thing to do is tackle it right away the moment Tara comes in,' she coached herself. 'I'll apologise, clear the air, and then suggest the meeting with Nisha.'

It probably would have been a good plan if Tara hadn't scuppered it, not showing up until just after eleven and, unusually, not bearing coffee and pastries. Also unusually, she stayed standing in front of the serving counter and didn't take her coat off, or make a move to join Charley at the till. A couple of women were browsing through the chocolates on the confectionary table so Tara kept her voice low as she spoke to Charley.

'I've decided to give up helping out in the shop.'

'Oh, no! Please don't,' implored Charley, also in a low voice.

Tara was adamant. 'I'm sorry, Charley. I've thought about it long and hard, and I just can't work with you anymore. I want to us stay friends, but working together is making that impossible.'

Glancing over to the customers, checking they were still out of hearing range, Charley said pleadingly, 'I understand what you're saying and why you're saying it, but we can make this work, Tara. We can.'

Tara shook her head and said, with what was for her an astonishing degree of understatement, 'We just don't see eye to eye on how things should be run.'

'I know,' Charley agreed, 'and I know I need to listen to you more, and take your advice more...'

She was met with a look of barely disguised disbelief and Charley couldn't blame Tara for her scepticism, since she had consistently quashed or opposed nearly every suggestion her mate had made to improve the business. Out of the corner of her eye, she saw the two women approaching the till, one of them clutching a small handful of items. Tara stood back to let Charley deal with them, and once they'd left, they carried on the conversation.

'I was going to ask Nisha to mediate a meeting between us. You, me and Pam,' Charley said. 'Please come. If nothing else, say you'll come to that. Give me one last chance.'

Tara took a deep breath then let it out slowly, clearly dubious. 'I don't know. There are some significant problems to resolve, Charley. I'd want to be properly involved in managing things, the decision-making and so on.'

Charley nodded. 'Yes, yes, I know.'

'And you'd have to renegotiate some deals,' Tara added pointedly.

'I agree,' said Charley. 'Starting with Angie's. You were right. It's a terrible deal. Even Angie says so! It's on my To Do list already.'

This last admission clearly surprised Tara and seemed to get her wavering. 'I'm serious about wanting to make some money out of the shop, Charley—'

'So am I,' cut in Charley. 'But I don't think I can do it without you. And in fact, I'm not even sure if I want to.'

The truth of this last statement hit home for Charley the moment she voiced it. Running the shop without Tara suddenly had no appeal for her. She wasn't cut out for being a 'sole trader', she realised, or a 'sole' anything, come to that. She was a people person; working on her own was dull and dreary, a drudge. She didn't just need Tara's expertise in the shop, she needed her company too.

'Can't we just try again? What have we got to lose?'

'Our friendship?' remarked Tara.

'It won't come to that, I promise. I value your friendship, and I value you, too much,' Charley told her sincerely.

'You've got a funny way of showing it,' said Tara, with uncharacteristic bitterness.

'I know,' admitted Charley. 'And I'm truly sorry. Things will change. I promise.'

'Okay,' said Tara, hesitantly, but the doubt on her face had begun to slowly dissipate and eventually she smiled at Charley and said, 'I suppose I'd better go and get the coffee and the croissants then.'

'No,' said Charley delving into her bag for her purse. 'I'll get them. You call Nisha and sort out the meeting.'

Nisha agreed to come round to the shop after it closed on the Saturday. In the meantime, she told them to spend the week privately, but candidly, drawing up a list of the problems they had working together and then, without sharing the list, they were to send them to Nisha by close of play on Friday.

'I'm going to need a sodding great big piece of paper,' said Tara.

'You can have a little bit of till roll,' joked Charley.

When Pam got in, Charley updated her. 'Will you be okay to stay on after closing on Saturday?' she asked.

'Yes of course, and I suppose I'd better send Nisha my list too.'

Charley's head whipped round. 'Wait! You have problems too? Please tell me they're with Tara and not with me?'

'It's a private list,' Pam retorted, her mouth twitching playfully.

The reconciliation with Tara lifted Charley's spirits for the rest of the day, until Ricky waltzed in, closely followed by Erica. Unnecessarily closely, in Charley's opinion.

'I thought I'd introduce you,' he told them. 'Erica's taking over the bike shop.'

Erica flicked her hair, flashed Ricky a blatantly flirtatious smile, then turned towards Charley and Pam, put out limp hand and said, 'Hi! I'm your new neighbour!'

There was a beat and then Pam stepped forward, shook Erica's hand and said, 'How lovely to meet you.'

'Yes. Welcome to Cargo!' cried Charley, a little overly brightly. Even to her ears, her tone sounded false and brittle. She was really going to have to get a handle on how to cope with this woman, she told herself.

'Thank you so much,' enthused Erica. 'It's *so* good to meet you. Ricky's told me how friendly and helpful everyone is.' She pulled a simpering 'lucky little me' expression and Charley's hands itched to slap it off her face.

'Have you run a bike shop before?' asked Pam politely.

'No. And I have absolutely no idea where to start!' replied Erica gaily. Putting her hand on Ricky's arm, she added, 'But Ricky's going to hold my hand and talk me through everything. So, fingers crossed, I should be fine.'

Charley stared at the woman, trying not to hate her. It didn't work. Erica's nauseating coquettishness just put her back up.

'So, is the deal all done and dusted?' asked Pam, possibly out of politeness to fill the awkward silence, but Charley suspected the older woman of fishing. Pointlessly, in her opinion, since, judging by the expression on Erica's face, it was clearly a done deal.

'Well... we're nearly there,' replied Ricky, cautiously.

'We're just working out the final details,' gushed Erica, gazing up at Ricky. 'Looks like Ricky's going to be a bit of a sleeping partner,' she said and then turned to smile sweetly at Charley.

Ricky looked as if didn't know where to put himself – whether it was because he hadn't wanted details of the deal to be broadcast so openly, or whether it was because Erica was so obviously being deliberately provocative, Charley couldn't tell. Either way, she could have happily throttled her.

They stayed for a few minutes, Erica asking Charley some questions about footfall, customer numbers and seasonal peaks and troughs which she did her best to answer, although she knew she was coming across as vague to the point of evasive. She could sense Ricky's dismay at her apparently unhelpful attitude. The problem was, she didn't actually know the figures, she'd never compiled any and, for obvious reasons, wasn't keen to admit that. When they left, Ricky looked back over his shoulder at her, a look of bewildered disappointment in his eyes, and she hated herself.

'When she says "sleeping partner" she means a *business* sleeping partner, surely?' said Pam. 'One that invests in the company but doesn't actually work there, yes?'

Charley didn't reply. Watching Ricky and Erica walking off together back to the bike shop she was suddenly overwhelmed by the realisation that his departure was not just inevitable, but was gathering momentum, like a plane hurtling down the runway before take-off, and she was powerless to stop it leaving the runway.

For the remainder of that week, every time Charley saw Ricky, Erica was with him, laughing at something he'd just said, and seemingly forever pawing at him. She told herself off for being pathetically jealous. And as for Ricky, she could hardly bear to look at him. She just wanted him to be gone. She couldn't wait for him to leave, so that she could begin to get on with living her life without him. Waiting for his final departure was agony.

—

After the shop closed on the following Saturday, Nisha came round as she'd promised to mediate the meeting. She cleared one of the display tables and put a pop-up flip chart on top of it, opening the cover sheet to reveal a chart with their names down one side and the words 'Strengths' and 'Weaknesses' on the other side.

'What's crucial, going forward,' she told them, 'is that you recognise your own and each other's strengths and weaknesses, play to the strengths and address the weaknesses.'

Which was, Charley thought, far more tactful and positive than kicking off by going through, and no doubt inflaming, the list of grievances they held against each other. It didn't take much imagination to guess what Tara would have said about working with her – although she had no idea what Pam's complaints were, and promptly censured herself for not knowing.

By the end of the evening they had, in theory, thrashed out an acceptable way of working together. Charley readily accepted the business needed to prioritise making enough for Tara to get a decent profit share. And since Tara had far superior business skills and knowledge than both Charley and Pam put together, they all agreed Tara should draw up a development plan which would enable them to achieve that goal. A tad begrudgingly, Tara acknowledged that Charley had better taste than her and knew which products would appeal more to the punters, so Charley should take the lead as product buyer. Nisha pointed out that Pam's strengths were diplomacy and objectivity and argued that in the event of any disagreements, instead of Charley and Tara slugging it out between them, they ask Pam to mediate. They all agreed that Charley should ask Angie for a twenty per cent cut in her artwork and then, at Nisha's insistence, they accepted that *everyone* should have at least two days off a week, *not just Tara*, and regular holidays – *again, not just Tara*. It was Charley who objected, declaring she was happy to work six days a week and didn't need holidays. Nisha candidly informed her *nobody* works well when they're overtired. Finally, after bluntly reminding them of the personal and financial investments each of them had made in the business, Nisha summed up with astonishing perceptiveness what they each had to lose if they couldn't make the business work.

'Tara, you'd lose the chance to have a term-time job you could love, rather than one you'd hate. Pam, you'd lose the chance to develop a new career late in life, in a supportive working environment, and Charley, you'd lose the chance to prove yourself, and find the successful business woman we all know you can be.' Nisha eyed them all sternly. 'Make it work, ladies.'

–

It was nearly ten by the time Charley headed home after the meeting, thanking her lucky stars that she had such wonderful friends, and not to mention a one-in-a-million mother-in-law, although she still didn't know what Pam's issues might have been, she mused. It was raining as she drove through the wet, lamp-lit streets, the wipers swishing across the windscreen, with the cockerpoo curled up on the seat next to her. She hadn't eaten yet and neither had the poor dog, she realised guiltily.

'Sorry, Bubbles, you must be starving,' she told him. 'I know I am! Never mind, nearly home.'

She was in a buoyant mood as she walked down the steps to her flat, with Bubbles bounding down behind her, although she wished she'd thought to leave the hall light on. The light from the street lamp on the pavement above didn't reach the last few stairs so she watched her step, not least since the concrete could be slippery when wet. Taking out her key she went to open the front door, but her hand froze in mid-air. The door was ajar. Had she forgotten to shut it? She very much doubted it. Living alone, and in a garden flat, had taught her to be vigilant about locking all the doors and windows. Cautiously, she pushed the door open. Bubbles immediately shot inside, no doubt keen to be out of the rain and eager for his supper. Flicking on the hall light revealed a trail of wet, man-sized footprints, heading up the hallway. Charley's heart nearly stopped beating, and her mouth went dry. *Shit! There's someone in the flat.* All of a sudden, there was a furious outburst of barking from Bubbles.

'Bubbles,' she called urgently. 'Bubbles!' Then there was a yelping, and a crash from inside. '*Bubbles!*' she yelled one last frantic time and then she panicked and fled, taking the steps two at a time, praying the dog would follow her.

Chapter Forty-One

Blindly, she bolted to the safety of her car, scrambled in and locked it, all the while looking out for Bubbles in the hope he would emerge from the flat. He didn't. Grabbing her phone, she dialled the first person she thought of, her hands trembling violently.

'Ricky, it's me. There's someone in my flat!'

'And where are you?' His voice was urgent but calm.

'In my car.'

'Lock the car doors and call the police. I'm on my way.'

Heart pounding, sick with fear, she dialled the emergency number and managed to give the police her details. Having checked that she was safe and had someone who could help her, they told her they'd try to send an officer round, but they didn't say when. She ended the call, not very optimistic that anyone would show up. Safe in the car, waiting for Ricky, her panic began to subside as her adrenaline levels dropped, and she consciously tried to control the hammering of her heart. She double-checked that she'd locked the car doors, then kept her eyes fixed on the front steps and one hand on the door handle, hoping to God that if anything came up the concrete steps it would be Bubbles and not a burglar. What felt like ages later, a knocking on the driver's window made her nearly jump out of her skin. It was Ricky, with Carlo on a lead. She rolled the window down.

'Stay here, I'll check out the flat,' he told her.

'Be careful! Please! Don't do anything… risky.'

'I'll be fine. I've got security with me!' Ricky waggled the dog's leash, then added more seriously, 'Don't worry. They'll have probably run off ages ago, as soon as you opened the front door.'

Despite what he'd said, all the while Ricky was inside the flat her heart was in her mouth. What if something happened to him? If he got attacked and hurt? Anxiously, she peered through the darkness to the front door.

A few minutes later, he reappeared to say the flat was empty.

'Thank God you're okay. I was worried sick. But where's Bubbles?' she asked, expecting that he would have followed Ricky and Carlo back to the car.

'Isn't he with you? He's not in the flat.'

'Oh no! No, no, no, no!' Charley exclaimed, clambering out of the car and rushing into the flat, calling the dog desperately. *Please, please, please don't let them have taken my dog.* Frantically, she searched the flat and the garden, calling his name, but there was no sign of him anywhere.

'Why would they steal the bloody dog?' she raged. 'Who steals somebody's pet, for God's sake! He's not even a pedigree.' She was nearly in tears. Then, from somewhere in the flat, they heard Carlo barking excitedly. He'd found Bubbles cowering under Charley's bed. Together, she and Ricky coaxed the whimpering dog out and then she wrapped her arms round the cockerpoo's trembling little body and hugged him. Ricky lavished praise on his lurcher and then led Charley through to the living room, steering her gently down onto the sofa, and made her some tea. While she drank it, he started to clear up the mess. The flat was trashed. In their haste to find anything worth stealing, the intruders had strewn the contents of drawers and cupboards all over the floors, and they'd smashed numerous ornaments and pictures. Glass crunched underfoot as Ricky walked across the living room carpet. Charley wondered if the breakages were deliberate, in vengeance, because she had so little of value to take.

It suddenly struck her that it had been a bit of a liberty calling Ricky and expecting him to drop everything to come over and rescue her. Or actually, to rescue her at all.

'Thanks for coming. I shouldn't have called you.'

'No, I'm glad you did. I wouldn't have wanted you to deal with this on your own.'

'The police said they'd try to send someone,' she added vaguely.

'Yes but not immediately. And I don't suppose there'll be anything they can do,' he replied, carefully picking bits of broken glass out of the living room carpet.

'Is that from my wedding photo?'

There was a beat before Ricky replied. 'Yes. I'm sorry, it is. I'll get it mended for you,' he promised gently.

Charley struggled to hold back her tears. Whether they were caused by the breaking of the photo, or Ricky's kindness, she wasn't sure.

—

When two uniformed officers arrived a short while later they issued Charley with a crime number for the insurance claim, told her to make a list of anything missing, not forgetting things like her passport and her driver's licence, and advised her to put new locks on the doors and windows if there was any danger the intruders might have found a key to the flat.

'They often return,' they warned her, 'after you've had time to buy new stuff to replace the old.'

Then they handed her a leaflet about burglar alarms, household security and personal safety. She thanked them, showed them out, then fished her laptop out of her bag, grateful she'd had it with her, otherwise the burglars would have nicked that too. Stoically, she started compiling a list of everything that had been taken – her tablet, the TV, the iPod speakers from the kitchen, the food mixer Pam had bought her, and even the bathroom scales, for crying out loud. Then, going through to her bedroom, she discovered they'd taken her jewellery box from inside the top of her wardrobe, and all the precious pieces of jewellery Josh had ever given her. She felt as if a part of her had been torn away. Sinking to her knees, she completely lost it.

'*You bastards!*' she howled, overcome by the sense of loss and violation. 'You bloody, bloody, utter bastards!'

Ricky came rushing in, knelt down next to her and gathered her to him where she collapsed against him, sobbing noisily and messily all over his linen shirt.

'There wasn't even anything valuable,' she managed to gasp between sobs.

Cheap, junk jewellery, worthless yet priceless. Irreplaceable treasures. A pair of coloured-glass earrings he'd bought her on their honeymoon in Venice, a cheap necklace with the word *Charley* suspended on a chain, which had been a Christmas present from him. A bundle of bangles, none of which matched, that he'd given her over the years, until her wrist had rattled if she wore them altogether. The memory of each stolen item brought another stab of pain, of grieving loss. Ricky held her while she wept.

'Bloody, bloody, utter bastards,' he agreed softly, stroking her hair.

Finally, she let out a last, juddering breath and pulled away from him, so he stood up, held out his hand and helped her to her feet.

By now it was way past midnight, and Charley realised she still hadn't fed the dog. 'He must be ravenous,' she said, going into the kitchen.

'Have you eaten?' asked Ricky, following her through.

'No, but I'm not hungry.'

'I'm not surprised, but you should eat something,' he told her, opening the fridge and scanning the shelves.

'There's bugger all in there,' she informed him.

'In that case, how about some bugger all on toast?' he said, getting out the butter, some cheese and the eggs. 'Otherwise known as a "Welsh Rabbit" for some reason.'

She laughed and, too tired to correct his English, added, 'Go on then, thanks.'

While she ate he sat opposite her at the kitchen table. Both of the dogs were, by now, flat out on the floor, Bubbles having abandoned his basket in favour of lying cuddled up against the lurcher's flanks.

'I think I should spend the night here,' Ricky told her. 'In the spare room,' he added hastily. 'I don't want to leave you alone tonight.'

Neither do I, thought Charley. *In fact, I don't want you to leave me at all.* Carefully, she put down her knife and fork, finished her mouthful, caught his eye and held his gaze. *It was now or never*, said a voice in her head, or possibly in her heart. She had no idea how he would react to what she was about to say. Maybe he would reject her, turn her down, tell her she'd left it too late. But whatever he said, she reasoned, she couldn't hurt more than she already did, by saying nothing and watching him walk out of her life forever.

'Actually, I don't want to be alone *any* night, not any more,' she said, tentatively reaching out to take his hand, her eyes searching deeply for his reaction. Gradually, she watched the full meaning of what she was saying dawn on him. But just to make things clear she added, 'I want you to stay with me. Not just tonight, always.'

He stared at her in silence, a whole range of emotions appearing to stream across his face. When he eventually spoke, his response rocked her.

'Let's just deal with tonight, shall we? You've had a traumatic evening, Charley, and you've been very frightened. It's not the kind of evening to make any rash decisions.'

'I'm not making a rash decision—' she started to protest, but he interrupted her firmly.

'Look, whatever you're feeling right now, it might be the shock talking, letting your emotions run away with you.'

Swiftly, she rose to her feet and reached out to him. 'No, no it's not. This isn't about what's happened tonight. I've been trying to tell you for a long time but...'

The guarded look in his eyes made her stumble and falter, but she ploughed on regardless.

'I wanted to tell you weeks ago, when you were in Italy, that I wished we could get back together and try again. I was going to call you but then you rang to say your grandmother had died and... well, it just so wasn't the right moment. And then I planned to tell you when I picked you up from the airport but... well, that day went horribly, horribly wrong and you said you were going back to Italy, and that there was nothing for you in the UK, so again, I shied off, and then... and then there was Erica.'

'Erica?' he looked baffled.

'I thought she was your girlfriend.'

There was a beat and then Ricky threw his head back and roared with laughter. 'Erica? Honestly? Can you *seriously* see me with a woman like her?'

Charley leapt to her own defence. 'But that's just the point! I *did* keep seeing you with her and, be fair, she was all over you, *is* all over you, forever pawing at you and gazing at you adoringly. You can't tell me you haven't noticed!'

Ricky had the good grace to look abashed. 'You're right. I know, but...'

'And what was all that... that stuff about being a "sleeping partner"!' Charley cut in, barely resisting the urge to add ironic air quotes round the words.

'That's not what you think!' he protested. 'It's just that she hasn't got quite enough money to buy the business out completely, so she suggested me leaving some money invested in it – for a share of the profits.'

Charley rolled her eyes. 'Oh? Sounds like the perfect solution all round then.'

Ricky looked even more sheepish. 'I didn't want to lose her as a buyer. I know I'm handling things with her badly, Charley, and I'm sorry.'

'You're not handling it at all!'

Uncharacteristically, Ricky leapt to his own defence. 'I didn't think I'd need to. I just figured I'd go back to Italy and it would all finish... fizzle out.'

Charley snorted loudly at his naivety. 'Ha! Good luck with that!'

'But I told you in the shop it was purely a business deal,' he countered. 'So why didn't you say anything after that?'

Charley sighed. 'Because you were so keen to get back to Italy. When you said you'd be gone in a month… I thought I'd left it too late.'

He paused and his eyes sought hers. 'So why are you telling me now?'

Charley's throat tightened, she swallowed hard and then said in a small, strained voice, 'I'm just hoping it isn't.'

He didn't reply immediately. And when he did, it wasn't to give her a straight answer. 'I think we should both sleep on this, Charley. I'll stay the night, but in the spare room, and if you still feel the same way in the morning…' He left the thought hanging in the air between them.

'Okay. Fine. I understand,' replied Charley and went off to make up the spare bed, resisting the temptation to tell him that, technically, it was already the morning.

It was well after one o'clock when she fell into her own bed. Her whole body ached for sleep and, given the high octane drama of the evening, she thought she'd drift off as soon as her head sank onto the pillow. Instead, the aftermath of fear crept up on her, leaving her fidgety, wide awake and restless. She lay on her back, watching the lights of passing cars sweep across the ceiling, hoping the gentle movement would lull her off. It didn't. Irritably, she resigned herself to giving up all thoughts of sleep and just getting through the night.

Dawn had barely broken when she heard a light tapping on her door.

'Yes?' she called out, propping herself up on her elbows.

Ricky pushed the door open and stood in the doorway in his T-shirt and boxers.

'Is it too early?' he asked tentatively.

Charley's heart flipped and then settled to trembling uneasily. 'That depends,' she said. 'Is it too late?'

Ricky's trademark easy smile spread across his face and settled deep in his eyes. 'No, it's not too late.'

'Then it's not too early,' she replied and pulled the duvet back to invite him into bed.

A few months later, in early spring of the following year, Charley arrived at the shop bright and early on a Saturday morning to find Pam already there.

'How was Tuscany?' asked her mother-in-law.

'Fabulous!' enthused Charley, and was moved see her mother-in-law's face light up with evident pleasure. Slipping off her coat, she dumped her bag behind the till and then swiftly glanced around the shop. It was immediately evident that it had been in good hands while she'd been away. The shelves and displays were all fully stocked, the floor hoovered, the surfaces clean. Which wasn't a surprise, but she was still relieved since the flight back from Italy had been a late one and Charley was decidedly short on sleep. She and Ricky had flown over to spend a few days with his family in order to announce their engagement in person, in the traditional way.

'His mum cried,' confessed Charley, 'and they both seemed genuinely thrilled.'

'And so they should be! They are gaining an outstanding daughter-in-law, and I should know!'

Charley grinned, until the significance of Pam's words suddenly hit home. *They are gaining an outstanding daughter-in-law.* The moment she married Ricky, *his* mother would become her mother-in-law, instead of Pam, and Charley would cease to be Pam's daughter-in-law. Which meant Charley would lose her role, her place in the older woman's life, and she'd become her... her what?

A small, fluttery panic started welling up inside her. Why was moving on so bloody hard? Why did it always involve having to lose something, or someone, in the process? Spontaneously, she went over to embrace the older woman, as if she wanted to physically hold on to her, to keep her in her life.

'I don't want you to stop being my mother-in-law!' she exclaimed, adopting a light-hearted tone to conceal her emotions.

'You can't have two mothers-in-law, darling, that's just greedy!' said Pam with mock severity, and Charley guessed Pam was adopting the same coping mechanism. The two of them stood in an affectionate embrace for a few moments.

Then Pam pulled back and, seeking out Charley's eyes, she said gently, 'Sweetheart, I'm ready, more than ready, to hand over the role of being your mother-in-law... but you do know it's just a label – a "job title", as it were? It doesn't have to change our relationship one iota, does it?'

Charley regarded the older woman carefully, then she shook her head. 'No. You're right. Of course it doesn't. I'll just have to start thinking of you as... something else,' she finished vaguely. *But what?* she wondered. How the hell could they sum up the unique close relationship between the two of them?

'Perhaps you could think of me as your business partner, or your colleague,' Pam suggested. 'Or maybe a stand-in mum, or your cheerleader and number one fan! Or... or a friend, even?' she finally ventured tentatively.

Charley smiled to herself, thinking how typically self-effacing it was of her mother-in-law not to assume – no, not to *realise* – that by now, after everything the two women had been through together, *of course* Charley counted her amongst her closest friends.

'Yes, a *friend*,' Charley agreed which, judging by the look on the older woman's face, seemed to delight her. 'A *close* friend,' Charley went on sincerely. 'A *wise and valued* friend.' Pam was beginning to look sheepishly gratified until Charley added mischievously, 'In fact, d'you know the term I think sums you up the best? An *old* friend.'

'Less of the *old*, thank you!'

'A *very* old friend,' stressed Charley, ignoring Pam's indignant protest and continuing mercilessly. 'In fact a *very, very* old friend... A *very, very, very*—'

'Tell you what,' broke in Pam abruptly. 'Let's go with "your previous-former-first-ex-original-mother-in-law"! That rolls off the tongue nicely!'

'Original?' Charley pounced on the term. 'You're that all right. One of a kind!'

They both laughed and went to open the shop to the first of the day's customers.

Acknowledgements

As ever, I owe an enormous amount to my wonderful agent Gaia Banks – on this occasion for guiding me through the perils and pitfalls of writing a sequel and for her crucial insight and input as first reader, not to mention her seemingly limitless encouragement. My thanks also go to Alba Arnau at Sheil Land Associates for her most excellent support behind the scenes. Thank you both.

I am, of course, greatly indebted to the lovely Emily Bedford, Senior Commissioning Editor at Canelo, not just for believing in me enough to commission a second book about Charley and Pam, but also for being open to exploring new directions for the characters. I can't thank her enough for guiding my debut women's fiction books to publication. It's been a hoot.

I absolutely love Sarah Whittaker's cover illustration, which is not just perfect for this book, but also fits so well with the signature of her cover of the previous book.

I am especially grateful to the talented Jennie Ayres for her sharp yet sympathetic copy editing and her excellent edits, comments and suggestions. She also has my apologies for stealing so many of her suggested changes outright!

I'd also like to thank everyone at Canelo on the production team, in particular Micaela Cavaletto and Nicole Abel, and everyone else involved in creating or promoting both books. I'm truly grateful.

Finally, my love and thanks to my four offspring who continue to enthusiastically crack open the fizz to celebrate every milestone in my writing journey.